ALCHEMY'S AIR

ALCHEMY'S AIR

BOOK TWO OF
THE EQUAL NIGHT TRILOGY

STACEY L. TUCKER

SparkPress, a BookSparks imprint
A Division of SparkPoint Studio, LLC

Published by SparkPress, a BookSparks imprint,
A division of SparkPoint Studio, LLC
Phoenix, Arizona, USA, 85007
www.gosparkpress.com

Published 2019

Printed in the United States of America

ISBN: 978-1-943006-84-7 (pbk)
ISBN: 978-1-943006-85-4 (e-bk)
Library of Congress Control Number: 2018959093

Cover design © Julie Metz, Ltd./metzdesign.com
Formatting by Katherine Lloyd/theDESKonline.com

The One with Fire in her heart,
Wind on her breath and Sea in her blood
will return the Divine to the planet. This is every woman.

For the Magdalen

THE BOOK OF SOPHIA

As Above, So Below.

I am the guardian of the Akash, the library of all that was, all that is, and all that will be.

I am the middle world, that of Imagination, your bridge between Heaven and Earth,

between body and spirit.

I am the fire that fuels you, the passion you deny.

I am the wind that holds the heavens apart from the earth, yet binds them.

I am the water that permeates you with love.

I wait in your sleeping heart, the time has come to hear me.

My Child of Earth and Starry Heaven,

When you restore the memory held deep within Gaia, you restore the past and the future.

You restore the wisdom of the Heart, the wisdom of Earth.

Remember Your Instinctual Truth, Your Divine Potential.

I feel your holy longing, Your pained desire to return home.

Your soul cries for nourishment. As your Great Mother, I am here.

Once the memory is restored, the great cleansing occurs.

The lines of the dragon will ignite,

Re-fuse the fire within all hearts. The desire behind all desires will come to light.

Sacred Masculine and Divine Feminine once more unite.

1

Skylar read the words again and the familiar tingle spread across the back of her head. She had lost track of how many times she'd read this page of the book in the last three months. Much of it didn't make sense at first but with each passing day came more clarity . . . and a heightened sense of dread.

"The Book of Sophia is an alchemical text," she told Ocean, the Great Mother of Fire. "It contains codes to assist humanity with the great changes happening on the planet."

"Well done grasshopper," Ocean said smiling. They sat on Ocean's back porch, shielded from the brutal sun. It had been over a year since they'd seen cooler temps in the Northeast.

"It's also a directive. Sophia talks about restoring a memory," Skylar said. "Do you know what she's talking about?"

Ocean paused and stared out at her vast lawn that hadn't been cut in months. "The ending of the last age was the time of the great flood. You've heard that story. It was eerily similar to the vibe of today's world. Technology of a different kind surpassed human consciousness and those in power were consumed with greed. My sisters and I knew we had limited time before all was lost. We gathered the entirety of earth's wisdom and placed it in the heart of a baby girl named Sophia. She became the living embodiment of the Great Sophia. She *was* Spirit in Matter. And in doing so, we ensured every woman from that day forward would carry the secret of Sophia under her heart, until the day it would be restored. This is that day."

Skylar looked down at the book in her lap. She hadn't let it out of her sight since Vivienne, Great Mother of Water, had handed it to her the night of Milicent Grayer's big show in June.

"How do I do that?" Skylar asked.

"Keep reading," Ocean said as she got up and went inside.

Skylar sighed. The world had become extremely tumultuous since that fateful night in the arena. It didn't go unnoticed by the Great Mothers that Milicent's scheme for world domination fell on the historical summer solstice of 2020. This solstice was exceptionally powerful with the alignment of the sun, earth, and moon during the yearlong syzygy of the planets Saturn, Jupiter, and Pluto. Such a planetary alignment happened every 734 years, and 2020 was spot on. The fallout from the intense energy was still being felt all over the planet and would be for years to come.

Old systems were breaking down all over the world. With many countries already in ruins, the government of the United States was hanging by a thread. But the Great Mothers saw it as an opportunity. They were intimately aware of the dark energies that had been controlling the US with puppet strings for over a century. But now, with the influx of divine energy and rare planetary alignments, a window of time had opened to wash the world clean of old thinking and usher in the Golden Age. Humanity was called to remember its divinity and use its power to aid the suffering planet. We had come to a crossroads . . .

Wake up to the truths within or die.

Skylar looked out at the Great Tree in Ocean's yard sensing the weight of this crossroads on her shoulders. When her mother Cassie died last year, she left behind a mystery for Skylar to solve, the greatest mystery of our time. How do we not only survive this tumultuous time in history, but also evolve into a species *worthy* of being the keepers of Gaia? Skylar would have to uncover the way. It was a tall order for a girl of twenty-two. She had extraordinary help from the Great Mothers of Fire, Air, and Water. Magda, the Goddess of the etheric realm often appeared to help as well. In her everyday world, Skylar relied on her best friend Suki to give her a dose of reality and a sense of humor, knowing they wouldn't survive without a few laughs.

And Argan . . .

Argan had become a teacher of sorts, helping with her physical training and meditation practices. So often she would search for a sign of the spark between them, but if it still existed, it was buried deep.

Skylar understood what the Great Mothers asked of her but questioned her resolve on a daily basis. It was all too much, too esoteric. What could one person really do? Even *with* the Book of Sophia.

She yearned to go back to a normal life, get her veterinary degree and get lost in the world of horses. She knew how to help in that world. *This* one of mysticism and mayhem left her scratching her head and she was convinced she defeated Milicent by little more than dumb luck.

"You don't think you can just return to that boring life of obscurity, do you?" Ocean asked from the doorway, reading her thoughts. She carried a tray of iced tea and coffee.

Skylar thought *yes, yes I do.* "No," she replied, taking a glass. Ocean sat back down in the rocker beside her.

The air that day was thick with electric energy. It felt like a coat of cellophane stuck to her skin. She assumed her grandmother, Beatrice, the Great Mother of Air had something to do with it. Beatrice loved to make her presence felt in a way that got under the skin. Skylar grimaced as she wiped away the dew that had accumulated on her forearm.

She rocked slowly in the wicker chair and looked out at the tree. This tree, neither living nor dead was another mystery to Skylar. It was completely blackened, as if charred by fire yet even from this distance, Skylar could feel life pulsing through it.

"Ocean, will you finally tell me about that tree?"

Ocean grabbed her mug of steaming coffee and sat back in her chair. She put her feet up on the railing, spotlighting her toenails, painted every color of the rainbow. "That tree is one of the *trees of the four directions*. It's the tree of the south, the direction of fire," she said. "But it is, in my opinion, *the* most important tree."

"Because it's yours?" Skylar asked.

"No, smart-ass," Ocean said. "Because it's also the tree of death, escorting souls onward to the next phase of their journey. Each leaf contains the record of each soul and the day it's going to move on from this world. It's a very important tree."

"Ocean, that tree has no leaves," Skylar said.

"I beg your pardon. It most certainly does. On the astral plane, or the celestial dimension that tree is alive, it has leaves, and it has color. On that plane of existence, the leaves contain all the information. But here, on the earth plane, it looks like this. So much of what we see here is a shadow of the truth. There are worlds beyond this one where this tree flourishes as the cycle of life marches on."

"Sophia is one key to those worlds," Skylar said, the tingle spread across the back of her head. "She connects the human experience to the eternal." She got up from her chair and walked down the back steps to the yard. With the Book of Sophia in hand, she crossed the tall grass to stand beside the great tree. The well that sat underneath had been replaced by Rhia's headstone. Skylar looked at it lovingly. Ocean had asked to bury Cassie's ashes under the tree but Skylar refused, not ready to give them up. They had their proper place in the library of her tiny house.

With an outstretched hand she touched the black bark with her palm. The pulse she felt from across the yard overpowered her here so close. She managed the energy as best she could. In her mind's eye she was transported to the astral plane where the tree stood in its true form. All around her were dream-like clouds, shielding her from seeing anything else but the tree. Its trunk was massive, thicker than a redwood yet the canopy was low enough for Skylar to touch. She released her hand and took a step back to stare at this incredible, living being. She expected it to start talking. The leaves were mostly green but for a few yellow and brown. A slight breeze went by and one fell to the ground. "Oh," Skylar gasped. She knew what that meant. She bent to pick it up but it disintegrated into the earth before she could touch it. All of the fallen leaves were quickly absorbed by the ground to regenerate and to be used as nourishment for the tree, only to be born again in future lifetimes.

As she stood there, a few more fell but one drifted upward, carried on the wind. Skylar watched it climb higher and higher until it disappeared from view. "How magnificent," she said aloud.

She bowed to the tree. "Thank you," she said. She knew she had been given the gift of insight from mother Gaia herself. With a shift of intention, like coming out of meditation, she was back in Ocean's yard.

"That was incredible," Skylar said. "My whole view of death is turned on its ear. It's such a natural, beautiful, quiet process, peaceful, even. Nothing like what we fear it to be."

"Nope," Ocean said. She had walked down to the tree while Skylar was on the astral plane.

"One leaf floated upward to the sky, not down to the ground like the rest," Skylar said.

Ocean looked at the Book of Sophia. "You had Sophia's book with you. What divine timing for that transitioning soul. The knowledge in the book carried that soul over the goal line, so to speak."

"Is this why Milicent wants my book?" Skylar asked. "Does it grant immortality?"

"Not to the uninitiated," Ocean said. "Trust me, no one would truly want to live forever. It's tiring," Ocean said. "The soul that was sent upward was probably very close to ascension. The kiss from Sophia was the last step in that soul's journey, as the kiss of the Holy Spirit is the last step for everyone. Milicent has lifetimes to go before she comes close to that opportunity." Ocean rolled her eyes. "The closest glimpse of immortality for humanity is your connection to the raw power of nature." She twirled around in the sunshine like a child. Skylar watched the rays of sun absorb into Ocean's red frizz, making it look like a fireball around her face. She stopped and held her face to the sun. "Getting outside, putting your bare feet in the grass and feeling the immortal force that runs through all life is what restores vitality. The longing to be one with the Creator, to *be* the Creator drives the human race, albeit subconsciously." She dropped into the tall grass and started making grass angels.

"Sophia is all about nature and the power of alchemy and the elements," Skylar said in agreement, ignoring Ocean's odd behavior. Childlike enthusiasm was not a phrase she'd use to describe her mentor. "And desire."

"You've progressed so much in the last three months, you're ready for this next step," Ocean said, sitting up from her grass angel and held out her hand for Skylar's help. Skylar pulled her out of the grass and Ocean dusted off her behind. "I'm learning it's important not to take yourself too seriously. My homework's been to do something silly every day."

Skylar stood in amazement. She opened her mouth to speak but Ocean cut her off. "Hope you enjoyed it. It's not for me."

They slowly walked back toward the steps. The heat had intensified in the short time they'd been outside and it made any physical exertion challenging. "What the heck is the temperature today?" Skylar asked.

"105," Ocean said.

"Is that a record?" Skylar asked.

"For today but not for long," Ocean said. "Let's get out of the sun."

They got back up to the porch and Ocean looked at her watch. "Lunch time," she said and poured herself a whiskey from her new bar cart. "Skylar, no matter the journey, the shortcuts or the frustrating long cuts, remember your destiny is a promise you made to yourself before you came into this world. It is stamped on a leaf on that tree. You are creating this life, no one else."

"I find that hard to believe," Skylar said. "This year has not been my own."

"You needed a little push but trust me, this is your show. All humans go through the veil of forgetting before coming back to earth. Figuring out your purpose is half the fun. But I'll tell you this; the book chose you. Cassie did as much as she could to prepare the way but it wouldn't have worked so beautifully if not divinely planned by Sophia herself." She put her hand on Skylar's shoulder. "We will continue our training. You will continue to work with the book. The answers will materialize. Until then, we prepare." In one gulp she shot the whiskey straight up and put her glass on the table. "You are being called to help humanity wake from its slumber, Skylar."

The words of Sophia and of Ocean started to seep into Skylar's heart like a wave of unnamed truth. "I can't do it alone," she said.

"Not *only* you," Ocean said. "You're not Jesus. But this *is* the second coming. And she's female."

Skylar's wound in her abdomen from Milicent's dagger had transformed into her own version of the mark of the Great Mothers, the ring of three doves. Its silvery sheen had a beautiful iridescent quality. She was actually grateful to have it and felt more connected to her lineage.

She had started training with Argan soon after the solstice. They had developed a rigorous routine, meeting at Joel's five days a week. At first their lessons were awkward and Skylar was hopeful of some glimmer of feeling from Argan. But he remained all business, coaching her on various techniques of Qigong, Kundalini yoga, and Tantric breath work. She lost track of the days they spent together. It had all become a blur of kicks, crunches, and painstaking hours in meditation. At first she would break out in a sweat if he got too close but his cold demeanor reminded her that ship had sailed. After a while, she was able to settle in and commit to a working relationship with him.

She had put her vet school plans on permanent hold. She loved equine life and it would always be a part of her heart. But she understood the demands of her new path and had vowed to all of the Great Mothers to see it through. Ocean was a fixture in Skylar's life most days and she came to rely on her as a surrogate mother figure. She was still struggling to find a path that worked with Rachel and welcomed the relationship with Ocean, despite her erratic, fiery temperament.

Vivienne, Great Mother of Water, had stayed in the States just a few days after Milicent's big show. She helped smooth things over with Devlin and his handlers. After Vivienne was finished, no one remembered much of anything about that night.

Skylar was in awe of Vivienne. She was timeless. It was virtually impossible to tell how old she was. She always wore a wrap around her head making it appear elongated, reminiscent of Nefertiti, and Skylar wondered if she had once been the Egyptian Queen. She also questioned how the exotic, dark-skinned Goddess begot Milicent as a granddaughter, who was white as snow. But she chalked it up to the magic of the universe and let it be. Skylar had yet to spend any time with Vivienne, which she desperately wanted to do. They were blood, and Skylar wanted to get to know her. Before she returned home to Italy, Vivienne invited Skylar to come stay with her. "Your quest will take you to Italy before it is through," she said. She didn't elaborate and Skylar was left with yet another piece to her puzzle.

Beatrice, the Great Mother of Air, was the woman Skylar had always called grandmother. As most of Skylar's life was kept secret until the past year, she learned there was a whole side of Beatrice she didn't know. Beatrice was the only one of the three Great Mothers that had fallen in love with a mortal man. She loved Arthur all of her life and when he died, she became a shell of who she once was, never recovering from his death. It was no secret that Ocean and Vivienne judged Bea for falling so helplessly into the trappings of mortal love. This shunning from her sisters was yet another reason for her bitter tongue, but Skylar accepted her grandmother's biting personality as part of her charm.

Skylar's father Joel wasn't happy with the direction her life was taking but he lost control of her long ago . . .

"I accept that you're taking this year off from school, Skylar, but I don't want you to forget about your career," Joel said. "Through Herculean efforts you got that first degree."

"I know, Dad," Skylar said. "But it would seem I have a few loose ends to tie up before I move on with that normal life we talked about."

Joel nodded. "Right. How are you feeling about . . . everything?"

"It's daunting but doable," she said, pushing a smile onto her face, hoping it reassured her father.

November 10, 2020: In the late hours of election night, polls were predicting Devlin Grayer was to be the forty-sixth president of the United States. Skylar, Suki, and Kyle sat around Skylar's TV in her tiny house watching in utter disbelief.

"I would have thought the country learned its lesson voting in a reality star last election," Suki said.

"Have you looked out your window?" asked Skylar. "The world is in shambles. I can only assume Milicent's black magic had something to do with their win. Although I'm not sure of her intentions. She wasn't keen on becoming First Lady. But what will she do now with access to absolutely everything?"

"I'm looking forward to finding out," Kyle said.

Suki shot him a look. "You were so down on her over the summer. Now you're a fan because they won?"

"I've never cared about politics, Suuk," he said. "But I need a job and this guy promises me one."

"Drumming not as lucrative as you'd hoped?" Skylar said.

"I never did it for the money, just the chicks," he said. "And now I have the chick but not the money."

4

Devlin Grayer stood beaming at the podium of his campaign rally. His wife Milicent stood regally by his side. She was stunning in her violet Chanel sheath reminiscent of Jackie Kennedy. Pillbox hat with veil, long satin gloves and purple stilettos completed the ensemble. The pundits were already enjoying jokes at her expense. She only wore shades of purple, except that fateful night at the arena in June, her only appearance in red. This night the crowd made the arena stifling hot. A line of sweat appeared under Devlin's recently dyed, perfectly coifed head of hair. Milicent, on the other hand was cool as crystal.

Standing on the other side of Devlin was Mica Noxx, his Vice President-elect. Together, they had succeeded in making history. The first female VP was an accomplishment sought after but never attained until this fateful election year, 2020. He secured her purely as a political move, having helped with the female and African American vote.

"This country has cried out for a leader that can restore its greatness and I have answered!" Devlin shouted. "America has seen great political and racial divide in recent years. But now the country has broken open in its pain. My promise to you is a future of great healing of what ails us. America was founded on vitally important principals that are just as relevant in the twenty-first century as they were in the days of our founding fathers. I vow to make this country what it was, what it truly is, and what it wholeheartedly can be." He looked directly into the teleprompter and recited his personal version of the last line of the Declaration of Independence. "And for your support, with a firm reliance on the protection of divine providence, I pledge my life, my fortune, and my sacred honor!" He left the podium in a fit of youthful exuberance, jumping down, pommel horse style, to the crowd of supporters.

The crowd continued to applaud as he walked by, shaking every hand. If Milicent was supposed to accompany him, she missed her cue and opted to stay on stage with the VP-elect. Behind her stood her overdressed assistant, Noah Maganti, in a cutting edge, skinny-legged, white tuxedo. His wavy brown hair held back by a stylish metrosexual black headband. Milicent had gone through assistants so often it wasn't worth learning their names until she stumbled across the job board at Delta Lambda Phi on Rosen's campus. It was a mystery to everyone what she was doing there that day in July, but shortly after, Noah showed up and instantly filled a very old hole. Now she never went any-where without him in tow.

"Mica," Milicent nodded in her direction. "You look lovely. You must let me borrow your designer." Milicent was lousy at small talk.

"Oh please, Milicent," Mica scoffed. "I'm sure Devlin and Cyril Magus aren't discussing their clothes right now." She gestured to the President-elect in an arm lock with a squatty, rodent-looking man in his late seventies. Magus was extremely influential in many sectors including banking, biotech, and energy. His ancestral line never made the lists of richest families as their fortunes were well hidden.

Milicent scanned the crowd but didn't see Devlin.

"He's near the stage steps," Noah said, feeding her informa-tion from a foot away.

Milicent frowned. "Oh, Magus burns my ass. He quite literally has all the money in the world and is still completely miserable. I hated dealing with him in the private sector and now he expects us to be in his political back pocket. He's sorely mistaken."

She returned her attention to Mica. "It was big of you to step in to the VP position so late in the campaign. What a shame about Sara," Milicent said. Sara Hendricks had been Devlin's original running mate but just a month before the election she pulled out citing health issues. Insiders knew there were concerns about her stability and recent erratic behavior caused the administration to lose faith in her abilities.

"Divine intervention works out for all of us," Mica said.

"Right," Milicent said speculatively. Her eyes followed Devlin as the two men walked through the doors to the private waiting area. Milicent and Mica gave the crowd a final wave and exited as well.

Milicent was met with an angry Devlin. "Millie, you really needed to be by my side," he barked. "How do you think it looks for you to be chatting with Mica while I'm greeting supporters alone?" He glared at Noah, miserable with the fact that this young man had quickly taken up so much of their real estate.

Milicent's face turned an uncharacteristic red. "Devlin, you jumped off the stage! Was I really supposed to follow you?" She shook her head. "I don't think so."

He turned to Mica. "You're going to need a refresher on protocol as well Mica."

"I don't take orders from you, Devlin. I told you when I accepted this nomination that I would come to the office on my own terms. Not yours. We both know you won this because of me." She smiled through her gritted teeth as all cameras were on them.

Milicent locked eyes with Cyril Magus from across the room.

"Don't tell me we'll be dealing with Cyril from the Oval, Devlin," Milicent scolded. "He has his own agenda."

"They all do, Millie," he said. "It's a game remember? We always play to see how far we can get. I'd say we got pretty far this time."

"Yes, but this is just the beginning. You actually have to govern the country. You know, fix things that are broken, improve people's lives, solve problems."

"That's what the Cabinet is for," he said.

Magus approached the President-elect with a scowl on his face. "Devlin, I wasn't finished talking to you."

"Sorry, Cyril, I'm only allotted five minutes a guest."

"I'm sure that's true for others," Cyril said. "Hello, Milicent. You're looking ravishing."

"Why is a comment on my looks your go-to Cyril?" Milicent said, her face stern. "Things are different now. Devlin's in public office."

"Things are far more the same than you realize. The big boys can handle things from here. I know Devlin let you play with his money in Seattle, but DC is no place for a woman, despite the charade going on in the public eye." He glanced in the direction of the VP-elect and returned his focus to Devlin.

"Cyril," Milicent took in air to calm down. "Your five minutes are up." She gestured to the line of supporters waiting for their photo op.

"I'll be in touch Devlin," Cyril said. "Mrs. Grayer." He walked away.

"Thank you for keeping your cool. I know he's an ass," Devlin said. "But he's right. Things are run a certain way here. If the downward spiral of the last four years didn't tip the scales of change, nothing can. *Washington doesn't change.*"

"You left that line out of your speech, dear," Milicent said with narrowed eyes. Another guest stepped up to shake their hands and the night played on.

Just after 4:00 a.m. Devlin walked out of the men's room with two security guards behind him. His driver opened his car door and he hopped in to find an impatient Milicent. Noah was forced to ride up front with the driver.

"I don't need such security measures," Devlin complained, not being able to pee in private anymore.

"Dev, this is our life now. You really need to follow the protocol. And not just because of the crackpots in the world."

"You mean you," Devlin said.

Milicent scowled. "For over a century, every twenty years the U.S. President has died in office or survived an assassination attempt. And you're *it* this time. You can't be too careful."

Devlin rolled his eyes again. "Yeah, Tecumseh's Curse. I know, Millie. Your little charade in June counts; we're good."

Now it was Milicent's turn to roll her eyes. "Dev, I was trying to prove a point and you weren't taking me seriously, I wasn't actually trying to kill you. If I were, you'd be dead and I would be President."

"Fine, fine," he waved her off. "I'll comply with all of this silliness. But how do I connect with the little people being so sequestered?"

"You'll find a way, my love," she cooed.

5

Skylar walked down the aisle of the new barn. She would always refer to it as the *new* barn. Her memories of the old barn were forever emblazoned in her memory, good and bad. The old barn was where she met Ronnie, and reconnected with Argan. It was also where Rhia died and life as Skylar had known it had ended.

The stables housed all of the horses Skylar had grown to love over her year at Rosen.

She was glad to see them thriving in their environment, despite Milicent's attempt to institutionalize the place. Even Cheveyo looked happy. He shook his head in greeting and gave her a hearty whinny. She wondered how long he would stay there. He belonged to no one and the confines of the Quine were no home for him. She doubted he would stick around but she had no idea where he'd go. She knew he would always be okay, no matter where he was. And so would she.

With Milicent preparing for her life in the White House, the Quine was left in the hands of Dean Thomas. Horses weren't his area of expertise and he had hired outside consultants to figure out what was best for the school now that the Grayers had moved on.

"Ms. Southmartin," the dean approached Skylar during a rare appearance at the stables. With the buttons on his suit jacket about to burst, he removed a handkerchief from his pocket to wipe sweat from his face. "Against my better judgment, it would seem you have been appointed permanent head of the Equine Facility. It's a direct order from the incumbent First Lady of the United States. I know you've had some experience with the position but you will have to get yourself educated on the financial side of this monstrosity and probably hire some folks to help you."

"That's great, Dean, but I'm not sure that's the right move for me," Skylar objected. She was unclear she could handle such an appointment with her new career, employed by the Great Mothers.

"I don't think you have much of a choice," he said. "It looks like you are called to serve at the pleasure of the First Lady-elect. You have the option of staying in your current office or picking another in the executive wing." He turned his back and walked down the aisle. As he rounded the corner he looked back at Skylar. "And Ms. Southmartin, this facility is a very small part of my life. See to it that it remains that way." He disappeared as Suki walked up beside Skylar.

"I miss *free will*," Skylar said. She filled Suki in on the details of her conversation with the dean.

"I'll stay," Suki said. "I have a good career trajectory now. Promote me to something good, with a lot more pay." Her eyes gleamed. "Kyle's still looking for work."

"What does his unemployment mean for the two of you?" Skylar asked.

"We're good," Suki said. "But he needs a job. I'm not dating a deadbeat."

"Are you channeling your grandmother?" Skylar asked. Suki's grandmother had passed late in the summer. It was bittersweet for Suki. Her grandmother was the only real family she had ever known but she did have a way of stifling Suki in all areas of her life. As much as she would miss her, she had a renewed sense of freedom.

"Probably," Suki said. "She was a wise woman. Only now do I understand her." She looked around the empty hall of the Quine. "Have you talked to Ronnie?"

"Not in the last few weeks," Skylar said. "She's been busy getting settled." Suki nodded. After losing Rhia and the events of the summer, Ronnie had decided India was where she needed to live full time. "I'm just two very long plane rides away," she had said the day she hugged Skylar goodbye.

In front of Cheveyo's stall hung one lonely eagle fern in a white plastic basin. "Why is this here? It looks so sad," Skylar said.

"I'd be sad too if I lived here," Suki said. "This place is so uninviting, which is saying a lot—it's a stable!" They looked around at the gray cement that walled each of the horses but for the small cutout each had for their head. One single barred window was fixed at the end of the aisle. "It's literally prison for horses."

Skylar looked at the struggling plant and it seemed to look back. It leaned in ever so slightly toward her.

"Did you see that?" Skylar whispered. "That plant is listening to our conversation."

"Of course it is," Suki said. "Plants are always listening."

Skylar reached out her hand and the fern responded by stretching to reach her hand. "Do they always do that?" she asked incredulously.

"Let me try," Suki pushed Skylar out of the way and reached toward the fern. Nothing. She deflated. "Must be all those magical powers have you really tuned into the source field."

"Source field?" Skylar asked. Again, she waved her hand in front of the plant and it followed her.

"The field of energy we're all connected to," Suki said. "Humans, plants, rocks even. Especially rocks. Ever since you had your *experience*, I started researching all sorts of stuff having to do with energy and consciousness. I've even been practicing."

"Practicing what?"

"Spoon bending," Suki said. "It's really all about focusing, or non-focusing your mind. You know, seeing things in a new way."

"That's pretty far removed from animal care," Skylar held a leaf gingerly between her fingers. The intricate veins of the leaf lit up like an energetic map. The same pathways ran in the veins in her hand. When she super-imposed them they were identical. Her eyes widened. "How about that? Tell me you see that electrical road map."

"Nice!" Suki said. She whipped out her notebook and scribbled feverously. "I'm learning it's not that removed from animals," she said when she finished.

"Miss De la Cruz!" a student came running over. "One of the mares is crowning, ready to give birth!"

"I know what crowning means, Justin," Suki said, instantly annoyed with his sophomoric enthusiasm. "She's had false labor a half dozen times already. I'm not convinced it's time."

"I see the bubble! And a foot!" Justin said in a panic and ran off.

"A foot is something," Skylar said. The girls rushed to the stall where Dune was staying. Milicent had brought the pregnant mare from Neshoba while she was ironing out her plan to resurrect the Executive Stables at the White House.

"Wow, I didn't think she would go today," Suki said. "But we are ripe with full moon energy."

Skylar gave her a look. "Since when have you blamed anything on the moon?"

"Again, *source field*," Suki said. "I'm learning the moon is behind a lot."

They gathered fresh hay and placed it around Dune. She took a few turns and clumsily lowered herself to the ground.

"Now what?" Justin asked.

"We wait," Skylar said. "They do most of the work." She gestured to the horse and soon-to-be-born foal.

Dune was the only female among Milicent's brood of five. Milicent was unsure which of her stallions sired the mare. They rarely socialized.

The girls beamed with happiness as the foal emerged. He quickly shook off the placenta and stood within minutes of entering the world. It was the magic of new life.

Suki took a step closer. "He's marvelous!" she said and did a quick evaluation. "Geez. Something's wrong with his eyes."

Skylar studied the foal, but didn't see what Suki was referring to.

"Holy cow," Justin exclaimed. "He doesn't have any!" To their mere mortal eyes, they saw eye sockets covered in a fine carpet of soft horsehair, a surface never needing an eyeball. Skylar leaned in toward the foal. She saw something completely different. His eyes were deep blue green with lightning bolts for pupils. She had never seen such eyes on a horse.

He cautiously wobbled toward his mother and began suckling like any other baby to his mama.

"What do we do?" Justin asked, starting to come unglued.

Suki looked at Skylar. "You can see his eyes, can't you?"

"Yup, and they're wonderful," Skylar said. She turned to Justin. "Justin, there's nothing to do right now. We'll test him after he's had time to bond with Dune. For now, he seems to be just fine."

Justin walked off muttering to himself and the girls continued to watch the horses. "You know Sky, at first I was envious of your new abilities," Suki said. "Then I realized I can develop my own powers . . . through learning. The world I thought was only open to you is actually open to all of us. We just have to work a little harder."

"How so?" Skylar asked.

"A lot of what Ocean taught you last year, meditation, focused intent is a big one. I've been really trying to stay mindful of the thoughts I allow into my brain." Suki said.

"Energy follows thought, she always said," Skylar repeated.

"It's a lot of retraining but worth it. I never paid attention to all of the negativity I put out in the world."

"Your negativity has its charm," Skylar smiled.

"Well, don't be surprised if that becomes the old me."

"Just don't become one of those positive affirmations people," Skylar said. "I hate those people."

"Inspirational quote memes, here I come." The girls laughed. "I'm meeting Kyle. Let me know when I can come pick out my new job title." Suki left Skylar in the aisle and she returned to Dune and the new foal. To her surprise, Cheveyo was standing with them in the stall, on guard as protector.

Skylar sucked in air over her teeth. "You . . ." she whispered. Cheveyo nodded slightly. Skylar smiled. The foal was his. She was so happy to see his family. He wouldn't be leaving anytime soon. He did belong here.

6

At home Skylar was flailing in her relationship with Rachel. Of all the secrets revealed over the last year, the fact that Rachel was her mother was the most devastating. Cassie was her mother, her childhood, her memories. Not Rachel.

Skylar knew Cassie would have wanted her to process it quickly but she struggled and usually avoided Rachel, exhausted from the sheer enormity of it all. But the holiday season was coming and she'd work on compassion if it killed her, which was highly possible.

Skylar braced herself for Rachel's bad cooking on Thanksgiving. She couldn't understand with all the catering options in the area, why she insisted on doing it herself, and why after all this time, her cooking abilities hadn't improved.

It was supposed to be the three of them, Joel, Rachel, and Skylar until the doctors had said Rachel's mother, Martha was well enough for a day visit. She had been diagnosed with schizophrenia decades ago, shortly after her husband, Rachel's father, Jonathan committed suicide. Rachel hadn't had much of a relationship with her own mother, who was in and out of hospitals. But the doctors said she had monumental improvement in the last few months. The day would now be spent waist deep in familial tension and dry turkey.

The front door opened slowly and Rachel came in with her arm wrapped around her mother. The frail woman was blanketed in wool despite the summer heat in November. She wore dark sunglasses and her salt and pepper hair was swept up in a messy bun. Skylar watched as Rachel got to work making Martha comfortable on one of the formal couches in the living room. "Is this okay mom?" she asked putting a pillow behind her back. Martha said nothing. Rachel moved the pillow slightly. "How about now?" Again, nothing from Martha. Rachel covered her legs with another blanket. "I'll be right back with some tea, Mom." Skylar could feel Rachel struggle to care for her mother.

Left alone with Martha, Skylar slowly circled the couch trying to read her energetic field. She couldn't remember the last time she saw Martha, if ever. As she studied her aura, it wafted like gray smoke around Martha's lifeless body. Skylar could see actual holes that faded into the blackness of another realm.

Skylar rested her hand on Martha's arm. The old woman didn't stir but Skylar felt her muscles relax at her touch. Moments later Skylar could hear the deep breaths in and out of Martha's lungs. Soon she was able to feel inside of Martha's body, feeling the pain she had shut off from all of her life. She observed Martha's inability to cope with the horrors of her early life. Once Jonathan took his own life, her brain compartmentalized her personality to save her from the same fate. Skylar could feel the dense pain buried in Martha's tissues, in every cell of her body. She felt the wall of her mental state, not as an illness but as armor against the terrors of living her life.

Martha stirred and slowly removed her sunglasses and looked at Skylar. Her stare was alert, piercing, keenly aware of her surroundings. "You see me," Martha said. "You see me."

"Yes," Skylar said.

"And what do you see?" Martha asked.

"I see your past hurts. And I see a future of possible healing, if you let the pain out of your body."

Martha shook her head. "This is all I know. I'm too old to release it now."

"There is still time to know joy," Skylar said.

Rachel walked in with a tray of tea. She looked at Skylar and Martha and the tray began to tremble in her hands. "Skylar, are you able to talk with my mom?" she asked wide-eyed.

"Yes, plain as day."

Rachel rushed the tea to the table and set it down. "This is miraculous!" She sat next to Martha and took her hand. "Mom, I've wanted to connect with you for so long." She searched Martha's eyes for understanding.

Martha looked at Rachel blankly. Rachel's hope dimmed.

"She isn't ignoring you," Skylar said. "A part of her died a long time ago and she's been carrying that dead person all this time. She doesn't know how to release her. If she can find a way, she'll come back to you. If she can't, she won't." Skylar reached out her hand and touched Rachel's shoulder as she wept. Skylar could feel her sadness run through her own veins. She stood between Martha and Rachel and gathered both of their hands. She felt Martha's grip tighten. The current between the women increased and flowed from one back to the other. Rachel looked in amazement at her mother. "I . . . feel her," she whispered.

"Love isn't dead," Skylar said. "Neither is hope."

Martha gave one final squeeze to the their hands and released them. She leaned forward and took the cup of tea. Skylar knew the moment had passed and hoped it wouldn't be too long before it returned, . . . for Rachel's sake.

"Thank you," Rachel whispered. "It's been decades since I felt my mother's love. But because of you, I felt it. It's still there. Thank you," she smiled and Skylar nodded lovingly. She was genuinely happy to help.

"Happy Thanksgiving Rain-gel," Skylar said.

"Happy Thanksgiving Skylar."

For the most part, the holiday season was pleasantly upbeat despite the outside world falling apart around them. The headlines seemed reminiscent of wartime yet all her visioning work with Ocean helped Skylar see the possibility for new beginnings in the crumbling social structures.

She felt a slight tinge of vindication when a scathing documentary surfaced exposing atrocities in the medical profession. It tied Big Pharma to secret government agencies withholding vital cures for diseases like cancer and Parkinson's. "I've always known those fuckers had the solutions in their well padded pockets," she told her father. "Mom didn't have to die." Joel pursed his lips and shook his head. He gave her a hug and walked out the door without saying a word.

Her sessions with Argan lessened. He mentioned something about holiday shopping, which sounded fishy, but she enjoyed the break from training. She and Suki decorated the Quine offices and were so bold as to put up a Christmas tree. She had done away with the round the clock feed of Joshua's concert footage and replaced it with Christmas cat videos.

As intellectual as Suki was, recent months saw an interesting turn in her area of focus. Her hobbyist enthusiasm of all things celebrity was now layered over her recent propensity for conspiracy theory, making for a dangerous combination. Skylar couldn't escape the alternative headlines Suki regurgitated on a daily basis regarding Big Oil, Big Pharma, and the government.

"Well maybe now Milicent can fix a few things," Suki said, shaking her head at the news feed on her phone.

"You mean Devlin," Skylar said.

"I doubt it," Suki said. She'd always had a girl crush on Milicent. The socialite turned political dynamo was the perfect blend of leadership and celebrity to make Suki swoon. "He *is* Big Pharma."

"Oh Suuk, I'm right there with ya, really. I know Cassie could have been cured. But I'll drive myself crazy living in the past and I have enough problems to fix in my current timeline," Skylar said.

Suki waved her off, reading something on her phone. She picked her head up a minute later. "Oh really?" her tone juvenile. "You might be interested to know that Big Pharma was in the news again, another celebrity overdose landed them in the hospital."

Skylar sighed. "You know I don't care about celebrities."

"You'll care about this one." Suki held up her phone for Skylar to read the headline. "Because it's Joshua."

7

Milicent paced the floor in the parlor of Neshoba, scratching her chest incessantly. She looked at her red skin in the hall mirror. Tiny hives had traveled from her chest up her neck to her jawline. "This is insanity!" she yelled at her reflection.

"I'm getting you some tea," Noah said.

"Make it the way I like it," Milicent barked.

"You finished the vodka last night," he said as he walked through the swinging door to the kitchen.

Milicent scratched the back of her neck anxiously and walked to the bar cart. Noah was right, no Grey Goose. She grabbed the bourbon and returned to the mirror. "What the hell is going on?" she examined the red bumps closer still.

"Stress," Devlin said behind her. He held her cup of hot tea.

"Darling, what a surprise," Milicent said, shifting her tone two octaves lower. She glanced at the kitchen door.

"I gave your man servant a forced break," he said.

She frowned. "I thought you weren't back from DC until tonight."

"I saw the news. Ryder is hospitalized. I thought I would come up and see you."

Milicent straightened her suit jacket and smoothed her hair back. She took the cup of tea from Devlin and put back the bottle of bourbon.

"That was kind of you to check on me," she said having a seat on the flowered sofa.

"He was an integral part of our life this past year," Devlin said. "Seeing this must be upsetting." He lightly touched a hive on her neck and she smacked his hand away.

She immediately tried to recover. "I'm sorry dear. They're just . . . irritating," she said, taking a sip of tea.

"Millie, is there anything you want to tell me?" Devlin asked, his eyes searching her face.

Milicent stared at him a long while before responding. "It's all just sad. I had no idea he was on drugs. That certainly wasn't the case when he was touring with us. Hopefully he will pull through and set a new course for his life."

"Should we pay him a visit?" Devlin asked.

"You're so busy with the transition, Dev. If I feel the need, I'll do that myself."

He continued to stare at her with a blank look on his face. "All right. But if you go, let me know."

She smiled and nodded. "All right."

8

Skylar walked the halls of Boston General with a large knot in her stomach. She swore she would never set foot in this place again unless she was setting it on fire, yet here she was. Everything was the same. Everything looked the same, smelled the same. She knew where all the restrooms were in case she had to vomit.

"Hey Tony," she said to the security guard at the main entrance. Tony was the only ray of sunshine Skylar took away from Boston Gen. He was old school Italian and loved a rich espresso. When Cassie was there, Skylar brought him a double shot every morning so he wouldn't have to drink the swill from the cafeteria.

"Skylar! Bellisima!" he got up from his chair and walked around the desk to give her a hug. "I've missed you."

She handed him a paper cup. "For old time's sake."

"Oh, you're the best," he said. "What brings you here? No more sick family I hope."

"No, Tony, a friend." She knew she'd be asking a favor of Tony. "Joshua Rider. He's probably in a private suite up top. Do you think you could get me in?"

He paused for just a moment. "For you? Anything." He returned to his desk and did a bit of investigating on his computer. He dug out a badge from the drawer and inserted it into a yellow lanyard. "He's in room 1542. Follow me." He led her to an open elevator and used a key to unlock the fifteenth floor. "If you have any issues, have them call me," he said, putting the lanyard around her head.

"Thanks, Tony. I appreciate it," she said as the elevator doors closed between them.

The doors opened on the fifteenth floor to another security desk. "Hello," she said to the portly guard scanning his phone. He glanced up and she showed him her badge. He waved her through without so much as an ID check.

The floor was eerily quiet. She passed two nurses having a conversation, and they glanced her way. She smiled but walked like she knew where she was going and they let her be.

A large laminated red paper sign stuck to the door of room 1542. It read:

Health Hazard, see Nurses Station before entering.

"My health or his?" Skylar asked out loud.

"His," a voice said behind her. Skylar whirred around.

"Sorry to startle you," she said. She was an older woman with a mop of curly gray hair dressed in a set of teacup dotted scrubs. Her nametag read *Ellen*. She had a kind face and gave Skylar a warm smile. "Are you family?"

Skylar thought about it. They definitely were connected. "Yes," hoping she wouldn't have to elaborate.

"I'm sorry," Ellen said. "Such a shame. He had a very bright future."

"He should pull through though, right?" Skylar asked.

"Only God knows, dear," Ellen said.

For the first time, the thought that Joshua might actually die crept into Skylar's mind. "I won't stay too long," she said.

She walked into his room as quietly as she could but then realized she wouldn't wake him. And if she did, it would be a good thing. He looked smaller, less intimidating. His hair looked recently cut. His face was smooth.

How odd it was to see Joshua stripped of his strength. His

power had always been in his eyes, now possibly permanently closed. She watched the bed sheets rise and fall with his even, slow breath and she poked his cheek. "You've had so much shit pumped into you your whole life, you should have been stronger than this. Wake up," she said.

She softened and shook her head. "What have you done to yourself?" she whispered within inches of his face, caressing that same cheek with the back of her fingers. The image of Joshua as a boy flashed in her mind. It reminded her that Milicent had done this to him. She saw the little boy so confused as to why his mother would hate him so much to subject him to all the tests, all the needles, all the changes. Skylar took in a large breath and sat in the chair next to the bed. "Can I help him?" she asked into the ethers. She expected Magda to reply but only the hum of the air conditioner answered.

"I forgive you Joshua," she said, taking his hand in hers. "I don't want you to die thinking yet another person hated you. We had a bizarre connection I might never understand and you were a lesson I needed to learn."

"Thank you," his voice said in a rasp. Skylar's head shot up and looked at his face. It was lifeless. "Over here," the voice spoke again from the foot of the bed. There stood his image, pure light, translucent, ethereal like Magda.

"Are you dead?" Skylar asked.

"I don't think so," he said. "But I wouldn't call this *alive* either."

She stood up. "So you're deciding."

"Yeah, I guess you could say that," he said. "I'm wondering what's left to return to."

"You've got a great career going," she said. "Just getting started. I bet the sky's the limit for you."

"From this vantage point, careers mean nothing." He drifted closer to her. "You know, you're the only visitor I've had."

"That can't be true," she said. "You're very popular. And don't forget, in a coma. Maybe you didn't see others."

He smiled a kind smile Skylar had never seen on him. "Nope, just you." He came even closer, within inches of her face and she felt heat coming off of his light body. "I'm sorry Skylar," he paused. ". . . for the way I treated you. You deserved better. I . . . wasn't taught any other way. Not that I'm making excuses but maybe I could have acted differently . . . better."

When Skylar reached out to touch this *being*, her fingers buzzed with small shocks. "Sorry," he said with a chuckle. All of the angst between them was missing. His soul was beautiful and Skylar wondered if he *should* return to his body.

"How long will you stay like this?" she asked.

"Apparently there's a process for ones like me. If I find a way to commit a selfless act of service, my soul is freed of my body and I will die. If I don't, I return to it with no memory and hope to discover that same act on my own."

"Wow, okay," she said. "I have a bit of a quest going myself. I'll keep you in mind if I see anything that suits you," she said.

"Thanks," he said.

"And I'll come back soon," she said.

"Don't," he said. "Go on that quest, save the world or something. I'll figure my shit out." He took a step back. "You know, you did capture a part of me." A look of surprise came across his face at his own revelation.

"I could say the same," she said, thinking that was an understatement. She actually wanted to hug him but a hundred shocks stood in her way. "Well then, goodbye for now, Joshua."

"Be well, Skylar," he said and faded.

9

The Winter Solstice, Dec 21, 2020: The week before Christmas, Skylar had trouble sleeping every night. She didn't need sleep the way she did before absorbing Rhia's heart light but it did afford her a break from all the incessant thoughts. She remembered staying awake at night when she was a child, excited for Santa. That was much better than this.

She hadn't been able to shake her thoughts of Joshua. How different he was without the drama of his ego. And how could she help him? Her list of mysteries was getting longer, not shorter.

The night of the Winter Solstice, Michael was up with her, pacing, yowling, determined to get outside.

Just after ten she acquiesced. "Fine," she said, opening the door. She never let him outside at night but he was driving her nuts. She followed him out into the hot night air and he settled down once he got out onto the tiny porch, tucking his feet under his body. "That's it? That's all you wanted?" she huffed and sat next to him. As she sat, she stared at the stars. The sky was clear and the planetary alignments were so obvious, she'd wondered how she'd never seen it before. How small she felt on earth, with a very big job to do. She looked for Saturn. It had been in the news that on this night of the solstice, there would be a historic alignment of Saturn, Jupiter, and Pluto. Skylar couldn't get into astrology but this alignment happened every 734 years and 2020 was it. How odd and fascinating that all of the cycles and alignments and endings and beginnings were convening at this time on the planet. As if it were all for her.

She could see Saturn, shining brightly in the east. Jupiter wasn't far behind it. She looked for Pluto but gave up without trying too hard. She climbed up into the porch loveseat and curled into the tightest ball, missing Cassie. For all the help she had from the women in her life, she craved the comfort of her mother.

"*I am comforting you, sweetheart,*" Cassie whispered in her ear as she held Skylar tight. "*Feel the thread between us, and you will feel me in your heart.*"

She closed her eyes, feeling drowsy for the first time in a week. There she remained for the night, blanketed in the love of her mother.

Christmas Eve was going to be festive at the Southmartin house. Skylar's prayers had been answered and Rachel had the meal catered. She was genuinely excited to be hosting a party filled with Skylar's friends. The house was tastefully decorated in fresh pine and red accents. Their tree was a modest seven footer with enough room for the only odd decoration in the house, Rachel's fiber optic angel. As a child, Skylar had nicknamed it "disco angel" as its dress and wings feverously flashed every color of the rainbow. Rachel always corrected her calling it the "chakra angel." Skylar liked "disco angel" much better.

They were expecting Suki and Kyle and also Argan. Skylar had invited Beatrice but she refused to make the drive. "I'll see you in the new year then," she told her grandmother over the phone. "We have lots to discuss."

Before any guests arrived, Skylar thought she'd pay her father a visit in his lab. Ever since she'd started morphing into an alien, Joel spent every waking moment searching for scientific breakthroughs in her blood, often finding a few. Her triple helix DNA was no passing phenomenon. He checked and rechecked with every draw of her blood and found the helix firmly intact. With no outside, biotechnical assistance, Skylar's telomeres regenerated on a consistent basis and her glandular system was functioning at an undocumented level.

"Hey Dad," she said, looking around. His lab never changed. She had thought maybe he would update his equipment or something but it was a perpetual throwback to the early nineties.

"Hey," he said distracted, his eyeballs attached to a microscope.

She stared at the classic periodic table poster that took up most of the back wall. It had yellowed from age and curled at the edges. As she stared at the poster, the boxes of each element quivered and started to circle about in a choreographed dance. She looked at Joel, who was oblivious to the magic show. The boxes slowed to form the shape of a human body. All 108 elements fit like a perfect jigsaw puzzle in an image of the Vitruvian Man.

A handful of elements burned brighter than the rest. Mercury, Salt, and Sulfur called her name.

"Dad, how many elements are in the periodic table?" she asked.

"108," he said, picking his head up from the microscope.

"And how many elements are in the human body?"

"108."

"So everything that makes up our outer world, also makes up our inner world," she said.

"That's one way to look at it," he said. "Why?"

Skylar blinked and the boxes returned to their original rows. "I've been into numerology lately and that seems like more than just a coincidence." She picked up a pencil and scribbled the words *mercury, salt,* and *sulfur* on a scratchpad. Joel read over her shoulder.

"The Tria Prima," he said.

"Hmm?"

"The three essentials, mercury, salt, and sulfur. The bases of alchemical creation." He took her pencil and drew lines from each word. They formed a triangle.

"Alchemy?" Skylar asked. "How magical of you."

"Have you had blood taken recently?" he asked, dismissing her comment.

"Not by anyone but you," she said.

"Let's do that now before you eat." He busied himself with preparing the needles.

"On Christmas? Really Dad?"

"Any new physical changes?" he asked.

"Not really. Except I seem to have a new relationship with plants. They are starting to bend in my direction, as if they are inspecting me or something. I thought it had to do with my new abilities but Suki said I might just be overly sensitive to the source field."

Joel looked back to his watch, taking her pulse. "Did you just exercise?" he asked, completely ignoring what she was saying.

"Nope."

He repeated the process. "Your pulse is high, 110 beats. That's off the charts. Are you feeling okay?"

"No different than usual."

"I'll run some tests for infection but we need to monitor this," he said concerned. He prepared her arm for the needle.

"Okay, Dad. But did you hear me about the source field?" she asked. "Are you familiar with a source field?"

Joel stopped for a moment and looked at her. "Can you stick to one subject please? You are all over the map with your interests. If you must know, the source field is a waste of time, discredited by numerous scientists. Tell Suki to stick to horses."

Skylar studied her father. This was the old Joel, the close-minded scientist that needed proof to believe something was true. She thought he had come so far from this.

She steadied herself and stared at his table of elements, but it was no help. The table had other ideas. Images of the planets swirling in the solar system spun in front of the poster. The earth shone the most brightly. They formed a pattern over the table, corresponding seven different metals to seven heavenly bodies; Gold for the sun, Silver for the moon, Iron for Mars, Mercury for Mercury, Lead for Saturn, Tin for Jupiter, and Copper for Venus.

Before she could make sense of it, she felt the needle enter her arm.

It pierced her skin like an arrow. Instantly, her body reacted like never before. Every cell in her body stood at attention. She could feel the life force draining through the needle. The dance of the planets stopped as her focus went inward.

"Please stop," she said, her voice only a whisper. Joel ignored her. "Dad, stop," she said a bit louder.

"Why? I'm almost done," Joel said dryly. "Let me finish."

"No, Dad!" she found her voice and ripped the needle out of her arm. She sprang out of the chair and fell backward.

"What?" he asked in the chaos. Blood poured out of the vile, spilling on the metal tray. Joel scrambled to save the sample as Skylar crashed to the floor.

"I think I have what I need," Joel said tending to his specimen. He handed her a cotton ball to cover the needle hole in her arm.

"Way to tend to me first, Dad," she said, splayed out on the floor.

"I'm sorry. What happened?"

"It felt wrong, like a violation. I couldn't get it out of my arm fast enough."

"Maybe you're hungry," he said awkwardly. "Rachel ordered the best dinner." He smiled.

"Great," she said, slowly getting to her feet. She was annoyed at her father's reaction, but could only assume he didn't know how to handle the situation. She still couldn't shake the feeling of panic she had when Joel drew her blood. It was like something precious was being ripped away.

She regained her breath and looked at the periodic table. The planets had vanished. The table had returned to normal.

Joel put all of the vials onto the tray. "I'll wait until tomorrow to work on this," Joel said. "It *is* Christmas."

"Good idea, Dad. When you're done, can Ocean take a look? I know you disagree on your methods but her perspective is helpful."

"Sure, we're all adults," he said. "Are you sure you're okay?"

"Yup." She looked at the daunting flight of stairs and wondered if she were telling the truth.

She made a full recovery from the blood drawing and the evening turned out to be very merry with a Secret Santa gift exchange. Skylar had picked Argan and had been looking forward to giving him her gift. Every man should own a pair of cowboy boots, especially one as handsome as Argan. It turned out he was her Secret Santa as well, and gave her a Siamese Fighting Fish.

"Wow, thank you," Skylar said slowly. "Michael really wanted a bird but a fish will do."

Argan chuckled. "I'll help you set up his tank. They're pretty easy to care for." The small royal blue fish had long flowing orange fins that dazzled the eyes with their luminescent color. Skylar wondered why in the entire universe of available gifts, Argan gave her a fish, yet another life to care for.

The rest of the gift exchange revealed all of the couples had each other and Skylar suspected Rachel had fixed it that way. Aside from the fish, the only non-clothing gifts were Kyle and Suki's exchange reminiscent of the Gift of the Magi. He had sold his autographed John Bonham drumsticks to buy her the gold chain she wanted for her grandmother's charm. And she pawned her gold charm to get a beautiful glass windowed box for his drumsticks. It was very touching to see their mutual vulnerability and Skylar felt they were a bit embarrassed. Skylar had no idea Suki was struggling financially. It did make sense as she was trying to carry the expenses of her grandmother's house and Skylar wasn't aware of any inheritance money.

To give them some privacy, Skylar corralled everyone else into the dining room for dessert, which was her only responsibility of the night. She had made a strawberry and banana trifle, an old recipe of Cassie's. The whole evening was surprisingly enjoyable but Skylar was glad when it was over. She had to admit she was more tired than usual and couldn't wait to climb in bed at Joel's.

She was so exhausted and couldn't remember if she'd brushed her teeth but she wasn't getting out of bed. She wasn't asleep long before her mind woke to an explosion of color and a sensation of being carried along a river of intense heat . . .

She stopped along the riverbank and hopped off, looking down to see the river was a snake of gold liquid winding along the earth. Skylar felt the energy from the flowing fire-like fluid. It ached with emptiness and scorched the earth where water once flowed. It wound back and forth upon itself, forever searching for the great sea within the earth's core from which it came. She saw herself dressed all in white, perched on a large boulder in the middle of the river. "Laughless Rock," she said assuredly. Her perspective shifted. She now stood on the rock, looking outward at hot liquid around her but felt no fear. Instead she closed her eyes and transformed into a beautiful white ibis. In one motion, she leapt into the air and flew from danger.

Skylar's eyes popped open but she remained still. She stared at the black ceiling until her focus started to shift. She stood up and the blackness in front of her eyes gave way to a collage of iridescent colors. *Beatrice was there, young and beautiful, like pictures Skylar had seen from years ago. She wore a gown of shimmering silver that reflected the light when she walked.*

Bea began to speak. "Laughless Rock is the resting place of the Goddess, where the veil between the Underworld and upper world is thinnest."

Skylar looked into a cobalt sky and clouds began to form. They wafted down close enough she thought she could touch them. They parted slightly and Magda appeared, serene and angelic. She gestured to a woman with long pyrite hair, cloaked in linen, now kneeling on Laughless Rock next to the river of gold. Deep red blood dripped from her eyes and pooled at her feet. She looked up at Skylar. Despite her suffering, her eyes shone with a bright light. The woman reached out toward Skylar, pleading without words. In bed, Skylar's physical body reached out her arms to help her. *She looked at Magda. "What do I do?"*

It is time to act. Restore the memory in the Akasha. Only then will her suffering cease. Magda said. You are a Daughter of the Rose, the bloodline of Sophia. You can heal the past and future. The Akasha is held deep within the earth, but it is also carried in your veins. Your blood is tied to the ore running deep in Mother Gaia.

"Of course, I will do it," Skylar said. She looked at the woman. She had seen her before. Her eyes were Argan's eyes. She locked on her gaze. "I will do it, I promise," she said telepathically. The woman bowed her head and Skylar felt her relief.

The scene faded and Skylar jolted up in bed. She moved her hands in front of her face and pinched her own cheeks to prove to herself she was awake. She stood up and took in a deep breath. *"Gaia's memory,"* she whispered. *"That was it."* Her eyes welled with tears as she remembered Cassie talking about the records locked in all of the crystals she had around the house. She used to say she was the keeper of the earth's memories stored in those crystals. It was a game they used to play, talking to the rocks and listening for them to talk back. "One day you will free the rock's memories and change the world," Cassie said emphatically.

It took Skylar a few minutes to remember she was at her dad's house. The sun was already high and she marveled that all of this happened during the light of day. She pulled out the Book of Sophia and started thumbing through the pages.

When you restore the memory held deep within Gaia, you restore the past and the future.
You restore the wisdom of the Heart, the wisdom of Earth.

She held onto the book and made her way to the kitchen for coffee. The reality of her dreams had been blending with her waking life and it was getting harder to tell which world she walked in. If she were lucid dreaming something would be out of place and she'd know.

A knock on the door made her jump as she walked by.

"Good morning!" Ocean chirped in uncharacteristic cheer. She stood at the door carrying breakfast items and a box of Joe.

"Wow, what are you so happy about?" Skylar asked. She scanned Ocean skeptically. Her good mood was definitely out of place.

"Things are shifting. I feel shift," Ocean said. "It's overdue."

"Shift happens," Skylar couldn't help herself.

Ocean's smile faded. "I don't enjoy puns." She walked into

the house and put her bags on the kitchen counter. Skylar wanted to talk to Argan before she brought up her dream to Ocean. For all she knew, Ocean was the one who put it in her head. "Did you have a good Christmas?"

"Yes, it was quite nice. We missed you." Skylar said.

"I'm sure that's true," Ocean said.

"Good morning, Ocean," Joel said entering the kitchen. He was smiling and looked genuinely happy to see her.

"Hello, Joel. I'm anxious to dive into that fresh batch of blood."

"I already ran my tests. Skylar's enzymes all seem to be stabilizing. And no infection to explain her high pulse rate." He reached for Skylar's arm to check again. "Still 110 beats." He creased his forehead. "I'm worried about tachycardia."

Ocean rolled her eyes. "Oh please, she's a child."

"Do you have an explanation?" Joel asked.

"I'd have to check the pulsation readings of the earth this week," Ocean said. "They've been spiking off the charts. She's probably just syncing with the telluric field. I wouldn't worry about tachycardia. Now let's see her samples. I have a full day."

The two retreated to the basement. Skylar thought about following but knew they would reemerge if they needed her. She accepted this was her awakened state and she fixed herself a cup of Joe.

10

O cean's woody perfume still hung in the air when there was
another knock on the door. She'd have to drink Joe black.

"Ready, I see," Argan said, looking at her disheveled hair and
sleepwear. They were only meeting once this week due to the
holidays.

"You're early," she said, facing him in the doorway.

"We said ten. It's ten."

"It's been a busy morning." She walked onto the front porch
to breathe the fresh air but there was none. She looked up into
the sky. The air was wet though no rain came. She felt the air
land on her skin. Humidity in late December made everything
damp.

She turned to face him. "Argan, I had a dream," she blurted.
"It was so real, as real as this moment. I was there, and I saw her."

"Saw who?"

"Your mother, I'm sure of it."

Argan's expression froze on his face.

"She was bleeding, Argan," she said. "And Magda said I have
to return the memory to the Akasha and your mother's suffering
will ease. I've confirmed that in Sophia's book. Much of it is in
alchemical language so I didn't understand it until now. I'm worried
for your mother. Have you spoken to her lately? Is she all right?"

"I'll give her a ring, Sky, but I'm sure she's fine. She's dramatic
but always fine."

"No, something is horribly wrong. Do you know what it could be?"

He paused. "Why don't you get dressed and I'll meet you out back. We can talk about it."

A prickling sensation crept up her head and she gave him a look of suspicion. "That . . . sounds . . . bad," she said. She was slow to walk inside but needed to get out of her pajamas. "I'll be five minutes."

She came out to the paddock with two bottles of water and offered one to Argan. "Thanks," he said as he twisted off the cap. She watched him intently as his lips touched the mouth of the bottle. He chugged it all at once and the muscles in his arm flexed as he raised the bottle to get the last drop of water out. "Still no end to the heat," he said. His eyes glanced toward her and back to the bottle.

"Ocean says we're shifting. That's the reason."

"Does she see an end date?"

"It could be years," Skylar tapped her fingers on the paddock fence, waiting for Argan to start talking.

"Years? Christ, that can't be true." He turned to the horse that had come to the fence to say hello to them both. "Hey Valor, it's nice to see you my friend." He gave the black stallion a pat on his flank.

"Argan, about my dream," Skylar started. "It's a sign of something I'm supposed to do."

"Yes, it is," he said, still staring at Valor.

"You're not surprised," she said. He turned to her with a pained look on his face and her sense of dread worsened. "What is it?"

"I don't know where to start," he said. He looked away and ran his hand through his hair in that familiar way. "I rehearsed this moment in my head a hundred times." He held the fence with both hands. "You had the dream," he said, glancing toward her again but couldn't hold her eyes. "You saw the snake of gold. You saw the sibyl, my mother."

The hot prickle had now traveled down her neck and seeped into her whole body.

He let go of the fence and started to pace. "She had been blessed, . . . or cursed with the gift of foresight. And not only have you dreamt of her, but she of you." He took in a deep breath and continued. "She sent me to find you, Skylar. We have important work and . . ." his voice cracked and trailed into a whisper. ". . . she sent me to find you." He shook his head.

Skylar stood in a daze. "I don't understand. You . . . you told me fate and destiny brought us together," she said in disbelief. "Not once did you say *your mother*."

"And I stand by that," he said trying to smile. "It *is* our destiny, Skylar. It is our job to transmute fate into destiny. There were just other forces. She saw the coming atrocities on our planet. It's of apocalyptic proportions. It's terrifying actually." He walked to her side and put his hand on her hip. "But in this chaos is a seed of opportunity and I have to help you find it," he said sincerely.

She stepped back and faced him square on. "All this time, that's been your motivation?" she asked. "You lied to me."

"We're even," he said.

"If you're coming clean, tell me all of it. What's your role in this, besides Cassie's messenger and the runner for your prophesying mother? You obviously know Ocean, and the truth about Rhia and all of the mysteries that have suffocated me for over a year. Did you know the truth about Rachel?" She hoped he wouldn't say it. *Don't say it*, she thought.

He looked far off into the distance, avoiding her stare. "I knew."

Her eyes widened. "Since when?"

"Always," he said.

"Always?" she held on to the fence for support. "We've known each other since we were eleven years old! You couldn't have known and understood something so complex then."

He slid his hands into the pockets of his jeans and leaned on the fence. "No. But my mother prepared me for this my whole life. Every opportunity she taught me the ways of the Goddess, and the Great Mothers. I've never known another way. So I do understand the complexities of the situation."

"Maybe you can explain it to me then," she said, sliding down to sit in the dirt. Argan slid down beside her. The image of their eleven-year-old selves sitting in the dirt, refusing to say a final goodbye came to mind.

"I was just a boy with no clue what love was," he said. "I only knew you made my heart full. You carry a part of me inside you, Skylar. And our time together was coming to an end. How was I supposed to live without you? It was heartbreak."

Tears welled in Skylar's eyes as he spoke. She stared out at the perpetually parched trees longing for a break that never came.

"My mother wanted to console me every way she knew how. Every night back in Greece she told me stories about how we would be reunited some day, when the stars were aligned and the Goddess was ready to return, she would oversee our reunion.

"I clung to that, Skylar. I had to. As I grew, she prepared me like a Spartan warrior knowing the day would come when I would be called to make the greatest sacrifice, to help you, regardless of your feelings for me. But my ego got in the way and I fell hard last year. The lines between duty and desire got blurred . . . real bad.

"I forgot my purpose and my commitment to my mother and to the Goddess. It took all of my strength not to make love to you over and over, so many times." She looked at him. His eyes couldn't hide his need for her. He looked away.

"When I saw you with Joshua, I saw red. I snapped. I couldn't continue. All that my mother asked of me dissolved in that moment." He picked up a rock and threw it across the yard.

"You were right, I did leave town. I left the country and returned to Greece. She forbade me to abandon all we had worked for and I came back a few weeks later. I got a handle on things. I promised Ocean I would train you and that's what I've been doing. You're coming along and my emotions won't get the better of me. You can be sure of it."

Skylar didn't know where to put this new information. Argan had always been her perfect hero, her soul mate who did no wrong. He didn't make mistakes. She did.

But now, this revelation was dumped in her lap. He had deceived her. It was her turn to forgive. Of all the emotions she felt, humility was at the top. *What was that saying?* she thought . . . *she who casts stones?* Or something like that.

She got up out of the dirt and brushed herself off. "Well, where do we go from here?"

"That's it? You must have questions, or a need to yell at me or something." He jumped up to meet her.

"No. I'm not casting stones today. To be honest, I don't want to. I've become the broken horse, Argan. In the last year, life has beaten me up so badly, I officially surrender. I'm not judging you. I've made my share of mistakes."

"I'm sorry, Sky," he said. He held her shoulders and made her look at him. "You've been put through every extreme this year. I'm sorry for the role I played in it. I . . . " he stopped talking and dropped his hands.

She could see his struggle. He needed her as much as she

needed him. "I forgive you, Argan. I've been doing a lot of forgiving lately." She gave him an encouraging smile and took his hands in hers. She clasped them together and raised them to her lips. She kissed each of his hands and let them go.

She stretched her arms in the air to shake off the rust. "Are we training today? I need to move my body."

He gave her a sympathetic smile. "All right. We can wait on meditation. Let's do some physical stuff."

They made their way to the backyard. Joel's petunias spilled over every surface and the pool hadn't been closed in almost two years due to the perpetual heat.

Skylar hadn't noticed much progress in the six months they'd been working together. Argan could still get her on the floor in one move. Today would be no different.

She spun around and threw her leg in the air. He caught it at the ankle and she dropped to the floor. "That needs some work," he said. "Your foundation is still unstable. An opponent can get you on the floor in seconds."

"Who am I fighting in this scenario, exactly?" she asked.

"Me," he said. He reached out his hand to help her up. She sprang up, refusing to take it.

"Again," he commanded. She repeated the process and once again he had her on the ground.

"No, really, who am I taking down? Milicent? That ship has sailed if you didn't notice, she's First Lady now . . . or soon will be."

"Skylar, you're right, there doesn't seem to be any actual opponent to fight but keeping your body in shape is key for that magic you're carrying under your ribs."

"So you're doing this to keep me in shape? That can't be the reason." She studied him, resting her arms on her knees. "You don't know the reason. You're just following orders. Just like me."

"Let's try again," he said.

"I don't want to," she got to her feet.

He grabbed her arm. "Come on, let's give it another shot."

She pulled away from his grip. "I said no!" and spun away from him and right into the pool.

After a minute, she came up for air. Argan was bending over from the side, concerned.

"You suck," she said, just able to stand on her toes.

"Very mature of you," he quipped back, failing to hold in a smile. He teetered on the edge and Skylar seized an opportunity. She pulled his arm toward her, knocking him off balance and right into the pool with her.

"Your foundation is unstable," she said when he came up out of the water.

"We've come full circle," he said, wiping the water out of his eyes.

"How so?"

"Remember that time you were crossing the brook when we were kids and fell in?"

She did, it was the day they met. She was so embarrassed. "Yeah, this is so like that," she grumbled.

They made their way out of the pool. "Let's run the drill again," he said.

"Soaking wet?" she asked with more grumbling.

"Yeah," his ire was up and they were going to do it again.

They ran the drill. She whirred around in lightning fast speed. Argan blocked her and she fell to the ground.

"Again," he commanded.

She got to her feet and tried it again. And again he leveled her.

"Again," he said.

With each subsequent blow, Skylar became more and more angry. And each time she was a little slower to get to her feet.

Seeing her grow weary, Argan suggested they take a break. "Let's recharge for a minute."

"No, I'm in it now. Let's go. Again," she said, now covered in wet grass and dirt.

"Sky, let's just take five," he said.

"No. Again," she said louder.

"Fine," he said. They ran the drill again and again he got her on the ground.

"Uggggghhhh!" she growled through gritted teeth, on her hands and knees. "Again," she barked, swaying slightly.

"Sky, I don't want . . ."

"Again!" she was on her feet, eyes closed, ready for his attack. None came. She opened her eyes to see him standing there. "What are you waiting for?"

"I don't want to hurt you," he said. "You need a break."

She took in a large breath. "Again," she whispered, standing tall. She turned completely inward and closed her eyes. She could hear the sound of Argan's breath. Once she focused on it, it howled in her ears as loud as the wind. She shifted her focus to the sounds of nature in the yard. She was acutely aware of the birds chirping, the insects buzzing. She could even hear the soft breeze floating through the treetops way above her. In her next breath, she tuned it all out. The only thing she heard was her own heartbeat pounding in her ears like a tribal drum. She moved her arms in concentric circles in the air with her eyes closed. She came to complete stillness and concentrated all her energy into her next movement, her roundhouse kick. Argan came at her and before she had time to think, she shot him clear across the yard and he landed in an exposed dirt pile earmarked for a new flowerbed.

She opened her eyes. "Oh my god, are you okay?" she ran to him.

"That was fantastic!" he said, springing to his feet.

"It really was," she said with a twinkle in her eye.

"Remember that feeling," he said. "It's your power."

She gave him a hand up and dusted the dirt off of his T-shirt. "I'm just making it worse," she said, feeling a hot prickle creep up her neck.

He smiled and for a brief moment she could see beneath his shell. "You had a breakthrough today. Great job."

She was still mad at his agenda but couldn't mask the familiar stirring below her heart. She tamped it down as usual. "I'll get some more drinks. We're empty." She almost made it to the kitchen and nearly ran into Ocean at the back door.

"Skylar, can you come down to your dad's lab please?" Ocean asked. Skylar glanced at Argan, already making his way over.

The threesome joined Joel in the small laboratory. "I have an explanation for your increased heart rate," Ocean said, "besides syncing to the earth's pulse, which is one factor. There are forces within the cosmos that mix with the earth's atmosphere and maintain it. Everything that happens on earth is a direct reaction to these radiations, a resonance if you will. Human beings are capable of harnessing these forces and using it as an energy source. Exactly fifty-four people on the planet currently do this. Your mother happens to be one of them. Rachel has always had a natural gift to control energy and transform it at will. Your heartbeat, now attuned to the earth's pulse gives you this power. The earth's pulse is increasing and so is yours."

Skylar slipped herself onto a stool for support.

"But that's not all!" Ocean mimicked her best game show host. "Besides your alignment with planetary energies, your potentiation is complete. It's all right here." She gestured to the microscope. "Your triple helix DNA is transforming again. Since you absorbed Rhia's heart light, it's been alchemizing from carbon based into a crystalline-based formation. In simple terms, your body is becoming multi-dimensional pure light. This is where dimension hopping becomes possible from your third dimension starting point."

Argan shuffled his feet to stand beside Skylar. She felt the warm pressure of his hand softly on her back and she gave him a smile of thanks.

"Last fall we watched your DNA transform you into a super-human but that did settle into a rhythm that let you function as a normal person. But you were still undergoing a process of reconfiguring your DNA, clarifying and cleansing all of the traumas you had held in your energy field. It's really fortunate you found out about Rachel and Cassie when you did. It gave your system a chance to clear that trauma from your memory in a way that you can move on quicker than the average person."

"I haven't forgotten that trauma, if that's what you're saying," Skylar said.

"Right, you won't forget but it won't get stuck in your cell tissue causing illness either. It took nine months, similar to a baby's gestation, but you are officially a clean slate, with no ancestral baggage to claim your youth, vitality, or mental stability."

Argan's hand dropped from Skylar's back. "Wow, can we all get that or is it just green heart girl?" he asked.

"It is accessible to everyone but next to impossible to activate in our current social climate. You need a completely open mind." She glanced at Joel, then back to Skylar. "Consider this process, triggered by your heart light, an initiation of sorts. Over the course of the past year, you have been purified and renewed on every level. You have completely removed your karma."

"Whoa," was all Argan said.

Skylar hoped to be a bit more eloquent than that. She took

a deep breath. "Ocean, thank you for the enlightening science lesson. I promise to use my superpowers for good, not evil."

The periodic table called to Skylar once more. The glowing boxes undulated like a snake to get her attention. "I have to ask you about the elements, the table on the wall," Skylar said, pointing to the poster.

"Giving you a show, is it?" Ocean said. "It ties into all this. The bodies of people only appear to consist of the same ingredients. They are actually made up of different levels of the elements corresponding to the type of spirit dwelling within. All people have fire, air, and water within them, in various combinations. These combinations express themselves as the different elements in that table. As the consciousness of a person deepens, their elemental formula changes. The Akasha is not only stored in the earth, and in the heavens but also in your blood. In the blood of all of humanity. It is what gives you your individuality and what ties you to earth."

Joel stood silently in the corner massaging the bridge of his nose.

"The mysteries of human blood are vast," Ocean continued. "And there are many human mutations happening on earth right now. The crystal and indigo children coming here are the start of a new species of human no longer willing to accept the hell we've created for ourselves. You have been called as a leader Skylar. This physical transformation is just one piece."

"Magda may have used the word *leader*. I don't see who I'm leading in any scenario."

"How about teacher?" Argan said. "You have learned so much with all you've been through. You could get your teaching degree."

"Hey, we were set on vet school," Joel chimed in. "What happened to that?"

"The Great Mother has bigger plans for Skylar than vet school," Ocean said.

"I thought you were a great mother?" Skylar said.

"Right, and I have bigger plans for you. And the kind of teaching you'll be doing, there's no degree on the planet that would qualify." She looked at Joel. "Skylar, you must combine the wisdom of Sophia with the knowledge of the sciences to bring humanity into the light. I'm talking about alchemy."

Ocean fished out a small clear vial from her bag. A shimmering gold liquid sloshed inside. "For starters, you'll need to drink this on a regular basis."

"What is it?" Joel grabbed it out of her hand.

"Hey!" she grabbed it back. "It's electrified gold. And if you touch it again, I'll flatten you."

"You want me to drink gold?" Skylar asked staring at the vial.

"It's either that or the menstrual blood of a high priestess," Ocean said. "That's a lot harder to find." She unscrewed the small black top. "It's electrified by the energy of the sun. If anyone else were to drink this, it would kill them on the spot, akin to being struck by lightening. But for you, this will amplify your will power and it will be stored in your body like an ankh. You will be the perfect marriage between the frequencies of the divine and physical matter."

"Perfect timing. She's found her center," Argan said. "She sent me clear across the yard."

Skylar smiled. She *had* found her center.

"You had the dream, didn't you?" Ocean said, studying Skylar through squinted eyes.

Skylar looked at Argan. "Yes," she said, staring into his eyes.

"Then our timeline is shifting," Ocean said. "When was the last time you saw Beatrice?"

"It's been awhile," Skylar said. "But we talked the other day and I plan to see her in the New Year."

"Don't wait. It appears to be *go time*," Ocean said. "Now drink up."

Skylar sniffed the thick shimmering liquid. "Smells like wood chips."

"I added a bit of cedar to help it go down. It's best to chug it all at once."

Skylar put the vial to her lips.

"Wait," Joel said. "Is her health at risk with all of this?"

"You have to see past the physical, Joel," Ocean said, her voice strained with annoyance. "What you perceive as physical is only one small part of the whole picture. She is exactly where she is supposed to be. You'll have to take my word for it."

Skylar took Argan's hand and he let her. She tipped the vial back and gulped the gilded liquid. She shuddered from the thick consistency. "Bleh." She stuck out her tongue. It was a bright metallic gold color. "Now what?"

Ocean took out a ziploc bag of two dozen more vials. "Once a day. Don't miss a dose."

"I don't want to know how you make this stuff," Joel said, leaning over the batch.

"Good thing. I'll never tell you."

"But what can I expect to happen to my body?" Skylar asked, sticking her tongue out again to see it in a scratched up microscope mirror.

"This will completely stop your aging process and now when you practice your skills, you will be much more adept, no matter what it is," Ocean said. "I have to run. I have a full day. Don't forget to see Beatrice!" she breezed up the stairs and was gone.

"Skylar, I don't like this," Joel said.

"It's okay, Dad. I'm meant for bigger things, remember?" She gave Joel a hug and looked at Argan. "Have time for another round of kicks? I'm feeling electrified."

"You feel different already?" Argan asked.

"Not really." The words hung in the air as a slow burn started in Skylar's belly. It felt similar to the feeling she would get when she had to stand in front of a class and give a speech. *Fear*, she thought. "I'm just going to get some air," she said, racing for the stairs.

She ran outside, sure she was going to throw up. Argan and Joel followed. "I'm ok, really Dad," she waved behind her. Joel got the hint and retreated back to his lab.

"How are you really?" Argan asked.

"It's like I swallowed a watermelon," she said holding her knees. "And it wants to come back up." The feeling spread from her belly, through her veins and soon covered every inch of her body. She heard Argan talking in a muffled voice. He sounded miles away. She focused on the acute feeling in her gut. *Fear*. She let herself feel its weight and she saw its color . . . black.

As she stood bent in half, she had an idea. In her head, she started talking to the blackness. Instead of letting it run wild in her mind and her body, she decided to give it some guidelines. She kept her eyes closed. "Now listen here," she said in her head. "I understand you want a voice and you've attached yourself to me to do it. But this feeling doesn't serve me. If you want to stick around, you need to change your tone." She imagined the blackness getting lighter. It slowly transformed into a swirling mass of gold and black waves that spiraled in her imagination. The blackness dissipated into the sea of gold and her mind filled with brilliant light. She smiled and stood upright. She opened her eyes.

Argan stood before her, his eyes wide. "That was amazing," he said. "Your skin shimmered and now you have this red streak in your hair." He reached out and touched her hair.

"Nice!" she said.

"What did you do?" he asked.

"I had to turn fear into excitement," she said. "They really are two sides of the same coin."

"Turning lead into gold already," he said.

She smiled. They were both completely dry now from their dip in the pool. "Can I interest you in some lunch? All this transmuting made me hungry."

"I'd like that," he said.

They went inside and Skylar started pulling out food from the fridge.

"Do you have any plans for New Year's Eve?" he asked casually.

She froze in place, her hand on the crisper. "Ummm, no," she said, still leaning into the fridge.

"I don't know if you remember, but it's my birthday and I thought if you didn't have any plans, you might . . . want to grab dinner . . . or something."

Skylar flashed back to last year's holiday season. They had seen each other on Christmas Eve and not again until Rhia's funeral in the spring. She had missed Argan's birthday.

She stood up and looked at him square in the face. "I would like that," she said.

"Great," he said. He looked away and walked to the kitchen desk littered with papers. Skylar's Book of Sophia lay casually on top. "You don't keep this in a safe place?" he asked.

"That is a safe place," she said. "I re-read it every day. I've asked Rachel to help but she can't read it. Sophia seems to only want me to know her secrets."

"May I?" he asked before touching the book.

"Sure."

Argan picked up the hide-covered book and slowly opened it. She was curious to see what effect it would have on him. She watched out of the corner of her eye while she pretended to fix a salad. He took a seat on a stool at the island and slowly thumbed through the translucent pages.

"It's really beautiful," he said. "I can feel her energy." He looked up at Skylar. "I can see why she chose you." He gave her an encouraging smile.

Her cheeks went pink. "Thank you," she said. "It really is quite something. But I'm concerned that it's falling apart. The pages are fraying."

He examined the pages. "Try keeping it in a safer place," he chided and she made a face at him. "You know, Ocean's right," he said. "Your book, your gift from Rhia, the Akasha in your blood, it's all given you amazing insight into how to navigate this new world we're entering. I'm truly honored to help you any way I can."

"Thank you," she said.

He leapt off his stool and hugged her. It took her by surprise. He'd been so cool these past few months and now it seemed a bit of his heart was melting. She inhaled deeply into his shirt and could smell his sweetness under the layer of pool chlorine. She smiled and hugged him tight.

"So what do you make of it?" he asked, releasing his hug.

She paused. He was asking *her* for the answers. "I have to restore a memory," Skylar said.

"Which one?" he asked.

"I have no idea," she said. "But this passage in particular sticks out to me." She picked up the book and started to read aloud . . . .

"Say, I am the child of Earth and starry Heaven. But my race is heavenly; and this you know yourselves. I am parched with thirst and I perish; but give me quickly refreshing water flowing forth from the lake of Memory. And then they will give you to drink from the divine spring, and then you will celebrate with the other heroes."

"Those are words from the Petelia tablet," Argan said.

Skylar's eyes lit up "You know this?"

"I do. I'm well schooled in Greece and Italy, remember? It's of Italian origin but right now the tablet sits at the British Museum."

"Why would those words be in Sophia's book?" she asked.

"All of mythology stems from the same root," he said. "My hunch is *this* is the original."

"So the one at the museum is a knockoff?" she asked.

"No," he said. "Just someone pulling it out of the ethers not knowing this already existed."

She smiled at the thought that Sophia's book just might be where the ideas of the world came from. "There are a few passages that discuss a map and a moon ritual, but there aren't any drawings, although they could have been back here," she said, flipping to the back of the book. "These last pages were torn out. You'd hardly notice. Ronnie pointed it out to me last year."

"Okay, well, where does the text reference? Any locations?" he asked.

"Just the Underworld," she said flippantly. She returned to the long forgotten salads. "Know how to get there?"

"Life experience is a guaranteed ticket to hell at least once or twice a lifetime," he said.

"Yeah, I hear ya," she said, thinking he was kidding.

"I'm serious, Sky. The Underworld is a journey everyone has to take to become whole. We must be willing to look at our pain and destroy the self we have created to become who we are meant to be. It is the true process of alchemy, the real meaning behind the Philosopher's Stone."

A light bulb went off in Skylar's head and she dropped her knife. She returned to the book and flipped pages until she found what she was looking for. "*It is an occult work of true wisdom to open the earth, so that it may generate salvation for the people,*" she read.

"Vitriol," he said.

"Guzunteheit," she said.

He smiled. "V.I.T.R.I.O.L. Visita Interiora Terrae Rectificando Invenies Occultum Lapidem. It's written on the Azoth, one of the great works of alchemy. Vitriol is also one of the symbols on the porta alchemica in Italy."

The familiar tingle spread across Skylar's head as Vivienne popped into her mind. "There are a lot of references to alchemy in Sophia's book," Skylar said.

"Sophia is a big idea in alchemy," Argan said. "She's the vitality of the world, where new ideas come from. She is the realm of imagination." Argan's face lit up when he spoke of Sophia. "It doesn't get more *alchemical* than that," he said. "But I'm sure a lot of it's confusing. Alchemical texts are meant to be cryptic to keep their secrets . . . secret."

"Yeah, there are a lot of blood references, and nature," she said. "And sex."

"Ahh, the original alchemy," he said.

"Yeah," she said, staring at the book. "I was suspicious that the Philosopher's Stone was just a metaphor all along."

"Yes," he said. "But fitting with your recent history, you've been granted actual, physical items and it wouldn't surprise me if you needed to go to the actual Underworld."

Skylar's face fell. "I think I know where that is. That night in the arena, when Milicent was concocting her craziness, she opened a portal. Ocean said it was the Underworld. It really seemed like hell."

"My guess is it looked that way as a projection of your expectations. Our thoughts create our world remember?" She nodded and started inhaling a box of chocolate chip cookies.

"I thought we were having a salad?" he asked.

"Right . . . stress eating," she said. She grabbed a handful more and picked up the salad bowl. "Let's eat outside. It's not that hot today."

They made their way to the patio table and Skylar sat. Argan took a seat across from her. "Going back to the idea of a map," Skylar said. "Italy makes sense. Vivienne is there. Am I supposed to go there to finish this?"

"What does Ocean say?" Argan asked.

"Apparently the one with the answers is Beatrice," she said. "I'm seeing her after New Year's."

"Great, we'll have a nice New Year's Eve and you can start 2021 with a new set of marching papers."

Michael trolled impatiently around Skylar's legs, yowling incessantly.

"You are making this a habit," she said, fussing with her jewelry for the tenth time in front of her full-length mirror. Argan had said to wear something formal but he refused to tell her where they were spending New Year's Eve. She had started to object, saying that this was his birthday, she should do the planning. But he insisted.

She bought a new red dress, mod-style with a flair skirt. It had a fun black underskirt that swished when she turned. Skylar let herself be excited. She hoped there would be dancing.

She heard a knock at the door and Michael dashed down the stairs, yowling until Skylar opened the door. Argan stood before her in a sleek, black tuxedo with long tie, tailored to a centimeter of his body. The waves of his hair were combed back and he flashed that dazzling smile that she hadn't seen him wear in over a year.

"I, a, I . . . wow," Skylar said. "Sorry, come in. You look great." Her face began to flush.

He reached for her hand and gave her a turn. "You look beautiful. Thank you for wearing that dress." He was serious and kissed her formally on the cheek. She felt like they were their eleven-year-old selves all dressed up.

"Happy birthday," she said.

"Thank you," he said, smiling.

Michael scissored between Argan's legs and in one motion, jumped onto his shoulder.

"Michael! How rude!" Skylar lunged to push the cat off of Argan.

"It's all right," he said, picking up the cat and gently placing him on the ground. Skylar looked in the driveway. A shiny black sports car waited.

"No truck?"

"We're riding in style tonight," he said.

She grabbed her purse and off they went. They drove in the direction of Boston and an hour later, they pulled up next to the Boston Harbor Cruise boat. A long line of people waited on the dock. Skylar's head turned this way and that, taking in all the sights of the dresses, lights, and sparkle that decorated the Harbor during the holiday season.

Argan gave the keys to the valet and Skylar went to the end of the long line of people.

"No, Sky, not there," he said. "Over there," he pointed to a large private yacht. Skylar could see a handful of crewmembers busy with activity.

She looked at him. "You are just full of surprises," she said, her mouth gaping. He smiled and led her carefully up the gang-way to the *Serendipity*. She looked back longingly at the party boat.

"What's wrong?" he asked.

"I had hoped there would be dancing." The words spilled out of her mouth before her brain caught up to her insensitivity. Argan had done so much.

He smiled. "There will be."

She relaxed and let him take her on a tour of the main deck. She felt she had stepped into a South Beach nightclub.

Everything was bright white, the furniture, the plush, fuzzy rugs. The overhead lighting bounced off of the chrome handrails in every direction.

"This is quite a departure from New England décor," she said, running her hand down the chrome rails.

"That's why it was a deal," he said, pouring champagne. "Some guy from Miami drove it up here and then died of a heart attack. It's a reasonable rental until they sell it." He was proud of his find.

"Wow, okay," she said, raising her glass to toast. "Here's to that guy."

"Cheers," he said.

The weather was exceptional and they could be out on the deck without coats. After a four-course meal they prepared to watch the fireworks at midnight. Close enough to shore, the symphony played as the lightshow above lit up the night sky.

Skylar watched Argan's face change color in the light of the fireworks. She never thought she'd get another chance to be here like this with him and she wanted to savor every moment. The music stopped and the sky went dark as the countdown of the last minute of 2020 began.

"This has been quite a year," Argan said, taking her hand. He turned to face her.

"That it has," she agreed, at a loss for words. "Thank you for all of your help." A thank you was all she could drum up.

"It was my pleasure," he said, still staring at her intently.

"I can only assume 2021 will be an even wilder ride." She lowered her eyes, unable to stand the intensity of his stare.

"I will be there to help you," he said, leaning close.

Cheers from the crowd on the mainland reached the boat. Midnight had arrived. "Happy New Year, Skylar." The music resumed and the grand finale of fireworks exploded overhead.

She looked up into the sky, beaming with joy. "Happy New Year, Argan."

He leaned in close enough to kiss her but stopped short of her lips. "Happy New Year," he whispered again and kissed her softly on the lips. He tasted sweet, with a bit of salt from the sea air. He released his kiss and looked in her eyes once more. She didn't move, frozen from the wonder of the moment. His mouth turned up slightly and he leaned in again, kissing her more deeply.

Instantly Skylar allowed herself to get lost in the joy, the perfection of the moment. She inhaled his delicious scent and the taste of his kiss. She allowed that door within her heart to fly open and accept the love Argan had to give her. If he changed his mind tomorrow, she would survive it. Right now, this moment with him was worth any price she'd have to pay.

"Now, how about that dance?" he asked. Still holding her hand, he led her to the large open bow of the boat. The crew had discreetly cleared the dining area to make room for dancing. With the symphony from shore complete, the music onboard resumed. Melodies from the bygone era of the nineteen forties wafted from the speakers.

Skylar giggled. "You always were an old soul," she said. She felt upheld by a mountain as he held her tight and led her around the deck.

"I like what I like," he said unapologetically. Skylar got lost in joy as they danced. Every so often Argan would lean in and kiss her. Some kisses were soft and slow, others more intense. As the night went on, he seemed to allow himself a similar return to the innocence of their initial relationship. They both allowed themselves to release the fragments of past hurts and return to the core love that had bound them over lifetimes.

Time passed quickly as they talked and laughed and danced until the sun came up. Skylar couldn't believe the night was over. The oranges and purples usually reserved for sunset made an appearance at sunrise.

"Happy Birthday Argan," Skylar said.

"Thanks Sky, but that was yesterday."

"Yes but I feel a new life coming into our relationship, you, me, this sunrise. Everything is changing. It's scary but the butterflies are exciting. And I couldn't be happier that we are facing it all together."

"Me too," he said and kissed her one more time. He pulled back and his serious demeanor returned. "Should I stop doing that, now that the night is over?"

She tugged on his lapels and drew him closer. She kissed him. "Never stop."

12

The fifteenth floor of Boston General was a bustle of activity. A skeleton crew usually worked on New Year's Day but not this year. Security was on its ear preparing for a visit from the First Lady-elect. Every staff member reviewed protocol dozens of times and when they were sure they had it down, they reviewed it again. Milicent was expected just before noon, but as the day wore on, an eager staff grew weary when she never came. Half past three Noah called the floor manager to send Mrs. Grayer's regrets that she would not be coming that day.

Routines resumed and the next item of business took over conversation on floor fifteen. At 4:00 p.m. the day shift turned over to night and at 11:00 p.m. only one first year resident lingered at the nurse's station, wearing headphones.

"Good evening," a mature female voice said to the resident. He startled at the sight of her and shot out of his chair. "Hello," he said. He glanced at the clock. It was a quarter past midnight.

"Christopher M." Milicent said, reading his nametag. "I'm here to see the patient in room 1542."

"Yes, ma'am." His head turned on a swivel, scanning the halls.

"I'm here alone, if that's what you're wondering," she said, Noah standing next to her.

"Yes, ma'am," he swallowed with a gulp, looking at Noah. "Please follow me." Milicent obliged and followed him the short walk to room 1542.

"Do you need any assistance inside, ma'am?" he asked.

"That should be all Christopher M. If I do need you, I will be sure to reach out."

He started to bow and a look of foolishness struck him. He turned on his heels and left Milicent and Noah in front of the door. "Noah, I need to do this alone," she said.

"I will be right here for you if you need me," Noah said, a look of puppy dog admiration in his eyes.

She took in a large breath and entered Joshua's room as if she were entering a board meeting. One look at Joshua lying still in bed and all airs fell.

She started across the room and was instantly confronted by the sound of her own stiletto heels. She abruptly stopped and slipped out of her shoes, walking the rest of the way silently in stocking feet. She stared at him for a good long while before she started to speak.

"I'm sorry this is the first time I've come," she said to his unresponsive body. "I've been so busy. Devlin won the election. It's just been a whirlwind since . . . and," she paused, visibly uncomfortable, "I hear you're getting the best of care." Her face fell and she slumped into the chair next to the bed. She rested her head in her hands as if she were confessing her sins to Joshua.

"I really am sorry," she whispered, a glimmer of a tear in her eye. "I've done what I swore I would never do. I became my mother and I've abandoned you, just the same." She touched his hand. "And now after everything, all the medicines I gave you to make you strong, invincible . . . you're like this!" She angered for a moment but despair quickly returned. "I don't understand. And there's nothing I can do to fix it." The tear broke free from her eye and she wiped it away. "Why did you take something to hurt yourself?"

"I was chasing pleasure," Joshua replied. Milicent looked at his light body, not at all surprised to see it. "Or love, I often confuse the two."

Milicent smiled. "It's good to see you well. This is how you should be. Not like this . . ." she gestured to the body in the bed. "Come back to us. I'll make things right."

"I'm not sure I can, but thanks for the offer. And thank you for coming." His body didn't move an inch. "In all these months, you're my second visitor. That shows me how shallow I've been living my life. And if nothing else, I've had a lot of time to reflect."

They stared at each other in silence, a lifetime of wrong decisions between them.

"I'm headed to DC next week," Milicent said, already wrapping up their conversation. "But I'll keep tabs on you. When you wake up, I'd like another shot at us."

He gave her one hard nod. She kissed the head of the body lying in bed and made her way toward the door. As she slipped back into her shoes she looked at his light body. "Who was your first visitor?"

"Skylar," he said.

She nodded and walked out of room 1542.

13

"Skylar?" Al Unger said, surprised to see his niece at his front door.

"Hey Al," she said. He had lost the title of Uncle after hitting on her a handful of years ago at her high school graduation party. He had reminded everyone in the room that she was legal, and they weren't blood related. "Happy New Year."

Skylar started through the open door but he stopped her. "Now isn't a good time. Mom's not receiving visitors," he said, partially blocking her.

"I'm not a visitor," she said annoyed. She pushed him out of the way and walked into the tired two family house.

"Nana!" Skylar called through the downstairs hall. Al followed behind her.

"In here," Beatrice called back from the porch. Skylar walked through the house that still smelled like Sasha, their Siberian Husky that had died over a decade ago. Her dog bed was still tucked into a corner near the TV. Skylar was sure if she looked hard enough, she'd find a few dog hairs. Beatrice was lounging on a wicker sofa with faded flower cushions watching Jeopardy at two o'clock in the afternoon.

"What is Epsom Salt?" she said to the television. "Back so soon?" she asked, fixated on the TV.

"It's been over six months, Nana," Skylar said. "Happy New Year."

"Happy New Year. And yes, but before that it had been two years since I'd seen you," Beatrice chided. She rolled to sit up and turned off the television. She got up without another word and walked into the kitchen. The pea green countertops had been replaced with white marble. The peeling cabinets had gotten a band-aid of an upgrade, painted a chambray blue. It was shabby, shabby chic.

"We're listing it next week," Al said from the doorway.

"She's not dead yet," Skylar said.

Beatrice gave her a dirty look and shifted energy to make some tea. "I know why you're here," she said.

Skylar looked at Al standing in the doorway. He shrugged. The secrets of the cosmos were old news to him. He skulked away to ruin someone else's afternoon.

"I'm not apologizing for all the deceit," Beatrice said nonchalantly. "What was I supposed to do, tell you the truth and unravel your entire existence? That was for someone else to do. I wanted no part of it."

"I understand," Skylar said, staring at the floor.

"Your mother died loving you," Bea said, eyes fixated on her teakettle. "Cassandra will always be your mother. Your oaf of a father did his share of screwing things up in your life but luckily he kept this together. And Rachel did what a scared teen in her position thought was best. We all make mistakes out of fear. Some are more extreme than others. Don't blame any of them, Skylar. They all had your best interest at heart."

"That's the nicest thing you've ever said about Dad," Skylar said.

"How 'bout that?" Bea said, pouring her tea. "Want some?"

"No, thank you, Nana. It's still hot as hell out," Skylar said. "Speaking of which, will the heat ever break or are we in Game of Thrones here?"

"Talk to Ocean. She's been in charge of the heat."

"You're joking," Skylar wasn't sure.

"Maybe. It really depends on the fall out from 2020. The effects will only now start to take hold. It will be interesting to see if Tecumseh's curse holds true. My bet is it does. He was a tough son of a bitch and would hold a grudge for eternity. He was a Scorpio. Devlin really needs to beef up his security detail. Every twenty years the elected president has died or been injured."

"You're making that up," Skylar said.

"I rarely tell stories, Skylar," Beatrice said dryly. She looked Skylar up and down. "Life is interesting enough. But look it up if you don't believe me." She squeezed the flesh of Skylar's upper arm. "You look good. You've been training." She tugged at her hair. "You should wear your hair back so I can see your face." She touched the red streak of hair. "Stick out your tongue." Skylar obliged. "Ocean's been busy." Skylar pursed her lips. She didn't know what to say. "Be careful with ingesting gold. Just the amounts she tells you, no more. We don't want your head to explode."

"Thanks for the advice, Nana. All of the crazy physical symptoms have seemed to settle down," Skylar said.

"For now," Beatrice said, ominously. She grabbed at Skylar's shirt hem. "And your scar?" Skylar lifted her shirt. Her iridescent circle of doves peeked out. "Ahh, your fate," Beatrice said lightly grazing the scar. "No escape."

"But not my destiny," Skylar said. "I'd like to think I still have some say in shaping my life."

"You'd think," Bea rolled her eyes. "Did you bring me that tea I like?"

"Oh yeah, it's in my car," Skylar said. "Give me a minute."

She went out to her car parked on the street and returned to the front steps with a shopping bag of her grandmother's favorite tea, the only present she'd ever given her she actually liked. Before she went back inside, a black town car rolled to a stop in front of the house. The portly driver quickly got out and walked around to the passenger side. He opened the door and one slim leg dressed in a denim capri and a sparkly white sneaker peeked out. "Hang on!" the voice attached said from inside the car. The girl appeared to be lying on the floor of the car, trying to find something under the seat.

"I can help you with that, m' lady," the driver said.

She waved him off. "Got it!" she said and popped out of the car. She couldn't have been more than twenty. Her thick jet-black hair, large brown eyes, and ample lips gave away her Indian descent. "Wait here, please," she told her driver.

"Miss, I had strict orders . . ." the driver objected.

"I'm telling you different. Wait here," she commanded. She approached Skylar still standing on the steps.

"Hello," Skylar spoke first.

"Hi," the girl replied. She looked down at a piece of paper. "Does Albert Unger live here?"

"You could say that," Skylar said, looking her up and down. This exotic beauty was impeccably groomed down to her French manicured nails. "Do you have a warrant? Or paternity papers?"

"The latter," the girl replied, not the least bit uneasy.

Skylar nodded, not surprised. "Of course you do. Follow me," she said. She stepped into the entry landing. "Al!" she yelled into the house. "Someone's here to see you!" she turned to the girl. "What is your name?"

"Britt," she said.

"Britt's here to see you!" she yelled again. "He should surface in a moment. Make sure to tell him you're *blood* related before he shakes your hand," Skylar said. "I'm Skylar, by the way."

"Pleasure," Britt said. For the first time, Skylar detected an accent.

Beatrice came in from the porch. Britt had a look of surprise on her face, recognizing Beatrice. "It's you," she said in astonishment. "I dreamt about you."

The enormity of what was happening sunk into Skylar. Britt was Beatrice's biological granddaughter.

Bea's face softened. "And I have dreamt of you, dear," she said with a kindness Skylar hadn't seen in years. Skylar felt instant annoyance. She didn't get that kindness.

Al came up out of his hole in the basement. "What's up?" he asked the group of women, now all in an embrace in the kitchen.

"Al," Beatrice started, "this is Britt Anjawal." Britt stared at Al in silence. It was apparent that this unassuming man with a severely receding hairline was not quite what she had envisioned in her reunion fantasies.

Al's eyes lit up in that all too familiar lecherous way. Skylar took one step toward him. "She's your daughter," she blurted, afraid of any time getting by them.

He froze and his smile quickly faded. Skylar expected surprise to take its place but it didn't.

"I didn't think this day would ever come," he whispered.

Twenty-one years ago, Al had a quickie marriage to a woman he hardly knew. He was knee deep in the illegal snake trade and spent quite a lot of time in India. He had taken up with a rebellious royal who was bent on defying her father. She married the unscrupulous American she hardly knew. It lasted less than four months—but long enough to produce a child. Talia's family made Al sign away any rights to the child and swear before a judge to never contact her or the family again. After being paid a handsome sum, he found it very easy to keep that promise. As far as he was concerned, he was happy to *be rid of the whole situation.*

But now, all these years later, a curious young woman was knocking on his door, looking for missing pieces to her puzzle.

76

"How I can help you?" Al asked, his attitude shifting to uncomfortably aloof.

"I'm not sure," Britt said. "I just wanted to put a face to one of the question marks in my life."

Beatrice thrust a hot cup of tea at Britt. She politely accepted it despite the high temperatures in the house. "Let's all go out to the porch," Bea said, leading Britt to the sunroom. "How long are you staying with us, dear?"

"I have flexibility with my schedule," Britt said. "I can stay as long as I want."

The doorbell rang and they all looked at the door. "Active morning," Bea said. "Get that Al, would you?" He reluctantly made his way to the front door and opened it without looking through the peephole. Britt's driver stood sweating in his heavy uniform on the top step.

"I need to speak with Miss Anjawal," he said with a heavy Indian accent. Britt saw him and headed in his direction.

"It's all right, Vihaan," she said. "I'm fine." She turned to Bea and Skylar. "He worries when I'm out of view." She turned back to Vihaan. "I do need some more time though."

"I insist on coming in," he said, speaking only to her. "Your father would have my head if he knew you were out of my sight."

"I am her father," Al said. Vihaan looked him up and down but said nothing.

"You can wait in the kitchen," Britt said, never asking permission from Beatrice. Vihaan hesitated then removed his hat and walked past Al. He awkwardly sat in a wire bistro chair in the corner by the sliding door to the postage stamp sized deck. He kept his hat in his hands and Britt returned to the sunroom. Beatrice had turned the TV back on for moral support.

As Skylar watched the drama unfold before her, she thought how odd this all was. She sat next to Bea, holding her leather-bound book in her lap. The strangeness of the past year bumped up against the strangeness of the past morning. It was all strange.

Bea started to speak over the droning TV. "Britt, I commend you for taking the leap to find your father. But I'm sorry to say he doesn't hold any secrets for you. He was merely a portal for you to enter this world. He is my son, you are my granddaughter."

The leather-bound book pulsed in Skylar's hands. "*Britt is one of us,*" she thought. This obvious but important fact had escaped her until now.

"I wasn't the one who arranged the deal all those years ago," Al said defensively. "You can ask your grandfather."

"He's dead," Britt said. "And my mother's gone mad." Her eyes already filled with tears. "At least that's what her sisters tell me. I don't believe it though. She is in there, somewhere. I'm sure of it."

Skylar glanced at Beatrice. Mental illness was a classic sign of denial of the lineage or aftermath of carrying the baby of Great Mother bloodlines.

"The world I come from is quite different," Britt said. "You wouldn't believe it."

Bea smiled. "I understand different," she said. "So does Skylar."

Skylar looked at Bea for answers to dozens of questions swirling in her brain. What did it mean that there was *another* granddaughter? She was supposed to be the only one, well besides Rhia. She still missed that girl terribly, even though her heart lived on inside Skylar.

"Things have changed in India," Britt said. "The spiritual heart of my land has vanished. I'm not the only one to feel it and it's causing great upheaval within my people and my family. That's part of the reason I've come." Vihaan appeared in the doorway, outwardly agitated at Britt's revelations. "The man who has been my father my whole life is claiming ownership of my family's dynasty even though it was my mother's line. With her being so incapacitated, I'm afraid he'll win and take everything my family has."

Beatrice smiled reassuringly. "You have already been through so much." She turned to Skylar. "Britt didn't come to find Al, Skylar," she continued. "She came to find you. You must see that."

"You have known for twenty years that this girl existed," Skylar said to Beatrice.

"Yes, but there was no action to take until now," Bea said. "She had to grow up, just like you." She patted both girls on the knee and pushed off to stand up. She glanced at her cane propped in the corner and left it where it stood. She wobbled to the kitchen and started to pull out pots.

She rummaged through a few cabinets but turned up empty handed. "Skylar, please go down to the basement pantry and grab me a large can of diced tomatoes," she said.

Skylar welcomed the chance to escape the drama and made her way down the basement steps.

The familiar scent of sage and mugwort filled her nose. *That's where mom got it from,* she thought, breathing deeply. She had never noticed it in this house. The basement had been finished many years ago when her Aunt Emily still had the top two floors. Beatrice had moved into the basement when Arthur died.

The corridor was lined with doors. It had been so long since Skylar had been down there, she hadn't a clue which door was the pantry. She opened a couple of linen closets and one filled entirely with dusty mason jars. "Hmm," she said aloud and shut the door. On her fourth try she found the pantry. She found the tomatoes among the countless other items with shelf lives longer than her own.

As she started toward the stairs, a light under one of the doors caught her eye. It glowed red. *How odd*, she thought. Nothing in her grandmother's house had ever caused her fear and this curious light was no different.

She twisted the nob and her nose instantly filled with the musty stench of reptiles. As her eyes adjusted to the low light, a wall of wet heat hit her in the face. Slightly dazed, she dropped the tomatoes and grasped at the wall for support. A dozen snakes in various sizes, all intertwined in one enormous floor-to-ceiling glass enclosure, stopped their intricate dance and stared at her.

Skylar was more fascinated than frightened. It took her just a moment to read their energy. She knew they meant no harm yet they held anger within, resenting their captivity. A handful slithered closer and she felt their desire to escape. As much as she wanted to help them, she had no idea what freedom looked like for these creatures.

One in particular caught her attention. Skylar walked up to the glass wall and knelt in front of the great white anaconda that parted the others like the sea.

Skylar sighed. "I'm sorry he has you locked up in here," she said to the snake. "He's an asshole."

The snake seemed to agree. She stared into Skylar's eyes, determined to tell her something. Skylar was well aware that the cobra is a symbol of knowledge and this one was desperate to share hers.

She heard the voice in her own head . . . *I see your heart, dear one. It is pure.* The serpent continued to weave back and forth over the glass, rising and falling with Skylar's breath. *The world began in a ssssssea of blood, the same life force that courssses through your veinsss. The numinous fluid is the answer you seek. It pulses from the heart, your center of wisdom. The ssssshift has begun. No man can stop it. Kundalini is rising. It is the energy of the earth that issss connected to your kind through your heart. Energy of the feminine is restoring balance to the earth.*

Skylar rested her palm on the cool glass. The snake flicked its tongue against it.

Look not on the destruction of an old regime in chaos from its own demisssse. Look to the future you can build and the planet you can create from the magic within your heart, in your blood.

A portal opened in Skylar's mind like a window. A golden white snake slithered over vast amounts of land. The ground left behind it shimmered with flecks of gold.

The snake rushed Skylar through the glass, and its energy engulfed her with enough power to knock her over. The image in her mind vanished and Skylar was left on the floor panting.

She could hear the words of the snake in her head. As the great white withdrew to the back of the enclosure, the other large snakes danced around her in ritual, in reverence, in unison. Skylar's eyes darted to each one. She knew they were all female, Goddesses trapped in form.

Al, that dickhead. He was keeping them all here for their power.

14

Skylar raced to the top of the stairs, her heart pounding. "You don't have the tomatoes," Bea said.

Skylar's face pained. "How could you look the other way while he keeps those creatures prisoner?" she asked horrified. "You know who they are, what they represent. And you let him keep them in a box!" She raced toward Bea as Britt entered the room. Skylar looked at her but couldn't see her face. It was blocked by a large oval of intense white light. Britt stepped toward her and she fell to the ground in fear. Her eyes darted around the room like a trapped animal. She could sympathize with the snakes. The women stared at her. "Don't come any closer," she warned, fear cracking her voice.

"Take deep breaths, Skylar," Bea said, slowing her step. "You know me. You shouldn't fear me."

Skylar regained her footing. "Know you? I don't know you at all. You've fed me nothing but lies my whole life. And now, you have that room downstairs? I don't know you." She rose to all fours and slowly stood up, now able to see Britt's face.

Britt stood awkwardly, not sure what had just happened. "She needs some water," Bea continued. Britt busied herself with getting a glass.

"We shouldn't have come, Miss," Vihaan said from the doorway.

"Don't be silly," Britt said. "This is getting good." She returned to Skylar's side with a cold glass of water. Skylar took it and gulped it down.

"The creatures in the basement are not his. They're mine and they need protection," Beatrice said. "They can't be set free in this world until the time is right. They know this. Ocean told you not to kid yourself, that we would reveal all the secrets to you at once. You can't handle it. You have no reason to trust me anymore but you have no choice. You're going to have to go on faith."

"Faith? In what? Who?" Skylar asked incredulously.

"Faith in the Divine Plan. Faith in Sophia. Faith in your destiny."

Skylar looked at Britt. "What does she have to do with this?" she asked.

"She is one of us," Bea said. "Like it or not, her destiny is at stake as well. She must go with you."

"To Italy?" Skylar assumed.

"To the past," Beatrice said. Skylar's face fell. She thought of the book and its call to restore the memory of the past.

"You read it in the book and had the dream of the Sybil," Beatrice continued. "You have connected with her son. It's time to act. You're ready. And there is only one way to move forward. The future is in our roots, dears."

"The ways of the Goddess," Skylar confirmed.

Beatrice resumed making sauce with the cans she had and poured chunky red liquid into a pot the size of a suitcase. She poured in various spices. "Silverwood calls for your return. You can make things right there."

"The boarding school mom went to?" Skylar asked.

"They were all there. Cassandra, Rachel, Milicent and Veronica. And you, briefly."

"Does it still exist?" Britt asked.

"On the astral plane, yes. Unfortunately on this physical plane, it resembles the past. But believe me when I say it is very much alive." Britt's eyes widened with enthusiasm. "You have one month to prepare. The portal will be thinnest on the eve of Imbolc and you can get in then."

"Imbolc?" asked Skylar.

"The Feast of the Goddess Brighid," Beatrice said. "We can call on her to bring you safe passage through the veil." She put her spoon down and took off her apron. "You will both have a long list of questions, but I'm tired. I need a nap before dinner." She turned on her heels and walked up the stairs to her bedroom.

Vihaan had lost all patience. "Miss, I must insist we go," he said with all the force his five-foot two-inch frame could muster. He took Britt by the arm. "Let us check into the hotel. You need rest."

Britt pulled her arm away from him. "Vihaan, you are this close to being fired, or beheaded, or something severe," she said. "You are driving me bloody bonkers!" She turned to Skylar. "I will leave you to the rest of your evening. If it's all right, I would like to work out the logistics to go with you, Skylar. I need this." She didn't elaborate.

Skylar was less than thrilled this intruder was now such a large part of her life. But Beatrice seemed to have expected it and she might prove to be helpful. "All right," Skylar said. "Leave me your number and we'll work something out."

Britt said her goodbyes as Vihaan pushed her out the door.

After her dinner with Beatrice, Skylar walked onto the tiny deck into the hot, damp night. Despite the heat, the sky was clear and she looked up at the ripe full moon.

"You have to find a way to come to terms with it, Skylar," Beatrice said, walking up behind her. This night she used her cane. "Your journey to Silverwood will help you move through it quicker than most. To be deceived by loved ones is a high act of betrayal, no matter the reasons behind it." She walked to her side and took Skylar's hand in hers. She glanced up at the moon. "The moon reflects our inner secrets back to us. She also reflects our mother within."

Skylar thought of Silverwood and Cassie and Rachel, both of them as teens. It was a time Skylar could only try to imagine but she would experience it soon enough if she agreed to go.

"There is no agreeing, dear," Bea said, reading her mind. "You must go. I understand your anger, your confusion. You are questioning which mother to see when you look at the moon. Cassandra? Rachel? Now neither as they are both clouded with hurt. But in time you will come to know in your heart that your ties aren't through genealogical charts, but through alchemy rooted in the stars. You are bound by the story that weaves between you."

They stared into the dazzling night sky. A rainbow glistened around the moon. "That circle of color around the moon is the

Goddess laughing at our silliness. She knows all is well and we have to go through our process to come to the end result." Skylar searched Bea's eyes for the answer. "Love," she said, giving Skylar's hands a squeeze. "The heavens contain our history just as much as the earth. It is quite a complex web we live in. And the forces of the planets weigh on each of us. Astrology wouldn't have mattered for thousands of years if it were as frivolous an endeavor as some make it to be."

She turned over one of Skylar's hands and traced the line of her vein up her arm. A light shone from inside her arm, lighting the map of her veins. "In your blood, you carry the Akasha. But that's not unique to you. All humans carry memory in their veins. That's why so often we repeat the patterns of our fore mothers. They are immortal in our blood. 'The living so often are ruled by the dead,' said Thomas Jefferson, and he was a wise man. One of the few I liked back then."

Skylar looked back to the swirls of clouds moving in the night sky. They changed color as they drifted across the moonlight. "The clouds are stories we tell ourselves," Beatrice said. "They are so different in the night sky, so filled with fear. They mix with tainted memories and create the true force behind all nightmares."

"Our memories also change with time. You've experienced that, yes? They talk of time healing all wounds. But time can freeze wounds just as easily. One can get stuck in the patterns of the past, or the manipulations of others. Those are the true tragedies, to be stuck in someone else's version of the truth. You feel that way now, stuck in your parent's version. But that was before. Now you know the facts; you can move forward in your own truth."

Bea waved her hand in the warm night air and swirls of clouds took human form. They danced about like children in the moonlight.

"But Skylar, there is a greater mission now. The memory of the Earth, the Akasha was manipulated long ago. We were there when it happened, Ocean, Vivienne, and me. We watched the world crumble before our eyes in the age of Aries. There was nothing we could do. Lucifer and the black magicians of Atlantis united to rule the world in the Piscean Age. This planet has seen great advances but has also suffered greatly. We've stood by powerless as the core of earth has been pillaged over and over through the course of time."

Bea's sylph-like clouds played out the drama in the night sky. Some grew taller and darker; others cowered with fear from an unseen force.

"Now the Aquarian cycle has begun. Aquarius is the revelation of the free spirit. You were incarnated at this exact time in history to fulfill the vitally important task of restoring that fractured memory of the Akasha."

Skylar stared at her grandmother with wide eyes. "That's what I gathered from Sophia's book."

"When you restore the Akashic memory, you will have fulfilled the destiny waiting in your heart."

"I carry someone else's heart," Skylar said. It was the first time she spoke of Rhia to Beatrice.

"This is so. Your burden carries with it the destiny of all women. We all carry the heart of another within us—our mothers, our children. I see your outward changes," she touched Skylar's hair. "But they are just a symbol that your spiritual eyes are opening. You are beautiful in your metamorphosis. Even if you do let that hair hang in your face." Skylar smiled. Her grandmother couldn't let a compliment go by without a dig right behind it.

The night sky had become a stage for Beatrice's grand show. The clouds wafted in front of the moon, creating shapes of women dancing by. Their wild hair flowed free and their demeanor, mischievous, playful. The diorama she created with her hands transformed from fearful beings into angels with wings and unicorns . . . all delights from the imagination of children.

The forms were so lifelike, Skylar was sure she could touch them. She reached her hand out but it breezed through, just like a cloud. "Those are the sylphs, my sky spirits," Beatrice said. "They are keepers of the stories we tell ourselves. Like clouds, they change and morph with time. They darken and lighten and are never the same twice. They commit to be true but so often they are mischievous. They love a good joke. Most looked to blame the gnomes and salamanders for the corruption of earth, but it was actually the sky spirits. I may have left them unsupervised . . . for a thousand years." She shrugged with mild concern.

Skylar's delight faded. "Wait, I was under the impression it was men who tampered with the Akashic memory. *It's your fault?* Or at least your minions?" Skylar was horrified. "Nana!" She started to pace. "Ocean knows this? Of course she does," she said answering her own question. "No wonder she rags on you all the time. I never understood it. Wow. And I've been assigned to clean up your mess. I get it now."

"Don't judge me, miss," Bea scolded. "Yes, they are under my watch but not my command. Long ago a few chose to help the dark energies invade earth. They are so easily swayed by charisma." She walked back inside and picked up a framed photo of Skylar's grandfather. "I chose my path and don't regret it. I am sorry that some of my duties may have fallen through the cracks of earth." The sylphs danced in one final circle and dissipated into the night. Skylar walked inside.

"I was shunned by my sisters, considered weak for falling in love. They were the weak ones, refusing to be vulnerable to another. I have been dead for a dozen years. Yet my body lives. That is the hell I must endure as punishment for going against my sisters. I gladly take it for the happiness I once had. And the happiness I will have again when your grandfather returns."

Skylar knew what she was referring to. Beatrice was the only one of the three Great Mothers who fell in love with a mortal man. The others had their men but they were for one purpose: to plant the seed of life in their wombs. They had no interest in love. Bea had been seen as weak by her sisters for falling for Arthur the way she did. But she never looked back. She found him in every incarnation he had, for a thousand years she loved him. Each time he died, she patiently waited outside of time until they could be together again. Each time she would plant herself in his life, waiting for the spark to re-fuse between them. And it always did. His last incarnation was as Skylar's grandfather. Bea loved him for half a century until he came to the end of his mortal life.

"You're blaming *love* for a lapse in your duties? Awwe, come on Nana! You have to take responsibility here." This time Skylar scolded. "Besides," she said, softening, "Grampy doesn't want this for you. How much longer are you planning to be on the planet?"

"I am here as long as earth exists," Bea said.

"You're going to spend eternity in this house, mourning your dead husband until he returns who knows when, letting the world fall apart?" Skylar asked accusingly. "You are living in hell and you're taking the world with you."

"No," Bea said casually. "I've seen hell. This ain't it." Bea motioned to the moon. "We're getting off track. This is about you. If anything, take a lesson from me on what not to do. Don't hold resentment in your heart. You are too young. The connection between mothers and daughters is never severed, Skylar. Cassandra lives in you, as does Rachel. Heal this memory."

Skylar had a headache and needed time to process all Beatrice had told her. "Nana, it's late. Do you mind if I stay the night?" she asked. "I don't have the energy to drive home."

"Of course," Bea said, giving her a hug.

"We're not done talking about this," Skylar said.

"Of course," Bea repeated.

Skylar's sight was clouded in the salty water. She could make out seven stone bird-like figures with massive wings seated in a circle. A faint light illuminated the sand at their feet. She stepped inside the circle and at once, they locked into place, anchored in the sand. Images of celestial bodies appeared above each bird. She looked down at her torso, illuminating from within, all of her energy centers were visible through her skin.

She shot up in bed from the rush of energy through her body. Was this an orgasm? An alien abduction? The tomato sauce? She couldn't tell but she scrambled out of bed, her nervous system in hyper drive. She got dressed quickly and did a few jumping jacks, suddenly craving a run, which was odd. She never ran. Enough light streamed through the window to be able to go.

She made due with her Keds, which she knew would be a mistake, but she hadn't packed running shoes. She didn't even own running shoes. It didn't matter. She needed to move her body.

She came back to the house when the sun was high in the sky, having run for miles. "I should enter a marathon," she said out loud. The thought left her mind as quickly as it entered. She stopped in the yard at the towering tree Cassie used to climb to get into the house. Something was oddly familiar about the windy roots that snaked along the ground as well as the branches that held the leaves.

She stared at the intricacies of the tree. She confirmed her suspicion; this was the exact tree in Ocean's yard, the same one in the etheric realm where she met Magda. She examined a few leaves, no names or death dates to be seen. As she studied the branches, she discovered that the exact same pattern of branches held the leaves as roots that snaked along the ground. They were a mirror image of each other.

"As above, so below," Beatrice said behind her.

Skylar whirred around. "I thought that was a heaven and earth metaphor," she said.

"It is, but that same paradigm lives among us. In this tree, in the human body."

"Huh?"

"Part of existence is to master the chakra system, or nervous system of the body, the heart being in the middle, the center of the body, the center of the universe. The goal is to balance those chakras below the heart with those above. One does that, one ascends."

Skylar was in amazement. "Have you done that?"

Bea shrugged. "I was never given the opportunity. I'm not originally from this plane so I'm not afforded the same chances as you are."

"This is the same tree as Ocean's, isn't it?" Skylar asked. "Although hers is black but I feel it's same essence."

"You feel *your* essence in the tree, Skylar," Bea said. "All of the descendants of the Great Mothers feel a connection to that tree. And yes, it is the same one. Vivienne has one at her home in Italy as well. But all of our trees hold different energy because of the wind. That would be me," she said smugly.

"My sisters each claim the throne of the hierarchy of the elements, both catalysts for transformation but they forget the *alchemy of air*. Air is the in-between. I hold apart *above* and *below*, as well as bind them. I am tied to earth through direction, sometimes called the four faces of the Goddess."

"That's beautiful, Nana. You made Ocean's black," Skylar said.

"She did that herself. It matches her personality," Bea said dryly. She handed her a piece of paper. "You'll need to get everything on this list to bring with you to Silverwood." Without waiting for Skylar to read it, Bea started toward the house. "I need to get ready for an appointment," she said already to the door.

"Are you still driving, Nana?"

"Yes," Bea said, with one eyebrow raised.

"How do they renew your license at ninety-five?"

"I pass all of their tests. What can they do?" Bea smiled and walked into the house.

Skylar looked at the paper. It read *288 Derby*.

She returned to the tree and put her hand on the trunk as she did at Ocean's. She felt its thick, brown bark with her hands. It was a strong tree. Skylar felt its power, its immense life-force flow into her hands. She smiled, feeling the connection all trees have to one another. She looked around to see if anyone was watching. When she thought she was alone, she gave the tree a hug. With her whole body connected to that tree, its energy poured through her in a constant current. She felt it's love but also it's anger. She saw in her mind the battles that nature fights among itself always trying to restore balance. Nature was volatile, but beautiful. Skylar felt unstoppable. When the energy began to diminish, she heard a faint song being hummed by the voice of an angel. She released her arms in surprise and the song stopped.

"Thank you," she said to the tree. No, it wasn't weird at all. She went back inside and Beatrice had already gone. She thought about seeing the snakes again but decided against it and dialed her grandmother's cell phone.

"Figure it out!" Beatrice's voice boomed in Skylar's ear. "Be ready to leave on the first of February." She disconnected.

16

January 20, 2021: Devlin Grayer stood at the inaugural podium, one hand raised in the air, the other palm flat on the Bible, King James edition. "I do solemnly swear that I will faithfully execute the Office of President of the United States, and will to the best of my ability, preserve, protect, and defend the Constitution of the United States."

This was the first Presidential Inauguration with a record-breaking temperature of eighty-five degrees. Presidents were customarily forbidden to wear overcoats, but today Devlin's light Armani suit was too heavy. Milicent stood by his side, stone-faced. Devlin had asked her to venture from her purple wardrobe for this one day. She resisted at first but just days before the inauguration, she agreed. Designers scrambled to work, with the freedom to use prints and other colors.

"No prints!" she barked. They settled on a muted emerald green silk shantung that should have become her new signature color. She wore it well. Noah stood at his usual post a few feet behind her. He also wore emerald green in solidarity.

Mica Noxx was the only one on the platform that looked genuinely pleased to be there. She beamed from ear to ear as the first woman to take the office of Vice President of the United States of America.

Milicent glanced at Cyril Magus. He had a prime seat on the grand stand next to many heads of state. It was unclear how he landed his seat on this historic day but it only added to Milicent's bad mood.

"The country has seen dark times this past year," Devlin started his inaugural speech. "and now more than ever, we must embrace diversity in our communities, our country, and our global family so we can return the United States to the leader it once was." An eruption of cheers ensued.

"You wouldn't know diversity if it bit you on the ass," Milicent said under her breath as she waved to the crowd of supporters. "You're from Connecticut."

She made quick work of settling into the White House, treating the move like any other. She brought in her personal decorators to redesign her office and they assured her it would be complete in a matter of weeks. Noah also made the permanent move to DC. He would have to put his senior year at Rosen on hold but *this* would make his mother so proud.

Just two days after inauguration, Milicent hosted the wives of many foreign dignitaries in the Rose Garden and was already bored. She did her best to feign interest in the polite conversations going on around her, but welcomed an interruption from her new Chief of Staff, Wren Riddle. "Mrs. Grayer? I'm so sorry to interrupt but there seems to be a . . . situation."

"Oh, please interrupt, Wren," Milicent said. Wren was in her late fifties and had worked in the White House in one form or another for almost three decades. She had seen the administration flip and flop and somehow always remained employed.

"You have a visitor. It boggles the mind how she got in your office. But she refuses to leave and none of the security officers seem to take notice of her. Her name is Beatrice Unger."

"Is that right?" Milicent's face brightened. "This day is picking up." She excused herself and left Noah to entertain the wives.

"What would you like me to do with her, ma'am?" Wren asked as they walked the hall to Milicent's office.

"I'll handle it. She's an old friend," Milicent said.

"Beatrice, it's been an age," Milicent said upon entering her office. She bent in half to greet her with an air kiss on each cheek. In her Manolos, Milicent towered over Bea's barely five-foot frame.

"You seem to be taking to your new environment well," Beatrice said.

"Hardly. I won't last four years, I can tell you that."

"It's been a long time since one of us had the keys to this place." She looked around Milicent's office like a tourist. It was a mix of mismatched furniture covered in fabric samples. Boxes still lined the walls waiting to be unpacked. "I know you've enlisted Skylar to help you back in Massachusetts but please release her from her duties. She's needed elsewhere."

"You came all this way to ask for a favor?" Milicent asked suspiciously. "That could have easily been a phone call. Why are you really here?"

"You have a rare opportunity to help our cause," Bea said. "Things need to get back on track. Through almost a hundred years of apathy in this office, the world sits in ruins. Skylar can't do it alone. I'm calling on all of the women in our circle to help, including you."

"I've been the black sheep for too long, Beatrice," Milicent crossed her arms. "You all counted me out years ago. I don't need to get involved."

"Oh, yes you do," she scolded like a true grandmother. "You weren't there for the fall of Rome, but I was," Beatrice helped herself to the only seat not covered in decorator swatches. "Those bastards couldn't be saved. I feel the same energy now. You know the Great Year is over. With it comes cataclysmic change. This will be far worse than Rome."

"It's the second coming," Milicent said emphatically. "I knew it! And this time Christ Consciousness is female."

"Milicent, you have to let go of this *female rule* nonsense. The feminine energies do not seek control, they seek balance." Beatrice wrung her hands. "It pains me to say this, but the world will lose millions of people from this upheaval. The apathy of the collective has grown too big. And only big change can correct it."

"Grandmother planning another flood?" Milicent's eyes showed great interest.

"That's her story to tell, not mine. Right now, I'm concerned with the task at hand."

Milicent didn't look like she was willing to help.

"You as much as anyone have known this day would come," Beatrice said. "You were well aware of what occurred on the Solstice and you used it to your advantage. You and I know that's the only reason you agreed to this whole charade." She gestured to the whole of the White House.

"I've already been doing my own digging around here," Milicent said, slightly perked. "I don't know if it's salvageable."

Beatrice stood up from her chair and leaned on the desk across from Milicent. "I'm not asking for salvage. I'm asking for decimation."

Milicent leaned her arms on her desk. She shook her head contemplating Beatrice's request. After her dramatic pause, she pounded one fist down. "What do you need me to do?"

17

"Suuk, I have to go away for a while," Skylar said as she patted Cheveyo. She couldn't look her in the eyes. "I know I was appointed by FLOTUS and all, but Beatrice has worked that out with Milicent. And apparently, the US Government has nothing on the Great Mother of Air."

"I've been waiting for you to say that," Suki said. "You have a world to save and mysteries to solve. And there's no room for the adorable, ethnically diverse sidekick to tag along."

"You are needed here," Skylar said. "No one can run this place like you can. Are you going to leave the horses in the hands of . . . them?" she gestured to two first-year students spilling grain all over the ground and trying to sweep it up with a dust broom. Enrollment in the Equine Program had returned to normal after Milicent's departure and they were back to training very green candidates. She cringed when the two students collided and their buckets crashed to the ground. "No, you belong here. You'll get that promo you were gunning for."

Suki shrugged. "I'm sorry I'm so boring," she said more to herself than to Skylar.

"There ain't no such thing," Skylar said, giving her friend a fierce hug.

"Whatever," Suki said, pushing Skylar away. "I assume you need someone to watch Michael."

"Hey, thanks for the offer."

"I want to go on your adventure."

"You have your own adventure here and his name is Kyle," Skylar said.

"Oh please, that could end tomorrow. You're doing something that matters."

Skylar thought about it. "I would take you Suuk, but it's not my decision to make. Out of the blue this girl shows up at Nana's and she fits right in to the insanity of it all. *Another granddaughter* . . . I can't believe it."

"Right, I've been replaced by blood," Suki said deflated.

"We're not quite blood, but close enough I guess," she said with a grimace. "Beatrice gave me a cryptic note and I have to decipher it before I can go." She handed the paper to Suki.

"Derby Street's downtown. Maybe it's an address," Suki said casually.

"Of course! You are so smart."

Suki was already busy on her phone looking it up. "It's the bong shop near the train station. I think Kyle knows that guy."

"That's great, Suuk," Skylar said. "And thanks for understanding about all this."

"I want to give you a gift," Suki said, pulling out a thin, curved sword from a stable locker. She removed its sheath and it shone in silver with intricate markings on the handle.

"Where the hell did you get that? And why was it in there?" Skylar asked.

"It was my grandmother's. Everyone has them in Japan. But you better learn how to use it. There's nothing more pathetic than a woman who doesn't know how to use a sword."

"You know how to use it?" Skylar was amazed.

"Of course! I was fencing champion at my boarding school, four years in a row."

"Where do you think I'm going? The Middle Ages?" Skylar

stared at the blade, eyes wide.

"This isn't King Arthur metal, Skylar, geeze," she said. "Think more . . . shogun. This is revered in other parts of the world. The US is so obtuse when it comes to the art of war." She held it out and Skylar took it awkwardly.

"Good God, give it to me," Suki immediately grabbed it back out of her hand. She stood at the ready, in parry position. She began dancing around the aisle in a figure eight wielding the shiny shaft of steel like a pro. She circled Skylar and spun around, landing the point of the blade at her stomach. Skylar felt it through her thin T-shirt.

"Impressive," Skylar said. "But I don't need a sword. You keep it for when I get back. We'll . . . go fencing or something."

"You're not taking my gift," Suki said dryly. "I really mean nothing to you."

"Wow, way to be dramatic," Skylar said. "Fine, I'll take the sword."

"Nope, forget it," Suki said.

"Suki, give me the sword!" Skylar's voice started to rise.

"Too late, moment's gone."

"Ugh," Skylar threw up her hands in frustration. "I do need your help you know. Can you take me to that bong shop? I could really use the company."

"Sure," her mood changed in a flash like a toddler who got her way. "I'll bring Kyle. This is his area of expertise."

Every college town has a bong shop. Rosen was no different. Off the main drag of Bay Avenue, the tiny storefront displayed rainbow bears and hookahs in all shapes and sizes.

The threesome adjusted their eyes to the dimly lit shop the following sunny Saturday. All of the shelves were lined with black felt to cushion the glass bongs and hookahs. A few low quality amethysts dotted the glass cases. Buckets of magnetic rocks lined the walkway, always a big seller for the wandering 'tween.

"Hey man," a heavy-lidded, twenty-something greeted Kyle with a man hug.

"Hey man," Kyle replied.

"I'm out of that really good shit until Tuesday," the clerk said. His bloodshot eyes and pot belly was all the proof Skylar needed that marijuana shouldn't be legalized.

"We're here for a different reason," Kyle said, grazing the countertop with his hands. "This is my girlfriend, Suki." Kyle put his arm around Suki.

"Hey man," the clerk said to Suki.

"Hey," Suki replied. Skylar had to purse her lips to keep from laughing. The tattoo on his forearm read *Jared*. She highly doubted he tattooed his own name on his arm but she was going with it.

"Her friend Skylar here is looking for something," Kyle said.

"Looking for what?" Jared asked.

"We're not sure," Skylar replied.

"Then why'd you come?" Jared asked in a haze.

"My grandmother gave me this piece of paper," she handed it to Jared. "We assumed it meant this address."

Jared nodded in understanding. "Got it," he said. "You wouldn't happen to be going on . . . a road trip, would you?"

Skylar's eyes widened. "Yes! How did you know?"

"'Cause I think you're in the wrong place," Jared said. "You need to go to Salem."

They were all surprised. "Salem?" Skylar asked.

"Yeah, I opened this place here 'cause it's the same exact address as a place in Salem. I figured it had good witchy energy. All numerology and shit. Try that one."

Kyle looked at the girls. "Salem's not an hour. Roadie?" he asked.

"I already have the secrets to the universe, why do I need witches?" Skylar asked.

"It was doubtful Beatrice would send you here to this shit hole," Suki said. "No offense Phil. Salem makes more sense."

Ahh, Phil, Skylar thought. "Beatrice is rarely about making sense, but it's worth a shot," she said.

The trio arrived in Salem, MA just after 1:00 p.m. that same day. They stared at the large worn wood building at 288 Derby Street.

"The Salem Wax Museum? Really?" Skylar scoffed in disbelief. She walked from the car to the entrance with her head on a swivel. The people-watching was exceptional although she found the commercialized brutality disturbing. Little kids in T-shirts and crocs skipped behind their parents waiting to snake through the velvet ropes to witness the various mechanisms of torture. No one seemed to notice anything wrong with it.

They went inside and paid their entrance fee.

"The tour starts this way," Suki said, pointing left.

"I think I'll start with the gift shop," Skylar said. "You guys go on, I'll catch up." She walked into the small shop with its rows of witch T-shirts, beer cozies, and souvenir spoons.

"You're late," the woman at the register grumbled behind a curtain of black hair hiding her face. "I expected you this morning."

Skylar's palms started to sweat. "I went to the wrong Derby Street," she said, wiping them on her jean shorts. "Does now work?"

"It'll have to," the clerk said, raising her head. She was pretty, about twenty-five, if Skylar had to guess. With tattoos up both arms, her skin was every color of the rainbow. Skylar glanced at her nametag that read "Tamsyn." She took a minute to tune in to Tamsyn's aura.

"I'll stop you right there," Tamsyn said. "No one reads me without permission."

"Sorry," Skylar felt caught stealing. She focused on Tamsyn's eyes. "Why are you here at the museum? Among all the tourists?" she asked.

"Classic case of hidden in plain sight," Tamsyn said. "I can carry on my business and no one cares. Those fuckers want to keep their secrets. I'll keep mine. They want to keep women prisoners. I'll keep them prisoners in their own ignorance."

Skylar's eyes widened. "I'm sorry you're still struggling with forgiveness," she said. "You've found no peace?"

"My peace will come when men burn for their sins." She spat into the fire heating a cauldron Skylar thought was a prop until it glowed orange.

Skylar shrugged one shoulder. "Revenge works too," she said optimistically. "Do you mind if I take a look at your collection?" Skylar motioned to the crystals and pendants that aligned one wall of the shop.

"Let me see your palms," Tamsyn said. Skylar held out both hands face up. It was pointless to wipe them again. The sweat returned immediately. Tamsyn studied them and eyed Skylar accusingly. "You've had sex with a demon," she said.

Skylar rolled her eyes and huffed. "In my defense I had no idea what he was at the time."

"What were you trying to do? Create the Philosopher's stone?"

"Again . . . I had no idea what I was doing. I was pulled toward that creature with a maddening force." She continued to spill the contents of her guilty conscience. "I'm just thankful I'm over it." Skylar saddened at the thought of Joshua.

"One is never *over* that kind of attraction," Tamsyn said in a tone that made Skylar feel small. "Manageable, yes; over it? No. What makes you think you're *over it?*" Tamsyn didn't give her time to answer. "The only way to beat the pull from your loins is to increase your vibration."

"I've been working on it," Skylar said.

"Work faster," Tamsyn said. She returned to Skylar's hands. "Despite dabbling with demons, you're clean. Don't bother with this fake stuff. Follow me."

She led Skylar to her back room. "Watch the puddles," she said, stepping over a large pool of water. "We flood quite a bit these days. The water's rising and our carpets get soaked every time we have a storm. I don't see us living another twenty years before this building's in the ocean."

"Wow, I'm sorry to hear that," Skylar said.

"Everyone on the coast is dealing with this," she sighed. "Watch your head too. The ceiling's low."

Skylar followed Tamsyn into a cluttered room just bigger than a storage closet. She could never understand why those who valued the secret mysteries let them get buried by worldly clutter and dirt. But she had to admit this room was much better than the gift shop. The pulse of energy from the stones was palpable. There were only a few but they were mighty.

"The gems of our natural world are pieces of our past," Tamsyn said. "They have energy we can connect to."

Skylar closed her eyes but still saw the stones in her mind's eye. A couple burned brighter than others. A citrine behind her and an amethyst to her left shone brightest of all. She opened her eyes and it all returned to normal. She picked up the amethyst and it pulsed in her hand.

Tamsyn's voice broke her concentration. "So you have the Book of Sophia?" she said. "That makes sense, given your dragon blood lines. You really are the perfect storm we've been waiting for. Don't screw this up." She leaned close to Skylar and looked down at the amethyst. "I know she reached out to you but that's just because she's bored here. The citrine too." Tamsyn talked about the stones as if they were people. "Don't confuse a *connection* with their desire for a change of scenery." She backed away and started rummaging through piles of average looking stones. Skylar replaced the amethyst to the shelf.

"You're going to need this," Tamsyn said handing her a bag of river rocks. "And this," a compass. "And this." She handed her a small smooth green stone in the shape of an egg. Skylar held it in her hand.

"What is it?" she asked.

"A jade egg," Tamsyn replied. "It's for improved vaginal blood flow. You're going to want to wash it first."

"Does my vagina need better blood flow?" Skylar asked, straight faced.

"We all need better flow, honey."

Skylar walked about the back room enjoying the rich colors and crystals on every surface. It reminded her of Cassie. Tamsyn rambled on. "I see you doing work with lunar energy. Did you know *menses* means *moon*? You should really pay attention to your cycles and the moon centers of your body. That will get you more in touch with your psychic abilities and help you master lucid dreaming."

Skylar had just let all of the chakra schooling sink in. She had no idea what moon centers were and wasn't sure she had the capacity to care.

"The jade egg will for sure help but only when your body is in its clitoris or vagina moon. Don't even think about using it when you are in your cheeks moon center." She went on as if Skylar had any idea what she meant.

"I'll remember that, thanks," Skylar said.

"But study the sun energy too, gosh . . . the lions!" Tamsyn's voice shrieked. She kept throwing information at Skylar and it was impossible to catch it all. "The lions have great wisdom to share." Skylar nodded again. She turned to a wall of pegs and saw a sapphire pendulum hanging by a silver chain. It shone brighter than any stone in the room, its light similar to the emerald in the Grotto. She had to have it.

"Can I see that pendulum?" Skylar asked.

Tamsyn stopped mid stride and slowly turned to the pendulum. She exhaled loudly. "My grandmother made that for a woman in the 1960s but she never showed up to claim it. It was paid for and everything. It's been hanging there ever since. No one has asked for it in all this time," She took it down from the wall. "It figures it's for you."

Skylar grasped her fingers around it and felt its energy course through her palm. "She made it for me, it just took me a while to get here," she said, trying to be mysterious.

The stone got hot in her hand and she released it. A bright red burn briefly appeared then faded back to normal pink skin. She untangled the chain and put it around her neck instead. The sapphire rested at her breastbone. The thin material of her T-shirt seemed to be enough of a buffer on her skin.

"Excuse me one moment," Tamsyn said. "I feel someone's at the register." She left and Skylar closed her eyes. She felt the pulse of the stone on her heart chakra. It seemed to amplify the energy of everything in the room. The stones on the shelves, even the shelves themselves pulsed with a heartbeat. The floor rumbled intensely and things started crashing to the floor. *Was it an earthquake?* Skylar's eyes popped open and she grasped a table for support. She looked around. Nothing had moved, nothing was broken. It had been all in her head.

Tamsyn returned and stared at her curiously. "Does it make you nauseous?" Tamsyn asked pointing to the pendulum. "You look sick."

"No, but I can imagine this is what ayahuasca is like," Skylar said. "Everything was moving and I'm seeing weird scenes in my head."

"Why are you wearing it like a necklace? A pendulum is held by the chain."

"This felt better," Skylar said.

"You might want to re-think that," Tamsyn said.

"How much do you want for it?" Skylar asked.

"I told you it was already paid for," Tamsyn said. "Even if it was before I was born." She scoured the back room for other items to throw at Skylar. "Take this aura mist . . . and these flower essences too." She held up a handful of small eyedropper bottles. "And planetary elixirs. The essence of Jupiter helps the seeker." They made their way back to the main gift shop and Skylar struggled to carry it all in her hands. Suki and Kyle were milling around with other patrons.

"You've been gone forever," Suki said. "We took the whole tour already."

"It's fine," Skylar said. "I can't say I'm sorry I missed it." She piled everything on the checkout counter. "Let me pay you for the other things at least," Skylar said to Tamsyn.

Tamsyn shook her head. "I can't accept your money."

"How about his money?" Suki said, referring to Kyle.

"Hey!" Kyle protested.

"We have to pay her," Suki said. "You can do that."

Reluctantly Kyle got out his wallet. "His money?" Tamsyn studied Kyle. "I'll take it."

Skylar took a few last minutes to look around the gift shop. A stack of tourist-like maps caught her eye. At the top of each one sat a star similar to the one in her Book of Sophia. So often it was confused with the star of David. She picked up a map. Many alchemical symbols dotted the intricate maze. A small Ziploc bag of door stickers was stapled to each map.

"Tamsyn, what are these?" Skylar asked.

"Ahh, the Magical Door game," Tamsyn said. "You have to find the five gates in the maze. When you do, you put a sticker on each gate. Once you find all five, you scratch off the secret inscription and obtain the ability to turn lead into gold."

"Can I take one?" Skylar asked. She could hear the sound of her own heart in her ears. This magic door was the Porta Alchemica Argan talked about.

"Take them all. They aren't selling and I'll be stuck with them forever." Skylar grabbed a few more and stuck them in her bag. She said her goodbyes to Tamsyn. Divine timing had brought them together and now she had a fair amount of tools in her toolbox.

"Thanks for coming with me today," Skylar said to Suki and Kyle as they walked to the car. "You were right, this was where we needed to go." She looked up and saw a large white bird sitting on a yield sign. "Do you guys see that bird, or am I hallucinating again?"

"I see it," Kyle said. "Is it a crane?"

"It's an ibis," Suki said. "They're usually in warmer climates."

"The whole country's a warmer climate," Skylar said.

"True," Suki said. "Is it Beatrice? Did she follow us?"

"Beatrice doesn't yield," Skylar said. "If it were her, she'd be on a *rough road* sign."

They chuckled and got in the car.

18

First State of the Union address: Devlin Grayer was well received by Congress. His first State of the Union gave him at least a dozen standing ovations. He called for a return to traditional values, a solid plan for the drug epidemic, and a focus on technology for alternative energy sources. With each emphatic initiative, the room rushed to its feet.

Milicent was bored. She sat in the mezzanine in watered down purple Chanel. Even her wardrobe spoke to her dissatisfaction with her current life stuck as Devlin's cheerleader. As if on cue, her mystery rash flared up, increasing in intensity as the evening wore on, almost to an unbearable degree. During the eighth standing ovation she took the opportunity to excuse herself from the room. Her absence would be noticed but she had to get away from all of the suits and get a handle on the rash.

She walked into the main rotunda of the Capitol Building and Noah greeted her, fishing through his shoulder bag.

"Cortisone or Grey Goose?" he asked.

"Cortisone, Noah," she said, grabbing the tube out of his hand. She headed to the bathroom as her security detail watched her every move. Once safely behind the ladies room door, she examined her rash. "Good God," she said aloud. "There has to be a better cream for this." She applied the cream and appreciated the few minutes alone, albeit in a public restroom.

She took a deep breath and exited back into the lobby. Wren

stood waiting with Noah. "Mrs. Grayer, are you all right?"

"Yes, Wren, thank you. I just had to let this rash cool down. I need another minute before I can go back inside."

"Of course, ma'am." Wren took a step back and waited silently.

Noah wasn't so silent taking the opportunity to discuss overdue decorating decisions needing to be made for her office renovation.

"Noah, I honestly don't care," Milicent said, taking a seat in the hall. "You handle it."

His eyes widened at the opportunity. *He* would be in charge of decorating the First Lady's office? Overcome with emotion, he needed his own alone time in the restroom and squeaked out an "excuse me" before bolting away.

As she sat on a bench rubbing the back of her tight neck, Milicent took in her surroundings. She had been in and out of DC as a child but didn't remember much of the architecture. The Capitol Building was supposed to command power but it was lost on her. She admired the cherry finishes but all of the dark green made her ill. She paused when she glanced at the ceiling, not sure exactly what she was looking at. "What the hell is that?" she asked aloud.

Wren was ready to assist. "What ma'am?"

"Why is George Washington floating on a cloud on the ceiling?"

Wren looked up. "That is the Apotheosis of Washington, ma'am," she said.

"Man becomes God," Milicent translated. "So George is a god in this place?" she nodded. "Makes sense." She squinted and continued to stare at the ceiling. "That is a bizarre painting though, don't you think?"

"How so, ma'am?" Wren asked.

"Really, Wren?" Milicent asked. "George Washington is in battle gear floating on the ceiling with Poseidon and Hermes. You don't find that odd?"

"It's Neptune and Mercury," Noah said, appearing at her side, his nose reddened. "Roman mythology, not Greek." He punctuated his clarification with a loving smile to appease his boss.

"Should you be getting back, ma'am?" Wren asked, motioning to the doors leading back to the Congressional floor.

"This is much more interesting than what's going on in there," Milicent said. "Noah, are you a history major?"

"*Art* history," he said. "Art tells the truth history hides."

His words sunk in and Milicent bounced up from her seat with atypical enthusiasm. "Noah, you are brilliant!" She quickly walked toward the Congressional floor. Before she went in, she turned back to Noah and Wren standing in the hall. "We have work to do." She pushed the door and went inside.

The next day Milicent's half-decorated office was considerably more congested with a dozen boxes delivered from the National Archives. Noah was fervently taking measurements of every corner of the room. He had relieved Milicent's decorators of their duties, insisting on doing everything himself. Milicent and Wren spent the greater part of the morning sifting through the vast amounts of information. The only piece marginally interesting was the original drawing of the Great Seal. The Bannu bird, the Egyptian symbol of the phoenix, stared up at her. Milicent recognized it instantly, having been well educated in Egyptian history. This was not news to her, being fully aware many of the ideas of the founding fathers came from Ancient Egypt. At noon, she concluded the National Archives were of no use to her and she sent the boxes back.

"Can you give me a bit more to go on ma'am?" Wren asked. "I can do some more digging."

Milicent studied her. "Okay. I'll give you a shot," she said. "You see we are living in a time when no one knows how to fix the problems because they can't find the root. The root of the problem in this country is buried deep and I want to uncover it. Find the root, fix the problem."

Noah groaned from the back corner, flummoxed over drape swatches. "Eggplant or raisin?" he muttered to himself. He walked to Milicent's desk and laid both before her. "Which one?" he asked.

She glared at him. "What part of 'you handle it' do you not understand?"

He slammed his clipboard down louder than he should have and let out a huff. "Milicent, I love you, but how can you be so obtuse? No one is going to wheel over their dirty secrets to you on a dolly." Wren's eyes widened at Noah's liberty with the First Lady. "You are forgetting the Native American influence, Mil," he continued, leaning his arms on her desk. "If you want to 'find the root' as you say, dig into American Indian art, or better yet talk to one. They never wrote stuff down. If anyone knows what went wrong, they do. Now . . ." he stood upright. "Eggplant or raisin?"

"He has a point, ma'am," Wren said. "But," she paused, treading carefully. "I'm sure you realize that's the whole idea. Not to fix the problems, but to manage them."

Milicent froze and stared at Wren. "What did you say?"

Wren met Milicent's stare equally. "I've worked in Washington in various capacities for twenty-eight years. Nothing changes because they keep their jobs if it doesn't . . . ma'am."

"Wren, please stop calling me ma'am. You're older than I am." Milicent got to her feet and started to pace. "I see your point. When I was in the private sector, we made a difference. We saved lives with improved healthcare and education. This . . . is archaic."

"The whole town's a dinosaur ma'—" Wren stopped herself and cleared her throat.

"So was Rome when it fell, Wren. And seeing people like Cyril Magus walk these halls burns me up. I thought I was done with him in the private sector."

"All do respect, you should settle in. Mr. Magus has been a fixture here as long as I can remember."

"That's not shocking. I'm not saying I'm an innocent party here. Devlin was a big roller in bio-tech. I'd be a hypocrite if I said we didn't look the other way a few times to get funding." Concern spread across her face. "It feels different on this side of things."

"You can't possibly be growing a conscience," a voice boomed from the doorway.

Wren rose to attention. Noah followed suit. "Good afternoon, Mr. President," she said as Devlin walked toward them.

"Good afternoon," he replied. He walked around the desk and kissed Milicent on the cheek.

"Wren's been in DC for decades, Dev. I've been getting quite a history lesson," Milicent said.

Devlin eyed Wren but she stood tall and nodded. "I'll leave you," she said.

"No, I just came to see how the decorating was going," he said and Noah stepped forward. "You should really get this office in order before you start taking on projects." He pointed to the raisin colored swatch on the desk. "That one." Noah wrinkled his nose.

"Thank you for your input, dear," Milicent said.

"We have a dinner with Cyril and his wife this evening, Milicent," Devlin said. "Please clear your calendar." Milicent said nothing and he walked out the door without a word. Wren relaxed slightly.

"I'm really the one you should be worried about," Milicent said, staring at the drape swatches.

"I gathered," Wren said and looked over her shoulder nervously. "There's quite a bit I could tell you if you were interested," her voice dropped to a whisper. "For starters, all the shelved patents for free energy inventions. Decades have been wasted enslaving the world to crude oil. I keep wondering when the whistle blowers will start coming out. It's time, don't you think?" Wren paused as if choosing her next words. "Now that the Great Year is over."

Milicent's head shot up from her swatches. "Wren, let's get some more coffee in here. It's going to be a long day."

19

Despite their whirlwind start to the New Year, Skylar hadn't seen Argan in weeks. His mother fell ill the first week of January and he flew back to Greece to be with her. Skylar couldn't help but think Leonora's health was intricately tied to the dream she had and the journey ahead.

Argan was slow to agree. "I can't say for sure," he said. "Given our history and the current state of things, anything's possible. I'll keep you posted."

She hated to see him go. She felt they had made so much progress over the holidays. But she understood he needed to be with his mother.

He made good on his promise to keep in touch. He texted often with updates and called a few times. Leonora had contracted an aggressive superbug from visiting her sister in the hospital. It had taken almost three weeks but she finally improved enough for Argan to feel comfortable returning home.

In that time Skylar tied up the loose ends of her life to prepare to go to Silverwood. She hadn't told him about her impending trip, never knowing how to approach it. And as the time drew nearer, it seemed harder to explain.

The Quine was officially in Suki's hands and Joel had accepted his daughter had gone off the deep end.

"When will you be back?" he asked.

"I'm not sure Dad," Skylar said and looked to Rachel for support. If anyone understood all of this, she did.

"Joel, it's . . . fine," Rachel said carefully. "We knew a day like this would come. Our job is to support Skylar any way we can."

He looked at them both as if stranger words had never been spoken.

Skylar didn't want to dwell on an emotional goodbye. "I'll come back in one piece, I promise," she hugged them both. Rachel gave her a reassuring squeeze and Skylar left them standing on the front porch.

Her car was already packed with her clothes and all of the supplies from Tamsyn. For some undisclosed reason, Beatrice had sent her off with two small duffle bags filled with white feathers that seemed to take up more space than they did the week before. All that was left was to say her goodbyes to Ocean.

"It feels like a lifetime ago that I was here," Skylar said, standing in the sparse yoga studio. It all looked the same. All that was missing was that odd crystal table.

"It was," Argan said, appearing in the far doorway. His chest and feet were bare. His only clothes, loose linen pants. He was more gorgeous than ever, darker from the Grecian sun. The sight of him made Skylar forget why she was there.

Her face lit up when she saw him. "You look great," she said, unable to hide her delight.

He walked across the room and stopped short of a hug. He lightly touched the pendulum around her neck. "New toy?"

"It was a must-have," she said as her throat started to close. Instantly a wall of heat hit her like an open oven door, engulfing her in his energy field. It was hot and stifling. Her eyes teared up from the enormity of it and she took a step back.

"Beware of shiny objects, Skylar," he said. "It's easy to bounce along all the divination tools, looking for a shortcut. There's no substitute for hard work." He lingered on her eyes, then leaned in and hugged her awkwardly. All the progress made at New Years seemed to have been forgotten.

She started to cough and tried to regain focus.

"Sky, you're choking."

"Swallowed wrong," she coughed out.

"No, there's something else." He took one step closer and she started to sweat. "What are you hiding?"

"I'm not hiding," she said defensively and took a step back. Something was drastically different in his energy field. *He* was the one that was hiding.

"You might want to take off that pendulum," he said.

She obliged and hated to admit he was right. She felt better. She put it in her pocket and took a deep breath to face the inevitable. "I saw Beatrice and I've been given my marching orders."

He said nothing, waiting for her to elaborate.

"She concurred with the Book of Sophia. I have to restore a lost memory in the Akasha." She took in a large breath. "And I have to go to Silverwood to do it," she said hoping he understood what that meant. She held her breath.

It took only a minute. "Silverwood, meaning when you were there the first time?" he asked. She nodded. "What? Why?" he asked more flustered and ran his hand through his hair. "Did she say *why?*"

"*The future is in our roots my dears,*" Skylar mimicked her best Beatrice.

"No, that can't be right," he said, upset. "Messing with the time continuum is very dangerous. Beatrice knows that. I'm surprised she suggested this."

"It was more of a direct order than a suggestion," Skylar said as Argan began to walk in circles around the empty room.

"I'll go with you," he said.

"You have experience with time travel?"

"No," he said. "But I can help you." The pains on his face increased as the minutes clicked by. "When are you going?"

"The eve of Imbolc."

"That's in two days!" He shook his head. "No. That's not possible."

"It's all done, everything's done," she said. She still felt a fear bubble surrounding him that prevented her from walking any closer but it didn't stop him. He got within inches of her and placed one hand on her hip and the other hand over her scar. The feeling of Argan's hand made Skylar shudder. She hoped he wouldn't notice the excessive amount of sweat on her skin.

His thumb rested on the ring of doves and she felt her pulse beat through it. He pulled away from her and rolled out two mats on the floor. "Your heart rate is through the roof. We need to do some breath work."

"To hell with breath work, Argan!" She hadn't seen him in almost a month and the last thing she wanted to do was close her eyes.

"Sit," he commanded.

Her anger grew. "You are not the boss of me," she said.

"Look, we have a lot of chakra work to do. You have to get all of your systems up to light speed as soon as possible. Now if we are able to get you beyond light speed, your body will cease to exist and traveling through the time continuum will be effortless. But I can't get you there in two days. We'll have to delay."

"I don't think that's an option," Skylar said. "Beatrice was on a definite time line."

"Your physical training this past year can only take you so far. All leaps of ascension start in controlling the mind. I need more time."

He took in a deep breath but his exhale was more exasperation, not relaxation. He pressed his palms together at his heart center. "Eyes closed. Take in slow, even breaths."

She played along but was more focused on him. She had gotten good at slowing her breath down, holding it quite a while these days. She'd play games and time herself, up to five minutes now. But Argan's breath was ragged and as they sat there, he seemed to have a harder time of it.

After about ten minutes of struggle, he gave up. Skylar had never seen him give up on anything. But something was making him tense and no amount of breathing helped. "Let's try camel," he said, getting to his knees.

"What is that going to get us?" Skylar asked, completely annoyed. She was going into the great void in two days and Argan wanted her to do yoga.

He glared at her and she obliged, getting to her knees. Camel had always been a tough pose for Skylar, usually ending in nausea. Today her ire was up and she nailed it. A little anger worked wonders to obliterated obstacles. Just before she lifted herself out of the pose, she felt a sensation like ice shattering throughout her body. Her eyes were closed but it was as if a match had been lit in her view and the edges of her frame of vision burned away, exposing a field of brilliant white light. She sat in camel pose as the light show danced in her field of vision. All of the rust had fallen away, revealing a connection to the etheric plane. Magda appeared in her mind, soon to appear in front of her eyes. Skylar looked around, Argan had vanished.

Your powers are getting stronger, dear one. I am so pleased. You struggle with balance but that will come. She reached out her hand and Skylar felt the corporealness of Magda. Her hand grazed Skylar's face lovingly. *The virgin will bring the light to the world,* Magda proclaimed.

"Ummmmm," Skylar bit her lip.

As if Magda read her mind, *Virgin literally means belonging to no man.*

Skylar's shoulders relaxed. "Oh, okay, that sounds right."

Stay true to what's in your heart, Skylar, and you will succeed on your quest.

"Right, I have to make up for my grandmother's indiscretions," Skylar said.

Do not judge what you don't understand, Magda said. *You do not have all of the facts. And even if you did, it would not matter. Your job is to move forward into what you cannot see. Stop looking behind you to blame another. Look within to be the answer to the problem. Thy word shall be done.*

Magda vanished and Argan returned in Skylar's sight, still in camel pose. His chest glistened with sweat in the extreme back bending posture.

"Argan, have you been here all this time?" she asked casing the room.

"Yup, camel makes me nauseous but I work through it," he said.

"You didn't see Magda," she said.

"Your spirit guide?" he asked, coming out of the pose to sit on his heels. "No, but I don't think anyone else can see your spirit guide."

"They all can, Ocean, Ronnie, Milicent," Skylar said.

"Well, maybe it's a female thing," he said innocently.

"Maybe," she said.

"What did she say?"

"That I'm the second coming of Christ and you should obey me," she said.

"The first Christ didn't want to be worshiped and you shouldn't either. I thought freedom of thought was your motto?"

"There will be no world domination with that attitude," she said.

She got to her feet and reached for her tote bag. She took out the Book of Sophia.

"I carry it around now," she said. She gingerly fanned the pages. "I wish I could still read about my lifetimes. That was handy."

Argan's head perked up. "Did you learn anything worthwhile?"

She studied him. "Not enough," she said. "It was mostly modern era stuff. And I was so consumed with my immediate future, I didn't have the foresight to read anything else. That was a mistake. Now, I'd really like to know about my lives in ancient times, Rome, Egypt, even Atlantis. Who was I? If I knew that, I'm sure it would help me know what to do now."

"You'll have to figure it out like the rest of us," he said, giving her an encouraging smile. He got up to grab his water bottle.

"I was wrong about camel," she said apologetically. "It was exactly what I needed."

"Good," he said curtly. He sat on the bench and put on his sneakers. "I can't seem to settle today, sorry."

She got off the floor and sat next to him. "You wont tell me what else's got you worried?"

He leaned his arms on his knees. "I'm sorry, Sky. I guess I'm just hesitant to really do this time travel stuff."

She knew that wasn't it. "I thought we were done lying to each other. What's really the problem?" The pained look on his face told her this was serious. "Is it your mom?"

"You could say that," he said. She waited for him to explain. "It's just this whole thing, I mean this WHOLE thing is really dangerous. Like we-could-die dangerous."

"You mean the vortex travel? Beatrice assured me that part would be ridiculously easy."

"I didn't even consider that. No, I'm talking about . . . well." He struggled with his words.

"Argan, spit it out. What did your mother tell you?"

"The dark energies. There are dark energies that control this planet."

"Yes, this I've known." She remained completely present with him, yet questioned what he could possibly tell her that she didn't already know from the myriad of mystical women in her life.

"The dark energies don't want that Akasha restored, Sky. It's the last nail in their coffin."

"Right," she said.

"But I know you've been called to do this. I will help you."

"Right," she said.

"But to do this, I have to be completely on guard at all times. My mother reminded me that I am a warrior, raised for this single purpose, to help you complete your quest. I can't be clouded with love, or whatever this is."

The fear in Skylar's heart carried through her veins to every inch of her body. Now she understood what he was saying. He couldn't be with her romantically and fulfill his promise to his mother. "Does it have to be so black and white?" her voice raspy. "One thing my Book of Akasha taught me is that no future is certain. I know you like certainty, Argan, but it's also important to embrace mystery. Magic is possible if we can trust the mystery, trust the love. Or whatever this is." Her last words were sharp. Her defensiveness set in and she felt that door to her heart shut tight. "You know for someone who preaches forward thinking, it surprises me that you lack the courage to face the dark." She knew her words hurt.

"Courage? You've got to be kidding me. I've spent my whole life learning about courage, preparing for this moment."

"Right, preparing," she slipped on her shoes and grabbed her things. "We'll see what happens when it all comes down." She walked out the door, not letting him answer.

She stood behind the door as tears stung her eyes. Each time they started to get close, something happened to reopen the chasm between them. She was tired of it. She had an important job to do, with or without his help. She put her leather-bound book in her bag and gasped. The pages had frayed even more. A sense of urgency and the knot in her neck quickly returned. She would have to say her goodbyes to Ocean over the phone. She was getting out of here.

She nearly dropped her bag when her cell phone startled her in the hallway. Her caller ID said "M. Grayer." She stared at her phone, waiting to answer it until she got outside on the street. She didn't want to be around when Argan came out of the studio.

"Hello Milicent," Skylar said, juggling her bag with her phone to her ear.

"Please hold for Mrs. Grayer," an unfamiliar, official voice stated. Skylar cringed at the reminder that Milicent was now First Lady and she would have to revert back to calling her ma'am.

After a short pause, the line came back to life. "Skylar, I hear Dune has given birth to the horse of the apocalypse," Milicent's voice boomed into the phone.

"Well, I don't quite see it that way."

"Listen, we haven't spoken in so long. About all that back in June . . . I'm so sorry to have put you in harm's way," she said. "I have goals you see and sometimes individuals must be sacrificed for the greater good."

"Right . . . great . . . good," Skylar said only half listening. She was still thinking about Argan. "I was happy to help with Dune and the Quine, and . . ."

"I appreciate your service," Milicent said cutting her off mid-sentence. "Your sacrifices won't go unrewarded."

"Thank you."

"But I think you know that I spoke with Beatrice. It would seem your services are needed elsewhere."

"Beatrice may have mentioned something about a trip in my future," Skylar said.

"Skylar, don't play games with me, it's useless. I'm looking into some things here in Washington. This place reeks of inadequacy. But that's not my problem. What is my problem is that I seem to be taken less seriously than I had anticipated and I hate that."

"Right," Skylar said with no idea how to respond.

"I understand we share the same bloodline. Unfortunately there is nothing I can do about that so I must work with it. I will help you, for Grandmother."

Argan walked out of the building and Skylar turned her focus to him. In the background she heard Milicent's voice but not her words. Argan raised his hand in a quick wave and headed to his truck. There was a long pause on the other end of the phone.

"Are you listening Skylar? Desire for the wrong reason is a distraction! Focus on your goal and you will succeed."

"Thank you for the call," Skylar said, ready to disconnect.

"Don't end up like me, Skylar," Milicent said in a soft tone that surprised her. "I pushed everyone away, selfish with my own desires. Now I'm stuck in the White House for fuck's sake! It's worse than prison. I have to finish what I started, but you . . . you can choose differently."

Skylar had no idea what Milicent was saying. "I'll keep that in mind, thank you." She watched Argan drive away and she felt empty. *How could they continually fail at connecting?*

"On a different matter, what do you know about the porta alchemica?" Milicent asked.

Her words jolted Skylar back into the present moment. "You

mean in Italy?" Skylar asked, wondering if Milicent was now having her tailed by a government agency.

"Among other places," Milicent said. "Let's cut the BS. We both know things about the mysteries of this world. I need to know what you know."

"I've only started researching alchemy," Skylar said. "There's a mountain of information to digest and most of it is written in riddles."

"Right, that book of yours should help, no?"

"You would think, but I've discovered knowledge and wisdom are two different things." She stared at the empty space where Argan's truck had just been.

"You're not using it properly. I could help you."

Skylar wanted to cut that idea off at the knees. "Again, thank you for your offer but I'm doing all right."

"Well then," Milicent's curt tone returned. "When you see my sister, tell her I want to talk to her." She disconnected the phone.

20

As Milicent hung up the phone, she knew she was no longer alone in her office. "The White House is seeing quite a bit of divine royalty these days," she said, facing out her large picture window.

"Hello Milicent," Ocean said. "This place suits you."

"You're kidding," Milicent scoffed and turned to face Ocean. "I find it impossible to breathe here."

"Even after Beatrice's visit? I'll have to let her know. Maybe she can come back and smudge it for you."

"I know why you're here," Milicent said. "Beatrice beat you to it. You've got someone on the inside now. I've already started digging, but the layers of security on the information you're looking for run deep."

Ocean walked within the second delivery of file boxes and helped herself to a seat on a grape colored office chair. She started picking at a delivery tag still attached to the seat cushion. "You and I both know the information we're looking for won't be found in any box this building can produce."

Milicent's eyes narrowed as understanding of Ocean's silent demand seeped in. "I hold no loyalties to you."

"True," Ocean said. "Where *do* your loyalties lie?"

Milicent paused. Ocean had hit a nerve. She trusted no one and her loyalties were to herself. She was a terrible mother, had a marginal relationship with Devlin, and had even been estranged from Vivienne more than once. She could truly count on no one.

"It's time to step up and make your life matter," Ocean said.

Milicent lashed out. "That's just like you, Ocean. So sure you have all the answers and revel in everyone else's foolhearted attempts in the darkness, when we're all just trying to make the best out of the miserable lot we've been dealt. You always were my least favorite. Even Beatrice has value in her naiveté. You enjoy the ignorance of others. How it makes you *Mother Superior*."

"Casting stones again, Milicent?" Ocean said, unfazed. She got up from her chair and walked to the large window overlooking the White House lawn. "You may be of Vivienne's ilk but you have always had my cunningness. It was one of the qualities I admired in you."

"I don't want your compliments," Milicent said. "Where were you throughout the centuries? When women were stripped of everything. The extermination of our dignity, our human rights? The allowance of the church to take over and commit atrocities in the name of love, of Jesus! And the state in the name of patriotism! You allowed the witch hunts! You had the power to change it, even prevent it entirely, and you did nothing."

Darkness overtook Ocean's face dimming the light in the room. The sky outside the window turned gray. "What power do you think I had? One to thwart the prophesies of the Great Year? This moment in time is twenty-six thousand years in the making." Ocean exhaled and afternoon sun returned. "Milicent, you surprise me. You of all people know the power of the divine plan. We wouldn't be on the edge of the light without having gone through the great darkness. Blame me all you want. I don't have to justify myself to you."

Milicent returned to her desk and sat down. She rested her forehead on tented fingers. "This would be career suicide for

Devlin and most likely actual suicide. He wouldn't survive it, and I'm not sure I would either."

"I understand there will be casualties," Ocean said.

Milicent lifted her head up. An unfamiliar look of despair crept across her face. "I'm so glad you care about my well being," she said. She stared into the void between them. "If I agree to this, will you get out of my office?"

"Happily," Ocean said.

"I can't get back to Rosen for the foreseeable future. I'll send Wren, my Chief of Staff."

"It would be best to involve as few outsiders as possible," Ocean said.

"She knows more than you'd think," Milicent said, making her case.

Ocean cut her off. "Suki can do it."

"Suki? Who's Suki?" The words no sooner came out of her mouth than she gasped. "You have got to be kidding me. And you don't want to involve outsiders?"

"She's hardly an outsider. Line it up. I won't call it an order but it's not a suggestion either." Ocean walked out the door and passed Noah in the doorway.

"Where were you?" Milicent snapped at him.

"I got stuck in the elevator!" he said, visibly worked up. "The lights went out and the elevator stopped and it was fucking unbelievable! I thought I was going to fucking die!"

"You were in there five minutes, Noah, get a hold of yourself and get me a seltzer," Milicent ordered.

The next day she walked the halls of the White House consumed by the stifling air that no one else seemed to notice. She was hyper aware of the staff, press, and interns that all walked around in a daze. Having been schooled in entrainment and the power of inhalants to induce cognitive insensibility, she knew this went deeper.

"Wren," she said, walking with her Chief of Staff, "why does everyone look dead?"

"It's interesting, if you had asked me that before the election of 2016, I would have said it was government mind control," Wren said frankly. "But now, it's more of a general malaise that has digressed into group depression, or hopelessness for the future. No longer can we pretend we are working in the right direction. We know we're not and have no idea how to fix or reverse it. These staffers believed in something once. Even if it was misguided, they still believed and that made the work worth it. Now, their internal compasses are waking up to the dread that they've been fighting for the wrong reasons. And that is a hard day."

Milicent watched the staff members walking by her. They all nodded in her direction and greeted her with half-hearted smiles but she could see the truth behind it. She had mulled over her conversation with Ocean for the past twenty-four hours and didn't like the conclusion she kept coming to.

"Wren, I need you to contact someone at my Equine Facility at Rosen."

21

Skylar held the fateful picture of her two mothers as teens. They were linked arm in arm in front of a picturesque lake. One majestic mountain stood on the opposite shore.

"No GPS on earth can find it," Beatrice had said the day they said their goodbyes. She had written down extensive directions with a hand-drawn map detailing how to get to Silverwood in the Adirondack Park of upstate New York.

Skylar studied the page. "Are these roads?" The concentric circles on the paper looked more like crop circles than a road map.

"Nope, sound waves," Beatrice said. "Sound waves never fully disappear. You can track them backward and forward for centuries. I gave you a general idea of where the camp is. The sound waves will guide you in the rest of the way. Oh, also, you have to leave the book behind." She extended her open hand to take it.

"What? Why?"

"It's already there," Beatrice said. "Your mother has it."

"Which one?"

Beatrice gave her a look. Skylar knew Cassie had it. She handed the Book of Sophia to Beatrice.

"It will be right here when you get back," Bea said. The book had disintegrated more and Skylar had concerns that wouldn't be the case. "It shouldn't diminish further while you're at Silverwood. In fact, it should be in its entirety there."

That was an encouraging thought for Skylar. Maybe the missing pages would be there. She hugged her grandmother tightly, inhaling the scent of cinnamon in her hair.

"I love you, Nana," Skylar said.

"I love you too. Now go save the world."

Britt arrived to Skylar's house just before 10:00 a.m. on February 1. Skylar and Suki were standing in the driveway. "I ditched Vihaan," Britt said. "He was driving me nuts. Is it all right if I keep my rental car here?"

"That's a steep bill but okay," Skylar said. She turned to Suki. "Britt, this is Suki De la Cruz."

"How do you do?" Britt extended her hand.

"Hi," Suki said curtly. She had reverted to her terse, standoffish manner she reserved for new people.

"I'll put my things in your trunk," Britt said. She opened the hatch. "Good Lord, what is all this?"

Skylar cringed. "It's a trunk load of feathers," she said. "Don't ask. I did and didn't get a straight answer." She returned her attention to Suki. "I wish I could tell you when I'm coming back. Truth is, I have no clue."

"It's okay," Suki said. "I have my hands full at the Quine as well as a visit to the White House in my immediate future." Suki crossed her arms and kicked a pebble in the driveway. "You're sure you have no idea what Milicent wants from me? I'm pretty freaked out."

"I've been the last to know on a lot of this stuff, Suuk," Skylar said. "I just talked to her and she didn't mention it. I really want to know though. But I don't think you can contact me where I'm going."

"You never know. I'll continue to work out the mysteries of the universe . . . from a scientific perspective, that is. None of that witchy crap you're into. Maybe I'll come across telephone lines to the past."

Skylar picked up Michael and gave him a squeeze. "Treat him right," she said.

"As long as he behaves himself," Suki said. Skylar knew Kyle would be staying at the house while Suki was in DC.

Skylar opened the driver door when Argan's pickup careened down the driveway. His door flew open as the truck came to a stop. "Leaving without me?" he asked as he hopped out. He grabbed his duffle bag out of the back.

"No. But I wasn't going to wait either," Skylar said. She was still mad at him but also relieved he would be making this trip with her.

He looked at Suki. "Hey Suuk."

"Hey Argan." A bright smile came over Suki's face.

"Britt Anjawal," Britt said to Argan, extending her hand.

"Argan Papadopoulos," he said, flashing his heart-melting smile.

"You know, Argan, I never cleared your tag along with Beatrice, or Ocean or someone with more rank than me."

"Done and done," he said, heading toward the trunk. "Want me to drive first leg?"

"There's no room in the trunk," she said, handing him her keys and self-consciously smoothing her hair. He put his bag in the back seat and Britt hopped in next to it. Skylar shrugged her shoulders as she gave a last goodbye to Suki.

The drive from Diamond Point to Silverwood was about six hours with a planned lunch stop, so they intended to get there in the late afternoon. "What do you suppose we'll find when we get there?" Skylar asked.

"Beatrice didn't give you any clues?" Argan asked.

"She said it would be as it was in 1998, the year I was born."

"*We* were born," Argan corrected.

"Sorry, but I don't think your backstory matters on this road trip," Skylar said.

"That's fair," he said, ignoring her tone. "I'll just make sure you stay out of trouble."

"You are not assigned as my protector, Argan." She felt the need to assert her independence.

"I kind of am," he said. "Remember I told you—"

"No, you're not," she said.

"Sky, I . . ."

"Yeah, yeah, your Spartan warrior story, I know. It just gets a little . . . parental."

"Parental? You should be so fortunate to have me. I'm a rare breed. Really evolved you know."

"Yes, Argan, you keep telling me," Skylar said.

"You two really need to have sex and get on with things," Britt blurted out from the back seat. "The electricity you're creating will short us out for sure."

The front seat fell silent and Skylar could think of no other topic to discuss. She took the last opportunity to surf social media, knowing it didn't exist in 1998.

After lunch, Skylar took the wheel and Britt sat in front. Within five minutes, Argan fell asleep in the back seat.

"Tell me about yourself, Britt" Skylar said. "We're going on an important trip here. It would be good to know more about you."

"Well, my family is from the island of Rajkesh, off the mainland of India," Britt said. Then nothing.

Skylar prodded her on. "Right, you said that the day we met. What else?"

"I was pretty sheltered in our community. We were royalty, well, are royalty and I had all of the gifts and trappings that brings. But my mother was sinking deeper and deeper into depression and the whole time, my stepfather was taking control of the family estate. Now, she's in that place, I can't ever see her, and I'm not sure I'll have a home to return to. He cast me out once I insisted on seeing more of the world. It's as if he was keeping me prisoner and now that I've been sprung, I'm not welcome back. Part of me is fine with that. When I finally visited the mainland of India, it was immensely eye opening. A shock actually. So much poverty and suffering right in the streets. It affected me so deeply. I couldn't sleep for weeks."

Skylar listened, realizing she'd also had a similarly limited view of the world.

"I committed right then to do everything I could to ease the suffering I saw. I wanted to use some of my family resources to help the poor but my stepfather has other plans, of course. I think he's glad about my mother's decline. Our society is matriarchal and unfortunately I am the next in line to govern the people of Rajkesh."

"Unfortunately?" Skylar asked.

"I don't want the job," Britt said. "I want to return to the mainland of India and continue the work of Mother Teresa. But before I do, I have to do something to help my mother, her legacy."

"Remind me again why you're on this road trip with me?"

"My mother's indiscretions with . . . my biological father always seemed odd to me. The story my stepfather told me, even if my mother was manic, I don't know. I never really believed it. Now, I see Beatrice was right. I was meant to meet her, and you. Not Albert. You are on a quest to return the Divine Feminine to the planet. That is the work of Mother Teresa."

"I'm pretty sure Teresa was all about working in the trenches," Skylar said.

"Yes, in the service of others," Britt said. "You might not realize it, Skylar, but that's exactly what you're doing. I have the impression you wouldn't be uprooting your life so dramatically if you didn't feel a sense of duty, or calling to help humanity."

"The Great Mothers can be very persuasive," Skylar said, dismissing Britt's comment.

Britt laughed. "Yes, but give yourself some credit. If you weren't up for this task, you would have found a way out. So that's why I'm on this road trip with you. I have my own quest but you will show me the way. To walk into the fire of uncertainty with absolute faith you are exactly where you are supposed to be. You will lead me into my own destiny."

Skylar choked on her own saliva and started to cough. "Sorry, wow. I may need you to write that down. I want to be that girl."

"You are, Skylar, even if you don't see it in yourself."

"Thank you for that." Skylar glanced into the rear view mirror at Argan.

"Old flame, I assume?" Britt said.

"Kind of," Skylar said. "We have a complicated history."

"He's handsome," Britt said.

"That's what makes it complicated," Skylar said.

As the hours went by, they watched the congestion of strip malls and fast food give way to the pristine landscape of the Adirondack State Park. The sea of dark green pine trees had a magic of their own, transporting them into another world, the magical world of nature. Skylar felt the pulse of life, she heard the hum of the earth. But what was first a pleasant connection to Mother Gaia became so loud it made her physically ill. "I think I need to throw up," she said.

"Pull over," Britt said, perked up.

In a minute the sound and the nausea subsided. "I think I'm okay," Skylar said, as she kept driving. "Just keep talking to me." She wanted to drown out the nagging hum. Britt continued to talk about her family and recount stories of her childhood as a royal. She hadn't much else to talk about, having lived in a gilded box her whole life.

Once off the Northway, they traveled over an hour before the lines on Bea's map started to make sense.

Britt did her best to navigate Beatrice's serial killer scrawl on white lined paper. "Her map is quite intricate," she said. "Will it guide us into another dimension?"

"Are you serious?" Skylar asked.

"Well she never quite said how we would get into Silverwood." She held up the paper in the afternoon sun.

"I'm going on blind faith the way will present itself," Skylar said.

As they continued deep into the ADK, the landscape started to soften and distort as if looking through a fishbowl. A few miles down the last remote side road on Bea's map, the car drove through what looked like fine gold strands, like a spider web that didn't stick. The strands hit the windshield like soft rain and tumbled off.

Skylar pulled over and jumped out of the car. The air was visible, like waves streaming off hot pavement. The concentric circles had been broken apart from her car, the gold lines floating with no direction. Skylar's eyes widened at the sight of them and reached out to touch one close to her face. It zapped her like electricity and she shook off the pain.

"Are we supposed to drive through them?" Britt asked.

"We already have," Skylar said.

The stilling of the car woke Argan in the back seat and he got out to meet the girls in the middle of the clearing. He looked around the desolate area. "We're in the wilderness, huh?" The girls nodded. His head turned on a swivel when he noticed the lighted waves around them. "This is incredible." He smiled in awe, touching one without a reaction. "It's. . . inviting."

"I don't get that at all," Skylar said. "It hurt to touch it."

Britt tried one. "Nothing," she said.

They were standing at the entrance of a road similar to Ocean's driveway back in Rosen. It was a minefield of potholes and grown over with a bramble of branches. Britt looked down the long drive, then back at Bea's map. "We're looking for . . . the 'mouth of the mother', it says. This may be it." She was delighted to see they had found it but Skylar was more distracted by the light threads in the air. "Let's go!" Britt said with enthusiasm.

The three of them hopped back in the car. Skylar started the engine but it wouldn't shift out of park. They each took a turn to satisfy themselves but the car refused to move. "Let's accept that we have to walk the rest," Argan said. He grabbed his duffle bag out of the back seat and Britt popped the trunk. Argan looked at all the bags. "Since when were you so high maintenance?"

"Bea had me bring all these feathers," Skylar said staring into the trunk. "They keep expanding." She shook her head. "I'll have to come back for those." She grabbed one of her rolling bags and the threesome started down the mysterious lane. As they walked, Skylar tried to avoid the gold threads of light. Every now and then she'd bump one and get a jolt. Argan seemed blissful on his walk and Britt didn't care either way.

Beatrice's map was not to scale and they walked for almost an hour before coming to something that resembled an entrance. Anyone could have missed it. Woven twigs formed an over-grown arch of dead branches among strangling brown vines.

"Silverwood" shone in small gold lettering on a tattered wooden sign, filmed over by time.

"Did she say it was abandoned?" Britt asked, wiping the sign with a tissue from her massive tote bag.

"She may have mentioned that it had been awhile since anyone had the *need* for it. She was pretty vague about it. She likes to be vague. It's part of her charm."

"This is exactly right," Argan said pressing on, seemingly guided by his own internal compass. "You have to feel it."

They continued down the long overgrown driveway. With each step, the air got colder and the ground harder. Before long, snow appeared along the path and in the canopy of the trees. The frigid air set in. "What the hell?" Skylar asked. "I didn't pack for Narnia."

"Why not?" Argan asked, pulling out a coat from his duffle bag. "It's February in the ADK."

Britt was prepared as well, pulling out a thin but mighty parka from her tote.

"Do you have magical abilities you aren't telling us with that tote?" Skylar asked.

"No," Britt laughed. "I'm usually prepared for any situation. You have no coat at all?"

"I have other layers in my trunk," Skylar said.

"Way-showers need to be better prepared," Britt said, handing Skylar a sweatshirt from her second bag.

"I'll remember that, thanks," Skylar said, accepting the sweatshirt.

As they walked, the snow became deeper.

"Got boots in that tote of yours?" Skylar asked.

"No. They're in my bag in your trunk," Britt said.

"It looks like we don't have much farther to go," Argan said. Just ahead were lights shining through the trees. They had expected to be there in the late afternoon but with the unexpected trek in the woods, they came upon the compound of buildings just as the full moon was rising in the sky. There was still enough daylight to see their way but it wouldn't remain for long. The camp was eerily quiet, aside from some sounds coming from horses in a paddock a short distance before them.

Skylar walked up to the railroad-tie fence. A handful of blanket-clad horses roamed the cold ground, white puffs of winter air billowed out their noses. There were no horns on their foreheads but they felt ethereal to her just the same. She knew none of these beauties still lived in 2021.

They left the paddock and approached the first building in their sights. It was a simple wood-framed, brown-stained building that blended into the landscape like a half dozen others.

"This feels like summer camp," Skylar said.

"I never went," Britt said.

"You didn't miss much," Skylar said, recalling the weeks she endured in the Berkshires because Joel insisted it would *broaden her horizons.* She knew it was a ploy to get her mind off of Argan and for that reason she made sure she hated every minute of it. She saw the irony that she was here at camp *with* Argan. Part of her desperately wanted to enjoy that.

As she looked around, she could feel the memories of this place in her bones. This was no ordinary camp, with ordinary kids. These kids felt left out of the *real* world and found their tribe here. She could feel the intense bonding and life changing experiences that happened here. It stirred in her heart and triggered the direct line to her tear ducts. Before a tear fell from her eye, she shook it off and watched it take flight and freeze mid-air. She chuckled to herself.

In the middle of camp stood the extraordinary tree that had now become so familiar to her. "*The Great Mother's tree,*" she whispered in astonishment. Skylar had never seen one in winter. It was completely white, trunk to canopy. This tree was the most magical of all, even more than the Tree of Death in the astral realm. Its branches sparkled with dazzling light from an infinite number of dangling icicles. Each pristine branch danced with life from the light reflecting the frozen water. Intricate snowflake designs wove among the branches.

She walked up to this great tree of the north and placed her palm on its white trunk. She felt the same energy from Beatrice's tree and Ocean's Tree of Death. They were all tied together, each an anchor of the Elements, all needed to complete the circle.

Welcome back, this great white tree said in Skylar's mind. *We've been expecting you.*

"Thank you," Skylar said aloud.

"Who are you talking to?" Britt asked.

"The tree," Skylar said.

"Oh," Britt said.

"You can learn great lessons here. Remain open, heart and mind." A flood of heat pulsed through her hand, down her arm, and rushed every inch of her body, removing all traces of winter in her blood. She felt invigorated. She removed her hand and bowed to the tree in thanks.

One small group of students walked by without any acknowledgment. "Are we invisible?" Britt asked.

"Highly doubtful," Argan said. "These are teenagers. We could set ourselves on fire and no one would notice."

"They're not even talking to each other," Skylar said.

The threesome continued up the steps of the brown building. The sign on the door read "Hospitality."

"That sounds like us," Argan said. He pushed the door and it creaked open. "Come on then," he said over his shoulder.

As they walked around the room, each of their footsteps gave way to the floorboard's age. Britt swiped her finger across twenty years of dust on a desk made for the Vietnam War. On it sat a lonely brass swing arm lamp that would now be considered *vintage*. "What now?"

"Get out your dust rags," a young woman said with a jovial voice from the entryway. She flipped the switch by the door to illuminate the twelve by twelve room. They turned to see a young Rachel staring back at them. "Just kidding!" she said as she made her way to open a window. "I don't know who's on cleaning detail. But they are behind schedule." Skylar stared as a lump formed in her throat. Rachel was magnificently beautiful. Her sun-kissed hair and features glowed from the inside out. Skylar could see she was pregnant, which would make her sixteen. She could see her cobalt blue aura dance around her like a halo around the moon.

Rachel turned back to face them. "Did you just arrive?" she asked.

"We did," Argan said.

"Are you counselors? I didn't get any paperwork on new counselors. And it's an odd time of day to be arriving." Rachel shook her head. "I beg your pardon. So rude." She seemed to be talking to herself. "It's just a bit unorthodox."

Skylar realized she was half dozen years older than Rachel. How odd it felt to be on the other side of their age equation.

"We had a bit of a mix up with directions," Britt said. "So sorry we are arriving late in the day. I'm Britt and this is Skylar."

"Nice to meet you both," Rachel said. "Who's the handsome Greek god?" She clasped her hand over her mouth. "There I go again!"

"Argan," he said with a chuckle and shook her hand.

"Welcome to Silverwood," Rachel said with confidence. She had a great vitality to her that was missing in her adult version.

"You'll need to get settled soon before it gets too late. Where are all of your things?"

"We had . . . car trouble," Britt said. "It's a ways back and most of our bags are still in it. And we didn't pack for snow."

Skylar continued to stay silent and gawk at Rachel.

"Why not? It's February," she laughed. "I can get you some help tomorrow with your car," Rachel said. "But you'll have to make do with what you've got for tonight. Come with me." They followed Rachel back outside. The center commons had been transformed from the previously deserted landscape into a bustling campsite filled with energetic teens. Britt and Skylar marveled at the sight of it. Argan didn't seem fazed. Small out-house-sized buildings became visible with interior light. Doors swung open in unison and students poured out, all walking in the same direction.

"Are you hungry?" Rachel asked.

"I could definitely use a meal," Argan said, already fitting in.

"I have to run back to my bunk, wait here," Rachel said. "We'll get you some food at the Mess, then figure out where you're sleeping." She sprinted away.

"How are you completely comfortable with *all of this?*" Skylar asked.

"How can you not be?" he shot back. "Did you think this trip was going to be life as usual? You were told to expect a wild ride. So here you go." He gestured to the scene before them like a game show host. "This, Skylar, is your life."

Skylar took a deep breath. "I just wasn't really prepared to see her and being pregnant and all."

"She's pregnant?" Britt asked. "How can you tell?"

"I see things, remember?" Skylar said. "And she's my mother."

Britt's eyes widened. "Woah, she's pregnant with you? That's wild. How are we not breaking the time continuum?"

"We can stay until Rachel gives birth," Argan said. "It won't be good if we're here then."

"What will happen?" Britt asked.

"We're all too young to know," Argan said.

"We have plenty of time," Skylar said. "My birthday's end of July."

Rachel came back to their group. "Ok, follow me." She started walking with the crowd toward the Mess. "Where did you say you all were from?"

"Diamond Point," Skylar said forcing a smile. She locked eyes with Rachel for just a moment. "It's in Massachusetts."

"Oh, great," she said mildly interested. "When I'm done here at Silverwood, I'm headed to the West Coast. I want to go to college far away." A hint of sadness colored Rachel's voice. She shook it off and walked them into the Mess. In true summer camp fashion, its wide-open space was lined with long wooden picnic tables. The food stations hugged the back wall giving lots of room for socializing. The threesome followed Rachel to the food line and each grabbed a warm dish.

Britt leaned over the scratched up sneeze guard and gazed at the various choices. She wrinkled her nose.

"They put tofu in everything," Rachel said, covering her nose and mouth with her hand. She shook her head. "It's all vegan."

Skylar stared at the white, spongy squares floating in a cauldron of pureed greens. "Mmmm, looks good," she said politely.

Argan dug right into the pile of veggie burgers and took three. He continued to fill his plate with exotic vegetarian fare. Skylar stared at him.

"What?" he asked, already a bite of burger in his mouth. "I'm starving."

She rolled her eyes and headed for the salad bar. She met Britt there, having a conversation with an extremely thin, extremely white young man in a blue turban.

"Skylar, this is Origen!" Britt squealed. "He's Sikh like me! He wasn't born Sikh, but converted two years ago." She turned to the man with pubic hair sideburns peeking out of his blue head wrap.

"How do you do?" he said rigidly.

Skylar shook his hand. "Nice to meet you," she said.

Rachel and Argan walked over with full plates. "Hello Origen," Rachel said. "This is Argan."

"How do you do," Origen said in the same monotone voice.

"Hey man," Argan said, juggling his plate on one arm to shake hands with Origen.

"We can all take the round table in the corner," Rachel said, her voice flat.

"I'm fasting today, Rachel," Origen said. "I was just passing through to get some broth. Another time," he said, holding his hands in prayer to bid them adieu.

Rachel exhaled loudly. "Thank God," she said. "He annoys the hell out of me."

The foursome made their way to a large round table in the corner of the Mess. Skylar looked around at the students. They were an eclectic bunch. Most were well decorated with body piercings and tattoos. She had to remind herself this was 1998. How different life was just a few decades ago. The twin towers were still standing, smartphones didn't exist, and there was a sense of security Skylar realized was missing from 2021. Yet it felt so real to be here, as real as her life in the present. Were they both real? Were neither real? She was starting to think like Ocean.

The minute Ocean popped into her mind, she appeared in

the doorway, looking exactly the same. She was right, she didn't age unless it served a purpose.

"Aging is in the mind, Skylar," Ocean said one day in her yoga studio. "All those needlepointed pillows can't be wrong."

Ocean saw Skylar and made a straight line to their table. Rachel stopped her conversation with Britt mid sentence and looked at Ocean. She rose from her seat in a very formal greeting.

"Good evening, Ocean," Rachel said respectfully. "These counselors arrived right at meal time, so I brought them here before coming to see you." She seemed nervous, as if this were against protocol.

"Counselors? Ahh yes. I expected you earlier," Ocean said with a smile. "Welcome." Her piercing stare made Skylar fully aware that indeed Ocean was expecting them.

Rachel made unnecessary introductions. "Where shall we put them up for the night?" she asked.

"The ladies will be in Cabin 3A," Ocean said. "And Argan will be in the men's dormitory."

Rachel nodded "I'll go now and make sure the cabin is presentable." She smiled and walked away. Ocean turned back to the group. "You're late," she snapped.

"We had car trouble," Skylar said non-apologetically. "Or something like that. Our car got us to the crop circles of light and then it refused to go any farther. Rachel has no idea who we are?"

"No," Ocean said. "None of them do. You have to keep that covered." She looked at Argan. "I wasn't expecting *you*."

"He insisted," Skylar answered for him. She glared at him. He told her Ocean cleared this. He shrugged, not taking a break from his disappearing meal.

"Well I don't have a cabin for you so you'll have to endure the dormitory." She looked back at Skylar. "I'm sure it's unsettling to see Rachel, especially pregnant. You know you have to leave before she gives birth or there will be a huge mess I'm not sure I can fix. And prepare yourself to see Cassandra too." She looked at the girl's full plates. "Not hungry?"

"Vegan will take some getting used to," Skylar said.

"Well, if you're done with dinner, come with me," Ocean said. "Rachel can resume her role as tour guide another time."

Argan quickly finished the remnants on his plate and they cleared their dishes. They followed Ocean outside into the crisp winter air, a new moon hung in the clear night sky.

"What's the date today?" Skylar asked looking up at the sky.

"February 1st. Same as 2021." Ocean said. "We are having an Imbolc celebration tomorrow night. You'll join in. You should thank the Goddess for giving you safe passage to the past."

They walked with lanterns to cabin 3A. It shared a wall with 3B and in total the whole building was half the size of Skylar's tiny house.

Skylar opened the squeaky door and peered inside without going in. "I have a few bags Beatrice made me bring. There's more room in my car than in here."

"Don't be so dramatic," Ocean said. "Those bags are for me anyway. I've been out of feathers for months and this was a handy way to get more." She glanced at her watch. "Lights are out at 10:00 p.m. The days start early around here. Six thirty meditation in the palladium. It's mandatory. I hope you packed your whites." Ocean turned on her heels and led Argan away to the dorms. He glanced back quickly to catch Skylar's eye. He gave her a tight-lipped smile and vanished.

"You first," Britt said, gesturing to the rusted screen door. Skylar opened it again with an ear splitting squeak. Britt immediately fished into her tote bag and pulled out a travel size WD-40. She gave the hinges a few squirts and in two rotations of the door, the squeak stopped. Skylar peered into Britt's bag to see what other goodies she had in there.

Britt closed it from Skylar's prying eyes. "I'm always prepared," Britt said.

"Yes, you may have said that before," Skylar said, walking into the primitive cabin. Two twin beds covered in 1965 bedspreads took up most of the room. One small burgundy swivel chair sat in the corner near the sliding bathroom door.

"I guess we should be thankful we have our own loo," Britt said, already spreading out her toiletries on the only piece of wood furniture in the room, a six-drawer dresser with mirror attached. "Don't they know it's bad Feng Shui to have the mirror face the bed?" She peered around the back to see if she could un-attach it. "I'll have to get that off."

"And put it where?" Skylar scowled. "There's no extra floor space." She sat on the bed closest to the door. Dry heat was pumping out of an ancient radiator on the wall, thick with old layers of paint. "It is so stuffy in here." She bounced up to stand on the bed and opened the window above their heads. Crisp air blew through the dusty screen. "Ugh, that's going to be a mess."

"It's frozen dust," Britt said.

Skylar shut the window in frustration. She twirled around and landed in a thud on her bed.

"Why are you in such a bad mood?" Britt asked, hanging her clothes on satin hangers she brought with her.

Skylar wasn't sure. Was it trying to reason the fact that they were in a land from the past? Seeing Rachel? Knowing she was going to see Cassie? Having to be around Argan everyday? All of the above? It was all so enormous and she felt alone. But she wasn't. She wished Suki were here. "It's just a lot," she said flatly.

Britt stopped puttering and sat on Skylar's bed. The slippery polyester bedspread slid under her when she moved and the girls giggled. "It is a lot," she said. "Look, I don't know you all that well but you have extraordinary things to accomplish. The rest of us are here to support you. Lean on us."

Skylar felt Britt's sincerity. "Thank you," she said with a slight smile. She felt tired and wondered if her sleep patterns would be different here, or back to normal. She welcomed the ten o'clock curfew and barely brushed her teeth before climbing in.

She didn't have any idea of the time when she woke to a steady noise in the room. Crunch, crunch crunch . . . crunch, crunch, crunch . . . crunch, crunch, crunch, crunch. They both stirred from the sound of munching. Britt whispered in the darkness. "What is that noise?"

"It sounds like a we have a visitor," Skylar said. She flipped on the lamp to see a long gray tail sticking out of Britt's tote bag on the dresser.

"Oh my God!" Britt shrieked and stood on her bed.

Skylar jumped out of bed and grabbed the bag. In a few seconds she had the door open and flung the bag out into the chilly night. It landed in a patch of snow.

"It can't stay out there!" Britt barked.

"It'll only take a second for the mouse to run out. You can get your bag," Skylar said. She looked at the clock. It was 5:30 a.m. and a familiar rush of energy shot through her nervous system. "As long as I'm up, I think I'll go for a run," she said. This seemed to have become a new thing with her.

"It's still dark out!" Britt said.

"Right, well, it'll be an adventure."

"In the snow?" Britt asked doubtfully. "You weren't prepared for the weather and you have no idea where the hell you are."

"I'll manage," Skylar said, feeling the urge to get outside. "The fresh air is calling to me and it'll wake me up before meditation."

She dressed in Britt's sweatshirt and running pants. Again, her Keds would have to do.

She started across the compound in the dark. Britt was right, she didn't know where she was going. *Possibly a run down the road to her car*, she thought. She could get a bag and hump it back.

She got a mile into her trek and a faint light started over the horizon. Two figures appeared in the distance, walking toward her.

"Where are you going so early?" the redhead asked Skylar once they got close enough.

"Hello," Skylar said. "I needed a workout. I'm headed to my stranded car."

"You can't get there from here," the blonde said. "It's beyond the arches. You'll have to wait."

Skylar slowed her pace and stopped in front of them. *Ronnie and Milicent*, she thought.

"No one said my car was beyond reach," Skylar said.

"They're not going to, but I'd like to see you try," Milicent said.

"How do you know where my car is?" Skylar asked suspiciously.

"You're new and old," Milicent said. "Both of those get noticed quickly around here."

"Can we help you?" Ronnie asked. Even as a teen she was kind.

"Oh, no thank you," Skylar said. "It was just an idea. I can wait for Ocean's help."

Milicent snickered and Skylar studied her. She tried to tune into the subtleties of her aura. It always gave her answers. But it wasn't working. She couldn't tell if Milicent was that good or things were different here and all her new abilities didn't work.

"You two always out this early?" Skylar asked authoritatively. She was starting to enjoy the role reversal.

"Yes," Ronnie answered. "We like to go to Laughless Rock before meditation." Milicent gave her a shove. "Hey," Ronnie snapped.

Laughless Rock, Skylar thought . . . *from her dream.*

The sound of footsteps made her turn around. Argan jogged toward them in a sleeveless sweatshirt and shorts. Puffs of cold air burst from his mouth and he slowed when he saw the trio.

"Silverwood is a matriarchal society," Milicent said pre-emptively. "We live outside of the patriarchy of America. That doesn't mean we don't have men here. We do for sure. They just know their place." She glared at Argan.

"Nice to meet you too," Argan said with a wink. "I'll keep that in mind."

"I didn't catch your name," Milicent said.

"Argan," he said, trying to get his breathing under control. He flashed her a quiet smile and she refused to let him dazzle her.

"We should get ready for meditation," Milicent said, pulling Ronnie along.

"It was nice to meet you both," Ronnie said, her eyes lingering on Argan as the two of them walked away.

He paced to slow his heart rate. "Milicent knows," he said. "Her powers run deep."

"Yeah," Skylar agreed. "But Ronnie doesn't."

"No," he said. "None of them are supposed to know but Milicent is involved with some black magic. I can smell it."

"Me too," Skylar said. "It smells like petrichor. I thought it was just me."

He gave her a quizzical look. "Petrichor?"

"The smell of rain," Skylar said.

"I know what it is. Just surprised you do," he said.

"Thanks."

She looked at him standing there dressed for summer in the snow, his fists resting on his hips and she started to laugh.

"What?" he asked, his face wrinkled.

"Aren't you cold?" she asked.

"Nope," he said. "I can sweat in a snowstorm." He smiled widely, uncharacteristically jovial. She liked this Argan. He seemed freer, more vibrant than who he was back home.

"I'd like to go see this Laughless Rock," she said. "It can't be this easy that everything falls into place."

"Maybe it can," he said. "Let's go," he grabbed her hand. "We'll follow the packed snow."

He led her up a steep pathway in the trees. They hiked only a few minutes before coming to a small clearing. A boulder the size of a Volkswagen sat in the middle of a circle of smaller stones.

"Not hard to find at all," Skylar said.

"That's not it," Argan said. "Let's keep going." Skylar glanced back at the large rock as they continued their climb. They hiked through ever increasing snow another ten minutes. The packed down path had turned to slippery ice. Right among the snowy maples and birch trees sat a small rock no bigger than a bean-bag chair. The hard ground around it was exposed from frequent visitors.

"Here we go," Argan said.

"How are you so sure? The other one looked more like my dream." No sooner had the words come out of her mouth than a vision came to her mind and she felt her heart constrict. This was Laughless Rock, the place where Demeter grieved the loss of her daughter, Persephone. Many travelers came to cry here, seeking respite from their grief. Skylar was overwhelmed by the feelings held within the rock and knelt in the frozen mud.

Argan knelt beside her as if he was expecting her reaction. "You feel it, don't you?" He took her hand in his and sat silently next to her. "The weight of the world . . . absorbed by this rock, you feel it."

"Yes," she said. It was 6:00 a.m. and Skylar didn't want to be vulnerable at 6:00 a.m. She stood up and brushed herself off. "Why is it here?" she asked. "Shouldn't it be in Greece or something?"

"It's a symbol of the myth," he said. "It can *be* anywhere." He stared at the horizon as the sun rose higher. "Are you going to be all right?"

"I'm always all right," she said.

"I'm sure that's true but you don't need to keep a brave face all the time. Part of the reason we fell apart was because you refused to let me into your heart. I know it's a pretty full place, carrying the weight of the world and all, but I had hoped there was room for me."

"Me?" she asked. "You were the distant one at Ocean's place."

He opened his mouth to say something but stopped. "We have to get back," he said. "We don't want to miss our first group meditation." He started down the mountain backward. "By the way, how long are we staying here?"

"Good question," she said. "How long can it take to replace the memory of the world?" She cracked a smile.

"See you there." He jogged off down the path and Skylar stood watching him. She took a deep breath. The cold air was refreshing after so many months of heat. She exhaled through her mouth and turned her face toward the sun just rising over the mountain that framed one side of the lake. She hadn't seen the mountain when they arrived. Its snow covered top glistened in the sun. Halfway down it turned a dark pine green. The clouds in the new day's sky were choppy and animated among the pinks and oranges of sunrise. The billowy swirls made her think of Beatrice and she wondered how many of her sylphs were watching.

Beyond the rock, beams of sun called to her through the trees. As she followed the light, the only sound was her crunching footsteps in the snow. The hum that had plagued her since she arrived was thankfully silent. The sun led her to the edge of a cliff, below sat the majestic lake. She gasped. It was the lake in her photo. She thought of those two girls, with the light of the world in their eyes, looking forward to making their dreams come true. She stared at the water. It was the same, but for one stark difference. It lacked the dazzling diamonds from the sun's rays. Instead thick, white steam hovered above it.

"It never freezes," Rachel had said the night before at the Mess. "It's too warm. There's a city of hot springs running underneath heating the water up to 110 degrees. It's like a giant hot tub this time of year."

Interesting, Skylar thought as she stared at the lake. She wasn't aware of any hot springs in the Northeast. And it was so different than the lake in their photo. *How much of this was the Great Mother of Air's doing?*

As if Beatrice answered her, a strong breeze kicked up over the water, temporarily carrying the steamy clouds away. The choppy water reflected the sun and the familiar diamonds appeared. As quickly as it came, the breeze stopped, and the steam returned. In it transparent figures danced on the water. Wild women with flowing hair and flowing dresses twirled in circles. They were mesmerizing. No two were alike, all free to dance as they chose.

Nature is a portal to magic, Magda said.

"I was wondering when you'd show up," Skylar said turning toward her. She always looked the same, timeless, changeless.

I'm never away from you, Skylar, Magda said. *You should know that by now.*

"Yes," was all she could muster.

I'm so pleased you've made it this far. Many way-showers give up.

"I never thought giving up was a choice," Skylar said.

It's always a choice. You obviously chose to keep going.

"So this is Vivienne's lake," Skylar said. Ocean had told her that Vivienne placed the lake over a portal. It was one of the places on earth connecting all worlds, the physical, the Underworld, and the fifth dimension.

Yes, Magda said.

"It's nice to see Beatrice's sylphs celebrating above it. It's as if the two Great Mothers are getting along."

All of the Mothers are represented here. You will see their creations everywhere you look. This camp *as you call it serves a grand purpose. Tucked away under the protection of nature, it serves as a sacred place to birth a new consciousness on the planet. Many see this as a last resort for wayward children. But these children possess the gifts of the sixth root race. They have a higher consciousness than most currently on your planet. In their teen years they struggle with fitting in, as you say. The fortunate ones end up here. The Great Mothers know exactly why they are incarnated at this time and help them navigate your unforgiving world.*

"I understand," Skylar said. "Ever since I've carried this heart, the pain of life is almost unbearable. Even my happiest moments hold a touch of sadness. It's wearing me out."

I have a simple solution for you, dear one, but I am not so sure you will accept it.

"It'll give me relief from this perpetual depression?" Skylar asked.

It will.

"I'm all ears."

Forgiveness, Magda said.

Skylar groaned. She had heard this before. "Thank you, Magda. I will take that under consideration."

Don't be so quick to dismiss me, Magda said. *Forgiveness holds the key to every door you wish to open. Especially that one you have locked around your heart. You are holding on to your judgments about past actions as a badge you feel condemned to wear. You hold guilt for your anger toward those that hurt you. You hold guilt for those you, in turn, hurt. Forgiveness of self releases you from the hell you accept as your home. If you do that, the heart you carry will lighten. It is that simple.*

"Right, simple."

Magda faded into the breeze leaving Skylar to stare at the water. The sylphs had moved on as well, returning the clouds to ordinary steam.

22

After morning meditation, Skylar, Britt, and Argan stayed behind in the palladium to map out their story with Ocean. The palladium was an octagonal shaped one-room building, decorated like a posh tree house, with piles of plush pillows in every corner and lavishly embroidered mandala quilts hanging from the rafters. Each of the walls had a large window inviting the outside in.

"You will all need to teach a class," Ocean said. "Or else, why would you be here? Any requests or specialties I am unaware of?" She looked at Argan.

"I'm schooled in the Goddess," he said.

"I already have Origen teaching the Goddess," Ocean said. "What else?"

"Greek mythology?" he asked.

"No."

"Quantum physics?"

One eyebrow lifted on her face. "Really?"

He slumped. "No."

"How are you with a shovel?" she asked. "I need a gardener. The greenhouse is overrun."

"Done, I like dirt," he said.

"Next, Britt, you are perfect to assist Origen in Eastern Cultures," Ocean said. "Hindu mythology, tantra, and the like." Britt nodded.

"Skylar, you will be teaching on the numinousity of blood," Ocean said. "I figure with all that's going on inside you these days, you can speak well on the subject."

"That seems like a pretty narrow scope," Skylar said.

"Hardly. Get out your biology books too because you will be recreating your DNA transformation for your class. I hope you remembered the specifics because there's no calling Joel from here."

"Now classes have been going on for a couple of weeks so you'll have to jump in and get caught up. It shouldn't take up more than thirty percent of your time because you have a bigger agenda here. We gather nightly for group before dinner. But as you know, tonight is special. We are celebrating Imbolc. The group tends to get a bit wild on these nights so hopefully I will have an opportunity to introduce you." In two steps she was gone, and the threesome discussed their new appointments.

"I don't know enough about what's going on within me to teach it to someone else," Skylar said.

"That's the whole idea," Argan said. "Only in teaching to others can we fully grasp what is within."

"Please stop talking in fortune cookies," Skylar said.

The day's classes were canceled to prepare for the feast, and Skylar and Britt pitched in setting up chairs and food tables. Every student was required to take part in preparation for the evening's events. A dozen kids were dedicated altar decorators, assigned to trim the commons with a display worthy of the Goddess Brighid. Rich green linen draped the long altar, tied underneath with white satin ribbon. The same students decorated the wooden arbor with pine and berry roping until every inch of wood had been covered. A few of the students wore silence badges on their clothes, taking the day off from communication with others.

They had been assigned the task of stick gathering in the woods to fulfill their participation requirement.

Skylar watched a female student drag one of the bags of feathers from the hospitality building to the decorated arbor. It had gotten so big it resembled a giant sac of bakery flour. The girl made it to the arbor and spread the feathers out neatly in a spiral. She stood back, admiring her design when the wind kicked up and tossed them around. She threw her hands in the air and started again. Skylar chuckled, wondering how many times she would do this.

Argan had followed orders and jumped in to greenhouse duties. There didn't appear to be a learning curve. He spent most of the day cutting hundreds of red and white flowers of every kind for the decorations. He quickly developed a fan base of female students, many using the most transparent of reasons to return to the greenhouse and collect more blooms. When they were finished, the commons had been transformed from barren winter into a lush garden fit for a goddess. The freezing air had turned temperate, almost pleasant and coats were suddenly not needed. Skylar wondered which Great Mother had played with the thermostat.

Everyone gathered in the commons as the sun set at 5:00 p.m. Ronnie and Milicent were together. Rachel sat alone. Skylar felt her heart constrict looking for Cassie. Part of her wanted to see her mother; part of her didn't. She counted fifty students she learned they called *cedars*, and Ocean said everyone was accounted for, but no Cassie. Skylar found Britt and Argan and took a seat with them. She looked at the spiral of feathers under the arbor, still packed neatly on the ground. Someone's magic must have been in play. Ocean stood in the middle of the great circle and began to speak.

"Thank you all for gathering this evening. For those that participated in silence, I hope you have enjoyed your day of introspection. For some, it may have been a day of struggle. It's all worth the effort, I can assure you. Silence represents the quiet of winter. We go within to replenish and restore. We nurture the seed within us that takes root and will sprout in spring. Tonight we are halfway and shift our sights to rebirth. We are in celebration! The Goddess Brighid has graced us with her fertile abundance and we anticipate a fruitful spring." She motioned to the colorful food tables adorned with various dishes of fruits and vegetables.

"Before we commence with tonight's activities, I want to introduce you to three new counselors that have come to Silverwood." She turned to the threesome and they stood up. "Skylar Southmartin will be teaching all things blood. Britt Anjawal will be assisting Origen in Eastern Culture." Britt looked at Origen and he bowed her way. "And Argan Papadopoulos will be getting his hands dirty in the greenhouse." The threesome waved around the circle to many whispers and stares.

Ocean continued her speech. "As many of you know, the location of our precious community was based on the manifestation of material elements. Wind . . ." the wind kicked up on command. "Water . . ." she motioned to the lake. "Earth . . ." she motioned to the ground. "And fire!" she said with a gleam in her eye and ignited the campfire in an instant blaze. "It is through these elements we connect to our vitality, the passions within us to create. Ideas come from the elements and our goal here at Silverwood is to help you open to these ideas, open to this magic, this power."

Ocean rotated in a circle. "For a moment let's close our eyes and focus on our breath."

Skylar hesitated before closing her eyes. She watched many

of the cedars sit up taller, straightening their spines. Some crossed their legs in easy pose. She continued to watch as an interesting energy was forming within her she couldn't name. She was too alert to close her eyes.

"Let us picture the winds of change that are upon us. Think for a moment, how do you want your future to look? Your intention and attention shape your life. The more you focus on what you desire, the more the universe yields to help you."

As Ocean spoke, Skylar could see beings forming in the air. They were slight and transparent at first, rapidly growing more dense. "Sylphs," Skylar whispered.

The milky white beings danced around the circle for a brief moment before each one leaned in to whisper into the ear of every cedar. She tugged on Argan's shirt and he opened his eyes. "Can you see them?" she whispered. "Tell me you see them."

"See who, Sky?" he whispered back. Ocean's eyes shot like a laser beam at Skylar. She knew she should keep quiet.

"Never mind," Skylar said. She looked back at Ocean. *If you think I am closing my eyes you are sadly mistaken*, she said in her mind. Ocean shrugged and moved on. Skylar continued to watch the floating spirits. Some spoke silent words, other actually transformed into steam and entered the cedar's ear. Some of the kids perked up as if struck with an idea. Some seemed excited, hopping in their seat a bit. Others seemed frightened and a few popped their eyes open. No one appeared to see the sylphs but Skylar.

Ocean began to speak again. "Beneath the current social conventions runs a deeper, truer river of ore within, where divinity is alive and pulsing. Our roots are in this unconscious. They are kept alive through our myths and oral traditions. They are kept alive through our rituals. Our inner world, meaning our Underworld has been repressed for so long it has become dangerous.

We are in imminent danger of losing the soul of the earth." She looked directly at Skylar.

"I call each and every one of you to wake up the KNOWING in your heart!" She pounded her fist into her opposite hand. "This knowing is what you feel in this very moment. You are called to write a new story, to listen to the voice within, and then take action. Be the change that will save our planet. I thank you, my future healers, leaders, nurturers, mothers, and fathers of a new age, a luminescent tomorrow. Thank you for heeding the call."

The now highly alert group applauded.

"And now let the fire feast of Brighid begin!" With a flip of her hand, the small campfire exploded exponentially. The flames leapt up twenty feet in the air. Once they died down to a respectable level, many cedars moved forward to bring their offerings of Brighid's symbols; her cross, potted daffodils and crocuses, red and white ribbons, and many, many candles. Each took a turn lighting candles from the great blaze.

Once every candle was lit, they returned to their seats and the crowd got quiet. Everyone focused their attention on the arbor. Soon the feathers began to rustle and the energy of the group rose with excitement but still no one made a sound. They all watched intently as an image appeared over the feathers. It was faint but distinct. The Goddess Brighid was making an appearance to thank the cedars for the short respite on her journey around the world. Her flaming red curls glistened in the firelight and the energy at her feet gave the feathers an aura of bright white luminescence. She raised her hand in greeting and faded back into the ethers. The cedars erupted in triumph, succeeding in bringing Brighid forth. They pushed their chairs out of the way and began dancing around the fire to music blaring from an old-fashioned beat box.

"That was amazing," Britt said. "Good thing we brought those feathers."

"Yeah," was all Skylar could muster. She looked up in the sky. The sylphs were circling high above them now. An ibis cruised within the circle. *Nana,* she thought. Skylar smiled. "Good thing." She looked back at Britt. "This is a much more positive Ocean than the one I've got in 2021."

"Is that so?" Britt asked. "It's hard to be angry here. We've just arrived and I feel lighter, happier among the trees. And the air is an aphrodisiac."

Skylar glanced at Argan and quickly looked away.

"Yeah, I feel it," Argan said. "The build up of rust from our lives back home seems to be melting away." He smiled at Skylar. She had to admit the fairy dust of Silverwood was starting to have an effect on her as well.

"That's because we are protected from all negative astral energies here," Ocean said, walking up behind them. "There is no fear here. You can't help but feel better about . . . everything."

"Your speech was very motivational," Skylar said. Her eyes told another story.

"I could use a meal," Argan said, with his hand on his stomach. Skylar looked at him quizzically. He had been obsessed with food since they had arrived.

"I wish the food was better here," Skylar said. "It's the only fault I can find with this place."

"Vegan really is the path to clean living," Britt said.

Argan and Britt walked in the direction of the food tables and Skylar pounced on Ocean. "Is that your plan?" Skylar said. "Or Nana's plan? To imprint the adults of tomorrow with ideas that come directly from you?"

"Where do you think inspiration comes from?" Ocean asked. "Not the brain. Not even the individual mind. Inspiration comes from *divine source*. The sylphs are messengers. One of Beatrice's few contributions. Don't get too peeved about the way things work, just because you're on the inside now. You should be grateful. Soon enough you'll be commanding the elements like the rest of us and share in the blame when things don't go the way they *should*.

You have six weeks until the Equinox. That gives you ample time."

"To learn how to harness the energy of the elements, are you crazy?" Skylar shrieked. "That's hardly ample time. I've had Sophia's book for over a year and I've barely scratched the surface."

"Then this would be the accelerated path," Ocean said, straight-faced. "Why do you think you came here? In six weeks, you can learn what would have taken lifetimes in linear time."

"I came here to restore a memory to Sophia's library," Skylar said.

"Who told you that?" Ocean asked, looking unnerved.

"Beatrice said—"

"Oh for Goddess' sake, Beatrice." Ocean shook her fists in the air. "She was supposed to get you here, not feed you with unattainable goals." She cursed under her breath.

"Your present day self knew this was the job," Skylar said. "Be mad at her."

Ocean shook her head. "Got a plan in place, do ya?"

"I'm using the headlights method, only seeing a few feet in front of me at a time," Skylar said.

"Sure you are," Ocean said. "Let's put that aside and focus on the elements. That's a realistic goal while you're here. Stick out your tongue."

"I'm still taking the gold if that's what you're asking," Skylar said, refusing to comply. "I brought all you gave me."

"Good." Ocean walked off leaving Skylar reeling. She had accepted the plan. She had accepted the task to restore the memory. She drove into the past, for goodness sake! Skylar was tired of Ocean calling the shots.

She caught Milicent's stare from across the common. "*Tell my sister I want to talk to her*," she remembered her saying. Milicent was her answer. Milicent could help Skylar get where she needed to go.

23

Present day: Back at home, Suki was poring over her computer at Skylar's house. She preferred the bright, welcoming décor of the tiny house to that of the depressing reminders of loss at her own. She had spent an inordinate amount of time cleaning out her grandmother's house before listing it for sale. She didn't want to sell, but it would relieve an enormous financial burden she didn't need this early in her life. Her time playing house with Kyle would be paused for a few days as she was headed to DC in the morning.

Michael jumped up on Kyle and immediately began kneading his stomach. "I love cats," Kyle said. "I know that's not macho but they're cool. If a cat pays attention to you, you've made it." Michael curled up and fell asleep in seconds.

"Uhh huh," Suki replied mindlessly, consumed with her research.

Kyle stared at her. "Hey, Suuk, are you in there?"

"Uhh huh," Suki said.

"Suki, will you marry me?" Kyle asked.

"Uhh huh," Suki said.

"Suki!" Kyle yelled in cupped hands. Michael leapt off of his stomach and Suki startled to attention.

"Sorry," she said. "There's just so much to absorb." She sat back in her chair. "I would die if Skylar knew I've been practicing the breath meditations she showed me last year. And this will sound insane but . . . I got in."

"In what?"

"*In!*" She bounced up and hurried over to Kyle. She put her hand on his heart. "Here. I can't really describe it—it's beyond words. It's more than a feeling. It's a knowing that I'm a part of a higher being. No doubt. Complete certainty, I am divine."

"Cool," Kyle said.

"Once Skylar finds out, I'll never hear the end of it. But I'm on to other things. There's a mountain of information describing the toroid field that blankets our earth as well as the electron diffusion regions between Earth and the sun. When the earth's magnetic field fuses with the solar wind, portals can open to other worlds! This information has been on dozens of websites, including NASA. But that's not all."

"I didn't think so," Kyle said.

She grabbed her laptop and sat on Kyle's lap where Michael just had been.

"I've overlapped this portal information with my new experiences in meditation and woo woo consciousness that Skylar touts." Her voice rose with enthusiasm. "I mean, I've experienced it myself now. I can no longer deny it's true."

"I'm glad to see you're coming around, Suuk. I've only been talking about these government cover ups for a year now," he said.

"No, Kyle. I'm not talking about that conspiracy theory crap. I'm talking about getting to the truth."

"I know!" he started to match her enthusiasm. "I've been watching all of these documentaries online about the truth that's been kept from us."

Suki got out of his lap annoyed at his point of focus. "Ok Kyle, suppose these things you're watching are true. Why the hell are they allowed to air? If all this was really happening, wouldn't they prevent those shows?" She sat on the coffee table.

"Ahh, the beauty of the internet," he said. "We've returned to the days of freedom of speech. It's been missing for almost a hundred years."

She dismissed him. "None of that matters," she said, returning to her research. "Once I connected the dots between the portals surrounding earth and the portals in the mind, I came up with the answer."

"The answer to what?"

"To everything Skylar's been talking about! The next step in evolution. All her cycles of time talk and divine feminine energies and great mothers, yada yada. It all fits like pieces to the perfect puzzle. Like an actual divine plan written by God. We have to evolve as a species. Or die."

"Suki, in all this time, I don't think I've ever heard the word God come out of your mouth."

"Well times are changing, baby!" She leapt up. "There's a ton of work to do. We are behind as a planet but I'm going to figure out how to catch up."

"Okay, when you've got it figured out, let me know. Most of this makes no sense to me."

"Unfortunately I have to put it on hold until I return from DC." She closed her laptop on the desk and sat in the chair. "I bought a new outfit."

"I'm concerned about this roadie to DC, Suuk. What if you never return? The government is a web of lies. This could be a set up. Why the hell does Milicent want you there? It makes no sense."

"Would you stop?!" she said. "You're making it worse. Enough people know where I'm going. If I turn up missing, you'll know who to call."

"Yeah, but it's the government. It won't matter if you turn up missing," he said, caught up in the drama in his own head.

"There's no talking to you," she said, giving up. She walked into the kitchen.

"Check in frequently please," he called after her.

The next day Suki sat in the security waiting room of the White House, visibly nervous. She had to bring three different forms of identification with her after an initial clearance interview that took place off site. As she waited, she thought about the first day she met Milicent at Rosen. She had been instantly smitten. Milicent was strong and assured in her goals, misguided as they were. Suki had always struggled with finding the right balance of assertiveness. She usually came across as cold or bitchy, especially to other women. Milicent was so unapologetic for what she wanted in life.

"Ms. De la Cruz?" a young staffer approached Suki.

"Yes," Suki stood up and smoothed her pencil skirt.

"Follow me, please," the staffer said. She led Suki down a handful of angular hallways. She tried to take it all in but it was complete sensory overload and she resorted to following the staffer like a sheep. They walked through a door that looked like a dozen others. "Wait here, please." Suki was left alone again to sit. This time she waited over an hour. "They *are* keeping me here," Suki said under her breath. Her phone continued to ping from Kyle.

"So sorry to keep you waiting," another staffer said, walking in to greet Suki. "Wren Riddle, I'm Mrs. Grayer's Chief of Staff." Again Suki stood up and smoothed her skirt. "Follow me."

This time it was a short walk to another row of doors and Wren led her into a large room resembling a seamstress's shop. Dozens of large reams of ornate fabrics were draped haphazardly over every piece of furniture. Some smaller fabric squares were tacked to the walls. All of them shared the same purple palette. A young man was kneeling on the floor in the corner, bent over thick three-ring binders.

"Hello Suki," Milicent said from behind her. Suki whirred around.

"Hello Mrs. Grayer," Suki said nervously. Milicent glided across the room to shake her hand as Wren closed the door behind her.

"I'd say *have a seat* but as you can see, my office is in flux." Suki remained standing as Milicent walked to her desk and sat in the only available chair. "Our meeting probably won't take as long as your wait time. I'm sorry to have kept you. Apparently that's how things are done around here."

"That's all right, ma'am," Suki said. "I'm excited to be here." She glanced at the young man and Milicent's eyes followed.

"Noah, can you give me the room, please?" Milicent asked. Noah stood up with a surprised look on his face but didn't say a word. He looked at Suki. They studied each other simultaneously in the way one does trying to place a face. He gave Suki one last once over and continued out the door.

"Suki, I need your help," Milicent said, clearing her throat. "I need you to do some data pulling of a highly confidential nature at the Equine Facility. That's why I called you here to DC. We can't have this conversation over any recordable device." She picked up an accordion folder sitting on her desk. "Are you familiar with the basement archives at the Quine?"

Suki's eyes widened. "No, ma'am. I wasn't aware of any archives."

"Good answer, it's not on the directory." Milicent opened her top drawer and pulled out a wooden box. She slid the cover off and lifted out a simple brass hex key. "You would need this to access the floor from the elevator. It also unlocks the main door. Call me old fashioned. I hate key pads." She twisted the piece of metal around in her fingers. "This key has opened the door to my most prized treasures for three decades. The doors may come and go, but the key remains." She replaced it in its case and handed it to Suki.

"Thank you, ma'am," Suki said, feeling the weight of the box in her hand. "I'm . . . speechless."

"Right, I'm sure you're asking yourself why I am entrusting someone as *inexperienced* as yourself with what I am about to share with you." Milicent was the queen of the backhanded insult. "Ocean insists you are the woman for the job and I have no choice but to take her word for it. Just know if anything goes awry, I will hold you personally responsible. And there's no saying no either. Apparently we all have our roles to play in this divine comedy." She pushed the accordion folder across the desk at Suki. "Do not open this until you get into the archives at the Equine Facility. Do you understand?"

"Yes, ma'am," Suki said, feeling a trickle of sweat drip down her breastbone.

"Yes, what? What are you not doing?" Milicent asked.

"I am not opening this folder until I am standing in the archives at the Quine, uh, Equine Facility, ma'am."

"Good, I will know if you do," Milicent said. "Also, I am sure I don't have to tell you the strictest of confidence needs to be adhered. If I get wind that you've told that boyfriend of yours, I will ask Devlin to bring back the death penalty in Massachusetts." Suki swallowed hard but nodded profusely. "Once done, contact Wren and she will get you back in here. Good day Ms. De la Cruz."

"Good day, ma'am," Suki said. Her hands shook as she picked up the file folder and let herself out. Just beyond the doorway, Noah was standing at attention with a clipboard in his hand.

"How do I know you?" he asked defensively.

"Lambda party two years ago," she said, looking at him square in the eye. Sometimes her photographic memory was a curse.

"Oh, yeah," a rare moment of shame overtook his face. "I've grown up a lot since then."

"I can see that," she smiled and walked away. She had enough on her mind and didn't feel the need to resurrect her one and only experience at an alternative frat party.

Once outside in the sunshine, Suki sat on a bench to catch her breath. She checked her phone and had over a dozen text messages from Kyle. He was going to want details, details she couldn't give him.

24

The first week at Silverwood went by quickly and Skylar had settled into a routine. She already felt healthier, eating clean, despite it being forced upon her. She was sleeping seven hours a night and waking up naturally at 5:00 a.m. She enjoyed the magic of the sunrise, as it intensified her morning meditation.

She liked to meditate at Laughless Rock. It held its own magic that made it easy for her to connect into her body. She felt vibrant, alive. At the rock, the hum in her ears shifted into her entire body. It gave her enormous energy and she looked forward to the "kick" every morning.

She sat down on the ground in easy position and closed her eyes. The air was quiet but for one cardinal singing in a tree. A few minutes into her meditation, she heard a loud rustle. Much bigger than a squirrel, she opened one eye to make sure it wasn't a bear. As the rustle got closer, Skylar heard more humming. It was the same song she'd heard when she'd hugged Beatrice's tree. She sprang to her feet just as the girl came out of the trees.

"Gosh, I'm sorry," the teen said. "I figured I'd be alone up here at this hour." Skylar hadn't been prepared to meet Cassie this morning, but apparently the Rock was the most popular "secret" place on campus.

"It's all right," Skylar said, her heart pounding. "I . . . a . . . recently discovered this place and I wanted to come back. It feels magical, like I'll get the answers I'm looking for." Skylar couldn't tell if the feeling in her stomach was butterflies or a need to throw up.

"You will," Cassie said, standing in front of Skylar unassumingly. "I know why you're here."

"Meditation," Skylar said, swallowing hard halfway through the word.

"No, I know why you're *here*," Cassie said. She stared at Skylar's face inquisitively. "I was away for a week and just got back late last night. I've already heard all about you. If it's a secret, you can be sure everyone knows." She laughed. "Let me see your palms." She grabbed Skylar's hands and turned them up. A strong wave of energy ran through Skylar's arms from the touch of her mother. Cassie dropped them. "What the hell was that?"

"You felt it too? I don't know," Skylar said, still frozen where she stood. Skylar *did* know.

Cassie stared at her with a concerned look. She wiped her hands on her pants and grabbed Skylar's hand as if on a dare. The jolt happened again. Before Cassie let go, Skylar got a glimpse of her ouroboros ring on her right hand.

"I take it that's not a common thing around here?" Skylar asked. It hadn't happened with Rachel.

"No," Cassie said. "Can I see your palms again?" Skylar showed her. Cassie didn't touch them this time. She stared at Skylar's palms. "The rumors are true; you are the one," she said in awe. Her smile showed hope. "You're to replace the memory. The world is desperate for you to do that."

Skylar thought how interesting it was that Cassie's words concurred with her original reason for coming here. *Why was Ocean denying this?* she thought. "I could use a map," she said.

"You don't know the way? It's through the lake," Cassie pointed to the cliff side. "The lake is covering the portal you're looking for. I know that much. Once you get in, the rest will be up to you." Cassie turned to leave but Skylar didn't want her to go yet.

"But how do I get in?" she asked to keep her talking. She stared at this young, beautiful Cassie and memories of her vibrant mother came rushing back. Skylar's eyes filled with tears. Most days she refused to let herself miss her. Today, there was no escape.

"Ask Origen. He's insane but you need his level of crazy to figure out this stuff."

"I had thought Ocean would have helped me," Skylar said.

"She's gone again."

Skylar's eyes widened. "Gone, where? Why?"

"She muttered something about a girls reunion in Italy."

Vivienne, Skylar thought. She had no way to call Beatrice. Maybe she was headed to Italy too. Ocean didn't even say goodbye.

"She should return before the Equinox." Cassie said. "She never misses an Equinox. What did you say your name was?"

"Skylar."

"Pretty. I always wanted to go to the Isle of Skye. It's in Scotland. They say the veil of worlds is the thinnest there. But they say that about here too." She shrugged. "I'm Cassie." She extended her hand in greeting then quickly pulled it away, chuckling. Beatrice was right, their connection transcended genealogy.

"You said you were away?" Skylar asked.

"I was on retreat. Came back last night," Cassie said.

"I thought this whole place was a retreat," Skylar said.

"Yeah, but there's always further to go," Cassie's eyes sparkled with a secret. "I'm sure I'll see you around campus, Skylar. Good luck with that quest. It's a doozy." She retreated into the same woods she came from and Skylar stumbled backward onto the Rock. Tears pooled in her eyes until they spilled out. Her body refused to keep in the pain she had been carrying for a year since

Cassie died. All of the grief she refused to feel in the naive hope of her mother's return came to the surface and overflowed. There was nowhere to hide. Skylar had to face this.

Look at this as an opportunity, dear one, Magda's voice rang in Skylar's ears. *Use it to explore and heal the relationship with your mother as you meet each other as peers. You feel you were robbed of time with Cassandra. Here is your chance.*

She let the pain move through her. Instead of stuffing it down, she allowed herself to feel the pain shoot through her heart. She sat there as long as it took to wring out the tears. When they finally subsided, she felt better, lighter. She thought of Magda's words and committed to try.

25

Much to her own surprise, Skylar's class on blood was going well. She thought the best route to take was blunt honesty and personal anecdote. She usually started the day with a story about one of her many physical transformations and an hour's worth of questions would ensue. She wasn't quite sure how she'd test them but she'd punt that down the timeline.

She quickly learned that Origen was an elusive character. He was either teaching class or meditating. Their original meeting in the Mess had apparently been a fluke. He rarely ate food. She figured the best way to get to him was to sign up for one of his classes. Professors audited other classes all the time at Rosen. She'd give that a shot.

Her choices were *The Sexuality of the Goddess*, or *Anger: An Exorcism*. Skylar wanted to avoid exorcism at all costs so she opted for the Goddess class. Britt was his assistant and Skylar was curious to see how that was going.

The class was held at the palladium and Skylar walked in as it was starting.

"The Goddess represents the union of flesh and spirit," Origen said, standing in a circle of seated cedars on the brightly colored pillows on the floor. They were mostly female. Of the two dozen participants, three were male. Origen wore a white robe and head wrap, both dingy. His beard looked just as scraggly as the day they met. She shuddered slightly. Britt stood next to him, dressed head-to-toe in flowing kundalini whites. She was stunning in a white headband that contrasted her dark waves piled high on her head. She had brought an obscene amount of cash with her on this trip to the past and had been doing extensive damage at the campus store. She nodded to Skylar when she walked in.

Skylar tiptoed quietly to a small opening in the circle and sat without a pillow. She tucked into a tight ball, arms wrapped around knees to make herself as small as possible.

"The Goddess lives in all of us," Origen said, climbing out of the circle. He walked to the stack of floor pillows and grabbed a yellow bolster. "She isn't meant to be worshipped! She's meant to be embodied!" He stopped in front of Skylar and handed her the pillow. "So glad you could join us! Welcome Skylar!" he said sincerely. He returned to his spot in the circle. "The Goddess helps us return to our ancient, magical roots. She celebrates the sensuality of the body and the glory of sexuality."

A slight tingle started in the back of Skylar's head. For what it was worth, Origen was telling the truth. His aura was bright. She could see he was definitely committed to his spiritual path. But he did have some dark patches around his lower chakras. *No one is perfect*, she thought to herself.

"As our time together goes on, we will discuss the coiled one, the serpent, at length. The kundalini energy within the spine is said to be the manifestation of the sleeping Goddess or Shakti energy. She is the source of our vitality. If one nurtures her, she can grant you immortality."

Skylar's eyes narrowed. She raised her hand and spoke without waiting. "I'm sorry, Origen, immortality?"

"Oh, yes, dearest Skylar. If you were to learn the secrets to move the energy of your spinal column through your chakras and out your tenth gate, theoretically this energy could keep you on the planet indefinitely."

"Will we be learning that in this class?" another female cedar asked incredulously.

"We will be discussing it theoretically, not practically, I'm afraid," Origen said. "One needs to go through great preparation, years of intense schooling before initiation of that order can occur."

Britt picked up the lecture. "As Origen mentioned, this force is called Shakti in the eastern philosophies, the female force of life," she said. "She is the energy that animates the Shiva, or masculine principle."

"Very good, Britt," Origen said. "We will continue our discussion on the chakra system of the body and deepen our exercises to get those energy centers working for you. During the celebration of Equal Night, we will dive deep into the branch of illumination called tantra." He rolled his *t-r* in the middle of the word, in a contrived way.

He continued for another hour educating the group on various incarnations of goddess energy, from the Virgin Mary to Marilyn Monroe. Skylar assumed most of these kids had a vastly open mind about theological interpretation.

After class she approached him to ask about the lake. He smiled as she walked toward him. "I'm so pleased you are studying under me, dear one," he said. "You have much to learn but also much wisdom to share." He leaned in and inhaled deeply. "I sense you are schooled in the Akasha."

"In a way," Skylar said.

"Good. Then you are aware that the cosmic union of Shiva and Shakti is representative of the creative energy of the Akasha."

"Right," Skylar said, not aware at all.

He studied her again, looking intently into her eyes. An awkward silence charged the air. "Something's amiss with your auric body," he said. "It's as if you are here, but not here. You're placement in the continuum is . . . out of order. Are you from the past? Or future?" He was so casual, as if he were asking if she took cream or sugar.

Skylar shot a look at Britt. *Damn!* she thought to herself. *How is she supposed to answer that?* Ocean said no one would know and it seemed that everyone knew. Milicent knew. Cassie knew. How would she answer Origen? He could probably tell if she lied.

"Origen?" Another female cedar interrupted. "You were just wonderful!" she bubbled with schoolgirl flirtation. The crush on her instructor was obvious. Much to Skylar's amazement, he ate it up and shifted his attention to the girl, abandoning his curiosity for an ego stroke. Skylar took the opportunity to leave unnoticed and walked out the door with Britt.

"Did he give you the same sniff test?" Skylar asked.

"Nope," Britt said. "You must be extra potent."

"I'll have to come up with something before I see him again."

"Tell him the truth," Britt said. "He might enjoy the fact that he has a fan from the future."

The girls had to pass the greenhouse on the way back to their cabin and Skylar thought of Argan. She hadn't seen him all day. "I just want to stop in for a sec," she said as Britt followed. They walked through the double metal doors of the immense building into a hot and steamy room teeming with life. A rainbow of color went back as far as she could see. Exotic plants with enormous leaves and deep jewel-toned flowers crowded the aisle.

"God, it's hot in here," Britt said.

"You're from India," Skylar said.

"Yes, but we've been in the snow. It's just surprising."

More than the heat, it was the energy of the room that Skylar found surprising. She felt her heart race, which always made her lightheaded. All of the plants closest to her turned their attention her way, leaning in to investigate. Britt's mouth dropped in amazement.

"I've been getting this a lot," Skylar said, no longer fazed. They walked down the aisle and each of the plants took their turn with Skylar.

"They're not going to bite, are they?" Britt asked, keeping her arms in close to her body.

"I honestly don't know," Skylar said. They got past the exotics and entered a vast area with rows and rows of vegetable beds. "Huh? Hydroponics. Who knew they'd be so advanced here."

They didn't get far in when a cedar approached. "Can I help you?" he asked. He was pushing an overflowing wheelbarrow that spilled over with each of his steps. The smell from the odorous dirt got stronger as he drew nearer.

"Wow, what is that smell?" Britt asked, wrinkling her nose.

"Duck manure," the cedar said. "It feeds the hydro plants."

"Gotcha," Skylar said. "I'm looking for the new greenhouse supervisor, Argan," Skylar said. "Do you know him?"

"Oh yeah," he said, setting down the wheelbarrow. Duck manure fell at their feet and the girls both took a step backward. "He's all the way down near the Dragon's Blood." Neither girl responded. "It's a tree," he clarified. "That way." He pointed down the aisle and manure sailed off his hand right onto Britt's white clothes.

"Oh my god!" she shrieked. "Oh my god!"

"Oh, man, sorry." He started toward her as if to help but stopped himself. "It's organic," he said. "It'll come out."

"Mother Teresa didn't mind a little manure," Skylar said, watching Britt overreact.

"I've got to go," Britt said, holding her shirt away from her skin.

"It's not that bad," Skylar yelled as Britt retreated down the long aisle to the front door.

"I'll see you back at the cabin," Britt said over her shoulder, already halfway out.

She left quickly and Skylar turned to the cedar. "There are trees in here?" she asked, looking up at the soaring ceiling. He nodded and returned to his wheelbarrow.

She continued on and made her way through the maze of nature. Every color had a heightened luminosity. The reds were redder, the greens greener. She could feel the magnificent over-load of oxygen in her blood being in this greenhouse. She had never experienced anything like it. And then she saw why . . .

The elementals were busy creating life. These keepers of the second dimension worked in teams at the gardens, meticulously infusing the plants with their energy. What most pass off as fairy-tale, Skylar was seeing first hand. As she walked slowly by, each one stopped to look at her, effectively bending the plant it was working on. She gasped. The plants weren't turning in her direc-tion, the elementals were. They were tiny creatures some might think were fairies.

"Don't call us fairies!" a cacophony of voices rang in Skylar's head. She chuckled at her circumstances and leaned toward a cascading trellis of red bougainvillea to get closer.

"Deva is the proper term," one said. It was no bigger than a fingernail with green skin and a long tail that came to a point like an arrowhead. Skylar thought she saw wings but they were faint and seemed to blend with the red haze of the flower.

"Most certainly," Skylar said, staring at this fascinating creature.

"Different spelling!" it snapped. It quickly lost interest in Skylar and returned to its task.

She took a step back and let them all get on with their work. The gardens gave way to a host of different trees Skylar had never seen before. How insular she had been growing up among the oaks and maples of the northeast. These breathtaking beings were from far reaching corners of the planet. She stopped to read the signs: Fever Tree of Africa; Weeping Cherry from Japan; Poplar from Ireland. She looked up, hardly able to see the top of the Poplar.

She had reached the end of the greenhouse and still hadn't seen Argan. She didn't see another exit door either. "This place would be an extreme fire hazard if there isn't another exit," she said aloud. She turned back to start the trek to the front door and Argan appeared from behind an odd shaped tree. Its branches grew straight up in a scraggly, witch's broom fashion. A thick carpet of black leaves covered the top.

She looked at Argan curiously. "Were you hiding behind that tree?"

"Yes," he whispered.

"Why?"

"Look," he pointed to the treetop. What Skylar had mistaken for black leaves were hundreds of crows. "Oh my gosh, how did they all get in here? There are hundreds of them!"

"I know," he said. "It's ominous. I don't know what to do."

The birds had been silent but once Skylar focused her attention on them they woke up and started squawking.

"I can't leave the door open," he said. "It's freezing outside. Ocean's gone, so I can't ask her."

"There's another door?" Skylar asked. Argan pointed to a grass and ivy covered wall with a small handle. "Cool," she said, relieved. She stood under the tree of birds, closed her eyes, and listened. What first sounded like noise was actually a precise language, each bird sharing its part of the whole message. The familiar hum in her ears transformed into the music of the birds. As she stood, each took their turn swooping down to her. Argan started swatting them away.

"No," she said. "They're memory keepers. They're trying to help me." She stood there until every bird was done and the room fell silent. She opened her eyes and looked at each shoulder. "Ha, not a speck on me." She smiled. "Open the door."

Argan followed her direction and as soon as he opened the door, the birds filed out in an orderly line. When the last bird left, he shut the door.

"Wow, I'm impressed, you can understand the language of the birds. In alchemy, the key to perfect knowledge."

"I'm full of surprises," she winked.

"What did they say?" he asked.

"They concurred with Cassie that I'll find what I'm looking for under the lake. I must have heard the word *lake* a hundred times. They really want me to know that part."

Argan stiffened. "You met her?" he whispered.

"Early this morning," she said.

"Wow," he said. "What was that like?"

"Good, sad, unbelievable," she said. "Like my life flashed before me and I was powerless to change any of the bad parts." She finally exhaled. "I had a feeling if I lingered long enough, she'd figure it all out," Skylar said. "Her suspicions were raised when we shook hands. Origen knew something was off too. He smelled the future on me. We'll never make it to the Equinox. Everyone will know by then."

They went outside and made their way down the hill toward the lake. Skylar inhaled the crisp air deeply. She expected more cedars to be enjoying the sunset but it was brisk and also dinner hour. There were patches of snow here and there, with much of the ground exposed. It had been a very cold winter in 1998 but not much precipitation. Halfway down the hill, it was too warm and humid for any snow to accumulate.

They sat against a large rock and watched the sun dance

about on the small ripples of the water between pockets of rising steam. The humidity from the lake heated the surrounding air to a comfortable temperature and they soon removed their coats.

"It's such an odd sight to see this giant hot tub in the middle of the forest," Argan said. "There's never been a record of this body of water here in upstate New York."

"That shouldn't surprise you, given most of this has been a dream," she said. "The lake is no exception."

Skylar admired her handsome friend as he stared off at the lake. He glanced at her from the corner of his eye and turned toward her, his eyes lingered on hers. He broke his stare and looked back at the water. "I haven't been in yet," he gestured to the lake. "You?"

"Nope," she said.

He nodded toward the lake as a silent invitation.

"I didn't bring a bathing suit," she said.

"We can improvise." He rose to his feet and pulled her up to standing. "Come on."

They removed their shoes and started to undress. She caught a glimpse of Argan's eyes darting across her body. He returned to his task of removing his pants and made a quick three steps to the water's edge.

He dipped a foot in. "It's great," he said, smiling.

Skylar followed and they stood at the edge together. He reached for her hand and looked into her eyes as if to say *trust me*. They walked a few steps into the warm, steaming water holding hands. Suddenly Argan released her hand and dove in headfirst. The warm water splashed onto Skylar's face and she tasted it in her mouth. "Salt," she said aloud. "Huh."

Argan sprang up. He was gorgeous in the fading light reflecting off the water on his skin. "Salt," he confirmed. "It's amazing under there. It drops off pretty quickly. I had my eyes open but the concentration was too much. We have to come back with goggles."

Skylar's white bra was quickly turning a shade of orange and she tried to rub it out.

"Don't bother," Argan said. "The minerals are turning it."

She dove in and came up a minute later.

"You were under a long time," he said. "Are you a mermaid now with your new super powers?"

Skylar looked behind her. "No tail, sorry to say." She pulled at her hair and examined the strands. "I was hoping the rest of it would turn red." She dove back in, this time coming up after three minutes.

"Skylar!" Argan yelled. "What's going on? You were under too long."

She shrugged. "Don't worry, I could have stayed down longer. I want to show you something." She took his arm and led him under the water. They swam down about twenty feet and Skylar wanted to keep going. Argan pointed up and gestured that he had to go up for air. Before he turned upward she pointed to the bottom of the lake. She wanted to keep going.

He returned to the surface and Skylar continued deeper to investigate. She didn't have a problem with the salt in her eyes. What seemed to be a long concrete road stretched on before her and ended in a complete circle of familiar stone figures. After a few minutes of investigating, she made her way back to the top.

Argan was pacing at the water's edge. "That was eight minutes!"

Skylar was out of breath, not due to oxygen but to excitement. "Argan, I had a dream about the figures at the bottom of the lake! They're there, I touched them," she said. "You won't believe it! I am exactly where I'm supposed to be." Validation was sweet.

"How far down were you?" he asked.

"I don't know, fifty feet?" she said. "I'm a horrible estimator." She wrapped herself with her arms and tried to rub away the goose bumps. Argan grabbed his coat from the rock and draped it around her shoulders. "Thank you." She looked up at him. "This was incredible."

His eyes lingered on hers as he rubbed her arms with his hands to help dry her with his coat. She felt a wave of heat roll off of his body. *He still cares*, she thought to herself. He looked up to the sky as she started to dress.

They walked back to her cabin in silence and stopped at the screen door. "I'd love for you to see what's under that water," she said. "Let's find some gear and go down ASAP. With a little luck I can find a way into . . . where I'm going."

"It's a date," he said. "Good night . . . Skylar." He lingered on her name as he brushed her cheek with his hand, then turned away.

"Good night, Argan," she said into the night air filled with the sweet scent of him.

26

A faceless energy hovered over Skylar as she knelt paralyzed on the floor. An invisible force pushed her arms up into the air. She was completely powerless. The being stood in front of her, black smoke billowed behind him. She couldn't see his face but the energy was dark and masculine. *Joshua? No, his soul is journeying toward peace.* As Skylar knelt powerless, the cloaked man stuck a needle into each of her wrists. She screamed out in defiance of precious fluid seeping from her veins. He was draining her power to revive his own. Her anger welled and she pushed her hands up to break free of the force and got one quick glimpse of his face.

She jolted up in bed, tearing at the covers. "It can't be. It can't be," she repeated over and over. Panting, she checked her wrists, all in tact. As her breath slowly returned to normal she rushed to look at her reflection in the mirror. "It can't be . . . Devlin Grayer."

27

Present Day: Suki held tight to the accordion file as she traveled the elevator two stories below ground. She had never been to the basement, as she would have needed this hex key for elevator access. The whole building modeled maximum-security lockdown, an eyesore on campus but the dean looked the other way as his pockets got heavy with Grayer funding. As she stepped out of the elevator, Suki saw that the basement stayed true to that design.

"Why won't you tell me?" Kyle had asked the day she came home from DC. The question had incited the first real fight of their relationship. She remained vague and downright combative when he probed for information. She didn't know what more to say than "I can't tell you."

He couldn't recover from hurt feelings and after a day of not speaking to each other, he moved out of Skylar's house, effectively causing a break up. Suki was more at peace with it than she'd thought she'd be, questioning his character if something so small could cause this reaction. She hoped now he would find motivation to get a job.

She sighed facing a pale gray cement door and took a deep breath. Inserting the key into the round doorknob, she took notice of the only touch of decoration, a ring of three doves circling the keyhole. There was no fanfare, no alarms, only silence as she turned the knob and entered.

A motion detector signaled the lights. Nothing fluorescent or harsh, the lighting was a warm wash of perfect glow. As Suki's eyes adjusted, an odd smell she couldn't place filled her nose. It was sweet and she inhaled deeply to take in more of the delicious scent.

She closed the door quietly behind her and marveled at the enormity of the room. It took up the footprint of the entire building and rows and rows of freestanding shelves went back as far as she could see. At first glance, it looked bigger than Rosen's actual library. The walls were covered in a dark plum fabric and the climate control system hummed in the corner.

She placed the accordion file on a research desk and took a few minutes to explore the nearest shelves. The first books she came to were ancient. *Book* was a generous description. These were unbound papyruses, rolled and tied with fine, braided gold rope. They sat stacked in triangles on each shelf.

With no map to navigate the vast library, she settled in for what would be an all-day project. She had wished she'd packed a cooler and without being clear if she were allowed to return another day, she committed to staying until her task was complete.

After some time walking the aisles, she figured out the sections were separated geographically, then by time period. Fortunately each script was labeled underneath, as she would not have been able to read any of the texts. Milicent's specialty, Ancient Egypt, took up at least half of the room.

Other ancient works from India, Greece, and Celtic lands occupied the shelves a few rows down. "This is a historian's greatest dream," Suki said aloud. "These should be in world museums, not horded in a billionaire's basement library." She put her hand to her lips. She was certain she was being recorded.

As she explored, she became more and more humbled by her findings. Documents allegedly penned by Hermes, Solomon, and even Moses were tucked away in the section of Jewish Cabala.

Other shelves held ancient parchment claiming to be authored by various archangels, Michael, Gabriel, and Metatron. "The Sepher Raziel," Suki said in awe. "This can't be."

Half a dozen shelves claimed to house documents from Atlantis. She gasped. "What did Milicent ever need with Skylar?"

She was afraid to touch any of it and returned to her accordion file to uncover her directive. Anxious, she slipped the rubber band off of the clasp. Inside there was one sheet of paper and a pair of thin cotton gloves. Her orders were to find this list of items in the library and to be sure to wear the gloves. At first she thought it was to preserve the parchment, but fear of incriminating fingerprints crept into her mind. She shook off Kyle's conspiracy theory nonsense and read the list:

· *Symbola Aurea Mensae Duodecim Nationum, Mary the Prophetess*
· *The Book of Lambspringk, Benedictine Abbey of Hirschau, Württemberg*
· *Astronomy, Hypatia*

Suki cursed out loud. The only name she recognized was Hypatia. Her photographic memory recalled her Hellenistic history but she was lost on the other two. It was impossible to call out or get any data on her cell phone as the walls blocked her service. She would have to do her research the old fashioned way, with elbow grease.

Three hours into her search she was empty-handed and starving. If she could just take a break and get some food, she'd feel refreshed and be able to press on. She could also do a little research above ground and return with a better plan.

She left the accordion file on the desk and locked the door behind her before she went upstairs. She sucked down various candy bars from the vending machine and a Mountain Dew to keep her alert. In ten minutes she had the information she hoped would help guide her to the books on her list and she made her way to the elevator.

"Ms. De la Cruz?" a voice asked behind her. She whirred around to see the dean standing at the end of the hall. "What brings you here on a Saturday?"

"I could ask the same of you, sir," she said before having time to stop the connection between her brain and her mouth.

"Excuse me?" he asked angrily.

"My apologies, sir, you just caught me off guard," she said. "I, a, had some paperwork to catch up on and took advantage of the weekend quiet time."

"The executive offices are three floors up," he said as he walked closer. He was dressed uncharacteristically in khakis and a polo shirt stretched to capacity around his large midsection.

"I was refueling," she lifted her empty soda bottle. "About to go back up."

"I'll ride up with you," he said. "I'm here for some paperwork myself. You can help me dig out the financials for this building. I need it for the auditors."

Suki's shoulders sunk. This detour would set her back considerably. But there was nothing she could do so she obliged and accompanied him to the executive offices. Fortunately she was very familiar with the financial documents and could get him what he needed rather quickly. After just under an hour of small talk and data pulling, he left her alone to resume her work, not the least bit apologetic for taking up her free time on a Saturday.

When she was sure he was out of the building she made her way back down to the basement. The key didn't work as smoothly as it had the first time and for a second she panicked thinking her access was one time only. She dropped to her knee and jiggled the key inside the lock and it finally clicked.

When she returned inside, everything was as she'd left it. She was now armed with chronological information to direct her to each of her manuscripts. She found the work of Mary the Prophetess in the first century Egypt archives. It had been one of the rolled papyrus documents she saw when she first arrived. She picked it up wearing the gloves. Slipped underneath the gold rope was a piece of plain, white paper with the word "The" typed on it. She looked at it for a moment but didn't give it too much thought. She left Mary's book on her research desk in search of the second manuscript. The Book of Lambspringk was in sixteenth century Europe, Germany to be exact. This extremely thin book was bound, also with a thin rope around it. The same white paper lay on top. This one read "Lost." Now Suki's attention was perked.

Her search for Hypatia led her to the Hellenistic era of fourth-century Egypt. She found the Astronomy book, it too with a plain white paper on top. This one read, "Word."

None of the works were lengthy, all less than fifty actual pages, she guessed. Each contained interesting symbols and pictures that made no sense to her. All fit snuggly in her accordion file as if Milicent had planned for it. Suki was pleased with herself and slightly sad this scavenger hunt was over.

Once back above ground she tracked down Wren at the White House. "I've been successful," Suki said, making sure she didn't say anything incriminating.

"Glad to hear," Wren said. "Sit tight. The First Lady has changed her plans and is returning to Rosen in the morning. She will contact you when she arrives." She disconnected the phone and a sense of dread came over Suki. She had to babysit these documents until Milicent arrived. Or did she? It was just as easy to leave them in the basement archives and they would be much more secure than at Skylar's house.

Now back in the archives for the third time that day, she was getting comfortable with the process. Although she hadn't seen the sun much, she enjoyed her day exploring the vast body of knowledge hidden under her nose. She couldn't read the ancient texts, no matter the language but she took a few minutes to peruse the seventeenth century European section. Many of the books were alchemical in nature, precursors to the birth of modern science.

She drifted into a section of American occult grimoires and even someone as left-brained as she could feel the pulse of energy barely contained in these books. They were the most beautiful and curious tombs she encountered in Milicent's stacks. The rich jewel and black bindings oozed with the mystery and abundance of nature and hinted to the indescribable power forgotten by most of humanity. All of Skylar's ramblings about the Divine Goddess came to mind. The energy of the stack had a distinctly feminine feel, be it light or dark. She touched the binding of one and got a substantial shock through her cotton gloves. Unfortunately none of these magical texts were on her list and she would have to pass them by.

The grimoires overlapped with a section of early Freemason writings. It was no secret the Freemasons were steeped in the occult when the country was formed and to this day many questionable rituals pepper their rites of ceremony. If any of the documents felt off limits to Suki, it was these. Maybe because this genre was one she was most familiar with, her impressions skewed by popular culture. If the grimoires felt *feminine*, the works of the masons were unmistakably *masculine*. This section was almost as big as Ancient Egypt and Suki wondered why. The masons wouldn't be in Milicent's good favor, having shunned women since their inception.

As she turned away from the stack, one masonic book caught

her eye. Among the sea of beige bindings, one of bright crimson red stood out. She read the binding:

The Lost Word by Devlin P. Grayer.

Suki did a double take. The mystery words on each of her pulled manuscripts formed *The Lost Word*. She quickly touched the binding. No shock. She removed it off the shelves and as she suspected, it had a piece of paper on top. She read it:

If you're reading this, take it with you.

She started to put the pieces together. This was the book Milicent really wanted. The others were just breadcrumbs to lead her here.

She opened it and scanned the cover page. Again she read the words *The Lost Word*, but on this page, the subtitle read *America's Future* by Devlin P. Grayer, Mason, 33rd Degree.

Suki shut the book and returned it to the shelf. "Holy crap." Devlin was the highest degree in the order of the Freemasons. Her shock gave way to instant acceptance. "Of course!" she continued to talk to herself. "He's a billionaire with his hands in everything." *And now he's President,* she thought. Many Presidents had been masons, most in fact. The piece of her puzzle that didn't fit was Milicent. She's been tied to Devlin for decades knowing their view on a woman's place. Would she really have sacrificed her beliefs for the comfortable life she'd been given? If so, all of Suki's admiration for the First Lady would come to an abrupt halt.

She looked at her watch. It was late in the day. She had stayed long enough and was getting tired. She assumed she was supposed to take this book too so she pulled it back off the shelf and in her haste, it fell to the floor. When she bent down she noticed this shelving was on a moveable track. She slid it sideways and was surprised to find a very different door behind it.

This door, weathered with age, must have been imported

from a foreign land. It looked much older than anything found in this country. It had geometric shapes chiseled around its border and inscriptions she recognized as Latin. On either side flanked two identical, gnome-like creatures carved from white stone. In all of her cross-referencing of Skylar's experiences, Suki had been spending her time researching outer space, not ancient space. She had no idea what she was looking at. The door had no handle and she lightly touched it to confirm its solidity. When she did, it easily pushed open to a darkened room.

Suki looked over her shoulder. She was certain this was being recorded and Milicent would have her head. She picked up Devlin's book and slid the wall back in place. But . . .

This was that life she had talked about—adventure. The past year she had been so envious of Skylar's exploits and here was the chance to have some of her own. She pushed the wall of shelves completely to the side and stared into the darkness. But if she were honest with herself, she wasn't prepared to go in. She had broken enough rules for one day and discovered enough secrets. She wasn't that adventurous.

Before she turned away, an image appeared, like an old-fashioned movie reel. Suki felt uneasy, feeling adventure thrust upon her. Through a scratchy lens, she watched herself bounce along on her father's shoulders, his hand holding her mother's. She couldn't have been more than three. She held her breath. This made less sense than anything she'd seen that day. She couldn't turn back. This place was showing Suki the part of her past she held most precious. She reached one hand out and combed the air with her fingers. It didn't feel any different. She stepped one foot in, the other still planted in the library. The image of her family pulled back a step. Frustration exhaled out of her nose. With every ounce of courage she could muster, she stepped both feet into the dark room. The image retreated as many steps as she took forward and she stopped, realizing it was an illusion she could never catch. Her parents had died before she had a full grasp of who they were. If she were honest, she'd admit she didn't remember them, but from what she'd relived through photos.

Her mother waved her forward, her kind smile inviting Suki to follow them a little farther. One more step in, Suki slammed into an invisible wall. The movie was so far in the distance now and this transparent wall stood between them. Like a still lake disturbed by a thrown pebble, the wall now billowed with soft waves coming out of its center. The movie of her family now blurred.

She touched the wall again. This time, her hand slipped through into some other place she couldn't see. She pulled her hand back. It wasn't wet. She put it through again, a bit farther. *Where did this lead?* she asked herself, feeling excited about all the research she'd done on space and time jumping. Now she was given the opportunity to try it out first hand. She took a gulp of air and poked her head through the shimmering wall. She was relieved when she could breathe on the other side. She looked at her surroundings and recognized *what* she was in, she just didn't know *where*. *Why would her parents lead her here?*

A certainty came over her. This movie reminded her she had her own destiny to play out and it was her time.

She reversed her steps out of the room and back into the library. Everything was how she'd left it. It was 10:00 p.m. and she was exhausted but figured she'd get little sleep. She rushed to pack her things and collect the accordion file. She would take it after all, wanting to learn what Devlin had to say about America's future. She locked the door and headed back up to the main level. Among all the questions swirling in her head, she knew one thing for sure. She was coming back tomorrow.

28

Skylar walked into the palladium for Goddess class, five minutes before start time. She was pleased with herself for making the trek with time to spare. The same group of cedars sat in a circle on the floor. This time, Origen sat among them. Britt was not in the room.

"Welcome, my flower," Origen said, raising his arms above his head, not getting up from the floor. He returned his focus to the group. "All, let's inch back to accommodate our sister." The group scooted back to open the circle for Skylar. The empty space landed exactly next to Origen.

"Skywalker, sit by me," he gestured with a pat to the floor.

"Skylar," she corrected him.

"Oh, but you are one who walks the sky," he said. "No, I've decided you are Skywalker." Skylar bit her lip and sat.

He resumed his lecture. "Today we are discussing the internal mandala." He clasped his hands together in prayer and bowed his head briefly. "We are all here on this planet, looking to repair the holes within. The mandala is a tapestry," he raised his hands to the hanging quilts, "tattered by lifetimes of abuse. The art of tantra is one path toward repairing it. It is where two halves, masculine and feminine are desperate to create a whole. This is the heart of tantra." Again, he trilled his tongue over the word and Skylar grimaced. Britt had snuck in without being noticed and sat quietly behind the circle.

196

"The act of sexual intercourse is the human desire to unite the two aspects of our being, regardless of sexual orientation." Origen said. "Each one of us has both of these principles within us and we seek balance. It is in sexual union that we look to complete ourselves and connect to the *love* force we desperately want to return to. Sometimes one is stronger, then it reverses and the other takes over. It is the dance of two becoming one." He stood up in the circle. "There is tremendous heat generated during sexual union. We use our bodies to transmute energy, we are alchemists!" His excitement rose. "We create life with this magic!" he shouted. "But creating life is just one result of sexual energy. It's actually a very small one. Most of the time, the energy of a climax dissipates, wasted in the act itself. But I ask you, what if one never climaxed? Where would that energy go? What would you create?" He pointed around the circle. "Worlds! I tell you! Worlds!" He shook his fists at the ceiling. Skylar looked around the room at the cedars all caught up in Origen's monologue, Britt included.

"I can tell you this," he said. "There is an energetic process responsible for the life force on earth. And it is has the same properties as an orgasm. And let me now introduce you to the white magic of tantra, my dearlings." Again, he closed his eyes and placed his palms together in prayer.

The group stared silently as he stood motionless for what Skylar guessed was at least five minutes. She was about to check for breathing when he startled the group, resuming his lecture. "The art of tantra turns our unchaste impulses into something holy."

He leapt over a cedar and picked up a sharpie at the white-board. "We take the basic formula of sex . . ." He wrote out the words on the board:

tension-buildup-release

"and pause the process in the buildup phase. When there is no release, our internal athanor continues to burn. In that burning, we generate energy. We are our own source of power. And I'm here to tell you, dear ones, that power sits in your loins."

There were a few giggles among the group but Origin pressed on. Skylar got up to stretch her legs and get some water from the bubbler. Instead of returning to the circle, she opted to sit with Britt in the back of the room. "This is a whole lot different than the sex-ed class I remember," she said to Britt.

"He's startlingly accurate," Britt said.

"We are in fact talking about the kundalini energy that lies dormant in every human body," Origen said. "It is sexual in nature. It makes sense, doesn't it? Sitting at the base of your loins? But there are actually two sexual poles in the body," Origen's elementary drawings on the whiteboard made Skylar laugh. She didn't think all the arrows pointing to the stick figure's crotch were necessary. Everyone in the room seemed to get his point. "One, the collective sexual pole, in the genitals. The other is the individual sexual pole, in the third eye. Women are fortunate enough to have an additional area in their breasts, embodying the magic of the Goddess. Men desire to unite with the Goddess through the female body."

"He's trying to justify men's obsession with boobs," Skylar said.

"Give him credit," Britt said annoyed. "He's the first man I've encountered with such an enlightened view of biology." Skylar knew she and Britt had opposing viewpoints on Origen.

"This creative energy gives birth to art or innovation," Origen said. "It is for so much more than making babies."

He put down his sharpie and walked back into the circle. "We are going to do an exercise. We have mostly females in the circle but that's all right. You can channel your inner male."

The group stood up and he waved to Skylar. "Skywalker, come back over. We will be partners," Origen said. "Everyone else, pair up."

Britt's face sunk. She remained in the corner and let the circle of cedars participate.

Origen positioned Skylar to face him. He leaned in and gave her a deep sniff. "Perfect, you are menstruating!" He clapped his hands together with happiness. "What a bonus! I can smell the rich earth in your loins. I would love to drink you in and be nourished by the Goddess." He closed his eyes and breathed in deeply with his nose. Skylar leaned away, horrified.

"I will teach you how to replenish your lost energy during menstruation," he said. "You lose life force every month and you must nourish yourself with the right foods and herbs to restore your vitality. Another amazing bonus of tantra is transmuting your monthly pains into a pleasure greater than orgasm."

He quickly faced the group. "Everyone remember . . . blood creates worlds. Let me show you." He put his hand on Skylar's abdomen.

"That's okay!" she said, putting up both hands to stop him.

"Why do you resist? Our culture has stolen the sacredness out of a woman's body," he said to the group, "making menstruation into something disgusting, instead of revered. It is our duty at this time on the planet to return it to its most high place of honor."

Skylar softened. That she could agree with.

He moved on. "This circle is inclusive of our whole selves. We come to the circle as imperfect and perfect beings at the same time. Unconditional love is scary but we all yearn for it at our core." Origen positioned each cedar to face one another. "We are going to conduct a power transfer ceremony. It must be done first to prepare yourselves for the tantra work ahead." He handed each of the males a Native American ceremony stick. They were each uniquely carved wood of various animal heads and painted with vibrant colors. Skylar recognized the ibis feathers dangling from each one.

"This rod represents your perceived power. Not your true power because you have no clue what that is. For now, I want all who are holding the rod to imagine every ounce of your power, your being, your ego to be sucked out of your body and into the rod. Take a few minutes now. Those without the rod, close your eyes and imagine yourself being purified in Vivienne's lake. You are being washed away of all hurts and mistakes to emerge anew.

"Now, when you are ready, those holding the rod, hand it over to your partner, thus giving up who you thought you were and giving it freely to a newly reborn soul."

Origen held his own ceremony stick and closed his eyes in contemplation. Skylar found the exercise intriguing and played along. She pictured herself diving into the lake and each time coming up freer from the rust of the material world. She kept her eyes closed and not one person in the room was making a sound.

When she felt ready, she opened her eyes to a room of tears. All of the cedars, boys and girls were crying. Skylar could feel the initial resistance, then the longing of the boys to let go of all they'd been taught men were supposed to be. The girls held extraordinary forgiveness in their hearts for those that trampled their innocence and identity over the years. She watched those with rods give away their egoic selves and those receiving them, accept them with openness. The whole exercise became an activity in letting go and being vulnerable with an open heart. Now it was Skylar's turn and she no longer wanted to continue. Origen gave his ceremony stick to her happily, having no real attachment to false masculinity. She on the other hand was reluctant to take it. It all became so personal so fast and she sensed if she took it, the shell around her heart would crack wide open. She was very attached to that shell.

"Won't you take it?" Origen asked her, reaching out his hand. Shaking off the spiral of emotion that temporarily consumed her, she took the rod. "Thank you," she said.

After that class, Skylar felt depleted but she wanted to ask Origen about the lake. Cassie said he was her ticket for information.

"Origen, may I have a word?" she asked. Britt scampered over.

"Yes, but before you do, you really need to work on your heart chakra. It is completely closed to men," he said. "I'm not one trying to get into your heart but I assume someone is or will be, and they will be met with a stiff arm. Being vulnerable to love is the greatest gift you can give yourself, Skywalker." He glanced briefly at Britt and returned his attention to Skylar. His words choked her heart, squeezing it down to the size of a golf ball, leaving her speechless.

"You never did answer me the other day," he chided. "You wonder why I call you that but you are not from this time. You do truly walk the sky."

She cleared her throat and found her voice. "There's no getting anything by you, Origen. You are most wise. I can only hope to enjoy the boons of your teachings and aspire to be one with the universe and accomplish a fraction of what you have done." He beamed with pride.

"Now, about the lake," she said, determined to get an answer. "I hear you are the wise one with knowledge about what's at the bottom."

He grabbed her by the elbow and pulled her close. "Why do you ask?"

"Remember all your talk about walking the sky?" she asked him. "I've been sent here on a secret mission." She lowered her voice to a whisper. "And I need your wise counsel." He nodded. "What can you tell me about that circle of stone figures?" she asked. He sucked in air over his teeth and looked at Britt. "She's with me, it's okay."

"You know about the governors?" he whispered.

"I saw them," she said.

"That's impossible," he said. "They are down over a hundred feet."

She smiled coyly. "Not only do I walk the sky, dearling, I walk the bottom of the sea as well." She liked playing this game with him. He was eating it up.

He closed his eyes and tented his hands. The breath in his nose became audible and Skylar waited. "The governors are waiting for the right time," he said slowly. "They are stone now but at the right time, they will awaken and bring everything back to the way it was." He remained still, never opening his eyes.

Skylar looked at Britt and she nudged her. "Can you show me how to get in?"

"The door opens for the one with fire in her heart, wind on her breath, and the sea in her blood." His eyes popped open and stared at Skylar. "That is you."

"There's a door under the lake?" Britt asked.

"Yes, there once stood five. Only one remains in the open, in Italia. The others are hidden. One is at the bottom of Vivienne's lake. Through it you will find the world you are looking for. I knew you were here for an extraordinary reason. I will help you."

"You already have, Origen," Skylar said sincerely. "Thank you."

P resent Day: "Why are you here?" The anger in Milicent's voice shook the walls, or so Suki imagined. She had been instructed to meet Milicent at Rosen. Suki's only alteration to the plan was they would meet in the library.

"Mrs. Grayer, please don't have me arrested, or worse," Suki said, twisting her hands. "I found everything you asked for . . . and then some." Milicent was uncharacteristically silent and her stare was impossible to read, so Suki rambled on. "Your collection is worthy of any of the best museums in the world or they are not worthy . . . I mean," she stopped to give her tongue a chance to untie and restarted. "I understand if you want to keep this knowledge hidden but I . . ." she couldn't believe her own boldness. "I . . . am asking for the opportunity to study here. To learn a fraction of what's contained in these books. This knowledge is priceless and I can't simply walk away from what I've seen. I will regret it for the rest of my life."

Milicent ran her hand over the research desk as if checking for dust. She found some and brushed it from her fingers. To look at her, one would think she hadn't heard a word Suki had said. She continued to wipe the desk with her hand until she was satisfied and then leaned on it with her arms crossed. "Fine," she said curtly. "It took fortitude to ask me. I admire fortitude." She scooped up the accordion file from the desk and turned to leave.

"Oh, thank you so much," Suki gushed but Milicent said

nothing. "Thank you. Thank you." She followed Milicent to the door. "There's an extra book in the accordion," she started to explain.

"It's not extra," Milicent cut her off. "Keep the key. It isn't my only one." She closed the door behind her. Suki couldn't believe it. No begging, no court marshall. Milicent agreed! Like a child on Christmas morning, she couldn't decide which treasure to open first. But she knew all of the manuscripts would have to wait. The door was priority number one.

30

There was a whole side of the camp Skylar hadn't seen yet. The great mountain that sat to the west was so tall it kept one side of camp in constant shadow. It was virtual wilderness, untouched by any human. Skylar had asked around but it seemed no one ventured to the west side of camp—ever. When she asked why, she always got the same answer: energy. She was told that once you start down the path to the mountain, the bad energy is so thick, it stops you in your tracks. The cedars called it the *barrier*. It was a bit of a game for new arrivals, Silverwood's idea of hazing. A lot of daring and big talk went on but nothing ever happened. No one could get near enough. But legend was if you broke through the barrier, all the secrets of the universe would be revealed to you.

With Ocean gone, Skylar had no idea of the real story. She was on her own and would have to check it out for herself. Continuing her routine of waking at sunrise, she headed out in her running clothes long before Britt stirred. The path to the mountain looked very much like the path to Laughless Rock, well trodden mud in patches of snow. About ten minutes in, the path abruptly ended with a distinct line between mud and snow. She stopped and waited for a feeling of doom or constriction or something dreadful. She felt none. With one step forward in the fresh white snow, still nothing. Through birch and ancient pine trees, she continued on alert for a shift in the energy. It never came.

She picked up her pace through the snow. Another mile into her run the trees cleared and the snow lessened, so much that she soon ran on bare ground. As much as the landscape changed, she never seemed to get any closer to the mountain. She was chasing a rainbow. She persisted, now too far to make it back in time for morning meditation. *But honestly, would it really matter?* She pressed on.

As the sun rose in the morning sky, she came upon a crude campsite with a hollowed out fire pit and primitive cooking utensils. Irregular shaped tin pots lay strewn about with wooden spoons decayed by years of weathering. It appeared she might have stepped even further back in time. She knelt over the fire pit and picked up a round pot. She knocked on the very real side of it and threw it back on the pit. Tall white pine trees edged the campsite and she caught a glimpse of a small cabin tucked behind them. *This* was the thing that made her stop in her tracks. The cabin was an exact replica of her tiny house. It had the same porch and windows flanking the front door. This one had been weathered by time but the structure was identical and so was the energy.

She stared at the door, unable to take a step further, needing some time to work up the nerve. But before she could move, the door opened and Cassie walked out onto the porch, the Book of Sophia in her hand. She was the mother Skylar remembered, beautiful and vibrant. Sunbeams found their way through the thick trees and reflected like diamonds in her hair. She gave Skylar a dazzling smile and waved a big, whole armed wave to come inside.

Skylar found her feet and ran to the cabin. She leapt up the two stairs and took one step through the decaying doorway.

"Mom?" she asked loudly. Cassie wasn't there.

The room was small and looked as if it had housed a smithy

or scientist at one time. Skylar couldn't tell. It was similar to Joel's lab but had a much more organic feel, less clinical. An odd shaped furnace sat in one corner; a pile of iron scrap lay next to it. Decades of dust blanketed the crowded countertops. Piles of rusty utensils and cloudy beakers lay strewn atop hardened burlap bags. A workbench below the shelving housed similar items. An actual cauldron sat on the floor next to the workbench. She touched it lightly, removing a bit of dust.

All around the room, heavily patina-ed copper piping lined the top of the walls like crown molding.

Skylar's eyes widened at the sight of the bookshelves. It was exactly like her library at home. The same horsehide journals lined the shelves and Skylar wondered if any were as precious as her Book of Sophia. Maybe they all were.

A kaleidoscope of light streamed through a small octagon-shaped stained glass window at the top of the book-shelved wall. She felt the tingle up the back of her head. This room, so far away from everyone and everything she loved, contained the same history as her childhood home. She looked closer at the books. *Sophia's book is here, I can feel it.*

The dust overpowered her and she sneezed. *No sage, no mugwort*, she thought. She closed her eyes and waited to feel the tingle between her brows, her "on button" to connect to her psychic abilities. She had hoped to connect to the time when this room was filled with life. But she got nothing. She opened her eyes and saw a pile of large swords in a corner. She picked one up and examined it. She traced the side of the blade with her finger and the tarnish gave way to the shining silver underneath, no elbow grease needed. With the lightest touch she was able to remove the years from the blade.

A startling sound rustled in the corner. A chipmunk scurried out from a pile of leaves through a hole in the wall that led outside. Skylar exhaled her held breath and relaxed her shoulders. The morning sun streaming through the stained glass created a large light beam of dust. She watched the light dance with the dust until it took form before her eyes. The mixture created a sphere similar to Rachel's ball of energy. As it got brighter, Skylar held out her hand. The sphere floated toward it, resting for a brief, enthralling moment. The ball became hot like a thousand prickers sticking in her hand. She broke away from it but it came after her. She ran around the room, bobbing and weaving out of the way of this antagonistic orb. Before she had time to run outside, it ran her down and she fell to the floor. She grabbed the tarnished sword with one hand and swung at the ball from the ground. It sliced the ball in two. She grabbed the handle of the sword with both hands and sliced at both balls, creating more and more balls of energy, all trying to attack her. She rolled to her feet and swung at the balls of light until they became too numerous and tiny to hit with the blade. The individual flecks formed into a cloud of glittery silver fish. She ran outside and the creature-cloud followed her. She turned to fight, unsure how. The cloud rushed her with immense speed and just before hitting her body, made a ninety-degree turn upward and flew toward the sky. Skylar watched the creature fly up until it was out of her view. Left standing in the dirt, holding the sword, her breath slowed and she walked back toward the cabin.

"Well done," young Cassie said, standing in the doorway. "They'll be back. You'll have another chance to practice."

"They were so beautiful," Skylar said, not surprised to see her. "It never occurred to me they might be dangerous."

"Beauty has a way of fooling us for it's own purpose," Cassie said as she stepped inside and Skylar followed. Her eyes lit up. The interior had come back to brilliant life. She didn't know where to look first. The room was a feast of vibrant color. All of the glass vials and containers glistened. Jars filled with fresh herbs and greenery lined the top shelf. The copper piping had been restored to a brilliant shine. The odd brick oven gave off a warm glow from its internal fire.

"Are you okay?" Cassie asked.

"Yes, but . . . sorry," Skylar stumbled for words. "I just, well . . . this didn't look like this when I was in here before."

"You passed the test. You handled the *light fish* beautifully. You can come in now."

"I've been practicing with a blade," Skylar puffed up.

"Keep practicing," Cassie laughed.

Skylar placed the sword on the pile, now shining with a blade of silver. Cassie picked up another sword from the pile. "So strange right? Why would this stuff be laying around an alchemist's laboratory?"

"That's what this place is?" Skylar asked.

"Yes, I practice here," Cassie said.

"I thought no cedar could get through the woods. The illumination barrier or whatever," Skylar said.

"Right, for most, sure," Cassie said. "But if you keep the secrets of alchemy alive in your life, there are no barriers."

"You do that?"

"I do. I've built up volumes of notes." She gestured to the wall of journals. The luster of the leather bindings had been restored.

"I don't think I do that," Skylar said. "Practice alchemy, I mean." She was distracted by one book in particular. It called to her with the familiar hum.

"You must or you wouldn't be here," Cassie said, oblivious to Skylar's distraction.

Skylar walked to the bookshelf and reached out her hand. "May I?"

"Sure," Cassie said. "Many are just drawings."

Skylar touched the humming book. She felt Sophia. "This one is humming, do you hear it?" She pulled her hand back.

"It better be humming," Cassie said. "It's my *Great Work*."

"Your thesis?" Skylar asked.

"No," Cassie said. She seemed slightly nervous to be sharing this information. "It's more like the culmination of all of my lucid dreams."

"Oh, I have no luck with lucid dreaming."

"It takes more practice than most lead you to believe," Cassie said as she took down the humming book from the shelf.

Skylar couldn't contain her enthusiasm. "It's so beautiful!"

Cassie looked at her crossly. "It looks the same as all the others."

"Oh, I don't think so," Skylar said. "To me, it glows."

"Really? That's weird," Cassie said. "Maybe you can read it then."

"Oh, I don't want to read your private dream journal."

"It's not private at all actually," Cassie said. "It's more like secrets dictated to me through my dreams. I wrote them down when I wasn't even awake. In another language no less."

"Secrets?"

"The secrets of the outer world, the secrets of the inner world, and how they're connected. The wisdom of the body runs deep. I love how the world tells us magic doesn't exist. How else can you explain this?"

"I can read Sanskrit," Skylar said. "It's a gift, from my mother." She had said too much. Cassie never mentioned the book was in Sanskrit.

Cassie studied Skylar but didn't say anything. She handed Skylar the book. "Give it a shot."

Skylar held the book in her hands. It was more vibrant, alive, and intact than her 2021 version. She skimmed through, now so familiar with the text of Sophia. "It's an alchemical treaty," she said staring at the fresh pages. "Many diagrams of the elements, metals, and the planets." These images weren't in her 2021 version. She stopped at the drawing of the Vitruvian Man. Her visions in Joel's lab were right here on these pages. "It's beautiful, as if the pages are alive."

"They are," Cassie said. "The true alchemist transforms within as much as without. These pages contain a part of me. It breathes my air and bleeds my blood."

Skylar held the book to her chest. "Why are you telling me this?" she asked.

"You are the one, Skylar. I knew it when we shook hands. You are the one that will help humanity move up the ladder of consciousness. This book can help you do that. Come read it, study it any time, often. Maybe we can study it together. It's hard to solve the mysteries of the universe alone. Invite Argan too. He can help. But please keep the book here."

"You've met Argan?" Skylar asked.

Cassie smiled a warm smile that carried up to her eyes but she didn't answer Skylar. She walked toward the door and picked up a sword. "Keep practicing with these too." She laughed. "I should be going."

"Are you going to try to make morning meditation?" Skylar asked.

"Nope," Cassie said.

"Thank you for inviting me in," Skylar blurted.

Cassie nodded and took one step through the doorway. On the threshold, she transformed into her forty-year-old self. Skylar ran out and watched her vanish into the trees. She felt lighter, happier each time she saw her mother. The pain of her loss lessened with each visit and for that she was thankful.

31

"I don't think I can stand another night of tofu," Skylar said, staring at her limp lunch. "Care to join me for a picnic tonight?" she asked Argan.

"Have a stash of meat, do ya?" he asked. His plate was picked clean.

"Sadly, no, but I'll come up with something," she said. "Pick you up at six?"

"Okay," he said, smiling.

That afternoon, Skylar investigated alternative food sources from the limited menu of the Mess. She had done some research and it turned out many of the cedars had stockpiles of contraband for late night snacking. That was great for a case of the munchies but she wasn't interested in making a meal out of cheerios and potato chips.

She walked into the completely silent Mess to find one cedar flipping chairs up off the floor preparing to mop. He hardly glanced up as she slipped into the kitchen. She rummaged through cabinets and opened the walk-in fridge hoping to find something worthwhile. She didn't.

She walked through a set of glass double doors and found herself in the middle of the familiar vegetable beds of the greenhouse. *More doors!* she thought. Giant purple eggplant, green peppers, and bright red tomatoes shone in the winter sunshine. The elementals seemed more subdued than her last encounter, hovering around the roots and soil, instead of on the actual vegetables.

"Hello," she said. They completely ignored her.

Hello, Magda said, appearing from behind the great sycamore. She never veered from her long gown with draping bell sleeves.

"Aren't you hot in that dress?" She was really getting familiar with Magda.

Magda smiled. *No*, she said. *Skylar, make haste to find your way under the lake. The night of the Equinox approaches. You must find your way by then.*

"Can I have a meal first?" Skylar asked, picking up an eggplant.

Just one, Magda said and she was gone. Skylar was beginning to think Magda enjoyed the drama.

She apologized to the eggplant and whoever may have been attached to it and popped it off its stem. After gathering a few more vegetables, she walked backward to the door of the Mess. "Namaste," she said with a bow and left.

"Why are we going to the other side of camp?" Argan asked as they trudged over a half hour in the direction of the mountain. He had insisted on carrying the heavy picnic basket and was now regretting it.

"There's a place I found I want to show you," Skylar said.

"If we go much farther, I'm giving you back the basket," he said.

"Oh, just give it to me," she said and grabbed it out of his hands. They walked another ten minutes and the alchemist's cabin came into view.

Argan stopped in his tracks. "Whoa, I can't go in there," he said.

"What? Why?" she said. "I need your help with something

and I thought it was better to show you." She stopped rambling and looked into his eyes. "You know this place?"

"You *don't* know this place?"

"Yes, it's an alchemist's lab. It's Cassie's. Doesn't it look like my tiny house?"

"It's also an omphalos. I can feel it in my bones." He stood near the campsite, just missing a pot with his foot.

"Okay, I'll bite. What's an omphalos?"

"A place on earth where two planes of existence converge. There are many around the world. I happen to come from the land of the plenty, Greece. The Isle of Skye is another, in Scotland. Kinda ironic huh?"

Skylar thought of Cassie's comment about the Isle of Skye. "America isn't known for it's ancient wisdom," Skylar said.

"You forget this area is ripe with Native American history. We are smack in the middle of Iroquois territory. And this camp was created by the Great Mothers. They put Laughless Rock here and if they happen to stick an omphalos here too, so be it."

Skylar couldn't argue with that. "Why don't you want to go in?"

"They have a way of . . . changing a person, when they enter," he said. "I had a bad experience once. I'd rather not repeat it."

"Oh," she said disappointed. "Cassie thought you could help me with controlling a sword. We can do that outside. Wait here."

She left the basket of food at Argan's feet and sprinted to the cabin. Once inside she let out a loud yelp. A large black jaguar sat perched on top of the bookcase. Oddly, she felt no fear, just surprise. She wasn't convinced he was actually real. His immense frame should have toppled the bookcase. If he moved, for sure it would fall. He glanced at Skylar with mild interest but she wasn't the reason he was there.

Argan came racing to the door. "What . . ." he tried to stop himself when he saw the large cat but it was too late. He had half of one foot inside and that's all it took. The feline wasted no time and pounced toward him. Argan lifted his arms as a shield and the jaguar disappeared when it should have knocked him to the ground. Instead it merged with him, as Rhia's heart light had done to Skylar's own chest. He dropped to all fours and let out a painful cry. It was a sound she'd never heard come out of any human, the sound of struggle between a human scream and a mighty cat's roar. It all happened so fast; she could do nothing but watch.

He remained on all fours and panted out of his mouth. "What can I do?" Skylar whispered. He shook his head but said nothing. For a moment she feared he could no longer talk. *What had he turned into?* she thought. She stepped toward him but he inched away like a scared animal, his eyes locked on hers. *Would he attack me?* she thought. She hadn't been fearful of the cat but now, she wasn't sure. She decided to give him some room and took a few steps back to wait. After enough time had passed, he regained his faculties and almost looked normal. He stood up and stretched his back. A crack shot up his spine.

"Is that *thing* inside you now?" she asked.

"Temporarily," he said, his voice raspy.

"When will it come out?"

"When it's called," he said.

"By anyone in particular?" she asked.

"The Goddess . . . of the Underworld," he said in between deep breaths.

"Oh, brilliant."

"Take it . . . as a good sign," he said, his breath still labored. "Things are moving . . . forward. The cat wouldn't have appeared if it weren't time . . . for you to complete your mission."

"How so?"

"The black jaguar is a gatekeeper to the Underworld. This

means the animals are rallying to help us." He finally stood straight up. He rubbed his stomach in a circle.

"So why did it latch on to you?"

His breath calmed and he could speak normally. "I'm your protector, Skylar. I don't know why you refuse to accept that. And I will be able to use his powers as my own."

"You said *like last time*. This has happened before?"

"Yup," he said, taking a seat on the floor. "It was soon after I returned home to Greece after my summer with you. I was withdrawn and my mother was worried about me. She wanted to teach me the hazards of avoiding pain. She said avoiding pain was toxic. And the jaguar taught me to sit in the discomfort of it and learn I wouldn't die."

"That's a pretty extreme lesson for a little boy," Skylar said. "She couldn't have signed you up for track or an art class?"

"We never *did* ordinary," he laughed and it morphed into a wheezing cough.

"Allergic to cats?" she asked.

"Ha ha," he said. He rested his arms on his bent knees and lowered his head to stretch it.

"Do you want to do this another day?" she asked.

"No," he said. "I'm okay." He jumped to his feet in one swift motion, jerked his head and his neck let out a loud crack.

"You are not all right," she said.

"My interior is now carrying a hundred and fifty pound cat. Nope, not all right."

"Ok well, should we head right to the Underworld or can we eat first?"

"I don't think I can eat right now. Give me a few minutes." He looked around the room and his eyes landed on the bookcase where the jaguar had perched.

"The Book of Sophia is here," Skylar said.

"I figured it would be."

Skylar walked over to the book. It hummed as usual. "I hadn't had a chance to look at the back when Cassie was here." She flipped to the back of the book. The pages were all intact.

"Oh, the pages are here!" She surprised herself with her own enthusiasm that quickly faded. "They're blank."

Argan looked over her shoulder, leaning one arm on the desk for support. "Huh, well that's anticlimactic." He cased the room and headed for the pile of swords. "This doesn't jive with alchemy," he said picking one up.

Skylar was still stuck on the blank pages, but decided Argan had the right idea. "I guess I shouldn't be too disappointed. I just thought maybe the ripped pages would hold the key to some secret." She looked around the room and almost chuckled over the road her life had taken. Here she sat, in an alchemist's laboratory twenty plus years in the past, entangled in the dramas of her mother's adolescence among others. With Argan by her side, she felt safe to plunge into this tumultuous world, only able to see a few feet in front of her at a time. She studied him, admiring his ability to take the absurdities of the day in stride.

"What?" he asked with an edge to his voice.

She let out her chuckle. "You are standing there with that cat somehow inside of you and you're already on to the next thing." She bent and picked up a sword. "I wish I had taken Suki more seriously. I basically laughed in her face when she brought me a sword."

He grabbed an old dirty rag and started to polish a blade. Skylar followed suit. "Swords are symbols of truth," he said. "They cut through deception and leave the fresh wound to heal with new awareness."

"I don't get that from a sword," she said. "I see death." She stared at the metal blade.

"It's death that makes life worth living," Argan said standing straight up. Skylar could see this took effort. He stood in the doorway. "Follow me."

They walked outside into the warm sun that danced on the snow-covered tops of the old white pines. Argan circled her in the clearing and came to stillness in front of her. "En garde."

She couldn't take it seriously. "I'll do my best," she said half-heartedly and stood straight.

"Mirror me," he said as he moved, always facing her. She kept pace and when he lunged forward, she was one step ahead, anticipating his movement. "The sword is ancillary. The key is how you move your body. What is your intention? Your body will follow your desire."

She released her expectations and let her mind connect to the tingle that gave her guidance. In her mind's eye, she saw herself proficient, enjoying the challenge of the fight, defeating her opponent. With each turn and thrust in the joust, Skylar met Argan's move and countered correctly. She was getting the hang of it, not convinced it was beginner's luck. She had hoped it was more than that. But in one moment it clicked. All of the hours, all of the lessons he had been giving her came rushing to her mind. The sequences that made no sense to her in Joel's backyard were vital to her form now. In her realization, she broke her concentration. Argan had her on the ground, the sword at her throat. "What happened?" he asked, releasing her immediately. "You had it."

She scrambled to her feet. "I've been your Ralph Macchio! All this time and you never let on." She growled. "You are just full of secrets."

"It worked, didn't it?" he said. He walked to the open doorway and threw his sword on the pile. "You look good . . . ready." He stood in the doorway, his arm leaning on the jamb.

"For what?"

"Anything that might come your way," he said. "You need a

dry run. Or a wet run. You have no idea what's under that lake, how to get in, any of it. You need a plan. You can't just show up, what do you expect to do? Who are you looking for? *What* are you searching for? Do you know any of the answers to these questions?" he asked.

She had no answer. "I've been in this situation before," she said, following him inside. "No plan. Just trying to use the force." She tried to be lighthearted. "It's gotten me this far. And I also believe help will present itself when I need it. This place wants to teach me what it knows."

She looked around the room, already enamored with the cabin. A small wooden box on the wall caught her eye. She stared at it for a moment before she realized what it was. "My grandfather's clock," she said in amazement. She lightly touched the dark cherry box. It was understated, a simple rectangle. The face and gears were protected by a glass window edged in one band of thin gold trim. No one would have ever given it a second look. That's why Arthur loved it. He took it in to his stable of broken clocks and knew he could get it running again. Once in good shape, he installed it on the wall in Cassie's house hoping it would help her be on time more. It didn't. There it remained in working order until the day he died. Then, knowing it's caretaker had moved on from this world, it stopped working in this one too.

She leaned in and heard its faint tick. "Any idea what time it is?" she asked Argan.

"I don't know, seven?" he said still trying to right himself.

The clock read five past seven. "Huh, it works," she said. She smiled feeling the connective thread to her grandfather. Argan walked over and put his hand on her waist.

"He would have loved you," she said to him.

He looked at Skylar and gave his neck another loud crack. "I'm ready to eat now."

32

Skylar came back to the cabin every day in the weeks leading up to the Equinox. A few times with Argan, most of the time alone. She studied the texts, and meditated on the sacred geometric images, hoping her enlightened DNA would decipher the codes. *Poring over someone else's words will never give you the wisdom found within your own heart*, the voice inside her whispered. She knew this voice. It was Magda's.

She was pleased with her sword wielding proficiency and actually enjoyed herself. It made her feel strong and confident. One evening as the sun was setting, she ran through her drills with her eyes closed. In her imagination she pictured Orks from Middle Earth, warriors of Aires, and the bitch mafia that made her life hell in High School. In the darkness of her mind she defeated every one. When she opened her eyes, she was startled to see Joshua standing in front of her. He had a luminescence and she could see the wall behind him. For a moment she thought his spirit had come to visit her but the image laughed and quickly vanished. Milicent took his place. Skylar lowered her sword and reached out to touch her, to see if she were *real* but she vanished into a fine mist. The mist swirled in the air, morphing into Joel, then Cassie, then Rachel. *Sylphs*, she thought. Skylar could never harm those she loved even in the privacy of her own imagination.

She closed her eyes and waited. She took in a deep breath. "Show yourself," she said into the air. She opened her eyes and a wafting cloud-like creature danced before her. It wasn't light and translucent like those she'd seen at Beatrice's house. This one was dark and thick with angry smoke. Skylar could feel it and knew this creature contained her own anger, no one else's.

The smoke recast itself into Joshua. She raised her sword and one appeared in his hand. They danced in a circle as she had done with Argan though this time she allowed the anger within her to swell. She lunged at Joshua, her sword held high. He met her with his own skill. They tussled for some time, never once did she falter or let up. She had thought she had forgiven him but had never released the anger underneath. She wanted him to feel her pain, her revenge for Rhia, Ronnie, and the baby she would never get to meet. She doubled back on top of him and sliced down the middle of his form. His smile faded and then so did he. The sylph returned as a wisp of a cloud within the room. It was less dense than before, slightly brighter but still held a visible darkness. It swirled like a small cyclone and Cassie appeared.

"I am not fighting my mother," she said to herself more than anyone else that may have been listening.

This sylph would not have taken her form had you not held the anger to make it so, Magda said in her head.

"Ugghh, no!" Skylar yelled.

Your honest emotions are the one thing your gifts cannot protect you from. Release this and move forward! Magda commanded.

Skylar refused to fight her mother, despite knowing it wasn't really her. She threw her sword on the pile and knelt on the floor. She expected tears but they never came. Instead she felt rage consume her and let out an angry, growling scream. She finally acknowledged her anger toward Cassie for abandoning her so young, leaving her behind to deal with the mountain of mysteries her life had become.

Her insides turned to fire that her body couldn't contain. The light that glowed green in her heart turned deep red. It traveled up to her eyes and her whole body released energy as powerful as the sun. The small cabin couldn't hold it. The pulse shook the walls and shattered every window.

The cedars back on campus all looked toward the beam of light shining from the forest. Argan dropped the wheelbarrow he was pushing and took off like a shot toward the cabin.

Skylar collapsed on the floor. She rolled onto her back barely conscious. Her eyes were open but she was unable to move any part of her body. As she stared upward at the circling smoke, truth seeped into her mind that had been in her heart all this time. *The one who walked before you sacrificed herself for the greater good. She could teach you no more in life. Her death will be your greatest teacher.* Cassie died so Skylar could live and complete this mission. It had been planned since the beginning of time. Cassie had passed her the torch from all the women before her. Now it was Skylar's turn.

Argan was there within minutes. He rushed through the open door as if he were entering a burning building. He held his arm over his mouth against the thick black smoke, making his way to the lifeless body on the floor.

"I need water," Skylar choked out.

He scooped up her limp body and carried her out of the cabin and into the clearing. He knelt down and placed her gently on the frozen ground. She propped herself up with one hand and took a few sips from his water bottle, looking back at the cabin. "Oh no," she groaned. "The windows are all broken."

"Yes, we'll fix that," he said. "You've discovered more of your power, I see."

"It turned out to be locked in my anger," she said. "But now, it's out. It's gone." She collapsed back onto the frozen ground. It was cool on her face. She turned on her back and looked up into the sky. She let her gaze relax to stare at the air a few feet from her face. The golden threads of time appeared. She reached out, this time no sting, but more of a strong tingle.

"The present," she whispered. "Do you see it?"

"I do," Argan said reverently. "It's reminding us of our timeline."

Skylar sat up and drank more water.

"Are you all right?" he asked. "I have a handful of cedars waiting for me back at the greenhouse."

"Sure, yes, the water helped. Thank you. I'll be here for a bit longer."

Argan left and Skylar watched the waves of the present mingle with the waves of the past in the air. Her vision softened and the clouds in the sky formed the face of a familiar horse. It was the long, statuesque face of Cheveyo. She missed him, and life back home. She thought of the enormous task ahead and wondered if given the chance, would she do all this again? With all of her anxious energy expended, all she had left was the resolve to try. She lay back and fell asleep on the frozen ground.

Skylar opened her eyes to see the setting sun. She had been asleep for hours but something stirred in the trees and she slowly sat up. A wolf sauntered into view. Skylar cocked her head and stared at the gray animal. She couldn't remember if wolves were dangerous. *Wake up, Sky! Yes, they are dangerous!* She wasn't frightened, she was curious. She had never seen a wolf in the wild. It was majestically beautiful.

"Her name is Neshoba," Milicent said from behind her. "It means *wolf* in Native American."

Skylar hopped up to greet Milicent. She ran her hands through her hair and wiped her face with her hand. She looked back toward the wolf. "She's magical," Skylar said. The wolf limped away and Skylar noticed her hind leg had a large gash.

"She has a hard time getting around but she has pups to feed," Milicent said. "So I bring them food from the Mess." She pulled out a brown paper plate of lunch food. "No one misses this slop."

"You're not scared she'll hurt you?" Skylar asked.

"Nah, she senses no fear in me so she isn't aggressive," Milicent said. "They feed on fear." She dumped the leftover stewed potatoes and vegetables on the ground. A moment later four furry little heads popped out of a hollowed out tree stump. Skylar's eyes lit up. They were as cute as any puppies she'd ever seen. They were so innocent and pure, scampering over to see what was for dinner. "They're probably the only vegan wolf pack on the planet," Milicent joked. "But it's all we've got."

Skylar enjoyed watching the wolf family eat and play in the last bit of sunshine. Neshoba kept her distance, studying the new human. Skylar made eye contact with the mother wolf and for a moment felt a connection to the animal. She was primal, raw, beautiful energy. She was Sophia, the power of nature in the wild.

"You're doing a good thing, taking care of them," Skylar said.

"They're helping me so much more," Milicent said. "Wolves have a fierce loyalty to their families, their loved ones. In ancient times they were guides for humans to the Underworld." Skylar's attention perked. "They know the way to freedom from the binds of our past, our pain. They know the way to the other side of it."

Neshoba limped quietly back to her den. Her pups followed. They were too young to hunt at night so this evening would be for sleeping.

"Will she heal to teach her pups to hunt?" Skylar asked.

"I'm not sure," Milicent said. "I've mixed together a paste of healing herbs for her leg but she won't let me close enough to apply it. If I can't treat it, I worry it'll get infected."

"Can I try?" Skylar asked.

Milicent's eyes widened. "It took me months to get this close to her. I can't imagine she'd let you touch her. You're crazy if you go near that den."

"I've been called crazy more than once," Skylar said.

Milicent opened her backpack and took out a jar of brown paste and handed it to Skylar. "Have at it," she said. "I'll use it on you when she bites you."

If I can connect to the vegetable kingdom, I've got to be able to do something with the animal one, Skylar thought. She walked the few yards to the den. The pups weren't quite ready to settle down and continued to tussle in a heap. Neshoba looked on as a proud mama. Skylar slowed a few feet before her. She could see the gash on her leg under bloodied fur and dirt. It looked deep. The jar had a small wooden spatula taped to its lid and Neshoba watched her intently but didn't move.

"You know why I'm here probably more than I do," Skylar said. "I want to help you. Will you let me help you?" She inched closer to the wolf. Neshoba let out a low growl, a warning not to come any closer.

"You know I mean no harm," Skylar said. "Your babies are busy. There's nothing for you to do. Please let me put this on your wound. It won't sting." She turned back to Milicent. "Is this going to sting?"

"Oh yeah," Milicent said.

"Shit," Skylar said to the sky. "Okay, so it's going to sting. You won't like it, but it'll heal you and then you'll be able to teach your babies to hunt. You want to do that, right?" She inched even closer until she could smell the scent of dog. She wrinkled her nose. Neshoba stood up and growled, this time showing her teeth. "Sorry!" Skylar said. "I'm more of a cat person but I do think you are exceptional." She reached the wooden spatula out with a generous amount of paste on one end. Neshoba circled three times and curled up in her pile of leaves. Skylar took it as an invitation and in one flick of her wrist, wiped most of the paste onto the wolf's cut. Neshoba bit into the air, just missing Skylar's hand but she didn't get up. Skylar quickly backed away. "I'm sorry again that it'll sting." She walked backwards and stood next to a stunned Milicent. The two girls watched. Neshoba stilled, staring at the cut that now fizzed with medicine. She gave it one lick and then stood up, shaking her head. Foam formed at the sides of her mouth as she wretched a few times.

"It tastes abhorrent," Milicent said.

"At least it's giving the paste some time to work," Skylar said optimistically. After a few minutes the wolf settled back down in her leaves.

"Let's leave her alone," Milicent said. "That's all we can do for now." Skylar nodded and they started on their way back to campus. "That was impressive. On your part and hers."

"I'm studying to be a vet," Skylar said. "Maybe I'll specialize in wildlife or something. I've been studying horses up until now."

"Have you visited the paddocks here?" Milicent asked, almost friendly. "Our horses are wonderful."

"You know, I haven't had a chance. I'll make it a point to do that soon."

They continued through the thicket of trees and came to the barrier, but from the opposite side. "I thought no one could pass the barrier?" Skylar asked.

"You did," Milicent said, looking straight ahead. "Speaking of barriers, have you found a way in yet?"

"In?" Skylar played dumb knowing Milicent would see right through her.

"Under the lake."

"No. I got down pretty far but didn't see a way in. It all looked so dead, from a time long ago."

"That's because you were without a guide. No doors to the Underworld will open without a guide. Like Anubis," Milicent said. "I love Egyptian writing. Even working on a few of their spells."

"Anything working for you?" In an instant, Skylar knew she went too far. "Sorry. You mentioned the wolves before. Do you think Neshoba knows the way *in*? Although she can't really swim." She answered her own question.

"I have seen stranger things for sure," Milicent said. "Start bringing her regular meals and see where it takes you."

34

Present Day: Milicent sat in her office and stared at the red book. She hated this book and everything it represented. For as much as Devlin turned the other way from her occult dealings, she did the same, pretending his life as a mason didn't exist. She could get on board with so many of their ideals, except one: no women. Their secret societies claimed to know the mysteries of the universe but how could they be so shortsighted as to exclude a vital part of that mystery—the feminine.

Devlin had his own predictions for the future of America and foolishly put them on paper. Oral tradition was the key to secret keeping. No one could track or expose a spoken word. The written word on the other hand, left a trail and Milicent was staring at it. She still wasn't convinced she'd do anything with it. She'd had it for over two weeks with no interest to act. She promised Ocean nothing and they hadn't reached the point of no return . . . yet.

A quick knock on her office door preceded Noah entering with a team of deliverymen. Her new furniture had arrived. "This way," he directed the men around her office. In less than ten minutes she had two leather couches in dark Byzantium, two herringbone club chairs in the palest lilac, and four sustainably harvested teak driftwood tables floating on a one-of-a-kind plum Persian rug in the middle of the room. The men left as quickly as they came, and Noah started primping yellow pillows.

"Yellow?" Milicent asked, one eyebrow raised.

"It couldn't all be purple or I was going to lose my mind. This complements it so well, don't you think?" He stood waiting for feedback.

"I don't hate it," she said. He beamed from her approval.

He clicked on the wall panel TV and gave her a side-glance. "I know you loath the TV but I have to check the entertainment report. *Inside D.C.* is running a feature on me! Can you believe it? Me! Well, really *you* and my road to the White House as your assistant but even still . . . " his words trailed as the TV screen came to life. "I'll mute until my segment comes on." He clicked the mute button and left the remote on her desk to return to his pillows.

He kept checking the screen every minute or so, knowing any longer and he'd miss it completely. His feature was only about thirty seconds long. After a dozen times of lifting his head, an image of Joshua caught his attention. "Mil, your boy's on," he said, unmuting the TV.

The entertainment anchor was halfway through his report. . . . "Joshua Rider is dead at age twenty-seven."

Noah froze and looked up at Milicent. The news was still ringing in the air when Wren came rushing in.

"Mrs. Grayer, I know you don't watch the news . . ." she saw the TV on and stopped. "I'm so sorry. I know he was a big part of your campaign. We'll have to prepare a statement and I assume you'll want to go to the funeral. I'll find out who's in charge of that."

Milicent stood staring blankly at the TV, now running Noah's segment. "I am," she said.

Noah took Milicent's hand, ignoring his thirty seconds of fame. "I'm here for you," he said.

Milicent looked between her Chief of Staff and her assistant, both eager to help her in any way possible. "Thank you both," she said, snapping back into the present moment. "I need a few minutes alone."

"Of course," Noah said, squeezing her hand before he and Wren walked out. Once on the other side of the door, they looked at each other with a mix of sympathy and confusion. Before either of them said a word, Milicent came charging out in angry stilettos. She blew past them and down the hall.

35

Milicent stormed into the Residence. "Devlin, Joshua's dead," she announced, her voice shaky but loud.

Devlin had his nose buried in a newspaper in a rare moment of free time. "Joshua who?" he asked without looking up.

"Rider, dear," she seethed through gritted teeth. "Remember, he helped you get elected to this fucking freak show?"

He looked up from his paper and cleared his throat. "Oh, of course, Millie what was I thinking. I'm sorry to hear that. He was so useful."

"Yes, he was," she said, walking to the wall of windows. With glazy eyes, she stared out at the handful of gardeners tending to the vibrant flowers below. It was a completely normal day in their completely normal lives and she hated them for it. She turned back and stared at Devlin. "His heart gave out in that coma."

"Huh," he said, returning to his paper.

Heavy lines appeared in her forehead. "I want to remind you that this all started with a drug overdose," she said, laying her hand on his paper, effectively stopping him from reading it. "Where are we with the regulation bill?" she forced him to look at her.

"Not again, Mil. I don't have energy to discuss Pharma with you."

"Dev, the misuse of prescription drugs in this country has spiraled out of control. You of all people recognize this. What are you doing about it?"

"Millie, I have a lot of people to answer to in this job," he said. "It's harder to get things done than I thought."

"You can't or won't? You have great power in two worlds, Dev. You can fix this."

"Do you know how deep Big Pharma goes?" he asked.

"He's DEAD!" she shouted. "It doesn't get deeper than dead."

He put down his newspaper and got out of his chair. "You don't give a shit about drug reform. What's the real issue here?" He stood waiting.

Her voice lowered. "I hate inadequacy."

He shook his head and gathered his things to head out. "I'm not rehashing this, Mil," he said. "Maybe next term."

"Next term? There's plenty of this term left." She followed him to the door. "I'm sorry you feel that way," she said, shutting the door behind him.

Milicent never went to bed that night and started with fresh coffee around 4:00 a.m. By six, Noah was driving her crazy with his frequent check-ins until she instructed him to be her press representative. The idea made Wren shudder but Milicent didn't care. She wouldn't be making a public appearance at all that day.

She broke her own rule and turned on the television. The morning news shows were already splashing the headlines of Joshua's death and one in particular was advertising an in-depth content piece on his connection to the Grayers. Milicent faltered momentarily. She was adept at hiding her tracks and was confident their history was well hidden.

A knock at the door drew her away from the television. "Ma'am, Madam Vice President to see you," the staff member said.

"Show her in," Milicent said, returning her focus to the TV. Her hand traveled to her neck and she started to scratch. "Not this again!" she thundered to the empty room.

Without so much as a "good morning", the V.P. made the reason for her visit crystal clear. "How confident are you that this won't come out?" Mica asked toward Milicent's turned back.

Milicent whirred around. "Very," she said.

"He was more than a ghost," Mica said. "And you paraded him around like a trophy. If your *interests* in him come out, you better be prepared to do damage control."

"Is that all?" Milicent asked emotionless.

"For now," Mica said. She turned on her heels and left.

36

The next afternoon, Skylar made the trek to the wolf's den with leftovers from her lunch run. Neshoba was laying in the sunlight as the pups wrestled in a heap.

"Hello Neshoba." Skylar approached her with the food ready to go. She examined her leg. The gash had a slight sheen, healing a bit overnight. "Your leg looks better. I'll see if Milicent has more salve. One more time should do it." She looked at the pups. "They'll be catching squirrels in no time." Skylar sat down a safe distance away and watched them eat. She could appreciate Milicent's affinity for them. They had a pecking order but Skylar also watched the biggest pup guard the food for the smallest. He was so much larger than the others, Skylar had named him Bear.

"So I'm hoping for a favor," Skylar said after their bellies were full. She couldn't believe how nervous she was asking the wolf for help. "I know water's not your thing but I thought you might know the way under the lake. You see I'm running out of time and . . ." She stopped mid-sentence sensing the uselessness of words. She bowed her head instead. When she picked her head up, the wolf was staring at her intently. Their eyes met and Skylar connected again to the spirit of the earth, the spirit of Sophia. She felt the energy creeping into her own veins. Neshoba lived in a fierce, wild truth, the vitality of now and the magnificence of this beast was completely humbling. The wolf looked away and the connection was broken. She went back to grooming in the sun.

Skylar brought the family dinner the following day. The gash had healed well overnight and the pups were already bigger than the day before.

"You are looking good. You'll teach them to hunt soon? I won't always be here to bring you meals. And Milicent is leaving soon too." She glanced at the pups. Their circle of play had expanded dangerously close to the edge of the cliff.

"Neshoba, your pup!" she couldn't get the words out before the littlest one started over the edge. Right before he fell, Bear bit him on the ruff of his neck and tossed him to safety. The loose pebbles gave out under his feet and he fell over the side with a yelp.

"No!" Skylar ran to the edge with Neshoba. They both peered into the water. "No!" Skylar repeated. She threw off her jacket and sneakers and jumped off the cliff and into the water. When she came to the top, she searched for Bear.

"Bear!" she yelled. She dove in and out of the columns of steam. "Vivienne, Ocean, someone help me!" She searched above and below the water. The pup was nowhere in sight but she refused to stop looking.

After a long while, she pulled herself to shore, hoping a different vantage point would help. She looked up to the top of the cliff. Neshoba stared down at her, then retreated away from the edge with the remaining pups. Skylar made her way back to the top of the cliff and looked down at the water below. No Bear.

She walked back and knelt before Neshoba. "I'm so sorry, mama," she bowed her head and cried. "I'm so sorry." Neshoba lay next to Skylar and put her head on the ground. There they sat in silence until sunset.

The wind picked up at moonrise and Skylar felt the chill of her wet clothes in the cold air. Neshoba got up and walked to the edge of the cliff. She looked over and then back at Skylar. *Follow that path. I cannot go but you have a guide now.* Skylar looked down at the lake and then back at Neshoba. Without a thought, she jumped back in. The water was warm on her cold skin and the salt concentration soothed her swollen eyes. Under the water, her perception of the lake had transformed. She could see the crystalline structure of each droplet of water. She was now swimming in the womb of creation, each molecule teeming with potential for life. The water was home and freedom, love and surrender, forgiveness and certainty all at once. It was a return to a love she felt was there all along. The clouds had to lift from her head for her to remember it. It was the wonder of nature.

She twirled and danced in the water and swam with great ease. For a moment, she had forgotten why she was there. And then she saw him. Bear was sitting at the water's edge in perfect stillness. He had transformed into a magnificent full-grown wolf but she still recognized him. He had the body of a beast but his eyes were human and penetrating. He watched her every move. She swam toward him but before she reached him, he got up and walked into the water. He submerged and she followed. *How odd it is to see this dog underwater,* she thought, swimming behind him.

I am not dog, he replied in her mind.

Sorry, she replied back.

He went deeper and her concern for him grew.

I am Spirit, immortal. No fear. She followed him onward, deeper still. Skylar waited for the moment when she would need air but it never came. Bear slowed at the bottom of the lakebed where the circle of stone figures greeted them.

This is it, Skylar thought. *This is the way in.*

This is as far as I go, Bear said. *You go rest of way.*

Yes, but how do I . . . she turned and he was turning back.

You have key to unlock stones and enter, he said.

His body started to fade into the darkness of the water. *Key? What key?* She patted her empty pockets. *Wait!* she screamed in her head. He had given the ultimate sacrifice, his life, to help her. He faded completely into the black water. *Thank you my friend,* she said.

She studied the figures, each at least ten feet high. There were seven. They sat tall on thrones of polished white ashlar, impenetrable. All were birds but all were different. Three were doves, each with distinguishing features, representing wind, water, and fire. Between the doves sat an owl, an ibis, an eagle, and a vulture. All had wings swept back behind them.

She touched the closest figure, the dove of fire, her wings sharp like flames. The dove was solid and smooth. No door to be found. She swam around each one unable to find anything resembling an entrance. When more time had passed, she swam between the eagle and the vulture and stood in the middle of the circle.

Once in the middle, a current picked up and circled around her feet. It spiraled up and images formed in the water; star gates, constellations, and planets appeared as if it were the night sky. Sacred geometric shapes and the concentric circles of the flower of life all swirled in the current. Skylar now stood in the wisdom circle of the great Goddess. Sand kicked up on the lake floor and sparkles of light shone underneath. Skylar knelt down and brushed over the beaming pinholes. From under the sand, three entwined rings of light emerged. In each ring sat a letter of the three Great Mothers—Aleph, Mem, Shin—Air, Water, Fire. Skylar felt the pulse in her heart and didn't have to look down to know the light within her chest had come to life. Her heart was the key to gain entrance to the Underworld.

The stone figures rumbled and the slightest movement stirred in their chests. They began to breathe. In one fluid motion, they all stepped to the right. Their wings fanned out, each touching the other, creating a wall of magnificent lighted stone. Once sealed tight, the wall became a vortex, draining out its contents of water into the rest of the lake. As the water drained, the light from the letters on the lake floor grew brighter. Skylar could now breathe air yet she looked at the water circling above her.

When all the water had drained from the circle, she heard an unfamiliar singsong voice call her name. "Sky-lar . . ." She looked toward the voice. No one was there but now she could see a door in the wing of the mighty eagle. The door was made of the same glistening stone as the great bird. Many of the geometric shapes she saw in the water current were carved into its border. On either side flanked two identical angel warriors carved from a pearlescent stone. The angels had an ominous appearance, their faces stern.

She felt the door. With no handle, she gave it a push. It opened with ease and a rush of air sucked her slightly forward and across the threshold. She took a deep breath. *This was it.* This was the reason she was here at Silverwood, here in the past. She got up her courage and stepped through.

The room was uncomfortably cold and completely dark. As her wet clothes froze to her skin, she knew she couldn't linger long. Unsure of her next move, she stood listening to the whistle of the wind coming into the room from the open door behind her. She closed her eyes hoping to connect to Magda or some help somewhere but when she did, the help that came was her own. With her eyes shut, she could see the interior of the room. It wasn't a room at all, but a cave of ice. The walls were thick and clear and curved up over her head and down the other side. The white puffs of air coming out of her mouth morphed into the birds from the circle. Each one beckoned her to move onward. Her only option was to follow them . . . with her eyes closed. No matter how daunting this journey or this cave was, she had to keep going.

The birds led her to the other end, which narrowed into a passageway of ice. They stopped there and motioned for her to go through. She stepped forward and took one last look behind her. The birds faded back into wisps of air and vanished.

Once through the passageway, she could no longer see with closed eyes. She felt warmth on her face and her clothes began to melt. She opened her eyes to a sun so bright, again she was left in the dark. She had to laugh, figuring this was part of it all. When her eyes adjusted, she looked down and noticed an iridescent quality to her skin. At first glance it looked like fine powder. She dusted it and examined it on her fingers. It shimmered with tiny specks of light. The more she dusted, the more it returned. It also covered her clothes, now almost dry. She dusted a few more times and then gave up trying to get it off. Around her, lush green foliage abounded. For all she knew, she could have been on a tropical island.

"Welcome, Skylar," the same melodic voice said from off her left.

Skylar turned to a tall voluptuous woman with a long dark braid woven with gold thread wrapped high above her head. A triple tower-like tiara covered the braids and a large blue crystal shone from the middle of her forehead, not held in place by anything Skylar could see. "Are you all right?" she asked.

"I'm not sure yet," Skylar said uneasily. She dusted her hands together but still had no luck removing the luminescent dust.

"It's *lucina*. It won't come off. You don't belong here so it's protecting you from our sun. If you didn't have it, you would be incinerated in seconds." After that information, Skylar stopped trying to dust it off.

"I am Diana," she said with a kind smile. Her demeanor took Skylar aback. She assumed the Goddess of the Underworld would be . . . formidable, at the very least, cranky. As she looked around, it seemed nothing here was as Skylar had expected. There was no darkness, no misery, no fearful souls she saw at the arena in June.

"Hi," Skylar said bewildered.

"You were expecting doom and gloom, I see," Diana said. "In the third dimension, your beliefs create your reality. Everyone thinks we live in a state of misery here. So when you have a small glimpse into our world, that's what you see. But that's not true. It isn't unpleasant at all." Skylar studied Diana. She was stunning, draped in a purple gown with an effulgent quality. Her skin shimmered as well, although the light seemed to come from within, not rest on top.

Skylar heard a slow drum in the distance. It was soothing yet nagged at her just the same. "I have to learn something only you can teach me," she blurted. Although things weren't scary or bleak here, an uneasy feeling stirred inside her making her anxious.

Diana smiled but her eyes were empty. *Her spirit is missing,* Skylar realized. Ocean had told her each of our souls contains a spirit. The soul is the feminine part of the equation; the spirit is the masculine. The soul receives; the spirit takes action. Diana had no spirit. She was completely female and Skylar could see the darkest part of the female in Diana's eyes.

The souls Skylar saw in the pit at the arena still had their spirits, their fears heightened as they were preparing to leave the physical world. That was the cause of their pain and chaos. Once a soul's spirit is removed, they find peace.

"Follow me," Diana walked down a sandy path between two trees with large green fronds. Her feet were decorated in jeweled roping tied to simple sandals.

Above their heads, a bolt of lightning flashed by. Skylar ducked.

"Telluric currents," Diana said, waving them off. "They are from your sun's electrical discharge. Your earth's core absorbs that energy and we see it here as lighting in our sky, even with the bright sun."

The sandy path led to a maze of buildings along a large body of water Skylar assumed was still Vivienne's lake, but she couldn't be sure. There was no land on the other side. The buildings were all white stone with abundant gold accents, capstones and pillars, strikingly similar to Ancient Egypt. Gold was plentiful, so much so, a wide river of the ore snaked between the buildings.

Ordinary people milled around doing ordinary things within the labyrinth. The only distinguishing characteristic was a type of uniform they all wore. Pebble colored, not gray, not brown, they were all the same. Skylar froze as a woman walked by with a lion tight to her side. She thought of Tamsyn and wished she had listened more closely to her rant about the lions.

"Am I really inside the earth?" Skylar asked, trying to take it all in. "Or on another dimensional plane?"

"Both," Diana said. "The interior of the third-dimensional earth has been well traveled by those that control your world. Cities such as this are not uncommon, although they serve a different purpose. Many were created as protection from disaster for your officials. Some were created to conduct experiments unnoticed. Some were devised to house great military complexes. None of these are fitting for our great Mother Earth. She has been repeatedly raped by the atrocities of man, fools that they are. They would be nothing without her yet force her to suffer at the hands of their ignorance."

They walked up the steps of a magnificent cathedral. It was gothic and pristinely white, almost ghostly. Its large archway led to a vibrant open-air courtyard. More people were mulling around, some working, and some leisurely conversing at tables overflowing with food.

"Cheese!" Skylar exclaimed staring at the food tables. Among the fruits and vegetables sat many broken wheels of orange and yellow cheeses. Large loaves of bread also dotted the table among the abundant plates of various cuts of meat. Skylar wasn't sure if she were elated or repulsed. It hadn't been that long since she'd been meat-free but her attitude seemed to have already changed.

"Are you hungry?" Diana asked. Skylar *was* hungry but she thought it odd to be considering eating food in this strange world. She wasn't quite that comfortable. "Thank you, I will pass for now," she said.

She followed Diana through another entryway to what appeared to be a throne room with an open ceiling to the sky. The river of gold pooled into a small lake before two massive seats made of green marble. An impressive wall of yellow citrine drew her attention. It pulsed with its own energy and Skylar had to squint to look at it. Diana walked up a few broad steps and sat on one of the seats. She gestured for Skylar to sit next to her.

"You want me to sit on a throne?" Skylar asked.

"It's just a chair, Skylar. And it's the only way you can see what happened," Diana said.

Skylar nodded and made her way to the seat beside Diana. Hieroglyphic-like illustrations covered the wall in front of them. They were vibrant, yet Skylar got the sense they had been there before time began. The images moved around the wall, telling a story as Diana spoke.

"Skylar, at the time of your conception, a great surge of energy from the sun was making its way toward earth. For the nine months of your gestation, exceptional things were happening to the planet with this influx of energy. Preparations were being made for the next evolutionary step for mankind. Now, twenty-two years later, we have reached the peak of that energy influx. This is why so many acts of insanity are occurring. As the vibration of earth rises, those that cannot handle it, literally go insane. Those in power in your world know this. They have created their underground cities, yes, but all the while looking . . . for this." She gestured to the great citrine wall. "This holds the answer to every puzzle. The memory of earth, the heart of Sophia, the heart of every human. They are all connected."

The pictures on the wall showed a young girl wearing a crown of gems holding the Book of Sophia. A chill ran up the back of Skylar's head; she knew *she* was that young girl.

"But Skylar, it goes much deeper than that. The Akasha holds our myths, our archetypes, and our patterns of behavior. It contains the inspiration for our dreams. This is where imagination lives. And in the collective imagination sits all possibility for human potential."

"Sophia," Skylar choked the tears back. She took her eyes off of the pictures to look at the great wall of yellow rock. Craggy branches of gold running through it framed a ten-foot tablet. Endless words in Sanskrit clicked by, recording the real time memories as life continued above. Skylar sat in awe, this was the Book of Sophia magnified beyond understanding.

"Your world is feeling the pressures of the end of the age of patriarchy. Dark forces are clamoring to find this wall. And if they do . . ." Diana's eyes darkened to black, her face paled, whiter than any ghost. "They will have complete control over the collective imagination, all dreams, all potential for humankind."

"That can't be possible," Skylar whispered.

"Oh, it is. And it is dangerously close to happening. Sophia is trying to return to earth but only can if this great wall is whole. Humanity is called to remember its divinity."

"That's why I'm here. I'm supposed to restore a memory," Skylar said.

"Which one?" Diana gestured to the wall. Pockets of holes darkened on cue to reveal the extent of its splintering.

Seeing so many holes, Skylar's confidence faltered. "I have to remind women who they really are."

Diana scoffed. "One person can't do that. Everyone's on their own for personal enlightenment. But take your best shot."

Skylar paused. She had more faith than Diana. She also knew that when we recover our strength, we can help others in finding their own. Yet here in this strange land, she didn't know what she was supposed to do. She got up and walked to the citrine wall placing her hand in one of the holes. At first, she felt nothing but closed her eyes and waited. Then she heard it.

An Underworld repressed . . . denial of what is within the earth, what is within the female, created this world. Time for change is at hand. Lead others out of the hell of fear. Expose the shadow, let the shadow be witnessed.

"Did you hear that?" Skylar asked.

"Yes, let the shadow be witnessed," Diana whispered. "It's been centuries since those words have been uttered here."

"What does it mean?" Skylar asked.

"The return of the Dark Madonna," Diana said.

On the wall, the Goddess Kali appeared. Her skin was dark, blue in color, and her eyes, red. She was fierce. But through her appearance, compassion showed as her true strength. She was protector of the young girl, the cosmic mother.

"She is the sacredness of the dark. She calls us to be one with nature, to our own divinity, our own depths. They are all the same thing."

The girl on the wall aged into a young woman. She stood between two mature women. "Know this about your pain, you will never be made whole unless you embrace the one who hurt you."

Skylar knew Diana was referring to Rachel.

"Do not wallow in sorrow too long. The Dark Madonna also encourages celebration. She is a part of Sophia and her passion for life and its bounty. She appears in Ancient Egypt as the Goddess Maat, the keeper of justice, balance, and compassion."

On the wall in hieroglyphic images, the golden scales of justice appeared next to the Goddess Maat. She was holding one large ostrich feather. Diana pointed to the same scales in the room. They were small and could be easily missed, sitting on a stone pedestal next to the citrine wall.

"We keep the fires of Maat alive here," Diana said. "Those are our own scales of justice used to determine the fate of each soul. The souls are weighed against the feather of truth. If they are balanced, the soul ascends. If it is out of balance, it must return to your world to try again."

"Try what?" Skylar asked.

"To live with compassion and forgiveness in their heart," Diana said. "That is the reason for life." Diana studied her. "I was there when you were born. I saw your path, your purpose."

"How is that possible?"

"The great tablet shows all," Diana said. "I can relive any moment I wish." She lowered her head. Skylar realized Diana would never make any new memories of her own. She could only protect those created by others.

"That is the ultimate sacrifice," Skylar said. "You can't make your own memories."

"No. But the Great Mothers depend on all of us to fulfill our part of the divine plan. We are all making sacrifices. This is mine. Returning the memory is not your only purpose here," Diana said. "You need to see something else." She walked Skylar to the tablet and touched a corner. An image appeared in the airwaves. It was the night Diana died. She was angry at her father, having just learned about his affair with Rachel's mother. The image showed Diana careening down a windy New England road in the dark. A young buck leapt out from the woods and she swerved into oncoming traffic. She hit a small car head on. Diana was still alive. The point of view shifted and Skylar saw inside the other car. A young woman with dark skin held the hand of a young Asian man. They were dead on impact. A lump formed in Skylar's throat. It was Suki's parents.

"I . . . I don't know what to say," Skylar said.

Diana touched the wall again and the image disappeared.

"We all have our regrets in life. This one is mine," Diana said. "My only hope for you is that your regrets are small."

Skylar nodded. Still at a loss for words, she looked around to take in more of her surroundings. Another river ran through the cathedral, this one of thick silver. Through the archway, Skylar could see people walking among lions, going about their daily tasks. The lions were uncharacteristically benign.

"Those great cats are not the same wild creatures you are accustomed to," Diana said. "They are in commune with us and we work together for a common goal. We all want the return of the Golden Age of Shambhala."

"If I succeed, will you come back to our dimension? To our world?" Skylar asked. "The way Milicent wanted?"

"My sister's actions come from a very conflicted place," Diana said. "I can't defend her but I understand. She conjured all of that sorcery, interfering with the divine plan of things. And that's why it didn't work. Nothing interferes with the divine plan. But Milicent always felt she was above everyone else."

"She still does," Skylar said.

"It's not Rachel's fault I'm here," Diana said. "I know Milicent believes that, but I have my own purpose. I am the keeper of the Akasha now," she said proudly. "I was never coming back. Why would I want to? I have too much work here. The time for the Underworld has come. *When* you succeed, it won't be the end of things, only the beginning. This is where the healing of the world takes place, on a global and individual level. Only exposing the shadow can anyone truly heal. Much of the healing of the Akasha happens in the individual human heart. Through forgiveness of others, selfless acts of service, and a willingness to accept others as they are, the great memory of earth will be restored."

Skylar started to see the plan crystallize in her mind. There was no magic formula, no shortcut. Each one of us had to do the work in the arena of our own life to heal our shadow, forgive our transgressions and live with an open heart.

"Skylar, the earth is behind schedule. The dark forces that have been in control have delayed the spiritual progress of most humans. Returning the memory will break the bonds of illusion and get everyone back on the right path."

"Any suggestions on how to do that?" Skylar asked.

A brilliant white light started toward them from the doorway. It was too bright for Skylar to make out the figure behind it. Slowly, the form of a tall man appeared within the light.

"Diana, you didn't tell me our guest arrived," said the voice of an angel.

"You don't need an announcement," Diana said.

"Welcome, Skylar. I hear you are completing my mission. I am so happy," he said. His face took shape into form. He was magnificently beautiful with white flowing hair, thick as Cheveyo's mane. His skin was dark, his eyes ice blue. He was eternal yet didn't appear older than thirty. "I am Lucifer." He extended his hand and when they touched, a bolt of energy shot from her hand to her heart and out to every cell in her body. She could feel the pulse in her fingertips and the hair on her arms rose up. All of the blood rushed to the surface of her skin. She was alive with electricity.

As he held her hand, Skylar saw a simple rock in her minds eye, *her* rock that she had given to Argan all those years ago. In its core, a solid mass of yellow sat protected from time's abuse.

Skylar gasped. "My rock," she whispered.

Lucifer smiled and released her hand.

"My rock!" She shouted. "That is the memory that will heal this wall!" She felt she should bow or kneel. She froze not able to do either. "Thank you. Why are you helping me?" she asked.

"I am the bringer of light," he said wryly. "Everyone forgets that." He turned without another word and disappeared.

Skylar looked at Diana. "I need to go now," she said with urgency. "I know where the rock is. I'll come back." She was now desperate to return home. She started for the door.

"Don't go yet," Diana said. "There's more to see."

Skylar hopped from one foot to the other, overcome with nervous energy to get home but she reluctantly followed Diana along the opposite end of the river. She looked behind her, hoping to get another glimpse of Lucifer. He had burned a desire on her brain she couldn't name.

"He has that effect on women," Diana said reading her energy. "He invented the idea of idol worship." Skylar blushed. "You are human, Skylar. Do not feel shame for your desires. Rejoice in them. They are pleasures of your birthright." The river led them outside of the throne room into a massive garden bathed in sunlight. It was eerily familiar, resembling the etheric realm she visited with Magda. In the center of the garden stood the familiar tree of Great Mothers. This one teamed with life and terrestrial energy. Its trunk was carved with many faces that appeared to be living as a part of the tree. The details were quite intricate and if Skylar stared long enough, she was sure they were breathing. Even in the Underworld, the tree of the Great Mothers flourished. It seemed Ocean's tree was the only one steeped in death.

"This is the river Mnemosyne," Diana said. "It grants eternal remembrance to those brave enough to take a sip." Its opaque, Aurelian water flowed under a great crystal structure that reminded Skylar of Ocean's grotto but more immense than she could ever imagine a crystal to be, stretching beyond her scope of vision.

"This crystal goes on for over a thousand miles," Diana said. "It is the true memory of earth, locked in iron core crystal."

Skylar was completely confused. "Then what was the citrine wall?"

"More of a mainframe, if you will. A place of contact," Diana said. "This great crystal would be impossible to navigate."

Skylar stretched to see the end but knew she couldn't. She looked around at all of the beauty in her surroundings. "This isn't the hell we've been taught," she said.

"This isn't hell. It's the Underworld," Diana said.

"I should be getting back. I know where my stone is. I will return soon and then we can get to work."

"You must return on the Equinox," Diana said. "The energies will be favorable then. Another time and I can't guarantee it will work."

"But that's in three days," Skylar's face fell.

"Then make haste," Diana said. She walked Skylar back through the throne room and the courtyard full of people.

Skylar stepped up her pace on her way back to the ice cave.

"No children?" she asked, looking around at only adults in the Underworld.

"No children," Diana said. "Their souls go straight back to heaven. There's no rust to work off."

That made sense to Skylar. They approached the cave entrance and she did a double take, recognizing a familiar head of thick silver hair.

"Grandpa?" she asked in amazement. The head turned and sure enough, belonged to Arthur. "What are you doing here?"

"Hey kiddo," Arthur said smiling, not at all fazed to see Skylar. "This is where they send me between incarnations. You knew I was a snowbird."

She rushed him with a bear hug embrace. "This is a little farther south than Florida," she said over his shoulder. He looked the same as always, with plump, rosy cheeks and a belly fit for Santa Claus.

"But what are *you* doing here?" he asked.

"Oh, I'm on a quest," she said casually.

"A quest?" he raised his brow.

"Yup." She didn't want to go into details. He would be mad at Beatrice.

"That grandmother of yours likes to play god," he said.

"Yes, I know but here we are," she said, playing it all down. "When are you going back . . . up?"

"Couple weeks, I get to do it all over again," he said with a sigh.

"You'll return to Nana. You don't seem happy."

"I love her, really, I do," he said. "But my lifetimes have lacked meaning for centuries. We have fun, sure, but I have no purpose on earth and I'm restless. And to be honest, I've grown tired of the whole process."

Skylar could see his point. "I understand. That's why I'm

here. It's my purpose." She smiled. It really was. "I don't want to leave you but I need to go now. I have to go get a missing piece to my puzzle. But I'll be back soon. How do I find you again?"

"I'll be waiting right here," he said. She hugged him tight and stepped into the passageway of the ice cave. She was not eager to retrace her steps but she didn't have a choice.

Diana called to her. "Tell my sister she's looking in the wrong place to find her answers. And bring reinforcements back with you. You're going to need them."

37

Coming out of the lake as quickly as possible, Skylar started running. She ran through the trees in the frigid night air, already accustomed to her freezing wet skin. She didn't stop until she reached Argan's cabin. He had recently moved to a single, as he was getting no sleep in the dormitory. She had no idea of the time but was certain it was after curfew. She stopped herself from banging on his door and peered through the curtained window.

"Looking for me?" he asked behind her.

She jumped and whirred around to face him, her wet hair smacking her in the eye.

"Midnight swim?" he asked.

"Argan, where is the rock I gave you?" she asked frantically. "I need that rock! It's the answer to everything."

He turned the doorknob and walked in. "You mean the magic rock, from when we were kids?"

"How many rocks have I given you in our lifetime?" she asked following him inside. His cabin was identical to hers but had one bed instead of two.

"It's back home, Sky. Sorry, I don't carry it at all times," he said.

Her shoulders sunk. "We're going to have to leave," she said. "I need that rock right away."

"Right away?" he repeated. "Who knows how long it will take to get back home. And it's pretty late to travel."

"It's the answer, Argan! It's the memory I need to return to the Akasha!"

"And what happens then?" he asked.

She paused. She didn't know. For all she knew it could mean the cosmos would implode and she'd be personally responsible for the end of civilization.

"Sky, I'd wait on the impulsive actions for just a second. Think about all of this. What is the end goal here?"

"The Akasha is missing a vital memory. I will return it and the world can heal."

"And then what?" his voice rose. "Sky, I'm right there with you, really I am. I came this far, didn't I? But restoring this memory will mean the altering of human evolution. Is that what you really want to do?"

Her mood shifted. "You said you were ready to do what it takes to help me," she said, her anger rising.

"Yes, I said that."

"And you're right. I don't know what will happen. But this task was given to me, by the Great Mothers of the whole freakin' world! I can't ignore that. And I can't run from it either. I have to see this through. I promised my mother. Both of them. There is no going back for me. I can't ask you to continue. You can take me home and I'll come back alone. I'll let you know when I've sufficiently saved the world."

He studied her and a smile crept onto his lips.

"What?" she asked, annoyed. "Why are you looking at me like that?"

"There's that *fire* I was looking for," he said.

"I'm of *water* lineage," she said.

"It's *fire* in your heart though, right?" he smiled.

"So you were just screwing with me?" she asked. "I don't like it."

"You are soaking," he said through a chuckle. He brushed her wet hair off of her shoulder. "And we aren't going anywhere until morning light."

He stared at her with his enormous green eyes and she shook her head.

"What?" he asked.

"Stop being so ridiculously good looking," she said. "I'm trying to be mad at you."

He wrinkled his nose to make a funny face.

"Better, thanks," she said.

He rummaged through a drawer and pulled out a pair of sweat pants and his Rosen T-shirt.

"You can change into these." He threw them at her and she caught them at her belly.

"Thanks," she said. She walked into the bathroom and started changing behind a partially closed door. She was happy to peel off her wet shirt and pants. Standing in the bright bathroom, she could see Argan through the crack of the open door. He glanced up at her and stared unapologetically for a moment, then turned away. She continued to watch him, waiting to dress. He walked back to his chest of drawers and stopped short of opening the top drawer. He seemed to be wrestling with something in his head.

She walked out of the bathroom, still not dressed in the clothes he gave her. "What is it, Argan?" she asked. "Is that cat causing you trouble?" She smiled and he shook his head. "What aren't you telling me?"

He froze where he stood. She reached out and touched his face with her fingers. She traced the line of his jaw and rested her hand on his chest. "You are so handsome, Argan. Yet I still see the boy I met when I was eleven. You're timeless and I'm in awe of you."

He took her hand to remove it from his body, but he paused and held it. He stared into her eyes so long she thought for sure she would lose her nerve. But she didn't. She leaned in and slipped her other hand around the back of his neck and drew his face close to hers. And he let her. Her lips grazed his and she waited, wanting to enjoy this moment between them. She needed nothing more than this. She felt his love for her in his eyes, in his heart, in his soul. She needed nothing else to prove that he loved her with his whole being.

Their kiss deepened and Argan let go of all of his hesitation, engulfing her in his strong arms. She took him into her mouth with urgency and need, quenching a desire she dared not admit until now.

He met her desire with a surprising fierceness. She wanted to give herself to this man who loved her, imperfections and all. There was no room for pretenses, no room for insecurity. She was exposed but knew it was worth the cost of letting him really see her, letting him in behind that door.

She shivered, sure it was from his touch and not her wet underwear. He slipped his hand under the strap of her camisole and it fell on her shoulder.

"Skylar, I—" he started but Skylar shook her head.

"Please," she said, her eyes pleading. "I need you, Argan." She so desperately wanted to make him understand. The only way she could begin to convey it was with physical intimacy.

He kissed both of her hands and led her to the bed without saying a word. He turned down the bed covers and slowly removed the rest of her wet clothes. "As beautiful as I remember," he said. "Climb in." She obliged and he followed behind her, fully clothed. "Come here," he gestured for her to snuggle in to the hollow of his arm. The warmth of his body made her melt like ice on fire. She collapsed, mind and body, from the emotional anxiety and the late hour. A tear escaped to his shoulder and she felt herself give in to exhaustion.

"Thank you," she whispered.

"For what?" he asked, his voice soothing.

"For everything you've ever done for me," she said.

"We're just getting started," he said as she fell asleep cradled in his arm.

The next morning she woke up to the sound of the shower running, dressed in Argan's T-shirt and sweatpants. She sat up, not surprised to see the white box on his bedside table. In fact she had expected it. She opened the box. The simple round stone looked very unassuming. She held it up to the light of the day hoping to see the citrine within. She couldn't.

Argan came out of the bathroom drying his hair with a towel and sat on the edge of the bed. "I wanted to give you some rest before giving you that," he said. "You were too hopped up last night."

She nodded, agreeing with him. "Thanks," she said.

He twirled her hair around his finger. "Sky, I'd like to go with you, under the lake."

"I was hoping you'd say that," she said. "Diana told me to bring reinforcements."

"Who's Diana?"

"It's a long story," she said. She spent the better part of an hour recapping her experience in the Underworld. Argan's interest didn't falter once. "I don't know how you're going to make the trip underwater."

"I'm very strong," he puffed his chest.

"Yes, and the Sibyl's son no less," she said. "We'll figure out a way. Then I will truly have everything I need."

38

When Skylar returned to her own cabin, Britt was waiting for her.

"You could have let me know you weren't coming back," Britt said coldly. "I assumed you were with Argan."

"I was, but it's not what you think," Skylar said. "I fell asleep there." She gave Britt the short version of her trip to the Underworld, assuming she was the other reinforcement Diana spoke of.

"I'll do what I can," Britt said in a hurry. "I have to run. I'm meeting Origen to go over some class notes." Her eyes lightened when she mentioned his name.

"Oh good, enjoy," Skylar said as Britt headed out of the cabin.

With her stone and reinforcements found, Skylar actually had a window of free time after class. She used it to make good on her promise to see Silverwood's family of horses. She half expected Cheveyo to make an appearance but she knew he had a family to watch over.

As she got closer to the stables, she heard a muffled voice over a tinny loud speaker. Someone was commentating a show of some sort. When she got there, she saw many of her young friends cheering Ronnie on a white mare, careening around barrels like a pro. Milicent watched from the sidelines.

"I made it," Skylar said to Milicent, her eyes wide as she continued to watch Ronnie.

"Do you compete?"

"God, no," Milicent said. "This is not my style."

"Right," Skylar said. "Looks fun, though." She moved away from Milicent and watched Ronnie intently. With no saddle and no stifling helmet, this was definitely wild woman territory. Just watching gave Skylar chills and she wanted in.

After another round, Ronnie hopped off of her mare. "Hi Skylar."

"Hi Ronnie, that was amazing!"

"Do you ride?" Ronnie asked.

"I do but haven't tried barrel racing," Skylar said.

"You should give it a go," Ronnie said.

"I hoped you'd say that," she said. "Can you suit me up?"

"No suit," Ronnie said. "You just get on and go."

Skylar took a deep breath and let Ronnie guide her to a black mare in the paddock. "This is Indigo. She's pretty accommodating. I don't see you getting into too much trouble with her."

Skylar pet the mare's flank. The late day sun shone on her black coat creating a cobalt sheen that dazzled the eyes. She mounted the horse and trotted out of the paddock to the race area. Five minutes later, the horn blared into the sky and Indigo took off. Skylar startled at first but it didn't take long to settle into the horse's rhythm. She closed her eyes and connected with Indigo's heartbeat and immense storehouse of energy. They rounded the barrels in perfect figure eight form a half dozen times, as if they shared one body.

Skylar let the horse do her work. In her mind's eye, she could see a bright yellow light engulfing them both. The light lingered in the actual air behind them and soon they were traveling back through it in the figure eight of energy. She felt so powerful she could lift herself right off the planet. In an instant the horse came to a halt and Skylar went sailing over the mare's head. She landed with a thud in the dirt but sprung up like a gymnast. The light of the infinity sign still lingered and Skylar gaped at her creation. Maybe she *could* create energy like Rachel. The onlookers were mesmerized. Oddities were common at Silverwood but nothing of this caliber.

"First fencer, now barrel rider," Argan said. "You've really stepped into your element here."

Skylar smiled at his attire. He dressed the part in a cowboy hat, white T-shirt, and jeans. She glanced at his feet. "You're wearing the boots I gave you!" she beamed. "New hat?" Her eyes lingered on his, recalling their night together.

"Ronnie gave it to me," he said. "I think she has a thing for cowboys."

"Who doesn't?" Skylar said with a smirk. "There is a wildness about this sport that's intoxicating," Skylar said as she led Indigo back to the paddock.

"You took quite a tumble, you okay?" he asked.

She was quick to blow it off. "Sure, nothing I can't handle. This really has been the most amazing week!" She was floating from the feeling of freedom, empowerment, and the connection to the earth all at once.

Argan couldn't keep from laughing at her childlike exuberance. "After all you've been through, you are the same as always," he said smiling.

She paused. "I'm okay with that." She twirled once more. "You're the same too. I'm so happy! For no other reason than for being alive! Can you feel it?"

"I think so," he said.

"No, it's a feeling. No thinking."

"Right," he said, smiling.

39

The next day Skylar woke up hardly able to move. She reached around and felt her sore backside. When she was able to get out of bed, she pulled her pajama bottoms down in front of the mirror. "Good lord," she couldn't believe the bruise that stretched from her lower back, down her right butt cheek and into her hamstring. "I thought I was above human suffering," she said over her shoulder. She took a step and pain shot up her leg into her back telling her that wasn't the case. "Yoga pants it is," she said, finding the softest pants available.

After considering skipping her teaching duties she hobbled in ten minutes late, surprised to see anyone still sitting there. Every seat was filled, many with cedars not currently enrolled in her class. From what she could hear of the whispers, they were all abuzz over her energy display the day before. She had powers they all desperately wanted to possess.

"Good morning," she said to the group. "I see some new faces. I can only assume this is a one-off thing and not a permanent add?" She didn't wait for anyone to answer. She tried to sit on the edge of her desk but the pain was too intense and she bolted upright. "Okay, let's pretend for a moment I could explain what happened yesterday." She leaned on the desk, holding herself up with both arms. "If I could, maybe I'd tell you, maybe I wouldn't. This is a class about blood. If that's what interests you, great. If not, there's the door," she pointed. No one moved.

"Okay, then." She stood up, one hand supporting her lower back and walked slowly to the blackboard. She loved the feel of chalk in her hands. "Today I promised to reveal the great secret of blood. Maybe that's why we have such a big group today." She cased the room of blank stares. "Yeah, I'll go with that." She drew a squiggle on the blackboard resembling a snake, topped with a small head with eyes. "There are two secrets actually that intertwine. My fabulous drawing represents the iron in your blood. Everyone knows blood has iron in it, but so what? Here's the magic: the iron in your blood responds to the iron in the core of the earth. That is the connection. There is a resonance that takes place that is important to life."

She drew another snake mirroring the first. When finished, her drawing looked strikingly similar to a strand of DNA. "This other squiggle represents the memory of earth. As iron in your blood is tied to the iron in the earth, your blood is also tied to the memory of the world. There are many reported cases of people recalling memories of others after a blood transfusion. They have actually been infused with the memory of the Akasha without having had the experience. This is proof that blood carries memory." She rested the chalk in its cradle and dusted the residue from her hands. "The Akasha is also carried in semen but that's another class." This trivia point caused a few giggles.

"There is also an untapped power in the blood of the female. Young women use their blood to create life. As they age, the potential grows to use that blood to create wisdom," She pointed to the two entwined snakes. ". . . divine wisdom." Skylar wondered where to go from here. "Questions?" Every hand in the room shot up. She sighed knowing it would be a long day.

40

Present Day: A few days after Joshua's death, the watchful eye of the media appeared to turn its gaze elsewhere and the Grayers made good on another obligatory dinner with Cyril Magus, this one without his wife. Milicent didn't understand why she had to attend and made no promises to be civil. She had also asked Noah to interrupt her at a respectable hour with a *First Lady emergency*. As Milicent was well aware such a thing didn't exist, she gave Noah permission to lie.

He handled his task like a pro and once Milicent was out of the room, Cyril's small talk took a darker turn. "Devlin, our hold is slipping. We need to re-establish control. Too much chaos is going in the wrong direction."

Not yet out of earshot, Milicent lingered in the hallway after sending Noah on a recon mission to the East Wing to retrieve the red book.

"I may have a solution," Devlin said pouring his vodka straight. ". . . access to some interesting information, a type of book if you will, of the same vein as our forefathers used."

"Don't speak so cryptically, what are you talking about?" Cyril asked.

"The science of the free masons," Devlin said proudly sharing his secret information.

"Alchemy? Oh please," Cyril scoffed. "We bled that knowledge dry long ago."

"Not necessarily," Devlin said. "A new, or should I say, old book, has surfaced. Sophia's book."

This got Cyril's attention. "That was a myth forgotten long ago."

"So we thought," Devlin said.

"Where did you come across this *book?*"

"My wife," Devlin said.

Cyril poured bourbon and started to pace. "I forgot she dabbled in the occult at one time," he said.

Milicent seethed behind the door. She did all she could to restrain herself from barging in. She had been played by her own husband.

"Do you have the book?" Cyril asked.

"No, but I know where I can get it," Devlin said.

"Devlin, you realize in the wrong hands, that book could ruin all we have created."

"I am well aware of that Cyril. *You* know I've been cultivating this plan for decades."

"Decades?" Milicent whispered. She held the wall for support. All this time, the life she shared with Devlin had been a rouse. He knew her bloodlines. He knew one day he would have the opportunity to get his hands on the Book of Sophia and wield nature and create energy. He would be the most powerful man on the planet and quite possibly live forever doing it. Her anger swelled, overtaking any sadness she felt about the final nail in the coffin of her marriage. It had been a sham for both of them.

Another night without sleep, Milicent promised herself a vacation in Italy when this folly was through. The next morning, one completely erroneous report about the last days of Joshua's life splashed on the television in the Residence, that now seemed to be on permanently. She was actually thankful, the more ludicrous the story, the further it got her away from the truth.

She called for Noah. "Tell the President I want to speak with him," she hollered.

"I'm right here," Devlin said, appearing from nowhere. "Where I've always been."

"What does that mean?" she asked.

"Our life together, these past thirty years," he said, his face, expressionless. "You never viewed them as a partnership. For you, I was always an accessory. Even in this place, the pinnacle of my accomplishments, you still see this as *your* story."

"I like to think your success had something to do with me," Milicent said.

Continued coverage scrolled on the screen behind them.

"You thought you were so good at covering it," Devlin said, gesturing to the TV. "And you were, when it was just the tabloids following you. But you're no match for DC."

Milicent stared at her husband blankly.

"I created an empire and gave it all to you," he said. "And this is how you repay me?"

"My motives never had anything to do with you," she said.

"Exactly," Devlin said. He looked at the television. "You have to fix this, Millie. I don't know how, but you have to." He turned and passed Noah on his way out the door.

"Where were you?" Milicent asked Noah.

"You texted me to get you that special latte you like," he said, holding the to-go cup.

Milicent looked at her phone. She hadn't texted Noah all morning. The realization that her every move was being watched and manipulated crystalized in her mind and she now understood the depth of the hole she'd created in this drama she called her life.

41

The day before the Equinox, camp was bustling with preparations. Ocean had still not returned and Britt had taken it upon herself to lead the charge. She was a natural event planner. Origen was also planning his own festivities and this gave her extra time to be with him. Skylar watched her moon over him and still couldn't understand the attraction. He repelled just about everyone else.

With no Great Mother on site, Skylar wondered how magical this event could possibly be. But Britt embraced the challenge and coordinated teams of cedars to transform the commons into a receiving ground worthy of a goddess.

"Which one are we celebrating?" Britt asked Origen.

"All of them," he said. "But this year is special. It is the dedication to the Emerald Ray of Sophia. Her return is imminent." He looked at Skylar and walked away.

The word *emerald* was all Britt needed to hear. She set her sights on everything green and trailed off after Origen.

Skylar soon learned that many of the cedars conducted their own ceremonies the night before the Equinox, everyone in a frenzy of hormones and enthusiasm. Fifty teenagers were given permission to let loose and *be free*. Similar to mischief night before Halloween, the night before Equinox was called Equal Night, honoring the dark before the light, the importance of the shadow. Here, the lines of duality blurred and were merged into oneness. This was one of the four nights of the year curfew was lifted.

"I'm not stepping out of my door tonight," Skylar said to Britt over dinner. "One can only imagine what will go on."

It was already dark when they walked the wooded path back to their cabin. Just over the hill before their porch, they heard a faint chanting coming from the woods.

"Let's check it out," Britt said.

"Let's not," Skylar said, then gave in to her curiosity and followed Britt. They veered off their path and looked through the thick branches. A campfire was lit and at least a dozen cedars were standing around it, all completely undressed. Skylar's eyes widened. They started to pair up. Only four were male so many of the girls came together and held hands.

"Oh my God, it's an orgy," Skylar said.

"No, it's a tantric rite," Britt corrected. "Called the Chakra Pûjâ."

"Really?" She continued to stare at the group of teens. She was familiar with all of them so to see them in such a private act felt wrong. "We should go," she said but didn't budge.

"The tantric practices use sex as a gateway to higher states of consciousness," Britt said. "This has more to do with spirituality than physicality. What you call profane, another can call sacred. You shouldn't judge what you don't understand."

"I may have heard that before," Skylar said. "And I'm not judging."

At that moment, Origen walked to the middle of the circle dressed in a dark red robe. Britt gasped then tried to recover. "There needs to be a guru," she said, her voice cracking slightly.

The circle of cedars returned to the fire and each passed a large gold chalice. "Wine," Britt said. "If they haul out a goat, I'm going to lose it."

Skylar looked back at the circle and there was Milicent in the middle of it all. Her face shone in the light of the fire and she looked radiant. She was partnered with another cedar Skylar only vaguely knew, an African-American girl named Nia. Skylar was fixated on Milicent's face, beautiful and vulnerable. She was glad to see her so free but felt sad that it was such a brief time in her life. She would live out the rest of her days so far away from this moment.

"The goal isn't orgasm," Britt said, continuing her tantra lesson. "In fact, orgasm is frowned upon. Lingering in the energy before climax gives the participants a window into the hidden divinity of the soul." Before Britt stopped speaking, a visible circle of light enclosed the group.

"Do you see that?" Skylar asked wide-eyed.

"I do," Britt said. "That's the goal of all of this. The transmutation of internal sexual energy into external power. Many occult groups do this for much darker reasons."

"I can't believe Ocean allows this," Skylar *was* judging.

"Ocean's not here," Britt said.

Something told Skylar this would still be going on if Ocean were here. She'd seen enough. "It's really rude of us to stay here," Skylar said. "I'm turning in."

"Right behind you," Britt said and Skylar left her standing in the woods.

42

P resent Day: Suki had spent the last few weeks practically living in the Quine basement. Many nights she brought her sleeping bag as it saved precious time. It would take decades to ingest the volumes of information at her fingertips but she wanted to give it her best shot. Much of it was beyond her reach, in a foreign or ancient language. Every so often she would peruse the ancients, just to look at pictures, but she would have to spend the bulk of her time on everything in English.

From Christian Mysticism to modern day witchcraft, each modality danced around a few universal subjects: the power of thought, the power of the individual heart, and the darkness hiding that knowledge from the masses.

She had also figured out a plan to go through the door again. She had come across a similar door in a book on seventeenth century Rome. From its markings, she determined this door was one of the lost alchemical doors from the villa Polombara, which made sense. Milicent had more than half of antiquity's secrets in this basement. A lost door fit right in.

So many of the door markings were celestial and Suki figured it tied to the natural calendar. Through her studies, she learned the best opening for slipping through the veils of time were during high points of the seasonal calendar, equinoxes and solstices. She would give it a go on the Spring Equinox, the next high point on the timeline.

43

March 20, 2021 and 1998 The Spring Equinox 5:37 a.m.: "Skylar," the voice whispered in the dark. Skylar stirred slightly in her sleep. "Skylar . . ." a little louder but still she slept.

A flick of the wrist of the Goddess and a flood of energy rushed Skylar's body. She jolted out of bed. "Skylar, it is time for the lush, green feminine energy to awaken. It will balance the masculine and return harmony to earth." Skylar knew this wasn't Magda.

"Magda is one of the countless Goddesses that carry my energy. They all inhabit a different part of me." *Sophia*, Skylar thought. "Yes. And when day and night are equal, I return from the Underworld. Today is that day."

Today was the Equinox, today she would return to the lake. She rushed to dress and stepped outside to catch the first glimpse of the day, stopping short of the ground. All of the snow had melted in the night, and greenery was coming to life by the minute. She could see the plants growing before her eyes and the sky ignited with a blaze of orange. Mother Nature was busy putting the finishing touches on the decorations for the Equinox Celebration. The beauty gave Skylar a rush of excitement and an extra boost of confidence to get over her goal line today.

She went back inside and took out the rock from her nightstand and sat it on the dresser. Argan was coming in a half hour to go with her to the lake and Britt should have been in her bed but she wasn't. *Maybe she took part in last night's festivities,* she thought.

She needed a few moments to breathe in the silence that allowed her to hear the drum of her own heart. With each breath, the air nourished her body and mind, calming her, lulling her into a safe space for expansion.

"I can't believe that asshole!" Britt stormed into the cabin, safe space squashed. "He said we had *a connection, a bond* that couldn't be broken." She whirred around the tiny room like a maelstrom littering every surface with items from her tote bag. She dug frantically looking for something. "I've got to get out of here. I don't know why I came."

Skylar's peaceful moment shattered, she turned to face Britt. "Trouble in paradise?" she asked, still sitting in lotus.

"He wanted me to have group sex!" Britt paused her feverous search. "This place is so hedonistic!" She continued to thrash around making no visible progress toward anything.

"Weren't you the one saying it was spiritual, not sexual?" Skylar asked.

Britt glared and growled but didn't answer the question. "I have to go. I'm sorry I can't help you find whatever it is you're supposed to find or do what it is you're supposed to do. I'll call Vihaan and he can come get me." She produced her cell phone from her purse.

"He's going to pick you up from the past?" Skylar asked.

"There's got to be a way right? If I want out of here, I can only assume there's some out clause somewhere. I can get myself to the road, where your car is." She got out her bag from the closet and shoved in clothes, very un-Britt like. She left a few things of Skylar's strewn on the dresser.

Skylar didn't press it. As she thought about it, she didn't particularly care if Britt stayed and wouldn't mind the extra space.

"Okay well, I'm headed to the Underworld shortly so I guess this is goodbye."

"I'm sorry I wasn't more help to you on your quest," Britt said, taking a pause from packing. "I guess I wasn't meant to be a part of it after all. I had no purpose to serve."

"That's not true," Skylar said, untucking from lotus. "You were great moral support. And how many people would be so open minded to jump in a car with a complete stranger and take a trip in time?" She was being sincere. "That took guts."

"Thank you," Britt said. "We're all just searching for answers, aren't we?" She held a pile of clothes in her arms. "Searching for the answer to who we are. I didn't think I found it back in Valhalla but maybe I did. Maybe I'm just the product of a mistake."

"There are no mistakes," Skylar said. "And you are a daughter of the Great Mothers. If nothing else, you should take that in and be proud of that."

Britt nodded and zipped her bag. "I'll take this for now and figure out the rest later. Every minute here tells me I don't belong."

"Sure, I understand," Skylar said. "I'll get in touch with you when I get back."

"I would like that," Britt said and they hugged goodbye. She walked out the door and it slammed behind her.

A few quiet moments forgotten, Skylar finished getting ready to meet Argan. She searched for her light sweater and before she found it, there was a knock. She looked around the room. *What did she forget?* she thought as she opened the door.

"Suki?!" Skylar was aghast. When would she stop thinking she'd seen it all? "How the hell . . . ?"

"Hey Sky!" Suki said, holding a small duffle bag. "Got room for me?" Skylar stepped aside for Suki to enter her cabin.

"Seriously, explain yourself—right now."

"Well you seem bent on believing you owe everything to magic and that's fine," Suki said, walking in. "I owe everything to research."

Skylar stepped aside as Suki walked inside. "Remember that source field I was telling you about? The one you never took seriously? Well turns out, portals connecting the field exist all over the place. Those Mothers of yours stuck one here. Through a few discoveries of my own, it turns out there's one at the Quine."

"That's all well and good but how did you get to *this cabin?*" Skylar asked.

"*Find my friends,*" Suki held up her cell phone. "Led me to your doorstep."

Skylar stared at Suki in disbelief, then broke out in a large grin. "Suuk, I actually don't care how you got here. I'm just so glad that you did. I have so much to fill you in on. And you wont believe it but I needed to use a sword! You were right! Gosh, I can't believe this, yes I can . . ." Skylar rambled on as Suki unpacked her things into the few drawers still warm from Britt's clothes.

"How do you feel?" Skylar asked after Suki tossed her empty duffle into the closet. "Acclimating to the past all right?" She bounced on her bed, still so happy to see her.

"No sweat," Suki said.

"What did you want to do when you got here?" Skylar asked.

"I really just wanted to see if I could do it," Suki said. "But also, the image that led me through the door was of my parents. I thought maybe coming to the past, I might be able to see them again. 1998 was the year they died."

Skylar held her breath before she spoke. "Wow, yes of course. Or maybe, I don't know, Suuk, that's huge," she stumbled on her words.

"I know, I thought I would at least try," Suki said.

"I'm meeting Argan, like right now, to head to the Underworld," Skylar said. "I have the stone and need to return it to the Akasha. Come with us." Skylar reached for the stone on her dresser.

"Wow, Underworld, no time to get settled, okay," Suki said. "How can I help?"

"I, um . . ." Skylar was distracted when she couldn't find her rock. "I . . . sorry Suuk, I just had it here before. And it's gone."

"Had what?"

"My rock!" Skylar searched the floor on her hands and knees. She pulled out the dresser to look behind it. Nothing. She picked up a wrinkled sweater that had been left behind in Britt's wake. She stared at it and a light bulb went off in her head. "Could she have?" she mused aloud. "No, why would she?"

"What?" Suki asked.

Skylar paused and leaned both hands on the dresser. *Britt took it*, she was sure of it. "What am I going to do? I need that rock. I told Diana I would come back on the Equinox with the rock!"

"Who's Diana?"

"Milicent's sister that died all those years ago and set Milicent on her path of revenge." Skylar did not want to bring up Suki's parents right now.

"Oh," Suki said. "Well let's go without the rock, we'll improvise."

"No!" She sat back on the bed. "It's the key to restoring the memory, the actual key!"

There was a knock on the door and Suki opened it. "Hey Argan!" Suki said, engulfing him in a big hug.

"Wow, Suki," he said, arms at his sides, frozen with surprise. "How did you get here?"

"Story for later. Argan the rock is gone!" Skylar announced loudly.

"What, why?" he asked.

"Britt, she took it. I know it. I don't know why but I'm sure that's what happened. And now what am I supposed to do? That was the key and it's gone. She's gone." She held her head in her hands.

Argan took a deep breath. "We still need to go," he said. "You need to go back and see Diana and we'll figure something out. Today is the day; it's the Equinox. We won't have this chance again." He knelt down in front of her and lifted her chin to meet her eyes with his. "It's okay. It will all be okay." He hugged her tight and she exhaled for the first time in an hour. She felt his sincere care for her and it made everything better, manageable.

"Thank you," she said to him. ". . . for making it better."

"Huh?" Suki asked, dumbfounded. "It's not like I *just* suggested that. But I guess I need broad shoulders and a sparkling smile."

"We need a plan to get in," Argan said. "We've come up empty on any gear that can get me to the bottom of the lake and Ocean's been away for any supernatural help."

"I have a few ideas or do you want to pee on those too," Suki said to Skylar.

"I'm all ears," Skylar said.

"Well, we could spin the mer-ka-ba," Suki said, like Skylar knew what she was referring to. "Or use the light body or . . . we could bypass the lake all together and use the portal that got me here. It's intention that directs where you go. The portal is just a doorway."

"Suuk, you're brilliant!" Skylar's enthusiasm returned. "Where did you . . . arrive when you got here?" Skylar asked.

"I landed in a small cabin on the other side of camp," Suki said. "It was a throwback to the heyday of alchemy. And it looks just like your tiny house. Even *I* felt the magic there. You should check it out some time."

Skylar raised her eyebrows.

"Oh, it *is* your tiny house, isn't it?" Suki asked.

"Yes, but it's good you landed there," Skylar said. "That means we've got another way in."

44

The threesome made the trek to the cabin an hour after sunrise. The landscape raced to reveal the glory of spring. Even the cabin was brighter. Vibrant fuchsia azaleas lined the outer walls and the window boxes cascaded with petunias and Spanish daggers. Skylar smiled at its transformation.

They walked into the cabin. All seemed the same, the books, the cauldron. The pile of swords still lay on the floor. "Feeling all right?" she asked Argan.

"Yeah," he said "Why?"

"I didn't know if that cat was stirring, sensing it's go time, or something," she said.

"Nothing yet," he said.

Suki went straight to the back corner and Argan followed her. Skylar took a quick detour to visit Sophia's book. Hanging from a nail tacked to the shelf was her pendulum chain, Cassie's ouroboros ring dangling from it, no pendulum attached. A note gouged by the nail read: *wear this.*

She glanced at the others and quickly slipped it on her finger unnoticed.

"Here we go," Suki said, staring at a blue velvet drape hung from an intricate metal rod woven of silver and gold. The woven pattern traveled down the drape in thick embroidery, silver entwined gold in luxurious braids.

"That curtain has never been here before," Skylar said emphatically.

"When the student is ready . . ." Suki said. She pulled aside the heavy fabric. A simple white stone door stood before them. It was the same door under the eagle's wing in the stone circle.

Skylar walked toward it with her hand outstretched, and felt the cool cement casing with her fingers. The cement felt hard in her hand but the energy of the doorway was malleable, almost supple.

"It is exactly the same as the original, but in much better shape," Argan said. The girls looked at him. "I've seen it," he said.

"So have I," Skylar said, describing the door under the lake. Alchemical symbols for the various planets and corresponding metals arched the doorway and down each side; Saturn, lead; Jupiter, tin; Mars, iron; Venus, bronze; Mercury; antinomy and vitriol.

"I memorized the translations of the Latin inscriptions," Suki said. "My favorite is at the top, *there are three marvels: God and man, mother and virgin, triune and one.*

"You've studied the Porta?" Argan asked Suki, surprised.

"Among other things," Suki said proudly. "I've made quite a few recent discoveries."

"The words on this door are the greatest puzzle of alchemy," Argan said. "Lifetimes have been spent trying to decipher them to gain the power the secret meanings hold. Only the rarest of individuals walked through the gate. It's stuff of legend actually." He stood there in awe. "Porta Alchemica," he repeated shaking his head. "The Great Mothers definitely have a sense of humor."

"The one at the Quine is exactly the same," Suki said.

"So Milicent has an alchemical door?" Skylar asked. "That

explains building that place with the security of a CIA torture camp. Where is it?" She hadn't taken her eyes off of the door.

"In the basement library," Suki said. "Behind a bookcase."

"I didn't know we had a basement library," Skylar said.

"You wouldn't believe it, Sky. But I have a strong feeling if I told you, I would have to kill you."

Skylar felt around the edges of the door and pushed it forward like she had under the lake. They each peered in.

"You know where we're headed?" Suki asked Skylar.

"Yup," Skylar said, tapping her temple. "I'll get us there." Skylar held out her hands, Argan on her left, Suki on her right. The threesome took as many steps as they could to the edge before taking the leap.

"Follow me." Skylar squeezed both of their hands and they all took one more step.

45

The darkness on the other side of the door was over in one blink. They had expected to fall but with only one step, they arrived through a door in the courtyard, in front of Diana's white cathedral. Suki beamed. "I'm really getting the hang of this," she said.

Argan was slow to recover from the shift in location. He knelt on the floor struggling to catch his breath. Skylar bent and put her hand on his shoulder. "Are you okay?" she asked.

"It's getting harder to carry this thing," he said.

"It'll all be over soon," she said kindly. Truthfully she had no idea how long this would go on. "Can you make it a little longer?" She searched his eyes for the strength she knew he had.

He nodded once and she helped him stand up.

"Why are we glowing?" Suki asked, mesmerized by her own luminescent skin.

"It's called *lucina*. It's a protective coating or you'd burn up from the sun down here," Skylar explained.

"There's a sun inside the earth?" Suki asked, squinting at it.

Argan's struggle intensified. "Something's changed," he said.

"Then let's get on with this," Skylar said. Suki and Argan followed her as she walked through the doors of the cathedral.

"I've failed," she announced to Diana and Lucifer sitting right where she had left them. "The stone is gone. I had it but it was stolen."

"You used the front door this time," Diana said. "And brought reinforcements, albeit questionable ones." Suki was still focused on the light shining off of her skin and Argan trailed quite a bit behind them.

Skylar ignored her snide comment. "Did you hear me?" she said. "I don't have the stone."

"Yes, we expected that," Lucifer said. His inner light shone so brightly Skylar couldn't look at him directly. He seemed to sense this and was able to tone down his brightness at will.

The sight of Lucifer pulled Suki back into the present moment. "After everything else, *he* is the freakiest thing ever," she whispered to Argan who didn't seem fazed.

"I knew you weren't worthy," Lucifer said. His voice dripped with disappointment.

"What was I supposed to do?" Skylar asked deflated. "I didn't know what it was until you told me."

"I had it actually," Argan spoke up in Skylar's defense.

Lucifer turned to him and stared curiously. "*You* have something that belongs to me." He got up from his seat and walked slowly to Argan. His intimidating form would have made a lesser man fall to his knees. But Argan stood and looked him square in the eye. "My cat has been missing. You have her." Argan swallowed audibly but said nothing, still standing tall. "Odd, she would have left at all, and now to see she is with you?" he pondered out loud. "Odd, indeed."

Skylar felt a hot prickle spread across her left hand. She looked down at Cassie's ouroboros ring. The citrine stone glowed with an inner light. Her eyes widened and she showed it to Suki. They both kept quiet. She turned the ring around and closed her palm over it. But that only lasted a moment; the heat was too much. She opened her palm to a searing burn on her skin. She used her shirt to slip off the ring and put it in the pocket of her jeans.

Lucifer returned to Diana's side and Argan stumbled slightly backward. Skylar started toward him but he waved her off. He almost knocked into the scales of Maat but caught himself on a column framing a sheet of bright gold leaf the size of an outstretched newspaper. He studied it. "Is this the Petelia Tablet?" he asked incredulously.

"I beg your pardon," Diana said with contempt. "The tablet found in Petelia was merely a replication of this one. I assure you this tablet has never left the Underworld."

Skylar walked toward the tablet. She read its words silently, now so familiar, in Sophia's book.

Diana stared at her curiously. "Can you read it?"

She could . . .

"Thou shall find to the left of the house of Hades a well-spring, and by the side thereof standing a white cypress. To this well-spring approach not near. But thou shalt find another by the lake of memory, cold water flowing forth, and there are guardians before it."

"That would be us," Diana said.

"Say, I am the child of Earth and starry Heaven," She looked at Argan and he gave her an encouraging nod. *"But my race is heavenly; and this you know yourselves. I am parched with thirst and I perish; but give me quickly refreshing water flowing forth from the lake of Memory.* Skylar looked at the Mnemosyne pooling near her feet. *"They will give you to drink from the divine spring, And then you will celebrate with the other heroes."*

A look of knowing spread across Skylar's face. "I need to drink from the water of remembering," she said. "That will make up for losing the stone."

"Can we all do it?" Suki asked. "Or does someone need to be on a quest?"

"Drinking from the water of remembering is not for the faint of heart," Diana said. "It opens your pathways to recall all memory of the Akasha. You will witness all of humanity, its love and its savagery."

"Oh Diana, you can be so dramatic," Lucifer said. "Knowledge is power. Witnessing the brutality of man is a small price to pay for what is gained. Let them all drink. If they struggle, there is always Lethe." He gestured to the silver river Lethe that ran parallel to the Mnemosyne.

"They won't remember their own names after that," Diana said. "No, only Skylar." She held out an ornate nautilus shell, encrusted with every jewel of the rainbow. "Use this."

Argan began to object and Skylar squeezed his hand. "I'll do it," she said reassuringly.

He looked at Diana. "Ma'am, may we have a minute?"

"One," Diana said.

Argan pulled Skylar aside and huddled with Suki. "I appreciate your willingness to jump in but you don't understand what's going on here. You are asking for the entire veil of obscurity to be lifted and you'll be inundated with every memory of mankind."

"Oh, is that what I'm doing?" Skylar snapped. "Thanks for explaining it so clearly."

"Argan's right, Sky," Suki said. "This is only supposed to happen when someone is about to die. Your head could explode."

A rush came to Skylar's head forcing her to sit down immediately. Her temple pounded with her own heartbeat and she took in a deep breath. "I think it already has." Argan and Suki exchanged concerned glances. As she sat there, a warm sensation stirred in her abdomen. It grew hot and she jumped up. "Yeouw," she yelled and looked down. Her ring had burned through her jeans to her skin. "I've got to do something with this ring or my fate will be death by a thousand cigarette burns."

"Why is it doing that?" Suki asked.

Skylar stared at the yellow stone. "Could this be the one we need?" Skylar didn't wait for an answer to her question. She ran to Lucifer and Diana and held it in the air. "Would this work . . . in the mainframe . . . tablet?"

"You're handing me a substitution?" Lucifer asked disdainfully.

With each moment, Skylar felt more confident this was the answer. Cassie had left it for her to bring here. "It's transforming on its own. That must mean something," Skylar said. "And it's citrine, like the great tablet. My rock wasn't citrine. You could have been wrong." Skylar bit her lip. She had just suggested to the Prince of Darkness that he might be incorrect. As she waited, a wave of clarity came over her. He hadn't been mistaken—he had been deceiving her.

"I don't think so," he said, his eyes piercing.

"There's no harm here, Lucifer," Diana said. "Let her try."

He bowed and stepped back as Skylar approached the citrine wall. Its energy roiled in waves she could feel in her stomach. There were so many holes; she didn't know where to place her ring. But its heat was now unbearable; she had no choice but to let go. She released her grip and the wall called to the ring like a homing beacon. It flew the rest of the distance to land inside one of the many pockets.

The threesome froze in place to see what would happen. They waited. But the earth didn't crumble and Skylar didn't feel any different.

After no progress, Lucifer began to speak. "Your *ring* was merely a rune," he said with slight relief on his face. "A hope of your mother's, laced with some undeveloped magic, to protect you from what she knew you must do to satisfy this quest."

Skylar was deflated.

"Have you truly sacrificed?" Diana asked. "The road to destiny is not true unless paved with great sacrifice. Your rune will mend the Akasha with one final act."

"Sacrifice? Are you kidding me?" Skylar could feel her blood heat up within her veins. "My mother is dead because of this *quest*. I live the rest of my life without her. That is the biggest sacrifice of all."

Now it was Diana's turn to anger. "I'm so sorry you lost your mum, how horrible for you. *I* lost my life at eighteen and took innocent lives with me. That couple had a small child. Think of her, that girl that has lived her whole life not knowing either of her parents." Her eyes shot to Suki and then back to Skylar. "You talk about sacrifice but you are selfish! There isn't a person walking the earth that doesn't feel the sting of loss. True sacrifice is in the courage to move forward in the love you give, not the loss you bear."

Skylar stood in disbelief. She was being scolded for mourning her mother.

"You are not mourning, Skylar," Diana said, reading her mind. "You are consumed by the cross you carry. A true warrior grows big enough to absorb it and become more than an old story."

Skylar was done talking. She walked back to the pooling river and knelt beside it. She picked up the jeweled shell, heavy in her hands. As she scooped the liquid, it slowly dripped down the side of the shell and onto her hand. How ironic to be drinking gold again. She raised the shell to her lips. *I'll give them sacrifice*, she thought.

Suki had moved close to Argan and clutched his waist for support. As they stood embracing, Lucifer's interest returned. "Courage, how interesting. I didn't see it in her," he said.

"I'd call it more of an *indignation*," Diana said. "But I'll take it."

Skylar's eyes narrowed at their comments, as she tasted the bitter gold liquid.

"Skylar, what *are* you doing?" a man's voice asked from behind her. Skylar froze and immediately stood up.

"Grampy. Don't try to stop me. I've made up my mind," she said without looking behind at her grandfather.

"Part of your *quest* is to drink from the Mnemosyne and obliterate your mind for eternity?"

"It's called *sacrifice*," she turned to look at him. "And it will ennoble my act of returning the memory to the Akasha."

"I see," he said. He clasped his hands behind his back and walked toward Diana. "Screwing with the living again, Diana?"

Skylar looked at her for clarification.

"I'm allowed to change the rules, Arthur. This is my domain," Diana said.

"Skylar's life will be ruined if she drinks that shit, but that's not your concern," Arthur said.

"The heroine's quest is fraught with sacrifice, not just one," Diana said.

Arthur looked at Skylar with the loving eyes of a grandfather. He looked at her young friends, everyone with their bright lives ahead of them. He turned to Diana. "I'll do it."

"*You'll* do it?" Diana repeated. "That makes no sense, Arthur." She waved him off. "You are due on the earth plane to return to Beatrice. If you do this, you can never go back."

"Is that enough of a sacrifice for you?" he asked.

"Beatrice will lose you for the rest of eternity?" Diana couldn't contain her delight. "It would serve her right, all caught up in selfish earthly love, if that's what you can call it. It was more like control. You should be angry that she makes you return to earth to love her over and over."

Arthur smiled his kind smile. "We make great sacrifice for those we love," he said looking at Skylar.

"I'm tempted, Arthur, but the answer is no," Diana said. "This is Skylar's job to do."

Arthur didn't look surprised. "I knew it was a long shot," he said with a shrug of his shoulders. He reached his hand around Skylar's back and drew her to him. "I'll hold your hand the whole time," he whispered in her ear. He released his hug and took her hand. She felt the unconditional love from her grandfather and she knew that no matter what dimension they lived in, they were never truly apart.

She scooped the shell into the ore once more and this time didn't hesitate. She swallowed the thick liquid until her stomach begged her to stop. The shell dropped to the ground and she looked at her grandfather.

"I love ya, kid," he said. "See you on the other side."

The room began to spin and the cast of characters faded from Skylar's view. Argan rushed toward her but Lucifer restrained him with a flip of his wrist.

"Let me help her!" Argan shouted.

"There is nothing you can do," Lucifer said. As Argan struggled behind a wall no one could see, his eyes went in and out of focus. Suki ran to him but was thrown back by the force of energy around him.

"Argan," she yelled. "Are you all right?" He didn't reply. He continued to writhe back and forth, struggling to break free.

Skylar's ears closed over and she could no longer hear anything going on around her. She sank to her knees and closed her eyes, waiting for the earth to move.

And then it did.

46

P resent Day: Milicent dropped her cup of tea as she walked down the hallway of the Residence. Hot liquid and porcelain flew in every direction.

"Shit, Mil," Noah said bouncing up from the sofa in the living room. "I'll get it cleaned up." Milicent held the wall for support as Noah picked up porcelain and rambled on about new responsibilities now that the office remodel was complete. He glanced up at her and dropped all the porcelain back to the floor. "You're paler than normal. Should I call the doctor?"

"No, Noah, I'm fine," she said, bending to get the porcelain.

"I'll get it!" Noah ordered.

She stabbed her finger with a shard. "Damn," she said. As she stared at the dark red blood on her finger she knew something had changed. They had all been schooled in how it would feel when the memory was restored to the Akasha but something was wrong. Milicent was expecting the contentment that eluded her for a lifetime. That wasn't this. Something had not gone to plan.

Ronnie sat in meditation in a simple Indian ashram, the only place she had found a shred of peace since Rhia died. Halfway through the seven hundred verses of the Bhagavad Gita, her eyes popped open. *No, no, no*, she thought to herself. She sprang up among the sea of pretzel positioned devotees. "Excuse me, sorry, pardon me," was all she could say to each person she stepped over until she found her way to the exit.

A sharp pain shot through Rachel's stomach up to her head and she bent in half at the kitchen counter. *Something went wrong.* One memory was to have been recovered . . . only one. This feeling was much more intense and dangerous. A rush of humanity's experiences flooded her mind and she dropped to the floor. *There's no way Skylar could take ownership of the entire Akashic memory. It's not humanly possible.* An image of Skylar as a young girl with a bright smile flashed in her mind before she passed out.

47

The ground beneath Skylar's feet rumbled with massive waves of energy. She was certain the walls of the cathedral were in jeopardy. The waves traveled up her legs, through her veins, electrifying her blood as they went. The heat within her core was familiar. She had felt it in training with Argan so many times but it was never this intense. All she could do was brace herself for the ride. The feeling traveled up her spine and came to rest at her third eye. As the heat began to build between her eyes, the pressure climbed to a dangerous level. No one could help her now. If it killed her, at least she died risking it all to help humanity. Her mother had done it; she could do the same. She continued to breathe from her belly to try to cool down but it was no use. She became lightheaded as she took in air faster and faster. Her heartbeat accelerated with her quick breaths out her mouth and she felt herself losing consciousness.

The tremors beneath Skylar's feet reached Argan and a low growl came from deep within his chest. The appearance of his eyes was no longer human; the eruption from his core was all feline. He stood paralyzed under Lucifer's spell as the jaguar within him clawed for release.

Suki stood in helpless horror watching her two friends struggle against forces she couldn't see. "Do something, please!" she pleaded with Diana.

"This is their initiation into the Underworld. It's never easy," Diana said wryly.

Suki's eyes widened. "Goddess help us all."

With Argan's last breath before bowing to the strength of Lucifer, he let out one blood boiling battle cry and the light body of the great cat leapt from his chest. It sprang through the invisible wall and pounced onto Lucifer, who stood motionless. He absorbed the jaguar with nothing but a strong inhale through his nose.

Lucifer's stare bore through Argan. "It would appear you are my equal," he said disdainfully. Argan met his eyes with the strength of a warrior king and ran toward Skylar.

The pressure in Skylar's head could no longer be contained and it took off like a shot through the spot where her fontanel once was. The ripple of energy blew Argan back to the floor. Already on her hands and knees, she stayed there to catch her breath. She was so thankful for the release from the indescribable force in her head, that at first she didn't realize everything was dark . . . and silent. Her eyes were open but there was no light. She heard nothing. *Could the intensity have left me blind? And deaf?*

It could have, she heard Magda's voice in her head. *But it didn't. You are adjusting to your new way of being. It will take a little time.*

"Why are you here?" Skylar barked at Magda. "You can't help me now."

I am always here, within you. And help is a relative term. So often you don't ask for it so I must sit by and watch you suffer needlessly. You don't need to solve the problems of the world by yourself even if you believe that's what the Great Mothers ask of you. They know one woman cannot do it alone.

"That would have been helpful information ten minutes ago," Skylar continued her conversation with Magda aloud.

You will still need help after this, Magda said. And Skylar sensed she was gone.

Through a pinhole, Skylar could see light begin to shine and she relaxed slightly. The vulnerability of blindness was terrifying. As the pinhole got bigger, she saw Argan crawl toward her. His form seemed two dimensional, like a paper doll. He reached her and held her shoulders.

"Sky, say something, are you all right?" he asked, searching her face for signs she was still in there.

She couldn't find the words to talk even though she had just spoken to Magda. She continued to stare at him and a flood of foreign memories took over her thoughts. Snippets of countries she'd never seen and people she'd never known flashed through her mind like a movie on fast-forward. She couldn't avoid the ugly images of human ignorance in her head and the retaliation of the earth if it continued unchecked. She now saw those in hiding, holding on to their last bits of power and the Great War that had already started that Argan had talked about.

"I . . ." she started to speak. Her voice was raspy. She desperately wanted water to drink. She cleared her throat. "I see it. All of it. You were right, Argan."

He smiled and pulled her into his chest. "You're talking sense now."

She collapsed in his arms and looked across the room at her grandfather.

"See you around, kid," he said and raised his hand in farewell. His body slowly faded into light and Skylar scrambled to stand up and Argan helped her. Only Arthur's aura remained, a deep blue similar to Rachel's. It soon faded and traveled upward.

"What happened?" Skylar asked.

Diana leapt out of her seat and raced to where Arthur had been standing. "That isn't right," she said, looking up into the telluric sky. "He was not supposed to go back to the third dimen-sion yet."

"He didn't," Lucifer said. "He went . . . up."

"He ascended?" Diana and Skylar asked in unison.

"Yes," he said bored with the conversation. "You got played, Diana. It would seem Arthur found a loophole in your system."

"And what would that be?" she asked, her eyes narrow slits.

He looked at the ancient scale of truth. The pans were even. "His connection with Skylar was enough to trigger the test of the feather of truth. His soul was light enough to earn ascension. He saw an opportunity and took it."

They all stood staring at the scale in disbelief.

Suki finally broke the silence. "Beatrice is going to be so pissed."

Dread seeped into every cell of Skylar's body. *Pissed* wouldn't begin to cover it.

48

Skylar gained her bearings and waited by the citrine wall. "Ohhh!" she gasped. The wall was repairing itself before her eyes. Darkened patches were disappearing, leaving only light yellow behind. She had done it! After all of the hurdles to get to a place she didn't know existed, no matter the consequence of drinking from the river, *she* had restored the memory of Sophia. Her eyes filled with happy tears. She had done it.

"Which memory was it?" Suki asked. "That triggered the healing?"

"My mother's," Skylar said, knowing it was as simple as that.

She looked at Suki and Argan. They had taken the leap into the unknown with her. She couldn't have made it without them. Argan was owed her love and Suki was owed the truth. . . .

Skylar took Suki's hand and led her to face Diana. "I've sacrificed, now it's your turn."

Diana's face grew dark with her secret. "I don't know what you're talking about," she said.

"You called me selfish but you are the selfish one, Diana," Skylar said. "You stay here holding court, with all your power but you're hiding. You are just like your sister. Tell Suki the truth or I will."

"Sky, what's going on?" Suki asked.

The anger faded from Diana's face and softened into remorse.

"Follow me," she said. She studied the citrine wall for a few moments before making a selection and removed a small piece. As it rested in her hand, the light from within intensified and a hologram formed in the air. A silent movie played for Suki. It was the night her parents died, the night Diana killed them and herself.

As Suki watched, a tear escaped her eye and fell down her cheek. The scene played on and she took Skylar's hand for support.

"I am sorry for your loss," Diana said solemnly.

"That's it," Skylar said. "That's all you have to say?"

Diana's face fell for a moment and then she met Suki's eyes. "For over two decades, I have drawn this memory from the wall over and over. And I will continue to do so for eternity. I never thought I would have the opportunity to meet the girl who was left without a family because of me. I see much suffering in this wall, but this one memory is my only regret."

Skylar no longer needed a hologram to relive the memory. She was now privy to every memory ever created in the history of the world. "You killed her parents," she said as rage welled inside her from a place she couldn't name.

"Sky, wait," Suki said. "I need time to process this and you're not helping with all of your toxic energy."

"My toxic energy?" her voice squeaked. "I'm defending you!"

"Thank you but you're not seeing clearly. I don't think I need defending. Diana isn't trying to hurt me. She's giving me a piece to my puzzle. And I'm . . . grateful." Suki turned to Diana. "I appreciate your willingness to show me the truth. I think I forgive you."

"Thank you," Diana said with relief in her voice. Her wrinkled brow softened. "I *may* consider retiring this memory to the wall permanently."

Skylar stared at the floor, trying to make sense of the barrage of feelings assaulting her senses. Suki was right, she wasn't thinking clearly. She was confusing all sorts of memories and feelings that weren't even hers. She stumbled back briefly as the enormity of what she had done to herself set in.

Argan came over, concerned. "I don't know how any of us are still standing," he said, visibly haggard. "But we may have overstayed our welcome." He pointed to the complete darkness that had overtaken the sun above them. A dark cloud of smoke descended from the sky. As it got closer, they could see the cloud was actually a group of individual beings. Skylar recognized them as shadow sylphs, Beatrice's dark army in charge of nightmares. "They're from Beatrice," Skylar said, too exhausted to be scared. "And they're not happy." One would think her grandmother's flock wouldn't hurt Skylar but she knew better.

Diana approached the threesome as the dark sylphs drew in. "They never show themselves here."

"Yeah," Skylar said. "This is an extreme moment for Nana."

"You have all passed every test thus far," Diana said. "Even Lucifer can't deny it." He couldn't deny but didn't acknowledge it either. With a tip of his head and hand he faded from view to the safety of the ethers.

"Coward," Skylar spat.

Argan scrunched his face. "Sky, we're going to have to talk about your new affinity toward rage," he said.

She shot him a look and turned toward Diana. Skylar now saw her in her true form and understood. Diana was the darkness, a necessary shadow to push humanity toward transformation. She *was* the Dark Madonna.

"You see the truth now, in all its forms," Diana said. "The dark benefits as much as the light. Through your act of great courage and sacrifice, you have restored Sophia's memory in the

Akasha. Great cleansing can now occur." She smiled eerily like Milicent and it jarred Skylar back to her present life.

"What do I tell your sister?" she asked.

"I am not returning to the earth plane," Diana said. "I have purpose here. Tell her to find her own." She waved to them all and started back toward the garden.

"What do we do about those?" Skylar asked.

"Skylar, they're just mist. For as much as Beatrice puffs up her importance, she's just a lot of hot air. At the end of all things, there is nothing she can do. Arthur made his choice willingly. He's gone." Diana waved farewell to Suki and Argan and retreated to the garden.

Skylar looked at the ominous sylphs and had no interest in another fight. She reached out her hand and commanded them to let her pass. Her authority stunned them and they shattered into smaller pieces. It reminded Skylar of the light fish from the cabin. Each piece disintegrated like ash and the sunlight returned to the sky. Skylar had mastered the element of air.

"That's right!" Suki said with her ire up, yelling at the sylphs dissipating before their eyes.

They walked out into a quiet courtyard. There was no one anywhere to be seen. Skylar, Argan, and Suki were left standing alone in this foreign land that had changed each of them forever. They ambled back the way they came, in silence, to the alchemical door. Skylar was looking forward to returning to Silverwood. It was one step closer to going home.

She turned and looked back at the beauty of the Underworld. It contained a lost magic desperately needed to reawaken the world above. She knew for certain, the darkness of Diana, of Lucifer, heaven and hell—they weren't outside of us, they are us. The good and the bad, the duality of our existence is necessary for wholeness. Once acknowledged, everything opens and bows to human potential.

49

Through the door, they fell into a heap on the floor of the alchemy cabin.

"Not graceful, but thankful we are in one piece," Skylar said. Argan found his second wind and jumped to his feet. He gave a hand to each of the girls and touched Skylar's hair. "Your red streak is gone. Back to brilliant white," he said. Age lines appeared on his face. She grazed his cheek with her hand. Somehow it made him more handsome.

Suki took a handful of her own hair, now tinged with silver. "Damn it! I didn't know that was going to happen," she said. "There were no physical changes when I came from the Quine."

"We've aged in the Underworld," Argan said.

"That makes sense, we've literally been through hell," Suki said.

Skylar looked at her grandfather's clock. It had stopped an hour before; just about the time Arthur left the Underworld. She touched it. "I love you, Grampy," she said, smiling.

She felt the call of Sophia's book from the shelf. She picked it up and it pulsed with a vitality she had never experienced. She felt passion, desire, and intention come off the pages in radical waves. The swell of intense energy rocked her body over and over. She dropped the book and gripped the table for support. Suki covered Argan's eyes in mock prudery. The waves subsided and Skylar returned the book to the shelf. "I'll have to come back tomorrow to handle that," she said and walked to the door. She held on to the doorjamb for support and immediately threw up.

"We can go back, you can drink from the Lethe," Argan said with worry.

The thought of forgetting all of her memories, all of her life, all of her love, made her heart ache. "No," she said immediately. "That isn't an option. I'll make this work, somehow." She threw up for a second time. The strain on her body had increased once they returned to the cabin. She could only imagine what it would be like when she returned home.

"Should I take you to the infirmary?" Argan asked.

"What are they going to do for me?" Skylar asked.

"I don't know, maybe they have a magic formula," he said.

"Okay," she said with little energy to disagree. He entwined her arm with his and they walked out into the fresh air.

Suki looked around the quiet room and took down the Book of Sophia from the shelf and held it in both hands. Nothing happened. "Damn," she said and she quickly ran after her friends.

The threesome passed through the main courtyard on their way back from the cabin, looking well worse for wear. Equinox celebrations were in full swing. Cedars were drinking who knew what and dancing dangerously close to each other. It was eerily similar to the previous night's happenings but Skylar was in no shape to analyze it.

Suki stared at the frivolity with no energy to smile. "I'm going to head back to the room. I need to lay down," she said.

Skylar looked up at her from her bent position. "You going to be okay?" she asked.

"Sure," Suki said. "I just need to process everything." She gave Skylar a smile and headed toward Cabin 3A.

Skylar continued on to the infirmary with Argan's help. "I'm sorry I'm not much of an Equinox date," she said.

"We'll celebrate when you're better," he said.

Rachel was on duty at the front desk and greeted them as they walked through the door. "Trip to the Underworld, I see?" she said, reading them both. She frowned at Skylar, and then shifted to Argan. "You look like complete shit and that's saying a lot. Are you sick? Did you drink anything weird? Get impaled by any foreign objects?" she asked.

"Nope, none of the above," he said. "I did get rid of my cat, though."

Rachel looked puzzled then shrugged it off. "Take two of these and get a good night sleep," she said, handing him ibuprofen. "You go, she stays."

"I really think I need to stay," Argan protested.

"No, only those that need it stay. Out!" she shooed him out before he had much of a chance to look at Skylar.

She found the nearest cot and collapsed. She didn't care if Rachel saw her at her worst. "Sit tight, I'll be back in a few," Rachel said and disappeared behind a half wall. The sounds of snapping lids and clinking glass distracted Skylar from her nausea but the ear-piercing whirr of a blender went right through her head.

Rachel returned with a tall glass of thick green liquid reminiscent of the smoothies she made in present day. She set it on the small metal table near Skylar's head. "Drink this within five minutes or it will start to grow." Skylar's nostrils flared when the smell consumed her and she watched yellow bubbles fester at the top. Rachel turned back. "I'm serious, five minutes." She looked at her watch. "Now four minutes."

Skylar didn't budge. Nothing moved but her eyes. They traveled between the bubbling liquid and Rachel. It took her a minute, one of the four, to register what she was seeing around

Rachel's midsection. A bright, circular wave of color spiraled around Rachel's belly. It was mesmerizing and gave Skylar butterflies in her own belly. She could see the tiny body of a baby growing, thriving within Rachel. Skylar's mind flooded with the feelings pouring from Rachel's heart. She felt Rachel's love for her unborn baby and also her concern for the life this special child would have. Skylar could see Rachel's pride, carrying the light of hope for the coming generations. She was honored to be the one to bring this baby into the world.

"Three minutes!" Rachel shouted from across the infirmary. Skylar glanced at the glass. *What would it do to her?* she wondered. *Improve her situation?* She couldn't imagine it much worse. She moved to pick up the glass but stopped when the door opened. Milicent slipped in quietly. She glanced at Skylar but seemed to look through her with glazed eyes, and headed for the apothecary. Skylar studied her, her aura was different than she'd expected. There were large pockets of dark energy around her lower abdomen and circling her head, but her stomach was a strong, vibrant yellow. Her solar plexus, the seat of her soul was resolute.

She helped herself to handfuls of unknown herbs.

"You can't take those," Rachel said, walking up behind Milicent.

"You can't stop me," Milicent said, carrying on with her task. She put a handful of leaves in a small plastic bag.

"Yes, I can," Rachel said, her voice strong. "In the wrong hands that stuff is lethal."

"Relax, it's just mistletoe," Milicent said, her back toward Rachel.

"I know," Rachel said grabbing the bag out of Milicent's hand. Standing next to each other as teens, there was quite a size discrepancy between them. Rachel was tiny and athletic; Milicent, tall and slender.

Milicent grabbed the bag back. "Don't do that," she said coldly.

"I can't let you leave with mistletoe in March," Rachel said. "You don't want it for kissing, I'm sure." She reached out her hand to take it again and Milicent grabbed her wrist. She held her hand up close to her face and studied it. She closed her eyes and whispered a few words Skylar couldn't hear. With a heavy, heated breath she blew on the back of Rachel's hand, exposing a tattoo of three entwined doves. Milicent's stare burned a hole in the image as she slowly crushed Rachel's hand. Rachel tried to pull away but couldn't escape Milicent's grip.

Skylar tried to sit up in her cot. She glanced at her glass of green liquid, now oozing over the side onto the metal table. Her five minutes were up. She stood up, only halfway, the pain engulfed her whole body, head to toe.

"You . . ." Milicent whispered in Rachel's ear. "You think you can hide who you are. But I know. I've always known. And you think you can hide that baby. I grow stronger here as you do, but one day when you let your guard down, I will come for her and it will be the end of life as you know it." She released her grip and walked out the door with her bag of mistletoe. Rachel fell backward and caught herself on the edge of the counter and slowly found her way to the floor. She began to sob.

Skylar gathered all of her strength and stood up. She wanted to help Rachel but first followed Milicent outside. "Milicent, wait," she called, holding on to the railing for support. Skylar knew she had a decision to make. She had an opportunity to change the future and change Milicent's mind about Rachel. She wanted to help, to improve the lives of everyone involved, including herself. But she wondered if intervening here would be helping. She couldn't be sure either way. She closed her eyes and saw a future memory where Milicent let her anger go and Rachel was free to raise her baby in peace. It was Skylar's future without Cassie.

"Save the lecture," Milicent said. "She owes me one life, I'll collect when that baby's born." She walked quickly across the courtyard to the Great Mother's tree. On the Equinox it had transformed from the sparkling icicle tree of winter into a familiar ethereal wonder. It was the tree on the astral plane she saw in Ocean's yard.

Skylar did her best to keep up with her. "Please, Milicent, please don't let the pain of the past harden your heart in the future."

"Too late," Milicent said, her tone biting. As her words came out, Skylar relived the memory of the night Rachel showed up at the Cannons and ruined their family forever. She felt for Milicent's loss and watched the tiny light within her heart go out.

"No," Skylar said. "That can't be the end. There's always a glimmer, no matter how bleak."

"Not here," Milicent said. She crushed the leaves of mistletoe and sprinkled them into a paper cup already brimming with brown liquid. With a pocketknife she sliced the pad of her middle finger and let the blood drip into the cup. "It needs a witness to work, so I guess you're it," she said. She gave it a quick stir and drained it in three gulps. She dropped the cup and placed both palms on the tree. And then she waited.

Skylar watched Milicent's aura turn gray and crack like dry serpent skin. As the grayness consumed her whole body, the yellow light of her solar plexus extinguished as easily as blowing out a candle. Skylar had no idea what it meant.

She's done her rituals and worked her magic, Magda's voice said. *This is the last step to actively detach her soul from her body. Only powerful necromancers are capable of this. Once a body is separated from its soul, it is free to commit the most heinous of crimes, without remorse.* Skylar's own heart felt the coldness of Milicent's intent. *She's preparing to kill Rachel's baby.*

Skylar had heard the story. She had even seen glimpses of it in her visions. But here, now, she felt the evil unleashed when a soul is taken by anyone but God.

One bright green leaf on a low branch of the tree shriveled unnaturally before Skylar's eyes. All color faded, leaving it charred for just a moment then it fell to the ground. Before Milicent could scoop it up, it vanished. The irises of her eyes went black and then back to normal. "Goodbye, Skylar," she said. "I'm leaving Silverwood. There's nothing this place can teach me."

Skylar stood motionless as she watched her walk away. Her only consolation was that she knew how the story played out.

Remember, Skylar, Magda said. *The future is malleable, even one you think you know.*

With an enormous weight on her heart, she went back inside to check on Rachel. Surprised to see her back at her desk, Skylar did her best to get there before resting on the floor.

"You should really get back in that cot," Rachel said. "You never drank the smoothie." They both looked at the smoldering table.

"That would be eating away at my stomach lining right now," Skylar said.

"Not really," Rachel said. "It has a counter effect once inside the body."

"You seem to have recovered from Milicent's visit," Skylar said looking at Rachel's bandaged hand.

Rachel shrugged. "It's nothing new," she said. "Her threats. There's nothing I can do to change the past. I have a plan . . . to protect my baby." She looked at Skylar and gave her a tight-lipped smile. This was her first mention of being pregnant. "It isn't ideal, but what would be in this scenario? She'll be safe and that's all that matters."

"You're having a girl?" Skylar asked.

"I have no medical proof, just a knowing in my heart," Rachel said, her smile a bit wider. Even amidst the horror of her situation, Rachel exuded hope.

"I'm sure you're right," Skylar said. For the first time, she felt true empathy for Rachel and the ultimate sacrifice she made to protect her baby. "Can I trouble you to make another smoothie? I promise to drink this one."

"Absolutely," Rachel said.

50

At the same moment, Skylar, Argan, and Suki appeared before the Great Mother's tree in the commons as if all called by a mysterious voice. Ocean stood beside it, waiting. She truly was a fiery soul, on the edge of a fight at all times. On this day, the first one after the Equinox, she looked radiant, different than Skylar had ever seen her. She never would have described Ocean as beautiful until now. But she was able to see all of the layers, all of the lives that Ocean had lived and the scope of what she had done for humanity over the millennia was unfathomable.

To her left stood Beatrice, to her right, Vivienne. Argan and Suki stared at them in awe. One Great Mother was impressive but the trio together was mind-blowing.

"I must be in trouble," Skylar said scanning them all. Beatrice looked even older than her ninety-five years.

"What did you think you were doing?" Ocean started in. "This is irreversible!"

"Ocean, don't start," Beatrice said. "Let me handle this."

"Handle this?" Ocean gasped. "You had her whole life to handle this and you didn't. Your time is up."

"Sisters, why must you have the same squabble for eternity?" Vivienne asked in a melodic voice that sounded like water falling over seashells. "It wastes too much energy." Vivienne truly embodied the magic of another world, the sea. She was stunning in blue robes that caressed her body like the flowing water she came from.

"It's just what we do," Ocean said.

Vivienne turned her attention to Skylar. "Child, you drank from the Mnemosyne."

"I had to Vivienne, uh, grandmother," Skylar reddened. "I lost my stone and then I had my mother's ring and that didn't work either . . ." she rambled knowing it was pointless. "I had to move to plan B."

"But now you can see where your stone is," Vivienne said.

"Britt took it," Skylar said. "I can't even be mad at her really. I understand her intent now. She's trying to save her mother's sanity. She thought the stone would help. But it won't."

Beatrice looked pained. Her granddaughter betrayed them all and her husband was gone forever. "You took Arthur from me," she said to Skylar.

"Nana, I am truly sorry. I had no idea that would happen," Skylar said. "Believe me when I say that Grandpa knew very well what he was doing."

Beatrice lowered her head. "He knew," she said like a woman who had learned her beloved chose another.

"I'm sorry," Skylar whispered, knowing there was nothing else she could say that would matter to her grandmother.

Argan stepped between them, looking tired but more rugged than Skylar had ever seen him. "Ladies, I know the road to our goal took a few wrong turns but you should be proud of Skylar. She completed her task even when it looked insurmountable." He smiled at her with love.

"No ill effects from drinking from the Mnemosyne?" Vivienne asked, one eyebrow raised with suspicion.

"I have to say the effects haven't been as extreme as I feared. I'm still standing," Skylar said. "I think Rachel's smoothie did the trick."

"This is highly unusual," Vivienne persisted. "Your nervous system should have shorted out on contact."

Skylar started theorizing. "Maybe with my potent blood and evolved DNA, I had the tool kit to handle . . ." Something clicked and she looked at Ocean. "Ocean?" she asked with suspicion. "Did you *know* I would be drinking from the Mnemosyne?"

"Knew? No," Ocean shook her head. "Hoped." She winked.

"That's why I've been ingesting gold all these months," Skylar said.

"A built up tolerance works wonders," Ocean said, straight-faced.

"So the line about anti-aging?" Skylar asked.

"Bunk," Ocean said.

"Well done, Skylar," Vivienne piped in. "By returning the memory to the Akasha, you have repaired the damage done by millennia of repression and abuse. You have paved the way for Sophia's return and the era of great cleansing will have a better chance of success."

"Cleansing," Skylar repeated as she slowly turned toward Vivienne. The word clicked in her mind like a key unlocking an old door. She remembered the words from the Book of Sophia:

Once the memory is restored, the great cleansing occurs.
The lines of the dragon will ignite,
Re-fuse the fire within all hearts.
The desire behind all desires will come to light.

The familiar tingle spread across the back of her head. It told her she was not done working for the Great Mothers. Not by a long shot.

51

The threesome had agreed to stay at Silverwood a few more days to rest but then head back to the present and get on with the future. Skylar considered staying until the end of the semester but the value didn't outweigh the cost of delaying her life in 2021. She had slept for twenty-four hours straight after seeing the Great Mothers and was ready to move her body. Suki was creating balance in the world by not sleeping the past twenty-four hours, taking round the clock meditation classes.

Skylar freshened up and left her cabin to go for a walk. It was dusk and the charge of spring fever in the air was invigorating. Campus was quiet; most cedars were still recovering from their Equinox highs. There was no urgency to *do* anything. Everyone was happy simply *being*.

After a short walk, Skylar found herself on the steps of cabin eleven, rapping on the door.

"Hey, you're up!" Argan said, his eyes bright with happiness to see her. "I didn't realize you were strong enough for the walk over." He glanced up to see if anyone else was around.

"Each day gets better," she said, walking past him into the cabin. "Ocean has me on a triple dose elixir. It's calming my nervous system so I can function normally. Although I'm losing some of the benefits of the Mnemosyne with cloudy visions. I'll have to tweak the dosage but all the body aches are gone. Thank goodness. I'll be back to barrel racing in no time."

"Ha, horses," he said, wistfully. "Seems like a lifetime ago." He shut the door behind them.

"It was," she said. His packed duffle bag sat on the bed. "Packed I see. I guess I should do the same. We've done everything we set out to do."

He leaned back on the low dresser and folded his arms as if he were studying her.

"What?" she asked self-consciously. A myriad of possibilities flashed in her mind and she tried to pick out one that might fit.

"You did it, Sky, you solved your puzzle. And here we are on the other side of it like the end of a movie."

"Act II, really," she said, trying to find something to do with her hands.

"Huh?"

"Everything gets buttoned up at the end of Act II. You think you're done but then a surprise happens to screw up happily ever after for a whole other act," she said, helping herself to a seat on the bed. She giggled when it squeaked and bounced a few times to exaggerate it.

"Since when were you a screenwriter?" he asked, still stuck in his stance by the dresser.

"Elective at Cornell," she leaned back on her elbows. "If horses fail me, film's calling my name."

He chuckled. "You'd be a natural."

"How about you, Argan?" she asked. "What do you see in your future now that all of this is over?"

"I should ask you that question, soothsayer," he said. He started to pace slowly, his arm still crossed.

"Please don't blow off my question," she said, following him with her eyes.

"I haven't given it much thought," he said.

"That can't be true," she said. "You plan everything."

"All of my plans got me nowhere. Along the way I learned this is the Skylar show and I'm just along for the ride."

"You don't really believe that," she said, standing up. "You're not supporting character material. You have Leading Man written all over you."

He shrugged off her comment. She walked to him and touched the new lines on his face. "You've literally come to the end of the earth for this quest you've been training for your whole life."

"You must know it was all for you." The truth in his eyes made her look away but he caught her cheek with his hand and forced her to look at him. "I know what you came for, Skylar, even if you don't."

"I'm omnipotent now, remember," she said, trying to lighten the moment but all she felt was heat.

"Then you know we're never going to be just friends," he said, refusing to release her from his stare. He cupped her face with both hands and leaned in with painful slowness. He stopped short of her lips. "Never," he whispered and kissed her softly.

He was right; this *was* why she'd come here.

He released her and pulled his shirt off over his head. She grinned as she took in the sight of his deeply tanned muscles flexing in the light of the lonely table lamp.

"Why now?" she asked. "What's changed?" her voice cracked.

He brushed her hair away from her neck. "Everything. We completed our mission. I did everything asked of me. And through it all I've felt your hunger and you've felt mine. It had no place before but now, I'm done fighting it." He buried his face in the cradle of her neck and every hair on her body stood at attention. She held her breath as his lips traveled upward.

He whispered in her ear. "For so long you closed your heart to me, pushed me aside, even got lost with another." He pulled her shirt collar aside and kissed her collarbone, "But here, now, I'm the mind reader and I see you're ready to let that go."

He pulled her shirt off over her head and traced her shimmering scar of three doves with his thumb. Unhooking her bra, he let her breasts fall open. Bowing his head in reverence, he caressed and kissed each one as they stood. He lifted his head to meet her eyes. "Will you give yourself to me?" he asked.

"Yes," she whispered. She couldn't speak another word. She was overwhelmed by him, his ability to command the moment, strong but tender.

"Good," he smiled. "I'm going to make love to you now," he said as his lips met hers with the desire behind all desires. The brush of his bare chest against hers made her shiver.

He walked toward the bed and gently settled her on the pillows, not missing a beat of their kiss. He let his pants fall to the floor and climbed next to her. Her hand shook as she touched the muscles of his stomach. Argan was love and his body was the physical expression of that love. She looked at him with wonder.

He explored her body with his hands, and she responded with overwhelming need at his touch. He was commanding yet nurturing, in charge yet vulnerable. A tear escaped her eye as her body succumbed to the yearning of her heart. She felt her sense of self slipping away, opening to a force greater than any she'd ever known.

He shifted his weight and lay gingerly above her, propped on his elbows. His body still as he caressed her hair with his hands.

She tried to move but he clasped her hands over her head. "Not yet," he said, his voice rough. "I still feel the part of you pushing me away. Please relax and open your heart to me." She felt his warmth, his love, his masculinity. He knew exactly how to move and how to love her. She looked into his eyes and saw their connection that spanned the ages. She felt the love that had endured pain and loss and held steadfast, leading them to the perfection of this moment.

She pressed her body to his, wanting him to fill the depth of her being with his love. Together they expanded beyond their bodies, beyond all boundaries, and connected to the grace and divinity of God. As the ripples of orgasm washed over her body, she felt their source. They radiated from her heart.

Her face glowing and her body trembling, she was almost afraid to look at Argan. For a brief moment, fear entered her mind. This was the reason she closed her heart to him from the beginning. This was the reason she had given herself so thoughtlessly to another.

"Skylar?" he said, his voice almost playful. "I see your mind tormenting you about the past. Let it go. There's no room in the future for those memories. Love is our true purpose."

She smiled, remembering her purpose. Was it all that she had accomplished? Or was it this? It was all of it and she was completely fulfilled.

They continued their love making throughout the night, barely stopping for any reason. Each orgasm seemed to fuel her energy, not deplete it. She let herself get distracted from the moment to think maybe she *had* learned a thing or two in sexual energy class. She chuckled at the thought.

"Something funny?" Argan asked, lying on his stomach, briefly satiated at the wee hour of 2:00 a.m.

"No, I'm just grateful for this night, so very grateful," she said.

"It's the first of many," he said. In that moment she knew she would never leave.

52

Skylar spent the last day wrapping up some loose items for her cedars and getting Origin up to speed if he chose to continue teaching her class.

"I'm sorry your time here is through, Skywalker," he said when she came to say goodbye.

She chuckled. What was once annoying now seemed almost endearing. "Thank you for all of your help," she said. "I hope we cross paths again one day." Skylar wondered exactly what he was doing in the year 2021. She reached to give him a hug but he cut her off with a bow of Namaste and was gone.

She considered leaving in the night, not having to say goodbye to everyone. Goodbye seemed so much worse than hello. She had grown to love and forgive Rachel. It had been so easy to judge her, denied the perspective personal experience reveals. But seeing Rachel's real struggle gave Skylar a precious gift: compassion. She knew Rachel had a painful and disheartening road ahead. But once she stepped back into 2021, it would be behind them both. It was a tough concept to grasp.

Ocean said she'd see them all back home. She handed Skylar a bag of ibis feathers. "These are yours now," she said and turned on her heels. She wasn't one for goodbyes either.

But there was one goodbye Skylar couldn't avoid. She returned to the alchemist's cabin with Argan one last time.

"Do you mind waiting here?" she asked him.

"Not at all," he said and kissed her.

She got to the porch and saw Cassie through the doorway. She was her vibrant teen self, eternally young. Skylar didn't know how to take a step forward or back. She stood frozen on the porch.

"We're heading out soon," she said from the doorway, her voice cracked. "I came to say goodbye."

Cassie smiled with wisdom beyond her years. "I know you're sad, Skylar, but you know this is all an illusion. The end doesn't last."

Skylar nodded and smiled slightly. She did know that. Her ability to see the divine plan showed her how the puzzle fit together beautifully. And one day they would be reunited as if only apart for mere minutes.

At a loss for words, she found the courage to move and rushed Cassie with a fierce hug. Today, there were no shocks. She was grateful for this second opportunity to know her mother and to feel her one more time. Once again, she could stay five minutes or five years and it wouldn't matter. Time truly didn't matter. She released her hug and turned toward the door.

"Wait!" Cassie said. She grabbed the Book of Sophia from the shelf and flipped to the back. Skylar's eyes widened as she watched Cassie rip out the last pages. "Finish it," she said, handing her the blank parchment. The pages vibrated in her hands just as the whole book had done so many times before. She looked up from her hands at Cassie but she was gone.

"Sky," Argan said from the doorway. "Ready to go?"

"Sure," she said. She took one last look around the cabin and knew it wouldn't be long until she'd be back in her own tiny house in 2021. They walked out into the sunshine and Skylar enjoyed the warmth on her face. "Hey, did you ever see Cassie here?"

"Nope," he said.

She nodded and glanced back at the cabin. Her mother leaned in the doorway with a big smile. She blew Skylar a kiss and waved. Skylar waved back. Argan was smart enough not to ask. He looked at the paper in her hand. "Any secrets?"

"Yes, many," she said. "But it turns out, they're my own."

53

"Are you going home your way or ours?" Skylar asked Suki as they walked out the door of Cabin 3A for the last time. The weather had quickly caught up to the heat wave back home and the girls dressed in shorts.

"My way," Suki said emphatically. "I don't think I'll ever take dense transportation again." She slung her duffle over her shoulder.

"You know how to get back?" Argan asked.

"Yup," Suki said. "I left the door open at the Quine."

"That was a week ago," Skylar said. "You don't think anyone's come along and closed it?"

Suki's face fell, she had obviously not thought that part through. "I have to try," she said. "If I have any problems, I'll come back." She walked off in the direction of the cabin and Skylar was confident Suki would be all right.

Skylar and Argan reached the car that had been sitting at the edge of camp for almost two months.

"It better start," Skylar said into the airwaves. "We're too far away from everything, magic included, to get any help." They hopped in and it started right up. She said a word of thanks.

Argan took the first shift driving home. Skylar sat in the passenger seat staring out the window. Her thoughts drifted to Britt. "How do you think Britt found her way out of here?" she asked. She didn't get any answers from her mind's eye.

"Probably that way," Argan said, pointing straight ahead at the dirt road lit up with flecks of gold. As they approached them, the flecks disappeared. They weren't actual flecks but little twinkles of energy. Skylar and Argan could see the telluric currents running under the ground, guiding them out of Silverwood.

"That's amazing!" She opened the window and stuck her head out. "Can you pull over? I want to get out."

Argan obliged and they both got out to take a closer look.

The mirage held as they bent to the ground and touched the iridescent dirt. It was earth. Dirt and stone ground together with grass, all materials of Mother Earth. She was showing them the way home. Skylar looked behind them. No light. She left no trail to the past, only that which she carried in her heart. "Okay, we can go. Thank you for stopping," she said.

"That's it?" Argan asked.

"I understand now," Skylar said. "There's no more looking behind. We've done that enough. I will carry the love of my mother with me always but the time for grieving is over. Forward is the only way."

"And so it is," he nodded and took her hand.

They climbed back in the car and the phosphorous path led them through twists of trees and fields and along the edge of one harrowing cliff. Argan used his four-wheeling skills to guide them safely to the highway. Their guidance faded and Skylar knew they were back in 2021.

"I expected to feel a time jump," Skylar said.

"You didn't?" Argan was out of breath. "I feel like I got punched in the gut."

"Let me drive then," she said. He rolled to a stop to catch his breath and she jumped out of the car. She opened the driver's door and Argan turned and vomited on her sneakers.

"Ugh!" she jumped back but it was too late.

"That feels better," he said standing up. "Sorry."

"I can't clean these!" She took off her sneakers immediately and wiped them in the grass, which didn't help much. She fished out a plastic bag from the back seat and put them in it. She hopped into the driver's seat barefoot.

"I'm good now, really," Argan said.

"I got this, thanks," Skylar said. "Get in."

Almost immediately Argan fell asleep. "Sure, you're good," she said to a sleeping Argan, his mouth already slung open. She looked at him and she felt peace. They were together at last. She had completed her mission. Her eyes had been opened to a world that existed within our own—the Underworld. She had gotten to see lost loved ones again, Cassie, Arthur. Even drinking from the Mnemosyne had become a positive experience. All was right in the world.

A few hours into the drive all that was right turned horribly wrong in the landscape. The bright green trees that lined the road were decimated from the top down. Skylar bent her neck to get a better view out the windshield. For miles trees were either chopped in half or burnt straight to the ground. Another few minutes clicked by and she realized they were the only car on the highway, north or southbound. Being alone was ominous and made her nervous. And then she saw why. . . .

A hole had opened from inside the earth, breaking the land in two. She rolled to a stop in the middle of the highway a few feet before the drop. Deeper dread filled her veins. She had a suspicion she hoped wasn't true. She got out of her car and walked to the edge of the crater. "Why didn't they shut down the highway?" she asked aloud.

"Emergency crews are too busy," a sole workman in an orange construction hat, said. "They haven't gotten around to it yet." He carried one cone and placed it in front of the massive hole.

"You're going to need a bigger cone," Skylar said.

He snorted a small laugh. "You'll have to turn around and backtrack through the rest area. You can get to the other side from there. Hope you don't have too far to travel though. The road's a warzone."

She looked back at her car. Argan was standing there, holding the passenger door. As she started back toward him, the workman got in his pickup and passed her, driving in reverse down the highway.

Neither of them said a word and hopped back into the car. As she put the car in reverse, she startled from the sound of her cell phone. She hadn't heard it ring in two months.

"Hello?" she spoke into the speakerphone.

"Finally," Suki said. "Where are you on the trip? I've been back for hours."

"We have another two hours to go," Skylar said. "And we've hit a bit of a snag."

"It can't be soon enough," Suki said. "We have big problems. Beatrice has been busy."

54

As Skylar continued to drive, the landscape became bleaker. The sun was low in the sky and a menacing wind had kicked up to blow the few trees still standing. She turned the radio on to get some news. An unprecedented number of natural disasters had plagued the planet for over a week. In the U.S. alone, the South was decimated by hurricanes, tornados in the Midwest, fires in California. The East Coast saw unprecedented wind activity. DC was currently under a massive scale tornado watch.

Talking to Beatrice couldn't wait another moment. She dialed her grandmother's number. "Nana, where are you?" Skylar yelled into the phone. The sound of the wind outside her car made it impossible to hear her.

"Rosen," Beatrice said calmly, almost serene. "I'm at Milicent's facility." It was an odd place for Beatrice to be. Skylar *should* have taken Suki's way home.

"Will you be there long?" Skylar asked. "We really need to discuss what's going on here."

"There's nothing to discuss, Skylar," Beatrice said. "You've heard the line about a woman scorned? Well this is that, but bigger."

"Oh Nana, really? You can't take the world down with you. I've seen the future and this isn't it."

"I don't have time to talk now," Beatrice said.

"I'll be there in a few hours," Skylar said. She glanced at

Argan and he shrugged. "Please stay put until I get there. We'll figure out how to move forward from this." Beatrice hung up without saying a word.

"Just focus on driving," Argan said. The wind brought heavy rain and Skylar was unsure she could stay on the road. The lack of fellow motorists was a blessing. They didn't have much to bump into when the wind pushed the car sideways except downed trees.

They managed to get back to Rosen with only a few unavoidable scratches to her car.

The landscape continued to show the brunt of Bea's wrath. On campus more trees were on their side, ripped from their roots. The welcome center was sliced completely down the middle, as if by a giant sword.

"Man, she's pissed," Argan said.

"I'm not convinced anger is the root of this," Skylar said. "It's loss."

They drove up to the pristine Equine Facility. It sat as an oasis in the sea of debris just outside its stone fences. Skylar and Argan found Beatrice straddling Shirl in the paddock.

"I'm glad to see you're getting exercise, Nana," Skylar said. "But do you really want to start with riding? There are safer ways to ease back into fitness."

"Always the smart-ass," Bea said, staring into the distance. "You see me now, all decaying, at the end of things. But I was young once. And beautiful."

Skylar saw a young woman in her mind's eye, strikingly similar to Cassie.

"And you think Grampy left you because you lost your looks?" Skylar asked. "We both know that's not true. You can return to your youth with the blink of an eye."

"You've aged as well, carrying the weight of the world in your head," Beatrice said, easing herself off of the horse. "There's no escaping the toll this job takes and I don't want to erase the reminder of all I've seen. My sisters reclaim their youth over and over because they have no desire to remember the love. I won't do that." Booming clangs of pain crashed around them disguised as thunder. Instead of offering cleansing rain, the clouds above them turned thick with smoke, sucking the oxygen out of the air. Skylar could breathe through the soot but Argan fell to his knees choking. With a whirl of her hand, she created a pocket of clean air for him to breathe and he sat on the ground to recover.

"Well done," Beatrice said. "You learned quite a lot at Silverwood." The smoke cleared and the winds calmed.

Skylar didn't think much of another new ability. It was more about focused desire than learning a new party trick. "What else, Nana? Besides a woman scorned. Are you trying to teach Devlin a lesson?"

"He's too far gone, corrupted beyond redemption and will not listen to reason. So I must continue with the Great Plan. The world needs to be purified Skylar. Humans are way behind spiritually. They gave away their power to external forces and this is where we are."

"I understand that," Skylar said. "I also understand that you are a Great Mother and all but you're not God. You don't command who lives and dies."

"Humans are already dead!" She yelled and the wind returned. Argan blew backward and hit the paddock fence hard. "What do they know of love? Of pain? They run from both and fill their days with distractions to avoid anything of meaning."

Skylar started toward Argan but he waved her off as Beatrice continued her tirade. "So now they will listen, as the world sits on the edge of ruin, *you* will listen. My sisters have always seen me as less than, but I am *everything*. The world was created from the WORD—I am that word!"

Skylar let out a deep breath. "Why is everyone so bent on taking credit?" she asked, her eyes darting to Argan and back to Beatrice. "Aren't you above the pettiness?"

"One would think," Beatrice said. "You search for Sophia, I am Sophia! I am the realm of in-between, the ether that holds the heavens apart from earth, yet binds them. Air is life, breath is life."

"You told me Sophia was in all women," Skylar said.

"I am in all women," Beatrice seethed. "The anger from oppression, abuse, ridicule, belittlement. To be treated like a joke by loved ones. I know this pain. I have carried the ancestral pain. It runs deep."

"Maybe, literally. But Sophia comes from within all of us. You can't claim ownership of that." Skylar softened sensing her grandmother's agony. "Nana, all this," she gestured to the chaos around them, "is your refusal to let go. You've been stuck in your own pain and all you want is for the rest of us to acknowledge it. We hear you, Nana." She used her minds' eye to visualize calming breezes but it did nothing to settle the maelstrom around them.

Beatrice turned her back and started walking Shirl toward the stable. Cheveyo came out to greet her. Skylar caught her breath at the sight of her old friend. He glanced in her direction and they locked eyes for almost a minute. "Thank you," she said when he broke his stare. She ran to Argan and whispered in his ear. He hurried off toward her car and she tried to appease Beatrice while he was gone. "Nana, I was one of those people you speak of. I ran from the love of a good man, thinking I was better off protecting my heart, but only when I allowed myself to be vulnerable did I truly come alive. I will never go back to living behind that closed door."

Beatrice kept walking and Skylar kept circling her. "When does this end, Nana? When the world is destroyed? Then what?

Taking the world down doesn't give you the peace you seek. You mock human denial of suffering yet it's your greatest affliction." She ran her hand through her hair. "I'm sorry, Nana. I am so sorry you've been holding the world up with your pain. But your willingness to let go will create a new world, one that can move forward in love and healing. It's time to let go, Nana." She put her hand on Beatrice's shoulder and the frail woman slumped forward. Argan rushed behind her with the bag of ibis feathers and scattered them at her feet. Skylar caught her grandmother in her arms and laid her down in the blanket of white wings.

She rested Beatrice's head in her lap and stroked her yellowed hair. "Oh Nana, I feel like Vivienne. She could never stay mad at Milicent despite her propensity for mass destruction. I feel the same way about you." She smiled slightly.

Beatrice's eyes popped open in an instant. "Help me up!" she barked. She dusted herself off, looked at the feathers and gave Skylar a stern look. "Well played. You're ready. I wouldn't have believed it but you are." She released Skylar's hand. "And so am I."

The sky opened up and a microburst of rain began. It was pointless to run, they were drenched in an instant. Skylar could see the energy of the raindrops cover Beatrice as she became lighter, more ethereal. At her feet, the drops animated each feather. They quivered as she raised her hand in farewell. "Remember I am always with you, just like Cassie," she said. "Call on us and we'll be there. And when the time is right, free the snakes." When only a faint outline of Bea was left, each feather became whole, turning into the bird from which it had come. They flew up, carrying Beatrice's soul on their backs to be reunited with her beloved.

"I thought she couldn't ascend," Argan said staring into the sky.

"The magic of love is that every rule is made to be broken," Skylar said with a wink. She went to hug him and discovered his dark shirt was not only soaked by the rain but also blood. She lifted his shirt. "This looks pretty bad," she said about the gash from the fence. "Do you have powers to fix it?"

"No," he said, wincing. "I'm not like you. I have no magical powers."

"You have many," she said softly. She rested her hands on his chest.

He grabbed her and kissed her hard on the mouth. "Come on, let's get out of here," he said, entwining his arm with hers as they slowly made their way to the car.

55

Skylar stared at the fresh tombstone next to Rhia's. She had known the moment Joshua had died but refused to admit it until now.

"How many more have to die before this is over?" she asked, feeling Ocean's presence behind her.

"Just one," Ocean said.

A strong breeze kicked up and Skylar thought of Beatrice. *She would always be there*, she said. And Skylar smiled. She knelt and touched the new grass growing over Joshua and wondered how Milicent ever agreed to put his body here.

"She didn't have a choice," Ocean said. The sun was hotter than Skylar remembered and the black tree offered no shade. "Ahh, speak of the actual devil. . . ." Skylar turned as Milicent navigated Ocean's freshly cut lawn effortlessly in stilettos. She wore a long-sleeved black dress that covered most of her skin. She was alone.

"I've mastered escaping my keepers," Milicent said to Ocean.

"Meet me on the porch when you're done," Ocean said walking toward the steps. As they passed each other, Milicent handed Ocean the red book.

Skylar returned her focus to Joshua. She had come up empty on helping him with that act of sacrifice he talked about. "I'm sorry I missed the funeral," she said.

"This is it," Milicent said, staring at the ground.

"Oh, I'm a bit underdressed," she said, glancing at her cutoff shorts.

"No matter," Milicent said. "Joshua said you were his only other visitor so I thought you should be here." They stood in silence and Skylar glanced at Milicent. She seemed somber, remorseful, human. Skylar didn't feel animosity toward Milicent. She felt pity.

"What happened?" Skylar asked, unable to handle the silence. "Did he give up?"

Milicent was slow to answer. "I don't know," she said, finally. "For once, I don't have the answer. He was so advanced, biologically, but was a child inside."

"I'm sorry," Skylar said. "After all of it, I *am* sorry he's gone."

Milicent nodded. The breeze returned and Skylar looked up at the black branches of Ocean's tree. On a low branch nearest to them, a bud emerged, green and fertile. "Look," she whispered. Milicent lifted her head and let a rare look of surprise escape. "Has that ever happened?" Skylar asked.

"Not that I'm aware of," Milicent said.

Its root quickly turned yellow and the bud fell onto the grass over Joshua. Their faces dropped, disheartened. Milicent bent to pick it up but stopped short as the fallen bud began to bloom in the grass. They watched as it formed into a full, green leaf. A smile crept across Milicent's face before she could stop herself.

The breeze picked it up from where Joshua lay to rest and carried it up into Milicent's outstretched hand. The leaf quivered for a moment then faded into her skin as if never there.

"Your soul," Skylar said astonished, forgetting her filter. But Milicent didn't care. She collapsed to her knees and cried. Skylar was overcome watching Milicent receive this most precious gift from Joshua. He *had* done it. He had found his sacrifice, he had found Milicent's soul in the astral plane and returned it to her.

One life for another had been Milicent's words at Silverwood. How true they were now.

Milicent's aura flushed clean as if washed from above. Its color now sky blue. She stood up and gave Skylar a genuine smile.

"What happens now?" Skylar asked.

Milicent wiped her cheeks and smoothed her dress. "I guess it's back to business," she said, her cool demeanor returning.

"Will you be returning to Rosen?" Skylar asked.

"I have a country to run," Milicent said. She turned and walked back inside.

Skylar smiled. She knew it was too much to expect the warm and fuzzies from Milicent, even with the return of her soul.

Before she left the yard, she bent and touched Joshua's stone, happy he was finally at peace.

56

Everyone involved knew this day would come; even Milicent who swore it wasn't possible. In the early days of April, an unscrupulous adoption advocate from Bulgaria sold his story to the highest bidder. The news was spilling out; as a toddler, Joshua had been adopted by the Grayers, Milicent to be specific. Devlin's name couldn't be found on any paperwork.

"I told you to fix this!" Devlin roared in the Residence living room. "And now it's too late. There is no amount of damage control to clean this up." He paused his condemnation to sit on the sofa and hang his head in his hands.

"You're right, Dev," she said. Her arms were crossed across her chest as a protective measure. "I'm sorry, there's nothing else I can say." She no longer wanted to hide the truth about Joshua.

He sprang up from the sofa and got in her face. "You're sorry?" His face contorted angrily and the pupils in his eyes widened unnaturally. For a brief moment she thought he would hit her. Instead his hand grabbed her by the neck and he started to squeeze. All of the anger built up over decades of being subservient to his domineering wife poured out of him at once and he lost control of his senses, squeezing harder.

Milicent clutched his hand with both of hers, her face turning bright red. She was unable to make a sound.

"I guess it's my turn to inflict pain, you miserable bitch," he said, his tone turned maniacal.

He released his grip on her throat and grabbed her hair. She gasped for breath. "Devlin, think about what you're doing!" she pleaded between coughs. She looked into his mad eyes and knew something was wrong. He would be angry for sure, but not enough to kill her. He spiraled out of control in seconds and she was too stunned to react. He removed a black cord from his pants pocket, little gold balls attached to each end. Still clutching her hair, he whipped the cord around her neck like a lasso. As he grabbed the ends to choke her, he was met by a blow to the back of his head. He released Milicent and dropped to the floor. Noah stood behind him, holding a large cast iron frying pan, his eyes wide, his mouth gaping open.

Milicent froze. "Noah," she whispered. "What have you done?"

He burst into tears. "I don't know, I just watched *Tangled!*" He let go of the pan and it crashed to the floor. "He was going to kill you, Mil! I could see it, he was enraged, like it wasn't him." He dropped to his knees and curled in a ball on the floor.

Milicent knelt on the floor to recover and checked Devlin's pulse. He was alive. Noah didn't have the upper body strength to kill a man. She sighed. "God damn it, Tecumseh," she said, her voice raspy. She looked down at Devlin's body. "I'm fixing this, my love." With an incantation and a focused surge of energy, she saturated Devlin's artery with electricity and the whites of his eyes flooded with blood. As Noah rocked back and forth, Milicent placed her hand over the bump on Devlin's head and it faded into his scalp. She turned to Noah. "Pull yourself together or you're going to jail." She picked up the Residence phone.

"Violet, the President seems to have had a stroke," she said calmly. "He needs immediate medical attention."

57

Skylar sat in her tiny house with a new appreciation of her surroundings. She was so happy to be back home, a plate of cheese and crackers on her lap. Suki was busy on her laptop, while simultaneously relishing in Entertainment Tonight. Her grandmother's house had a buyer and in a few weeks, she would be homeless.

"Stay with me until you figure it out," Skylar said. "But there's no room for Kyle."

"Thanks, Sky," Suki said. "And that won't be a problem. I don't see us getting back together. He was my first real boyfriend. I think I want to play the field."

"Okay," Skylar said. " I won't be joining you."

"I'm glad you and Argan worked everything out."

On the TV, Entertainment Tonight was interrupted with a special report. The anchor spoke, "We have just received confirmation, President Devlin P. Grayer is dead at the age of sixty-two. Extensive autopsies are being conducted but sources are citing a massive stroke as cause of death."

Skylar and Suki stared at the TV. "Oh, dear god," Skylar said. "Milicent."

With the White House submerged in chaos, Skylar questioned how to get to Milicent. But she knew she had to. Devlin was a huge obstacle that she didn't fully understand and now he was gone. *This is the beginning of the great cleansing,* she thought.

It sounded mad but Skylar knew Sophia's book could help. For so long she kept the book from Milicent but now she would hand it over willingly. Vivienne said there was one last piece to finish, and Skylar knew this was it. She would come full circle and join forces with the First Lady. She didn't have anyone to bounce the idea off of; Beatrice was gone, Ocean was gone. Skylar finally woke up to the fact that Ocean disappeared on purpose to make her solve her own problems. Argan would tell her she's crazy and she really didn't want to hear the word *no*.

She had tried Milicent's personal line for hours and it always went to voicemail. When she resorted to calling the White House main line she was connected with a second assistant who told her it was out of the question to speak with Mrs. Grayer in the foreseeable future.

"I have the number for her Chief of Staff," Suki said casually, her nose again buried in her laptop.

"Why didn't you tell me earlier?" Skylar asked.

"Because I don't think this is a good idea but I love you so I'll help you," Suki said.

Skylar was astonished when Wren answered her own phone. She explained who she was and how it was vital to see the First Lady as soon as possible. Wren concurred and Skylar was amazed at how easy it fell into place, as if divinely guided. Wren had informed her that the First Lady was vacating the East Wing now that the president was dead and she would soon be returning to Rosen. She said that Mrs. Grayer's personal assistant was on a leave of absence and she would see to it that Skylar got on her calendar early the following week.

58

Skylar waited nervously in the heavily air-conditioned Quine conference room for Milicent. She appreciated the two bonsai wisterias she had placed there the previous fall. They had flourished over the winter despite their environment and were each now in full bloom. The room had one small window that allowed the eastern sunlight to shine through.

She hadn't been sitting long before the door opened and a short, weaselly man walked in. His dark energy made Skylar instantly nervous. "I'm sorry, I'm waiting for Mrs. Grayer," she said. It was useless to try to read his aura; it was locked down tight. Her eyes darted around the room for an escape. She couldn't fit through the window and there was only one door in and out. She glanced at Sophia's book but knew there was nowhere to hide it.

He didn't introduce himself or offer a hand in greeting. He closed the door quietly and sat down across the table. He also acknowledged the book with his eyes. "With all of the turmoil in Washington right now, Mrs. Grayer is not inclined to meet with you. She sent me instead," he said, folding his hands.

"We're not *in* Washington," she said, trying to keep focused on the conversation while planning her exit. "I'm sorry to waste your time but I will reschedule with her." She stood up and held her book to her chest. He stood to meet her. To anyone else, he would have appeared harmless, meek even. But Skylar knew he was lethal.

"You're not leaving yet," he said.

"I'm sorry, I didn't catch your name," Skylar said.

"Magus," he said. "But we don't need to waste time with introductions. I understand you have something very valuable."

Skylar said nothing, clutching her book tighter. She heard Cheveyo's angry whinnies from the paddock below. He couldn't help her now.

"Your book has no value to me. I want the true gem you possess," he said.

"I don't know what you're talking about," she said.

"No games, young lady," he said. "I am old enough to be your grandfather. And I know the power you carry."

"What value is it to you?" she asked.

"The world is cracking open, you know this," he said. "In the right hands, that force will restore order we desperately need." He stepped toward her.

"We don't need order," she said, her voice quiet with fear. "We need healing. That's all I'm trying to do." He came closer still and she backed up. "And I need to leave."

"Not quite," he said. He lifted his hand toward her chest. A force she had never experienced began pulling her toward his outstretched hand. Confusion swirled with intense pain in her chest. This assault caught her off guard and all of her training had been forgotten. *Who was this man?* she thought. In her mind's eye she saw glimpses of Lucifer and Diana. She saw the citrine wall restored to its brilliance. She saw her heart light join with its twin flame. Once whole, she saw Sophia's emerald bring immortality to humanity. She saw Magus in his true form, ageless sorcerer, waiting through the millennia to capture Sophia's stone to capture the fate of humanity and harness all potential.

Her awareness returned to the room and she felt her body resist his force to take the heart light. He blew her back against the wall, chairs knocked on their sides. He pulled her back up and threw her across the room as if she were a ragdoll. She crashed into one of the wisteria plants, smashing the porcelain planter to the ground.

"I have plenty of time," he said. "I can wait until you crack."

This isn't right, she thought. *This isn't how it ends* . . . She could see his intent to use the energy from her heart light to return the world to shadow. "You're too late," Skylar's hoarse voice whispered. "There's no more controlling society. It's been broken open."

"Maybe," he said casually. "But I'll give it my best shot." He stood up and pulled one last time on Skylar's chest, propelling her forward. Unable to make any progress, his frustration grew and his face contorted with rage. There was no use. The heart light was not coming out.

"Well then," he said, lowering his hands and taking a final step toward her. "If I can't take it from you, I'll take *you*." He locked his grip on her arm and dragged her out the door with a disproportionate amount of force for his small frame. Sophia's book lay strewn on the floor. She tried to pull away but his sorcery was too great. He led her into the elevator and pulled out a hex key from his interior blazer pocket. He inserted it into the panel on the elevator and pressed the button for the basement.

"People know where I am," Skylar said.

"Not for long," he said as the doors opened. He pulled her toward the library door. The ring of doves shone brightly on the knob.

"You aren't worthy of this—any of it," she said.

He ignored her and opened the library door. Motion lights came on and he sped up his pace, making his way to the back wall. He let go of her briefly to slide the bookcase aside and she lunged for the door. With a flip of his wrist, he yanked her forward. He pushed the alchemical door open, an abyss of unlimited destinations awaited.

Skylar looked around at the bookshelves, thinking of Suki. She had known this was a bad idea. How right her friend was. Magus stepped through the alchemical doorway and pulled Skylar in with him. She held on to the doorjamb for only a second before the force was too great and pulled her through. She was gone.

59

Milicent walked into the Quine conference room with Noah. She had an appointment with Skylar.

"Typical," she muttered. "She thinks she can keep me waiting."

Noah looked around the room. "Mil," he said, righting the overturned chairs. "Look at this place. Something happened."

Milicent saw the broken pot. She trailed the pieces to the Book of Sophia on the floor. She knelt and picked it up. "Oh my god," she whispered. She felt the book pulse in her hands. It was everything she had wanted. It was the missing piece to everything in her collection. Her head snapped up. "The library!" She dashed out of the conference room, carrying the book. Noah followed, in awe of her newfound agility.

They stepped out of the elevator to the open door of the library, a hex key still in the keyhole.

"Shit," Milicent said, sprinting to the back of the library. The bookcase had been pushed out of the way of the alchemical door. She peered into the darkness.

"Where does it lead?" Noah asked.

"With the right expertise?" she asked with a pained look on her face. "Anywhere." She slammed her palm on the doorjamb in frustration. "We're too late. He took her, I know it."

"Who, Mil?" Noah asked.

"I'll explain it to you on the way up," she said, handing Noah the book. "Keep this safe, we're going to need it." He hugged it to his chest and they ran out of the library.

There was a massive caucus at Ocean's house later that evening. Everyone was there. Rachel and Joel sat in the corner of the parlor; Ronnie was trying to console them. Argan was laboring solemnly on the piano while Suki mindlessly fixed drinks for everyone. Milicent paced, Noah right behind her. Ocean had initially objected to letting him through her doors but Milicent insisted, holding her responsible for her dead husband and said Ocean owed her one. Ocean shrugged and let him through.

Rachel and Milicent exchanged glances and Ronnie stepped between them. "It's all right," Rachel said. "It seems we're on the same side now. The poles really have shifted." She shook her head.

"I'll make this quick," Ocean said to everyone. "We have work to do and not a lot of time. I've had to deal with Magus in just about every century." She paused to think. "Maybe not the eighteenth, I can't remember." She shook off the thought. "This is the closest he's come to getting what he wants. The good news is he only has half. And Skylar's body is wrapped around it. He can't do too much damage with half. He needs this . . ." she slipped out a stone from a small velvet bag. It was the half of the emerald from the grotto. Everyone in the room stared at its brilliant green light. They were all familiar with its origin and its purpose, except Noah. He cased the room and grabbed the back of Milicent's shirt for comfort. She immediately swatted his hand away. "The memory has been restored. It's time to finish this and bring forth the last element." She held up the stone. "The Great Year is over and the golden age has begun. I am the past; you all are the future. Skylar is the future and we have to work together to get her back. Lucifer doesn't want his crown restored. If it is, he is no longer trapped on earth. You would think he would want that but he likes it here. He has great control. Once the crown is whole, so is humanity, and he must leave earth."

Noah grabbed Milicent's shirt again and twisted the lavender silk in circles around his finger. She gave him a look but let him do it. Joel stood up and started to object. "This is preposterous, she's been kidnapped and you're going on about the devil? I've gone along with this nonsense all of her life but as her father, I'm not going to sit by and do nothing while you all run around chasing ghosts."

"Joel, you have a lot to learn," Ocean said. "First off, Lucifer is not the devil. And I'm glad you want to help because you have a job to do," Ocean said. "We all do and we'll stay here until we iron it out." Her already serious manner turned grave. "Unfortunately, one of you must make the greatest sacrifice of all." She paused a beat and then looked at Milicent. Noah gasped. Ocean walked toward Milicent and passed her to reach Argan sitting on the piano bench behind them. She handed him the shining stone. "You know what to do," she said. "Go get our girl."

He nodded with tears in his eyes. "I hope we're not too late," he said.

"You'd feel it in your bones if that were true," she smiled tenderly. "Magus now knows he needs Skylar alive until he gets this half. He won't hurt her . . . yet."

The lighting in the room took on a bluish hue and Vivienne appeared in the doorway. She swept in like the tide, commanding and powerful, harsh yet soothing. She was the embodiment of divine grace. Noah had had all his nervous system could take and passed out. He collapsed onto the floor and no one moved to help him until Ronnie's conscience got the better of her.

Vivienne blew past everyone and marched toward Milicent. "Child, why in the hell did you put a witch in the White House?"

"Grandmother, we have bigger problems," Milicent said. "You can't stay in hiding anymore." She wrung her hands. "We need you."

Vivienne was intrigued by this rare moment of vulnerability from her granddaughter. "I'm listening," she said.

ACKNOWLEDGMENTS

Thank you to my husband, who tirelessly supports my dreams in whatever form they take.

ABOUT THE AUTHOR

Stacey L. Tucker uses the action/ adventure genre to bridge science and spirituality in The Equal Night Trilogy. Tucker's first book in the series, *Ocean's Fire*, took Gold at the Living Now Book Awards, and she's looking to make magic again with Book 2, *Alchemy's Air*. She has written for *Women's World*, *Working Mother*, and *Pop Sugar*, and speaks to teen groups about self-empowerment and awareness in today's saturated climate of social media. You can find her at **www.staceyltucker.com**

SELECTED TITLES FROM SPARKPRESS

SparkPress is an independent boutique publisher delivering high-quality, entertaining, and engaging content that enhances readers' lives, with a special focus on female-driven work.
Visit us at **www.gosparkpress.com**

Deepest Blue, Mindy Tarquini, $16.95, 9781943006694. In Panduri, everyone's path is mapped, everyone's destiny determined, their lives charted at birth and steered by an unwavering star. Everything there has its place--until Matteo's older brother, Panduri's Heir, crosses out of their world without explanation, leaving Panduri's orbit in a spiral and Matteo's course on a skid. Forced to follow an unexpected path, Matteo is determined to rise, and he pursues the one future Panduri's star can never chart: a life of his own.

Resistant, Rachael Sparks, $16.95, 9781943006731. Bacteria won the war against our medicines. She might be evolution's answer. But can she survive long enough to find out?

Ocean's Fire, Stacey Tucker, $16.95, 978-1-943006-28-1. Once the Greeks forced their male gods upon the world, the belief in the power of women was severed. For centuries it has been thought that the wisdom of the high priestesses perished at the hand of the patriarchs—but now the ancient Book of Sophia has surfaced. Its pages contain the truths hidden by history, and the sacred knowledge for the coming age. And it is looking for Skylar Southmartin.

The Infinite Now, Mindy Tarquini, $16.95, 978-1-943006-34-2. In flu-ravaged 1918 Philadelphia, the newly-orphaned daughter of the local fortune teller panics and casts her entire neighborhood into a bubble of stagnant time in order to save the life of the mysterious shoemaker who has taken her in. As the complications of the time bubble multiply, this forward-thinking young woman must find the courage to face an uncertain future, so she can find a way to break the spell.

Above the Star, Alexis Chute, $16.95, 978-1-943006-56-4. *Above the Star* is an epic fantasy adventure experienced through the eyes of three unlikely heroes transported to a new world: senior citizen Archie; his daughter-in-law, Tessa; and his fourteen-year-old granddaughter, Ella. In this otherworldly realm, all interests are at war, all love is unrequited, and everyone is left to unravel the truth of who they really are.

ABOUT SPARKPRESS

SparkPress is an independent, hybrid imprint focused on merging the best of the traditional publishing model with new and innovative strategies. We deliver high-quality, entertaining, and engaging content that enhances readers' lives. We are proud to bring to market a list of *New York Times* best-selling, award-winning, and debut authors who represent a wide array of genres, as well as our established, industry-wide reputation for creative, results-driven success in working with authors. SparkPress, a BookSparks imprint, is a division of SparkPoint Studio LLC.

Learn more at GoSparkPress.com

www.ingramcontent.com/pod-product-compliance
Lightning Source LLC
Chambersburg PA
CBHW022248211224
19369CB00003B/18